Tree-House Comix Proudly Presents

DOG MAN
BRAWL of The WILD

WRITTEN AND ILLUSTRATED BY DAV PILKEY
AS GEORGE BEARD AND HAROLD HUTCHINS
WITH COLOR BY JOSE GARIBALDI

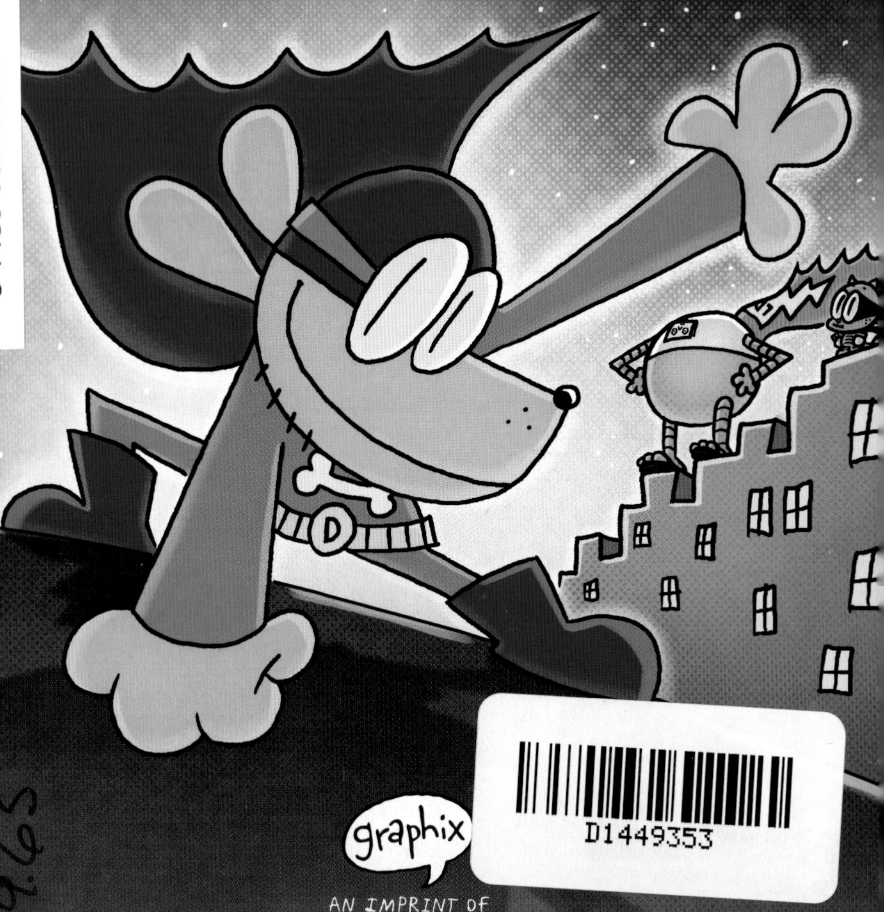

graphix
AN IMPRINT OF
SCHOLASTIC

FOR LIZETTE SERRANO
THANK YOU FOR YOUR STRENGTH, COMPASSION, AND DEVOTION TO LIBRARIES AND KIDS

Copyright © 2019 by Dav Pilkey
www.pilkey.com

Library of Congress Control Number 2018945989

978-1-338-23657-6 (POB)
978-1-338-29092-9 (Library)

10 9 8 7 6 5 4 3 2   19 20 21 22 23

Printed in China   62
First edition, January 2019

Edited by Ken Geist
Book design by Dav Pilkey and Phil Falco
Color by Jose Garibaldi
Color Flatting by Rachel Polk
Creative Director: David Saylor

CHAPTERS

Fore-Foreword: Dog Man: Behind the Profundity
—5—

Foreword: George and Harold's Recap of Our Story Thus Far
—8—

1. Two Messages
—13—

2. The Sad Guys
—31—

3. Things Get Worse!
—54—

4. A Buncha Stuff That Happened Next
—69—

5. Dog Jail Blues
—85—

6. Even More Stuff Happens!
—101—

7. Girl Power!
—115—

8. Help Is On the Way
—124—

9. Dog Man: The Major Motion Picture
—149—

10. The Great Cat's Bee
—173—

11. March of the Misfits
—203—

Sarah Hatoff News Blog
—212—

How to Draw
—214—

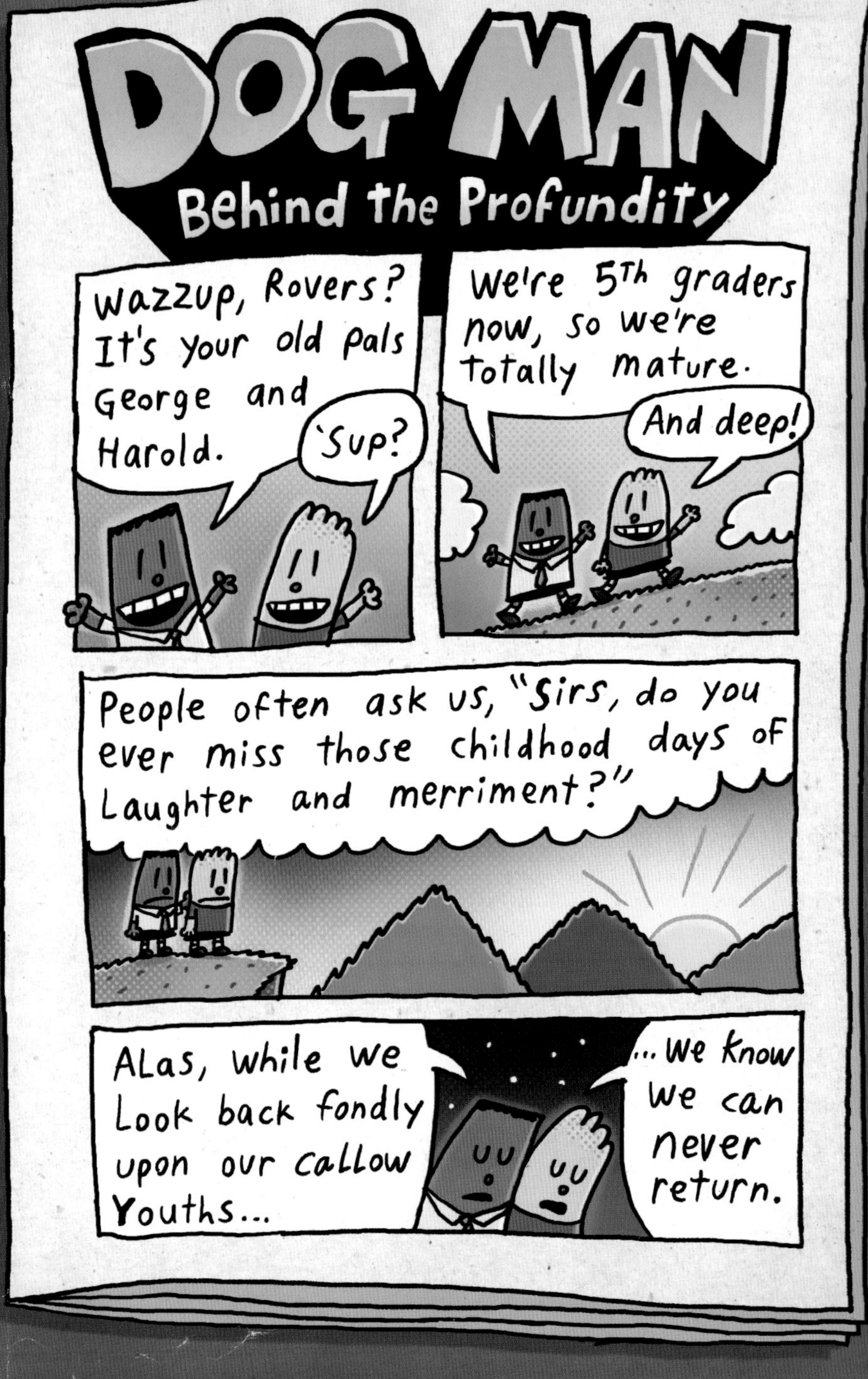
DOG MAN
Behind the Profundity
Wazzup, Rovers? It's your old pals George and Harold.
`Sup?
We're 5th graders now, so we're totally mature.
And deep!
People often ask us, "Sirs, do you ever miss those childhood days of laughter and merriment?"
Alas, while we look back fondly upon our callow youths...
...we know we can never return.

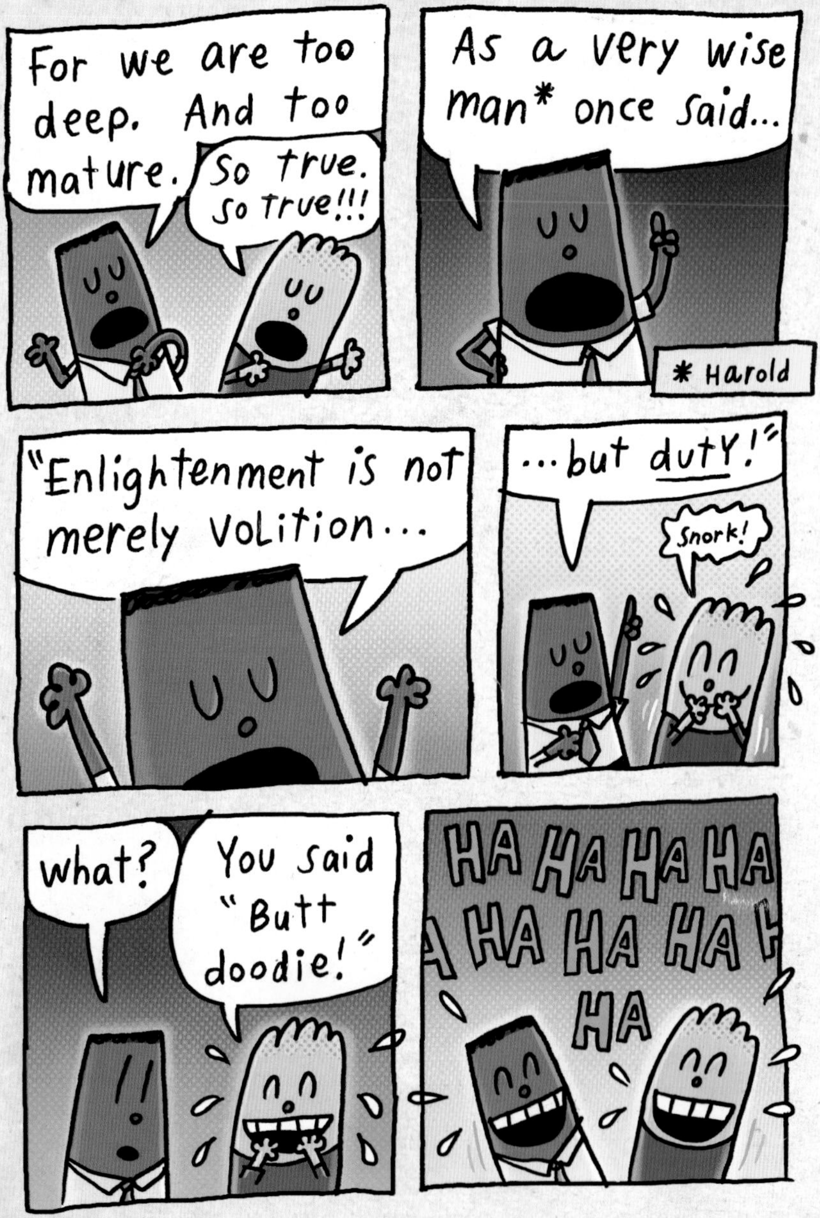
For we are too deep. And too mature.
So true. So true!!!
As a very wise man* once said...
* Harold
"Enlightenment is not merely volition...
...but duty!"
Snork!
what?
You said "Butt doodie!"
HA HA HA HA HA HA HA HA HA HA

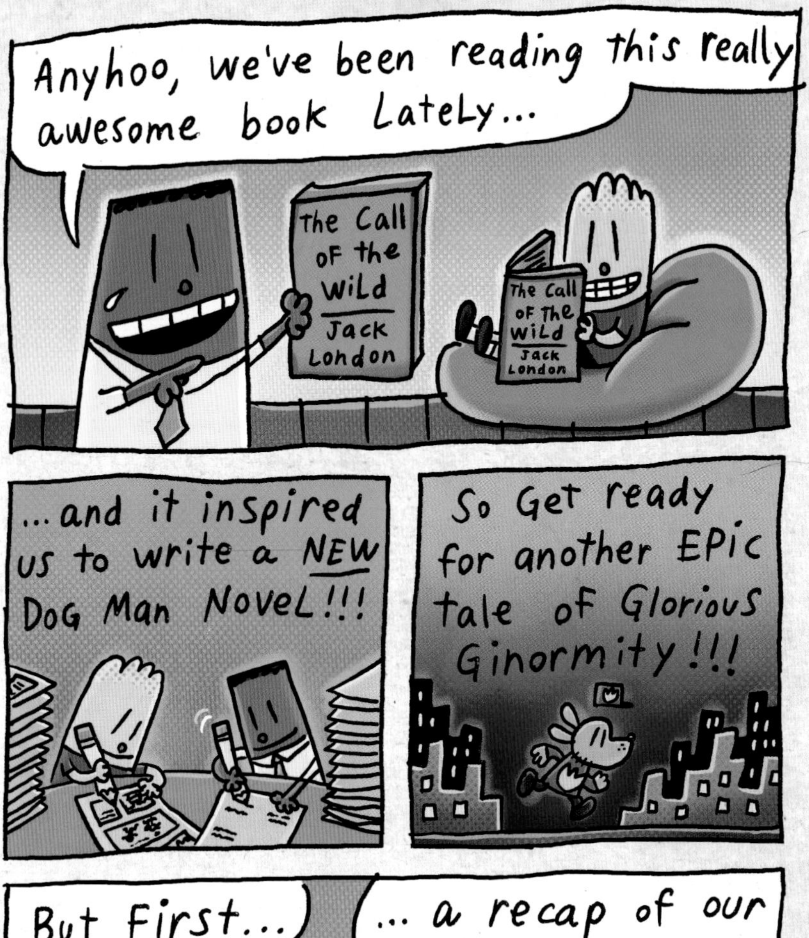
Anyhoo, we've been reading this really awesome book LateLy...
The Call of the WiLd
Jack London
The Call of The WiLd
Jack London
...and it inspired us to write a NEW Dog Man NoveL!!!
So Get ready for another EPic tale of Glorious Ginormity!!!
But First...
... a recap of our story thus Far.
Turn the page...

George and Harold Present:
A George And Harold Production of
George and Harold's
Recap of our Story Thus Far By George And Harold

"We're George and Harold, and we approve this recap."
©2019 by George and Harold.

One time there was a cop and a police dog...

...Who got hurt in an explosion!

KA-BLAM!

They were rushed to the hospital...

wee-ooo-wee-ooo

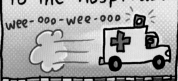

...Where the doctor had very sad news:

Boo Hoo Hoo!

I'm sorry, cop, but your head is dying!

Bummer, dude!!!

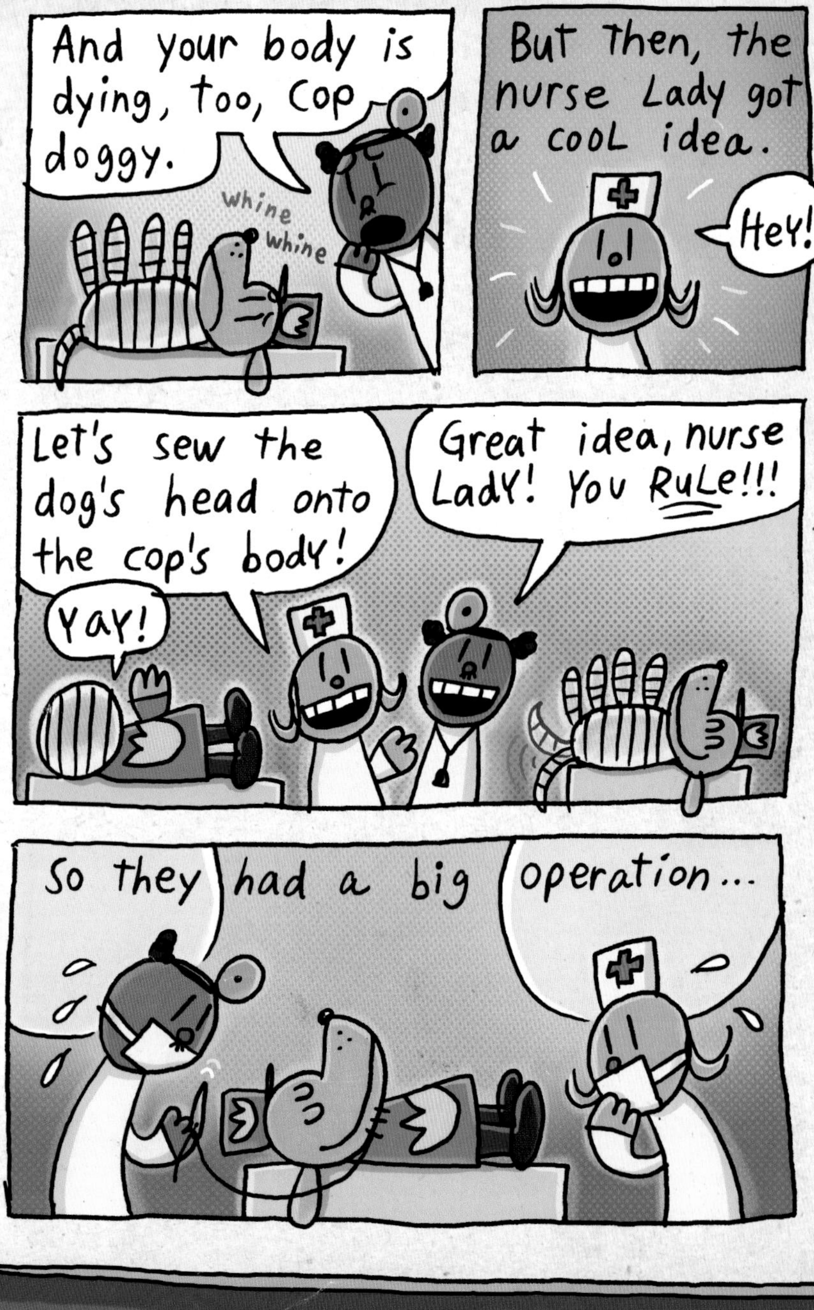
And your body is dying, too, Cop doggy.
whine
whine
But then, the nurse Lady got a cool idea.
Hey!
Let's sew the dog's head onto the cop's body!
Great idea, nurse Lady! You RuLe!!!
Yay!
So they had a big operation...

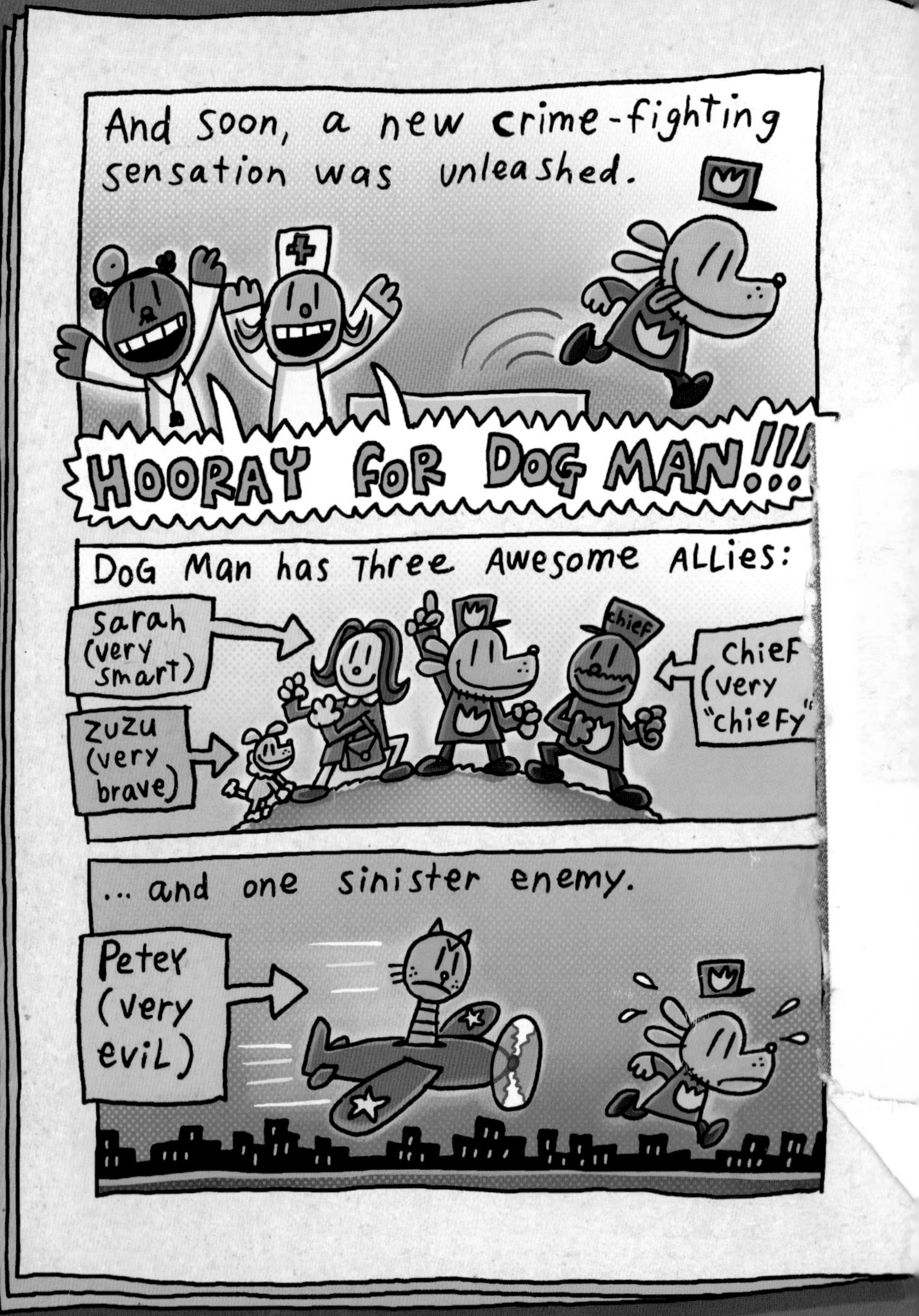
And soon, a new crime-fighting sensation was unleashed.
HOORAY FOR DOG MAN!!!
Dog Man has three awesome allies:
Sarah (very smart)
Zuzu (very brave)
Chief (very "chiefy")
Chief
... and one sinister enemy.
Peter (very evil)

But Petey's evil heart is beginning to change...

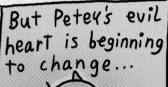

...because of one little kitten.

Li'L Petey (very good-hearted)

i'L Petey lives with Dog Man...

DOG Man

...and their Re-markable Robot PaL, 80-HD.

Most of the time, they're a Family...

...but Sometimes, they're Superheroes.

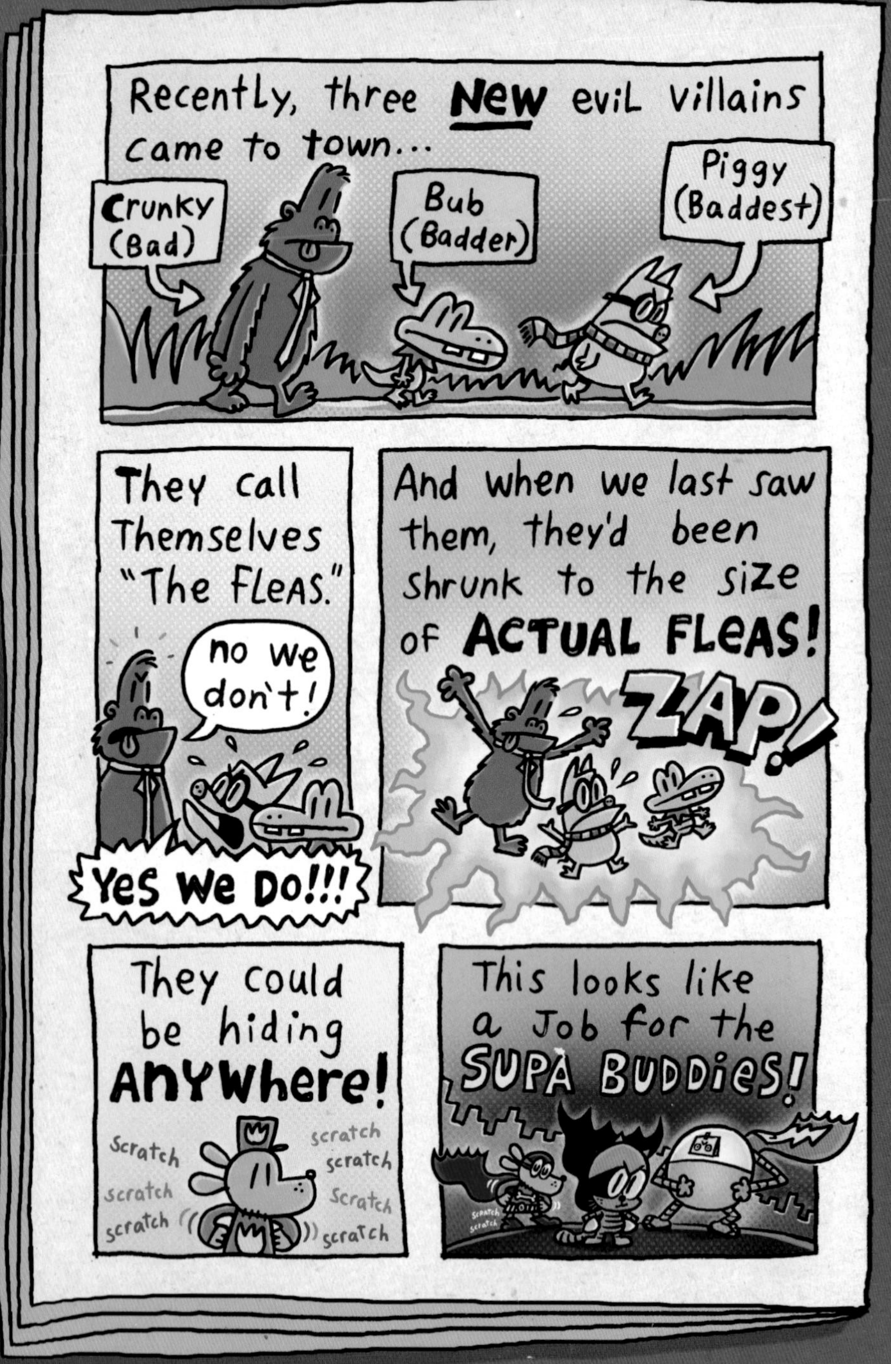
Recently, three NEW evil villains came to town...
Crunky (Bad)
Bub (Badder)
Piggy (Baddest)
They call Themselves "The FLEAS."
no we don't!
YES WE DO!!!
And when we last saw them, they'd been shrunk to the size of ACTUAL FLEAS!
ZAP!
They could be hiding ANYWhere!
scratch
scratch
scratch
scratch
scratch
scratch
scratch
This looks like a Job for the SUPA BUDDIES!
scratch
scratch

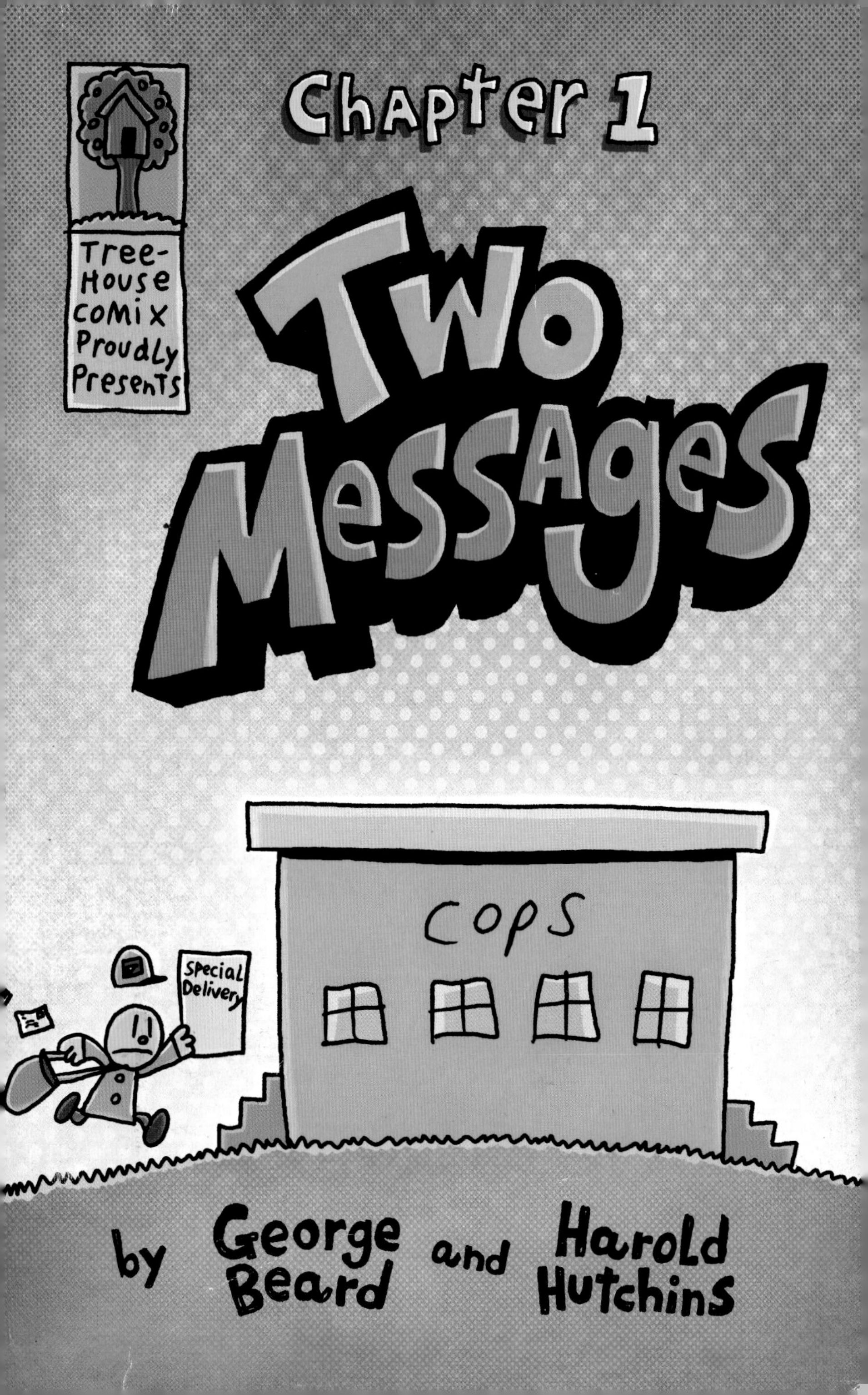
Tree-House Comix Proudly Presents
Chapter 1
Two Messages
COPS
Special Delivery
by George Beard and Harold Hutchins

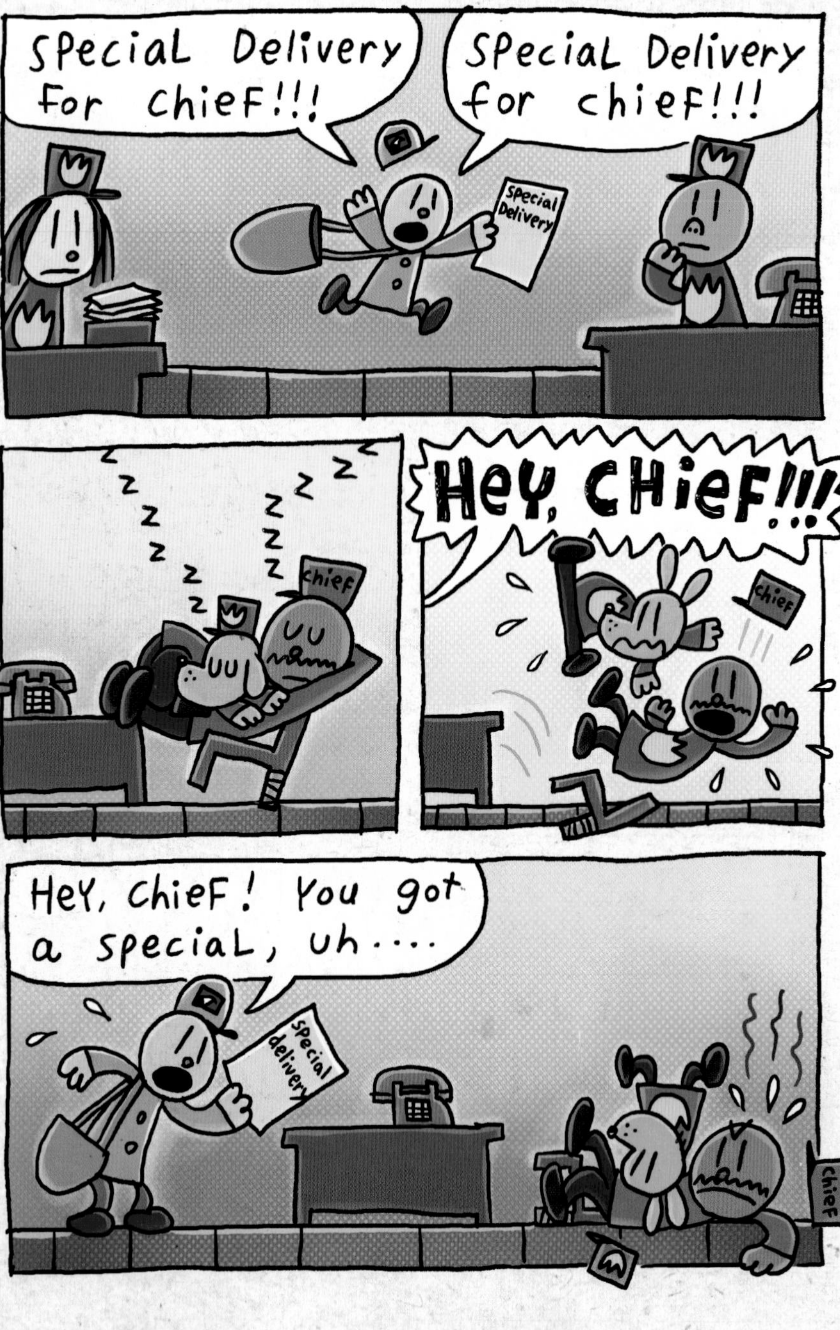

SPecial Delivery for ChieF!!!
SPecial Delivery for chieF!!!
Special Delivery
Z Z Z Z Z Z Z Z Z Z Z Z
chief
HEY, CHIEF!!!
chief
HeY, ChieF! You got a special, uh....
special delivery
chief

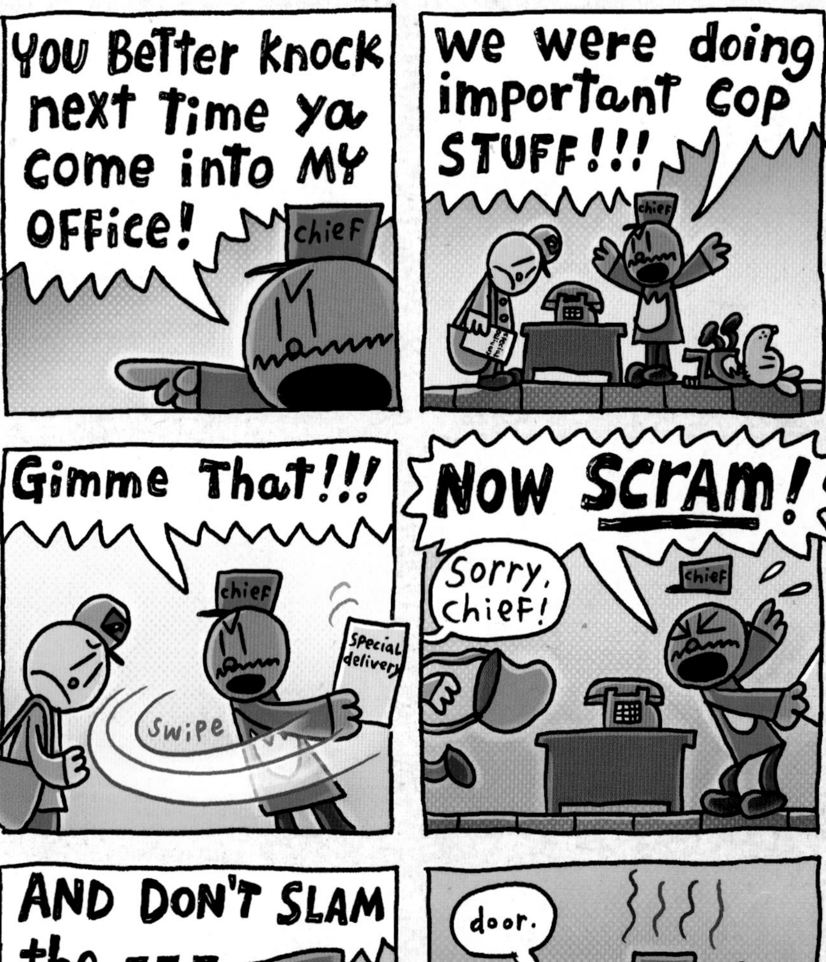
You Better knock next time ya come into MY OFFice!
chief
We were doing important cop STUFF!!!
chief
Special delivery
Gimme That!!!
chief
Special delivery
Swipe
NOW SCRAM!
Sorry, chief!
chief
AND DON'T SLAM the ---
chief
SLAM!
door.
chief

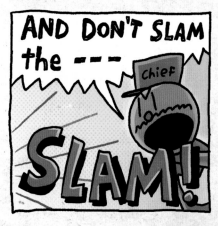

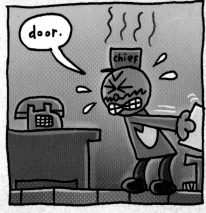

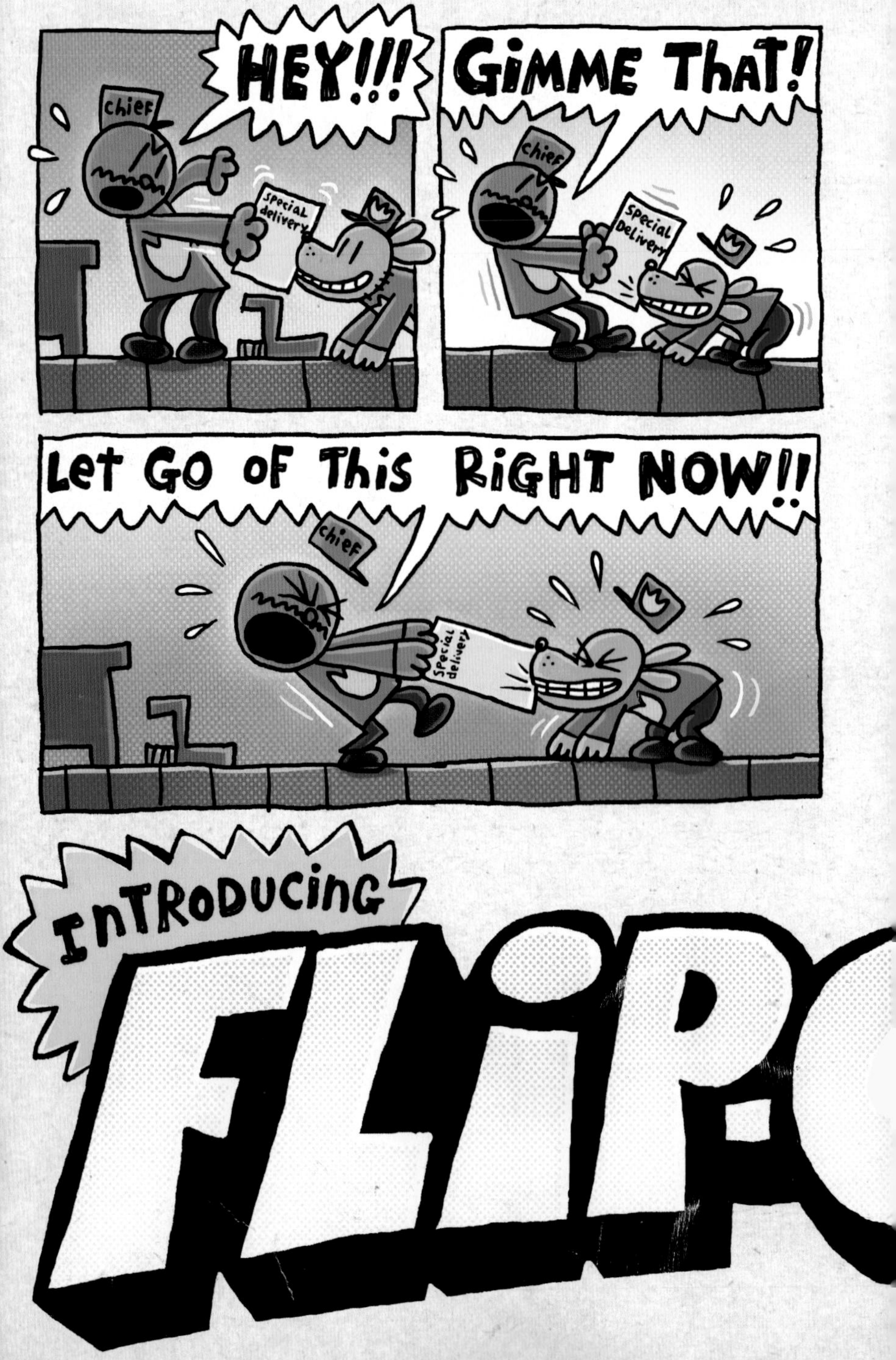
HEY!!!
chief
Special delivery
GiMME ThAT!
chief
Special Delivery
Let GO OF This RiGHT NOW!!
chief
Special delivery
InTRODUCinG
FLiP

STEP 1.
First, place your left hand inside the dotted lines marked "Left hand here." Hold the book open FLAT!

STEP 2:
Grasp the right-hand page with your thumb and index finger (inside the dotted lines marked "Right Thumb Here").

STEP 3:
Now QUICKLY flip the right-hand page back and forth until the picture appears to be Animated.

(for extra fun, try adding your own sound-effects!)

O.RAMA

Remember,

while you are flipping,
be sure you can see
the image on page 19
AND the image on page 21.

If you flip quickly,
the two pictures will
start to look like
one **ANimated** cartoon!

Don't forget to
add your own
sound-effects!

Left
hand here.

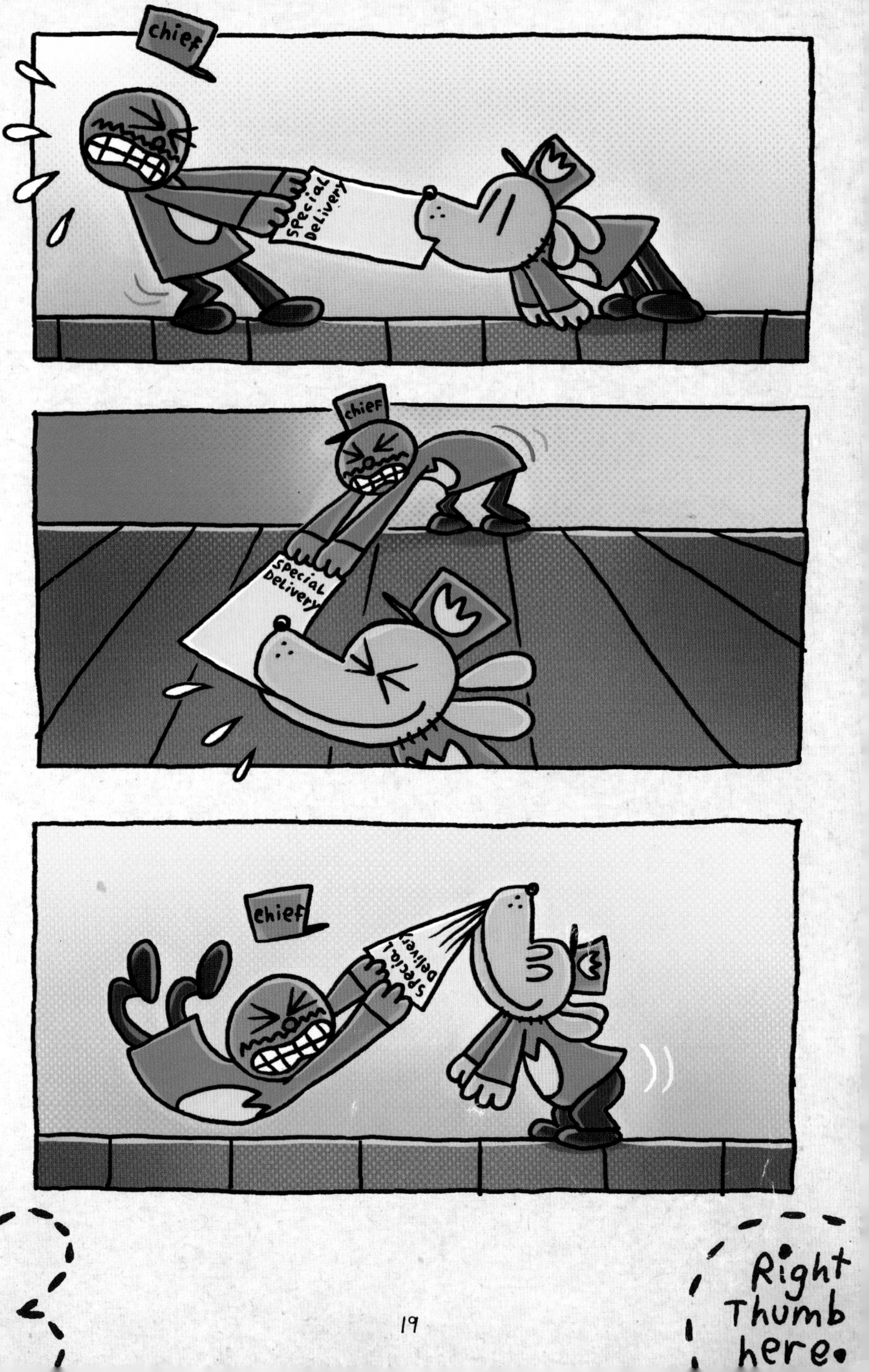
chief
Special Delivery
chief
Special Delivery
chief
Special Delivery

Right Thumb here.

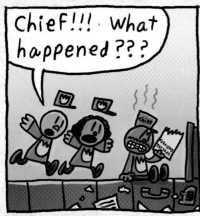

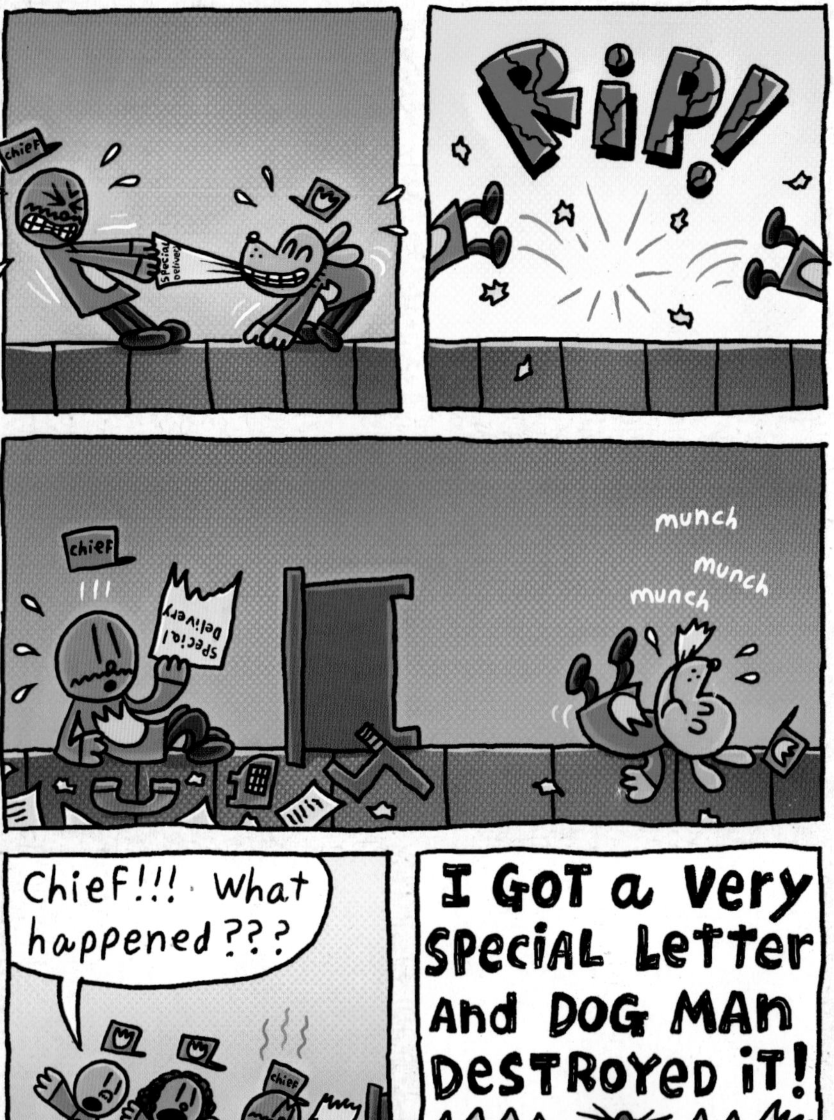
chief
Special delivery
RIP!
chief
Special Delivery
munch
munch
munch
Chief!!! What happened???
chief
I GOT a Very SPECiAL Letter And DOG MAN DESTROYED iT!
Special delivery

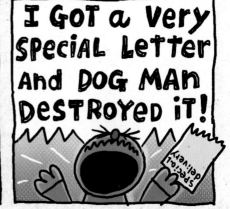

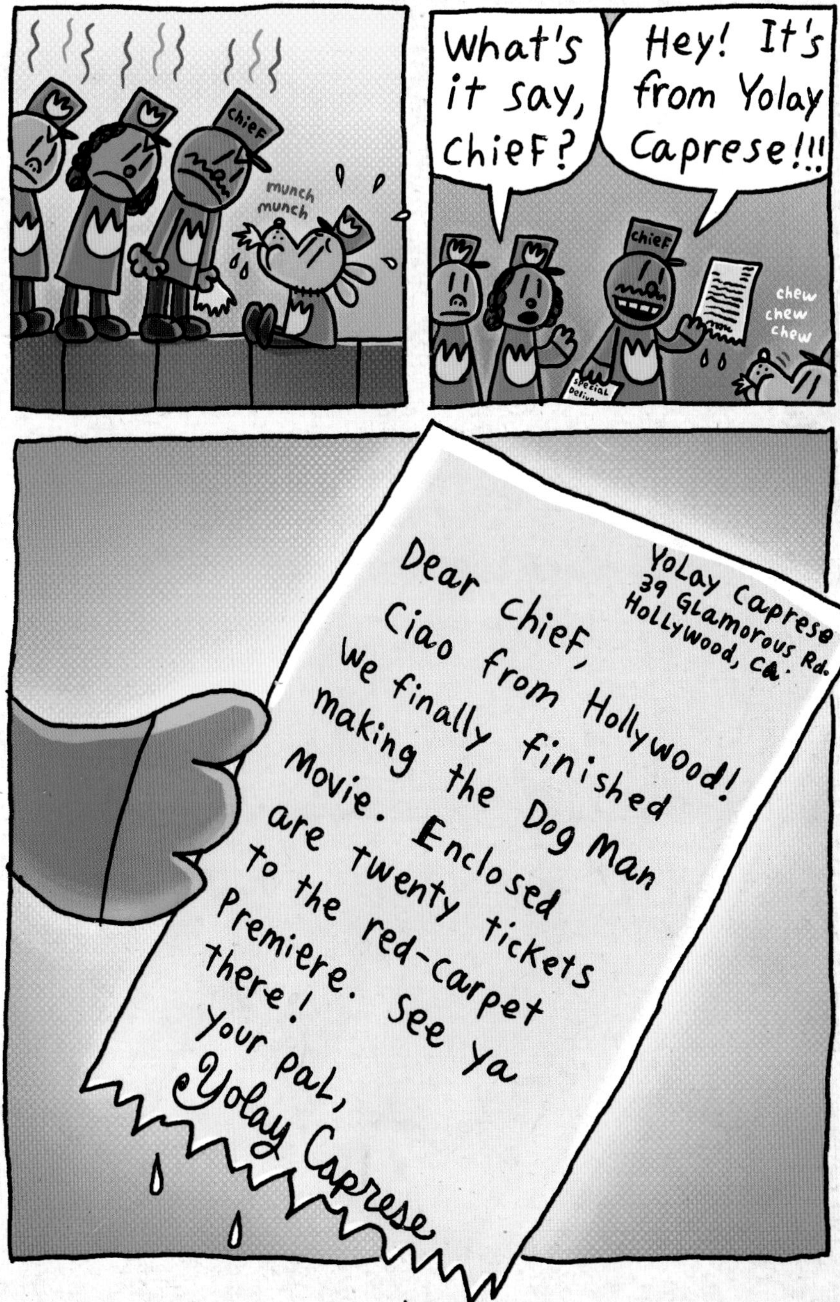
munch munch
What's it say, chief?
Hey! It's from Yolay Caprese!!!
chief
chew chew chew
Yolay Caprese
39 Glamorous Rd.
Hollywood, CA.
Dear chief,
Ciao from Hollywood!
We finally finished making the Dog Man Movie. Enclosed are twenty tickets to the red-carpet Premiere. See ya there!
Your pal,
Yolay Caprese

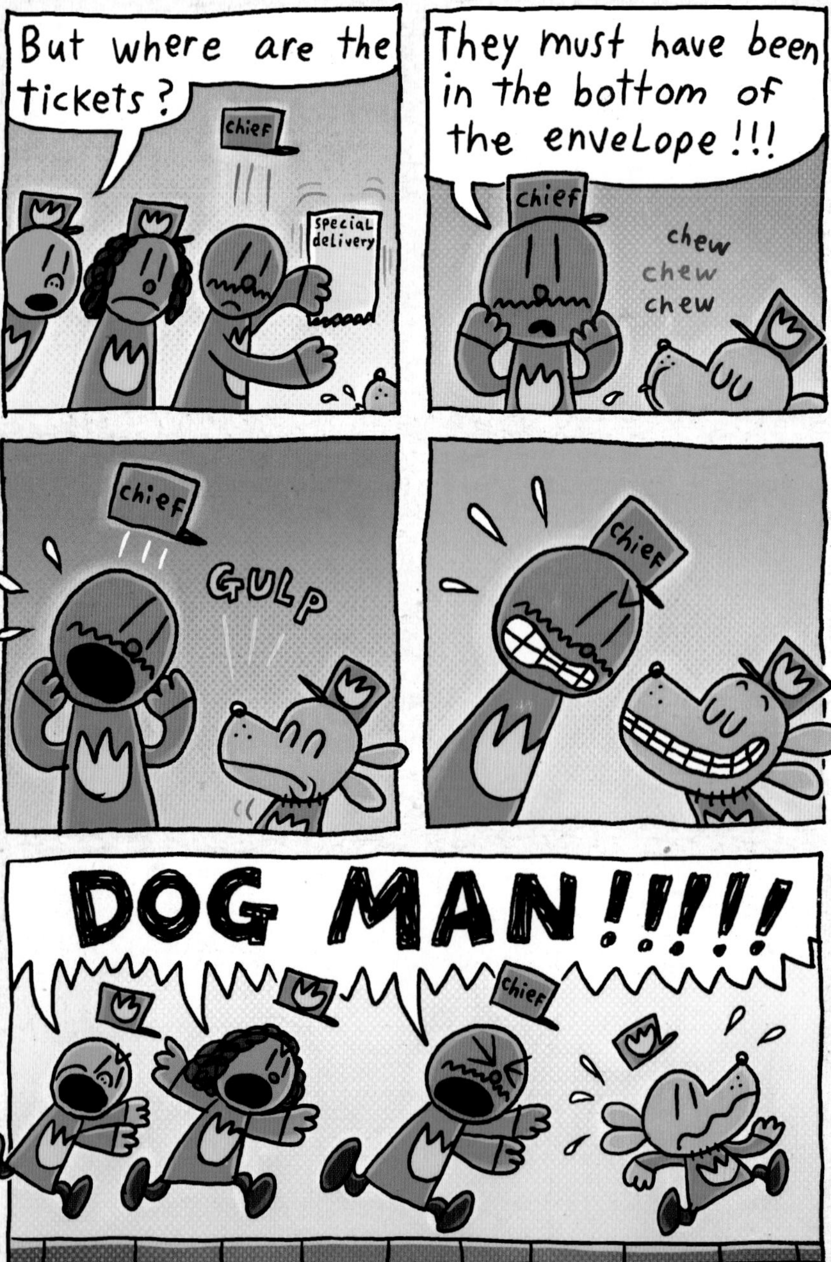
But where are the tickets?
chief
Special delivery
They must have been in the bottom of the envelope!!!
chief
chew
chew
chew
chief
GULP
chief
DOG MAN!!!!!
chief

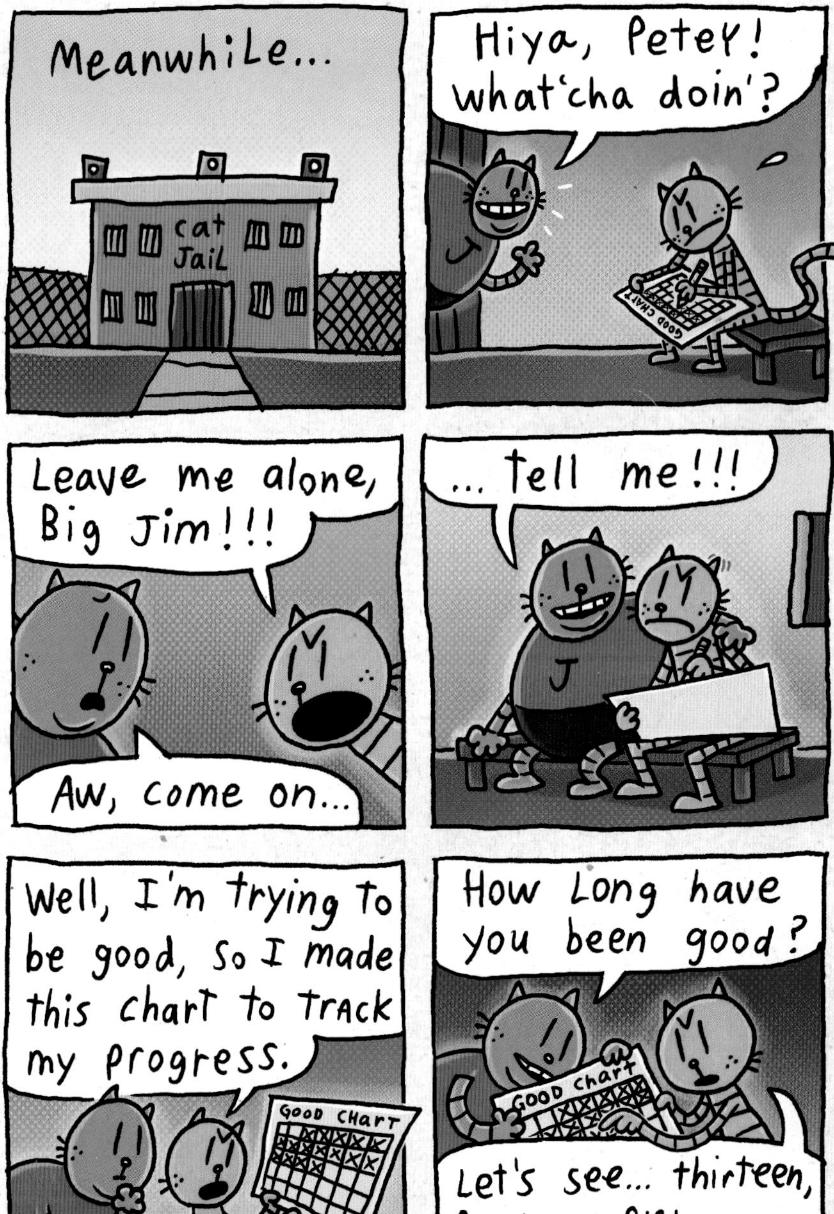
Meanwhile...
Cat Jail
Hiya, Petey! what'cha doin'?
GOOD CHART
Leave me alone, Big Jim!!!
Aw, come on...
... Tell me!!!
Well, I'm trying to be good, so I made this chart to track my progress.
GOOD CHART
How long have you been good?
GOOD CHART
Let's see... thirteen, fourteen, fifteen...

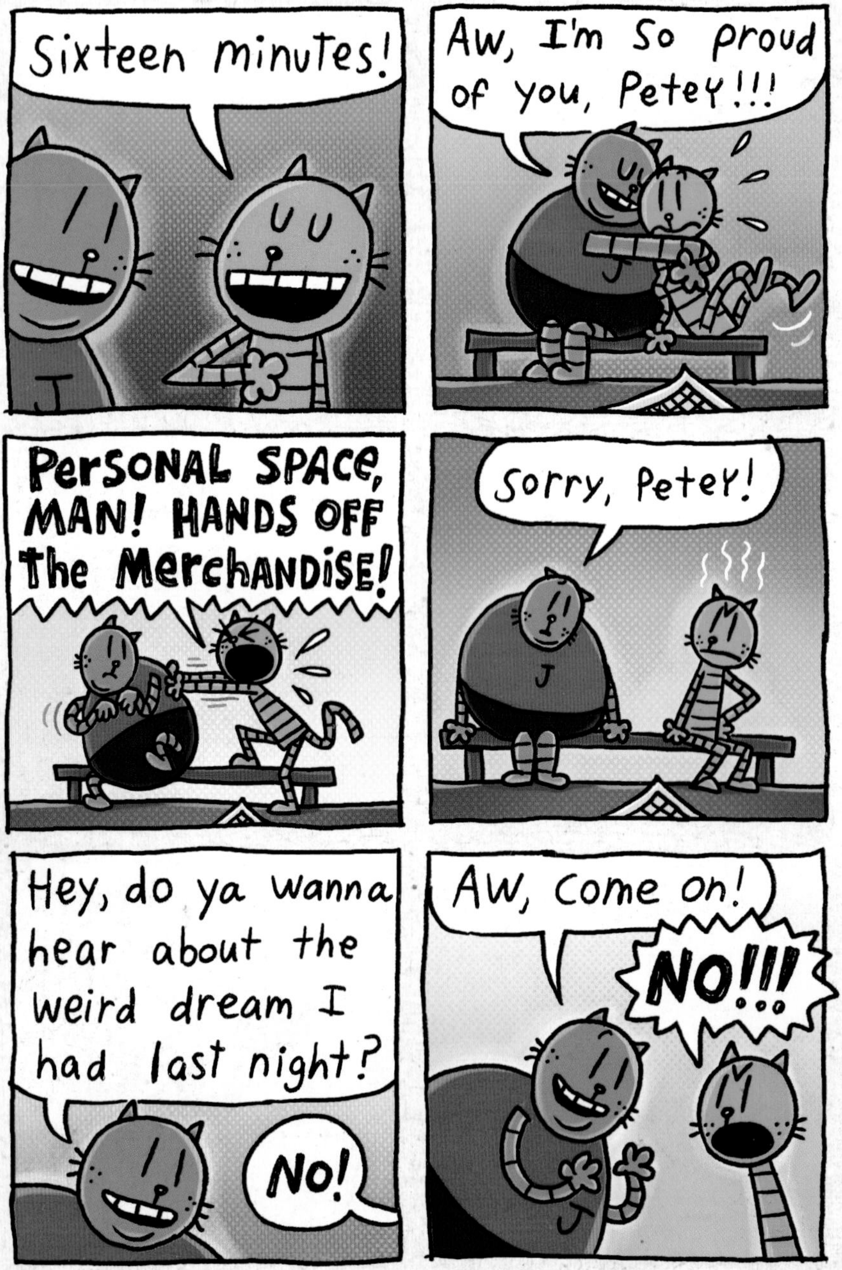
Sixteen minutes!
Aw, I'm so proud of you, Petey!!!
PERSONAL SPACE, MAN! HANDS OFF the MERCHANDISE!
Sorry, Petey!
Hey, do ya wanna hear about the weird dream I had last night?
NO!
Aw, come on!
NO!!!

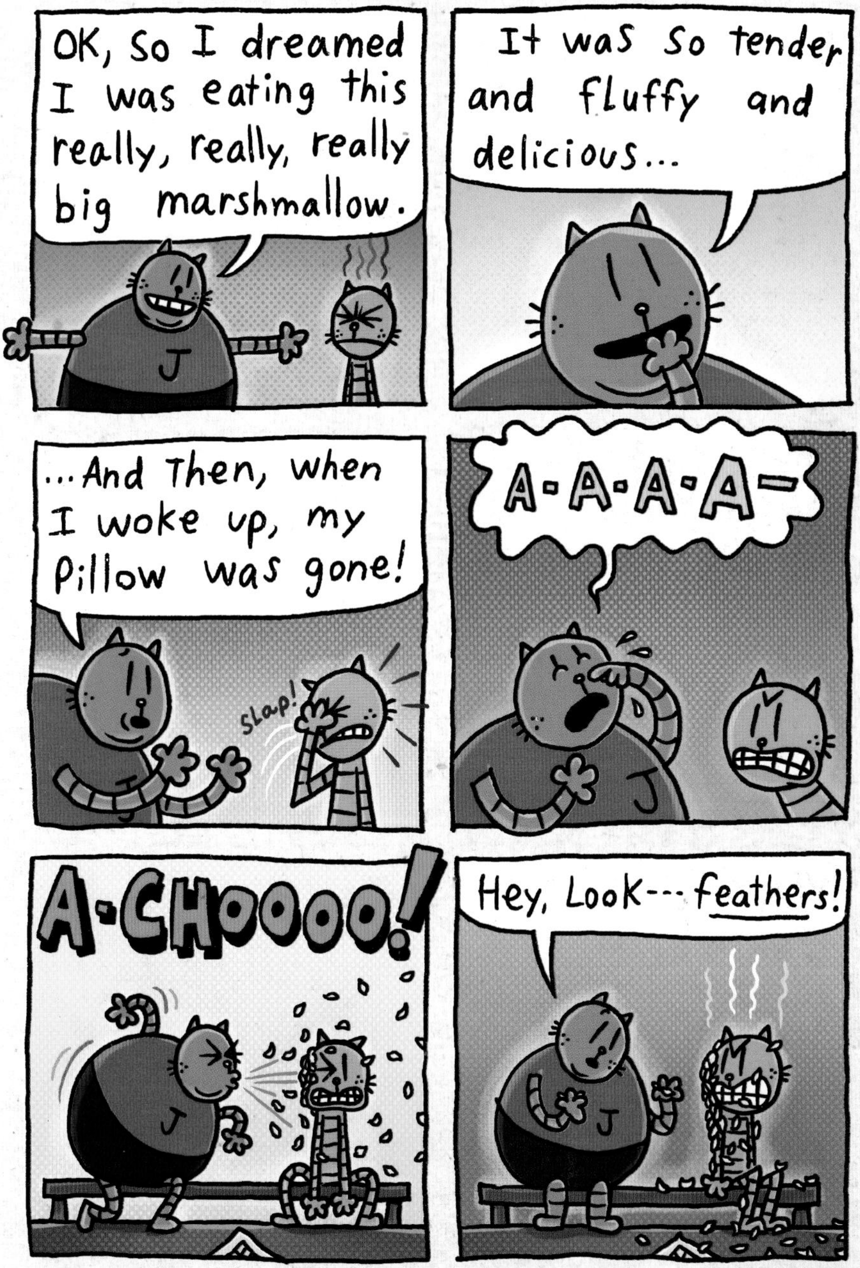
OK, So I dreamed I was eating this really, really, really big marshmallow.
It was So tender and fluffy and delicious...
...And Then, when I woke up, my Pillow was gone!
SLAP!
A-A-A-A-
A-CHOOOO!
Hey, Look--- feathers!

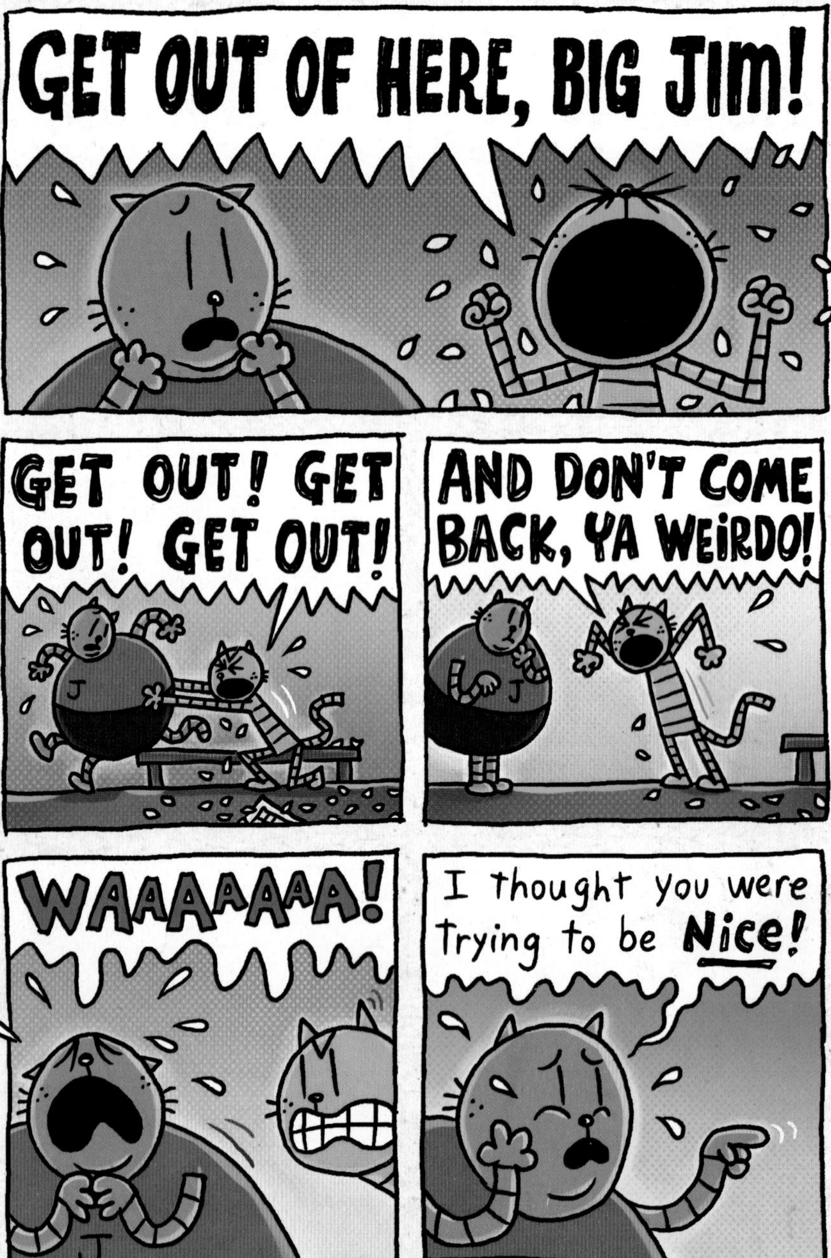
GET OUT OF HERE, BIG JIM!
GET OUT! GET OUT! GET OUT!
AND DON'T COME BACK, YA WEIRDO!
J
J
WAAAAAAA!
J
I thought you were trying to be Nice!

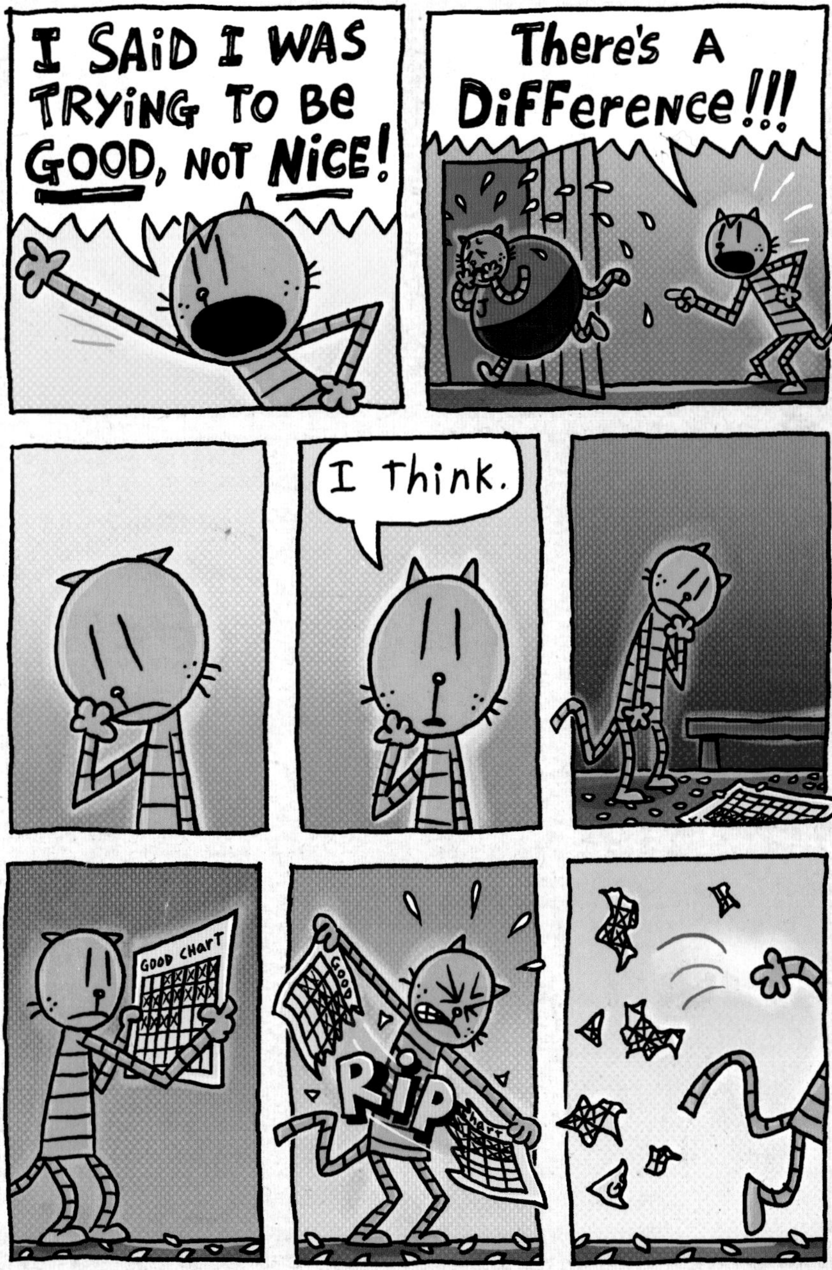
I SAID I WAS TRYING TO BE GOOD, NOT NICE!
There's A DIFFERENCE!!!
I think.
GOOD CHART
GOOD
RIP
CHART

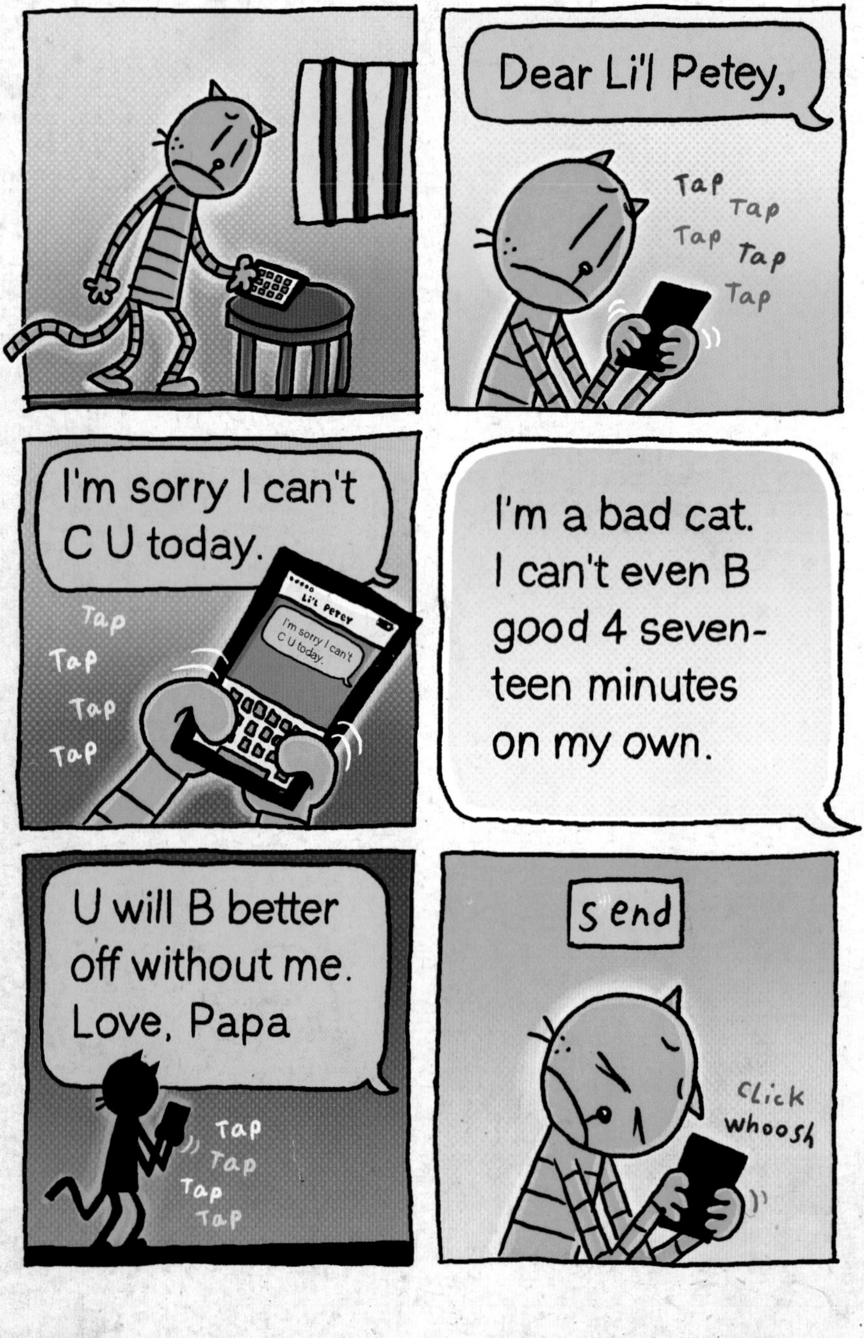
Dear Li'l Petey,
Tap Tap Tap Tap Tap
I'm sorry I can't C U today.
Li'l Petey
I'm sorry I can't C U today.
Tap Tap Tap Tap
I'm a bad cat. I can't even B good 4 seventeen minutes on my own.
U will B better off without me. Love, Papa
Tap Tap Tap Tap
Send
Click whoosh

Chapter 2

The Sad Guys

Flip Flop Flip

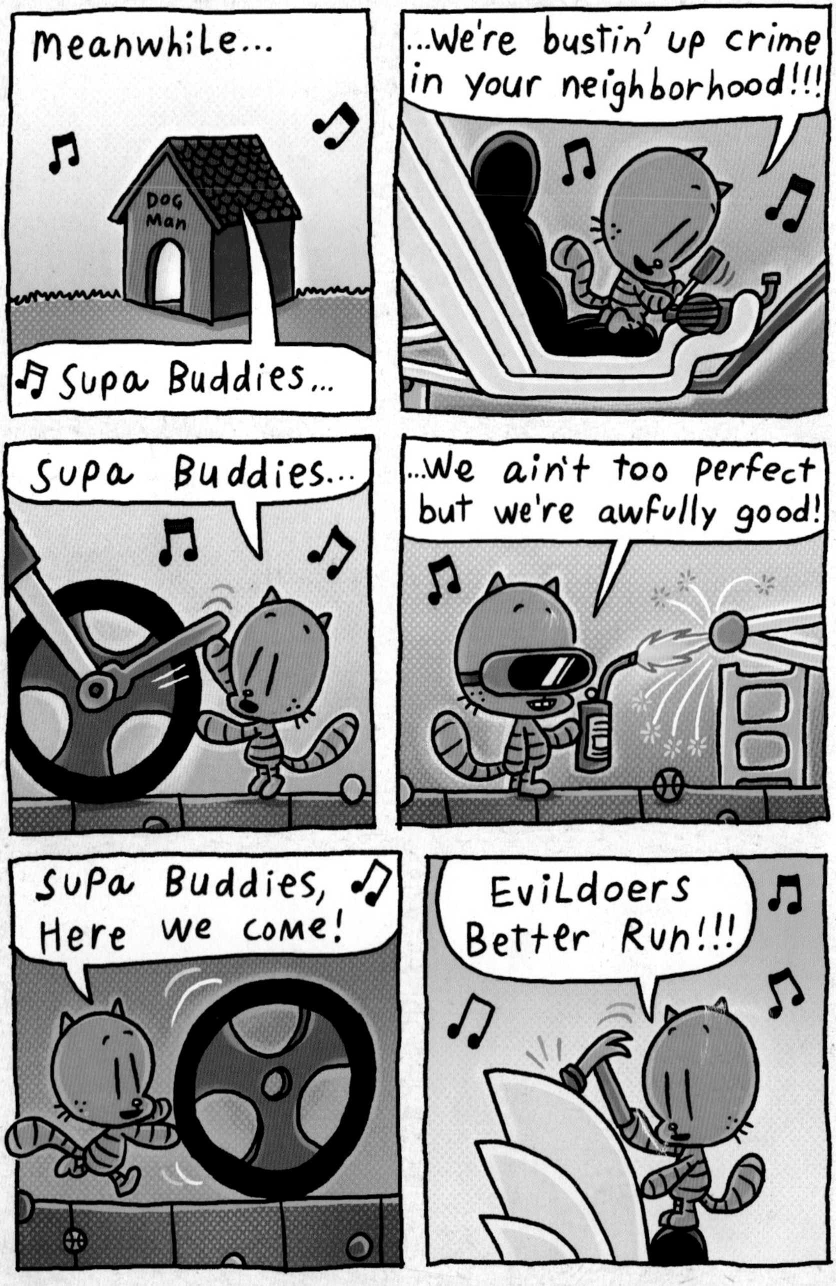
Meanwhile...
♫ Supa Buddies...
...We're bustin' up crime in your neighborhood!!!
DOG Man
Supa Buddies...
...We ain't too perfect but we're awfully good!
Supa Buddies, ♫ Here we come!
EviLdoers Better Run!!!

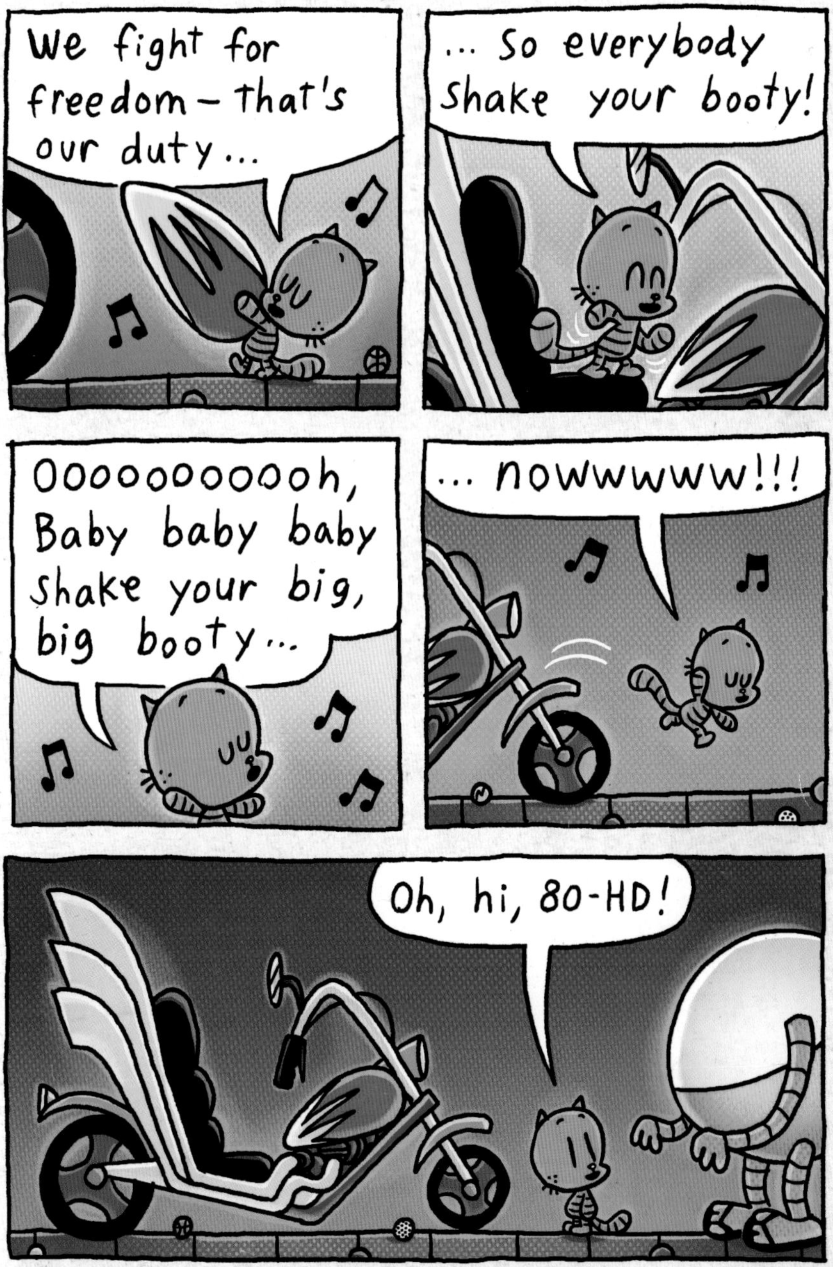
We fight for freedom—that's our duty...
... So everybody shake your booty!
Oooooooooooh, Baby baby baby shake your big, big booty...
... nowwwwww!!!
Oh, hi, 80-HD!

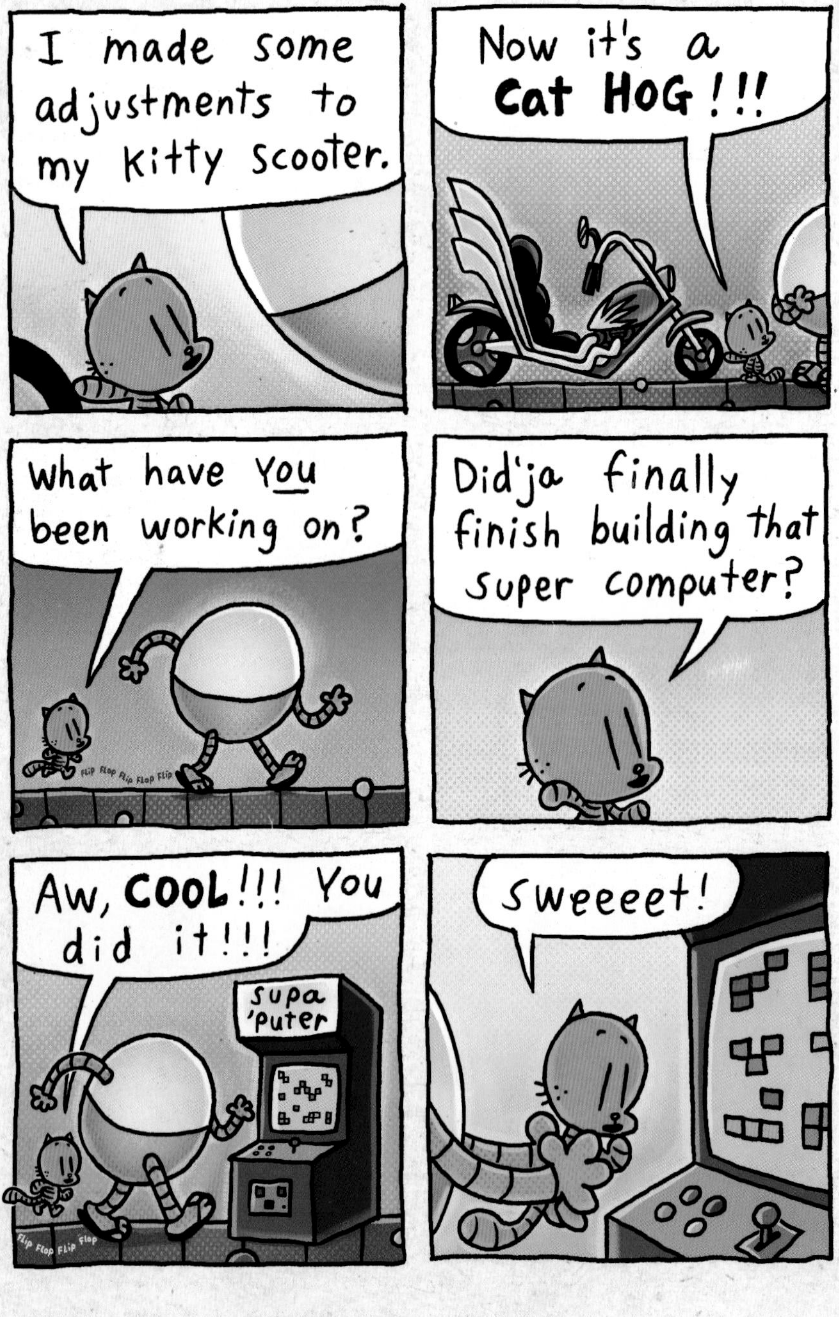
I made some adjustments to my kitty scooter.
Now it's a **Cat HOG**!!!
What have YOU been working on?
FLIP FLOP FLIP FLOP FLIP
Did'ja finally finish building that super computer?
Aw, **COOL**!!! You did it!!!
SUPA 'PUTER
FLIP FLOP FLIP FLOP
Sweeeet!

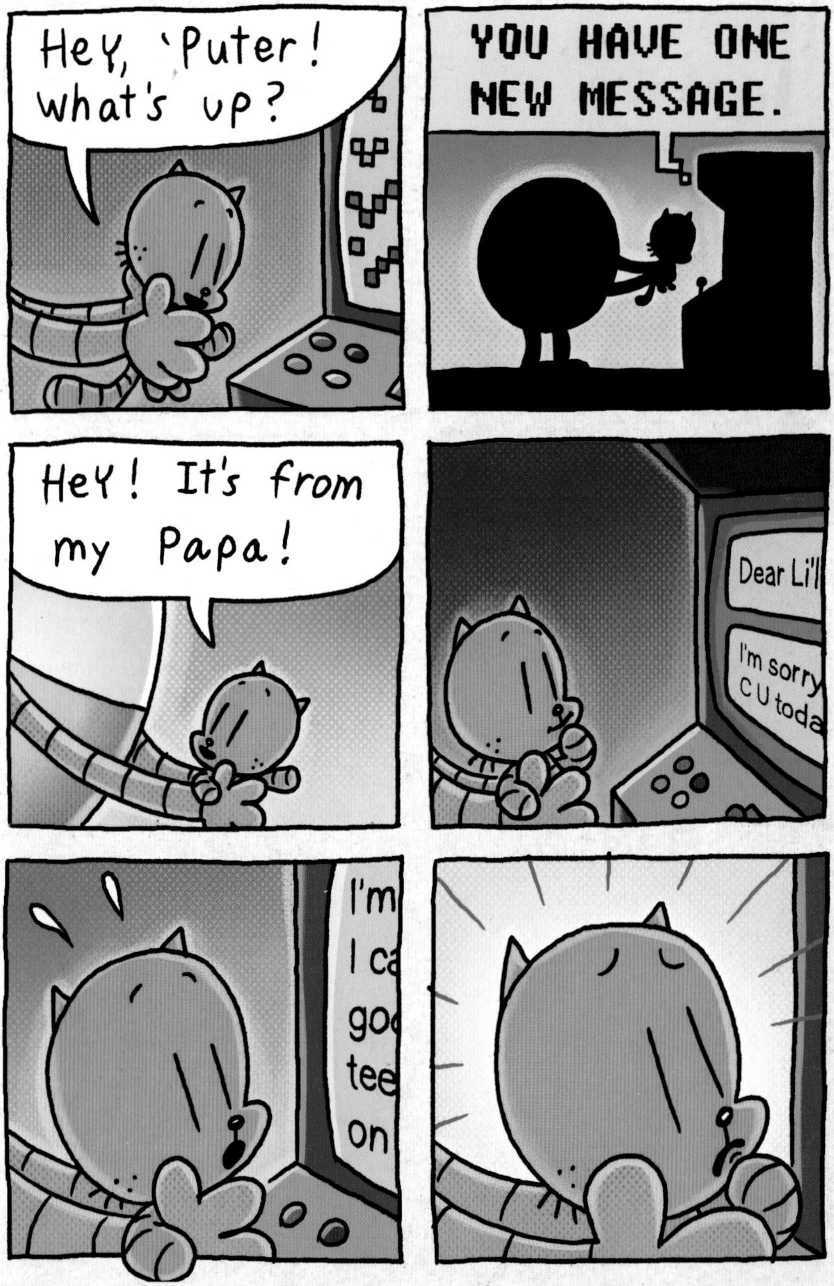
Hey, 'Puter! what's up?
YOU HAVE ONE NEW MESSAGE.
Hey! It's from my Papa!
I'm sorry

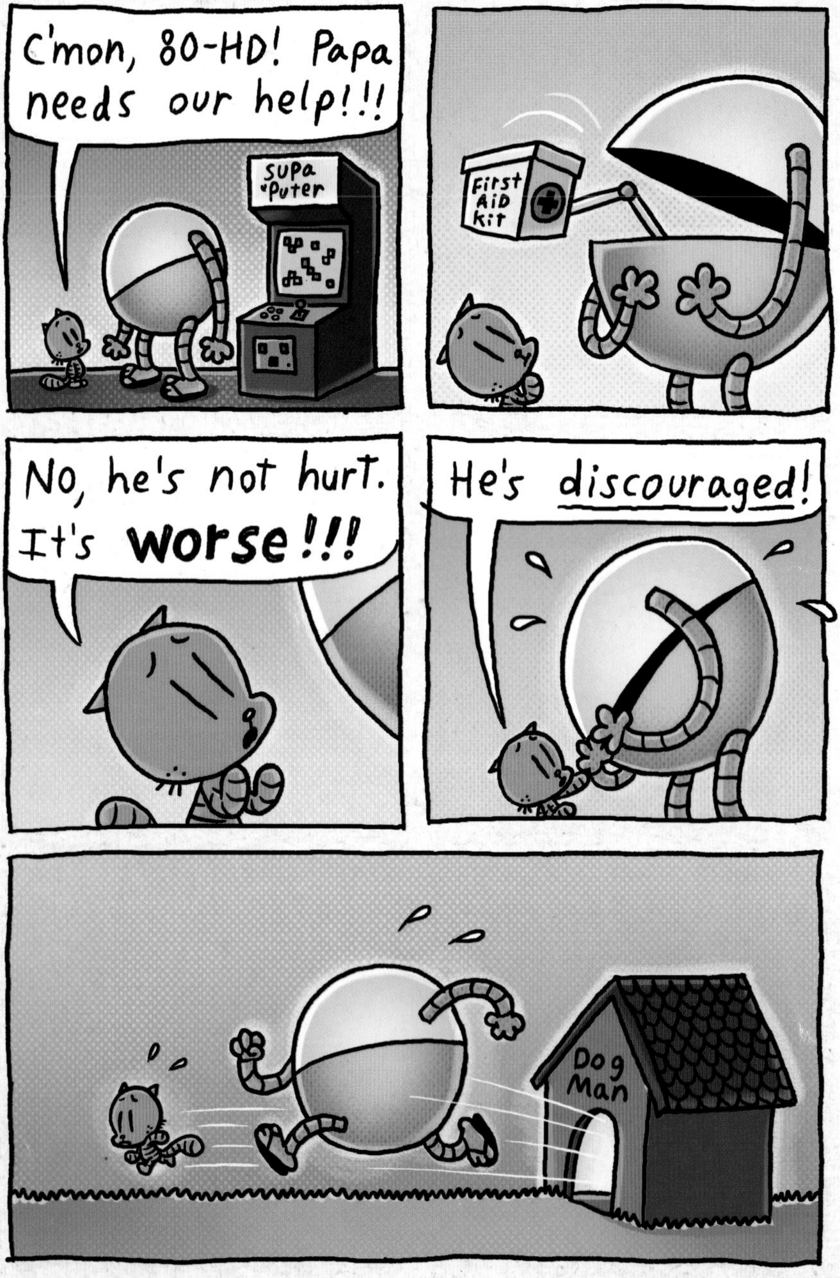
C'mon, 80-HD! Papa needs our help!!!
SUPA PUTER
First AID Kit
No, he's not hurt. It's **worse!!!**
He's discouraged!
Dog Man

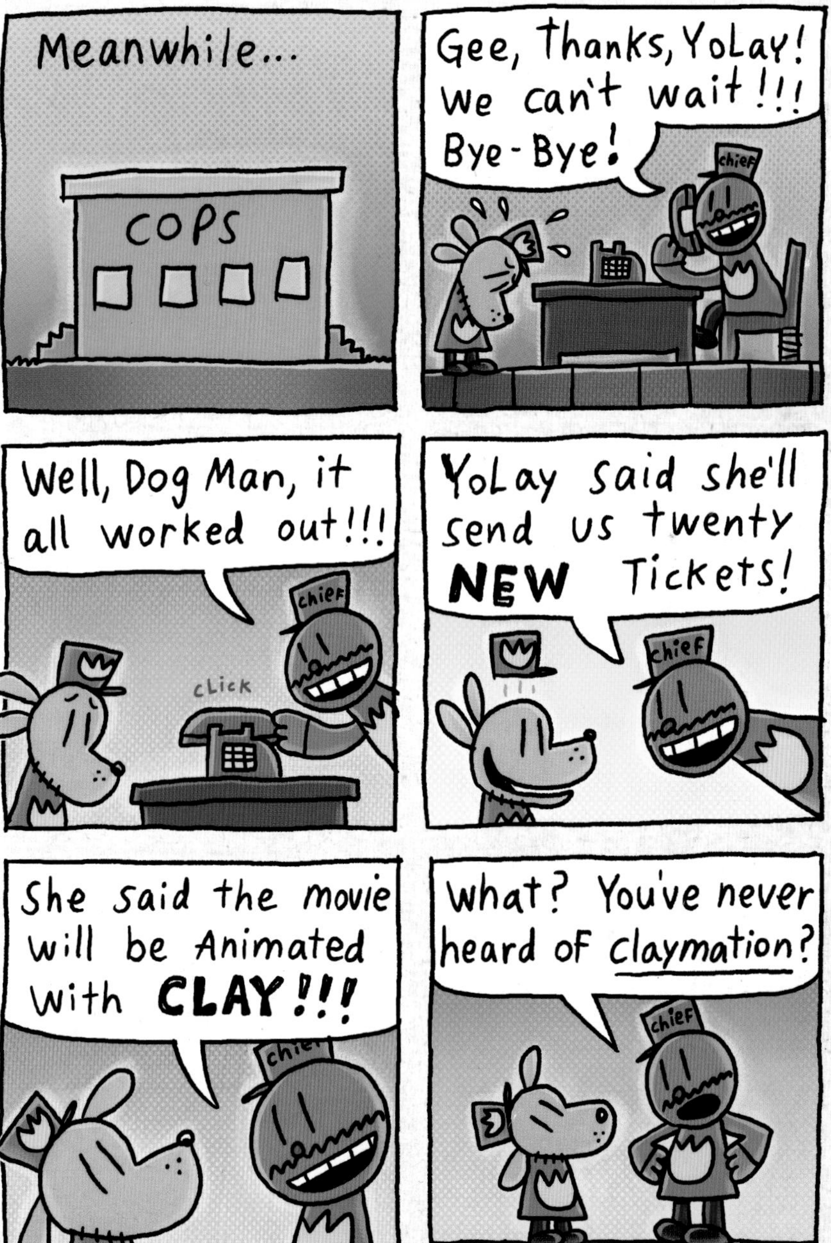
Meanwhile...
COPS
Gee, Thanks, YoLay! We can't wait!!! Bye-Bye!
chief
Well, Dog Man, it all worked out!!!
chief
cLick
YoLay said she'll send us twenty NEW Tickets!
chief
She said the movie will be Animated with CLAY!!!
What? You've never heard of claymation?
chief

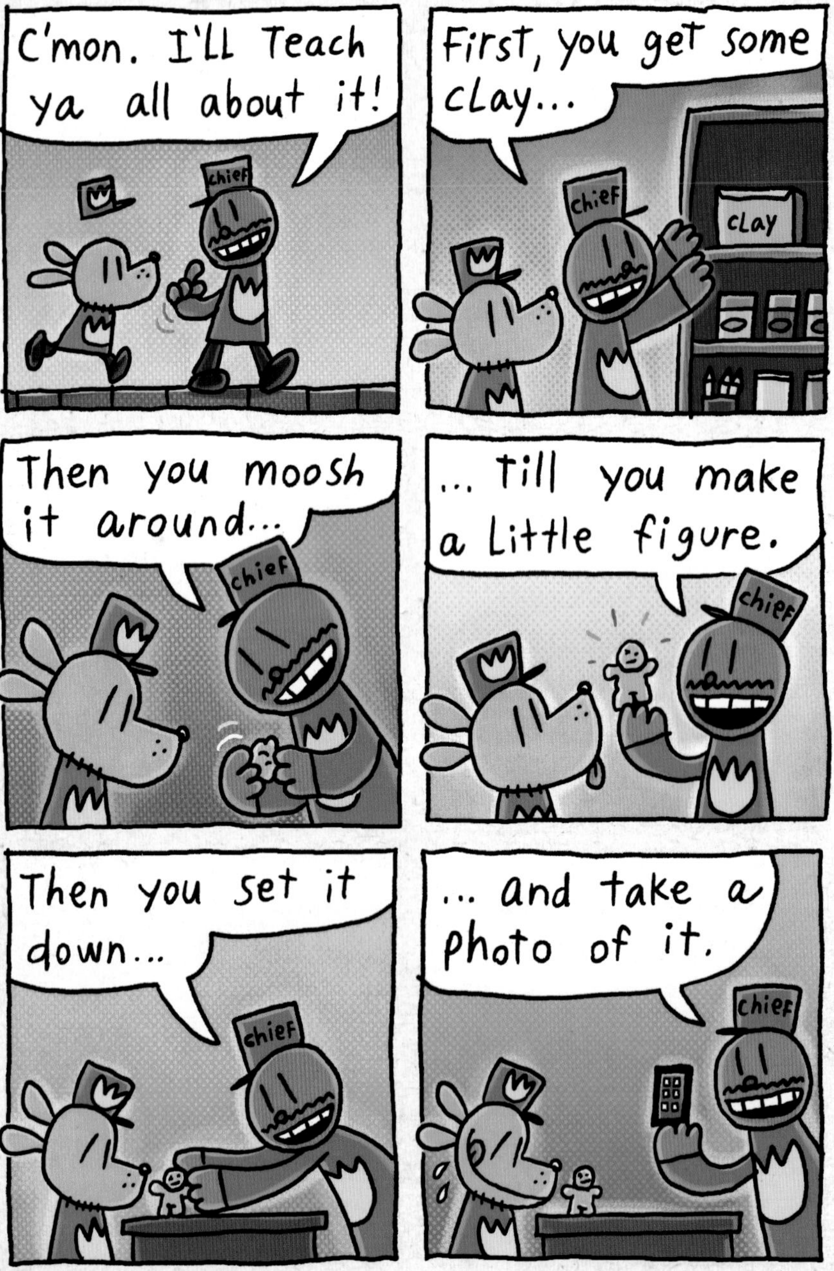
C'mon. I'LL Teach ya all about it!
chief
First, you get some cLay...
chief
cLay
Then you moosh it around...
chief
... Till you make a Little figure.
chief
Then you set it down...
chief
... and take a photo of it.
chief

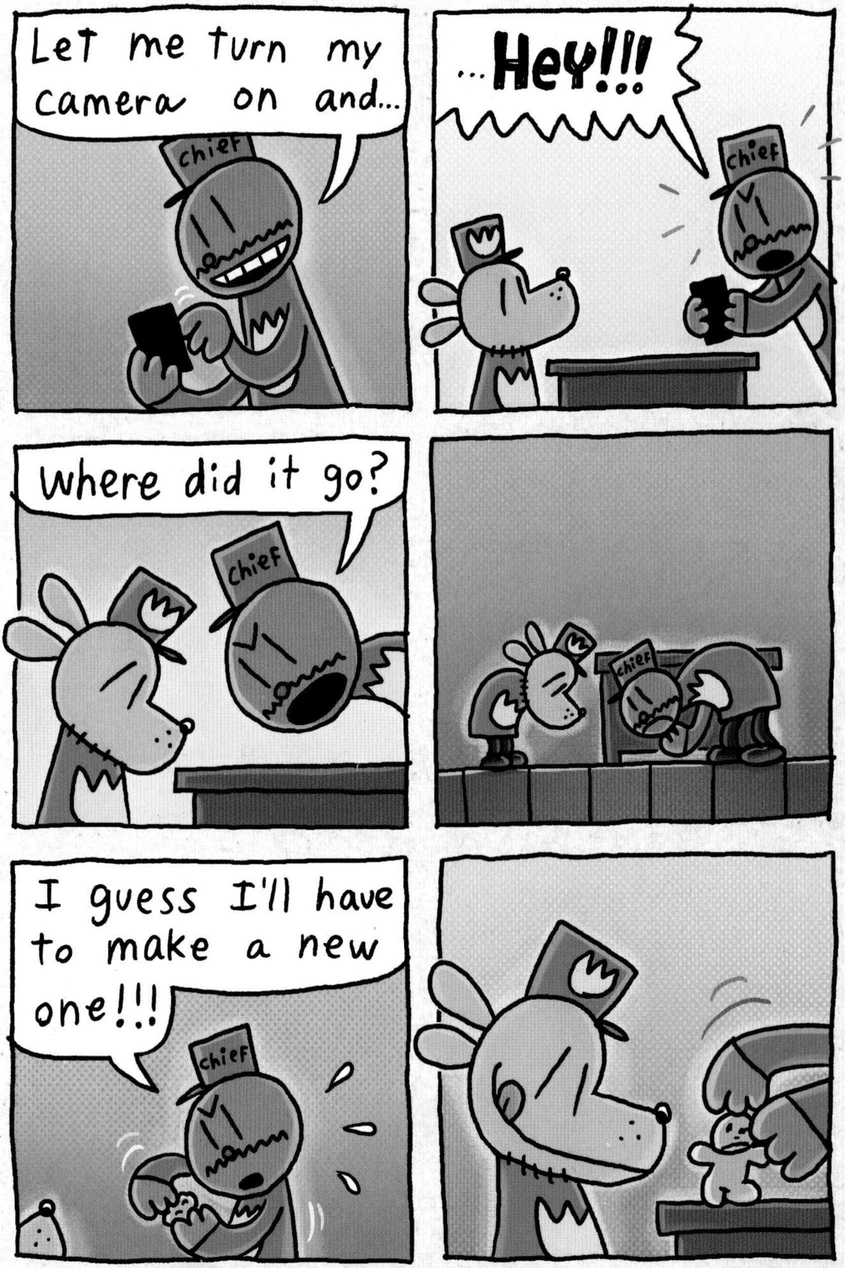
Let me turn my camera on and...
...Hey!!!
chief
chief
Where did it go?
chief
chief
I guess I'll have to make a new one!!!
chief

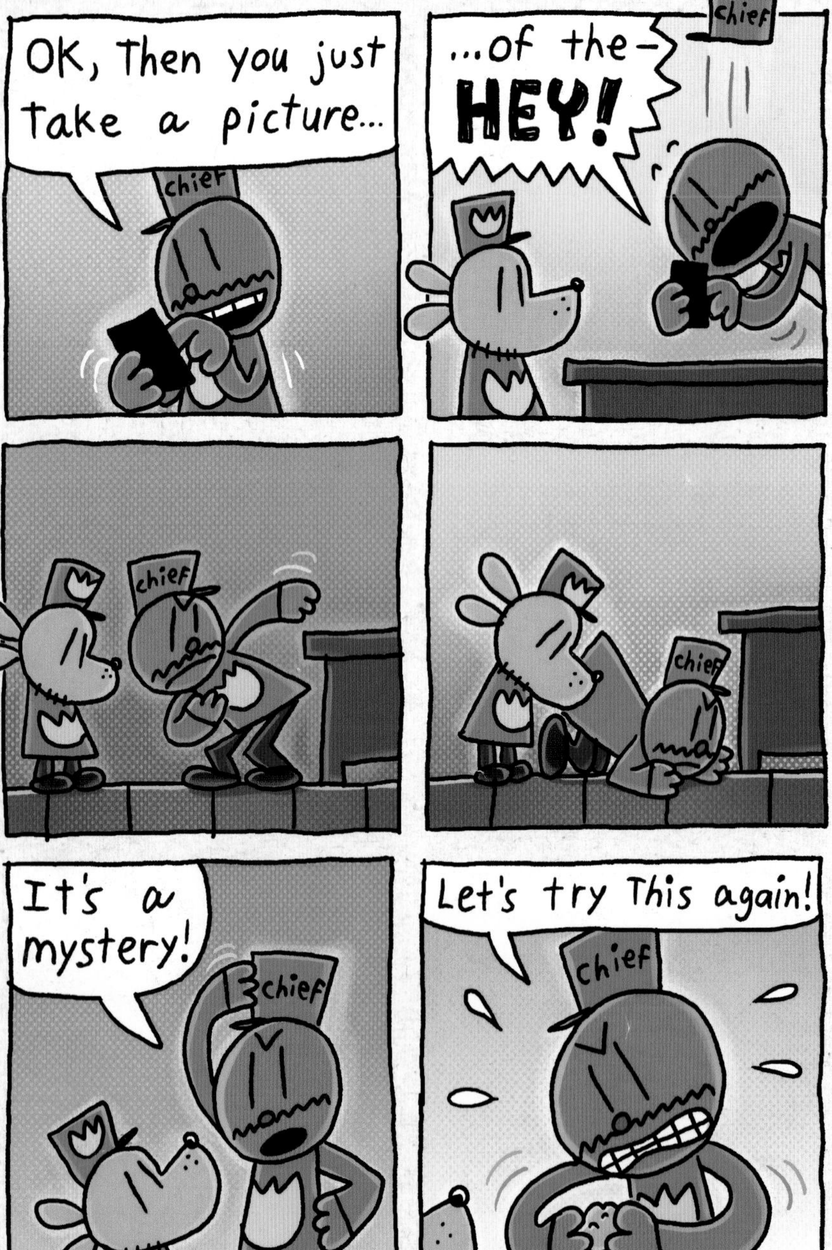
OK, Then you just take a picture...
chief
...of the–
HEY!
chief
chief
chief
It's a mystery!
chief
Let's try This again!
chief

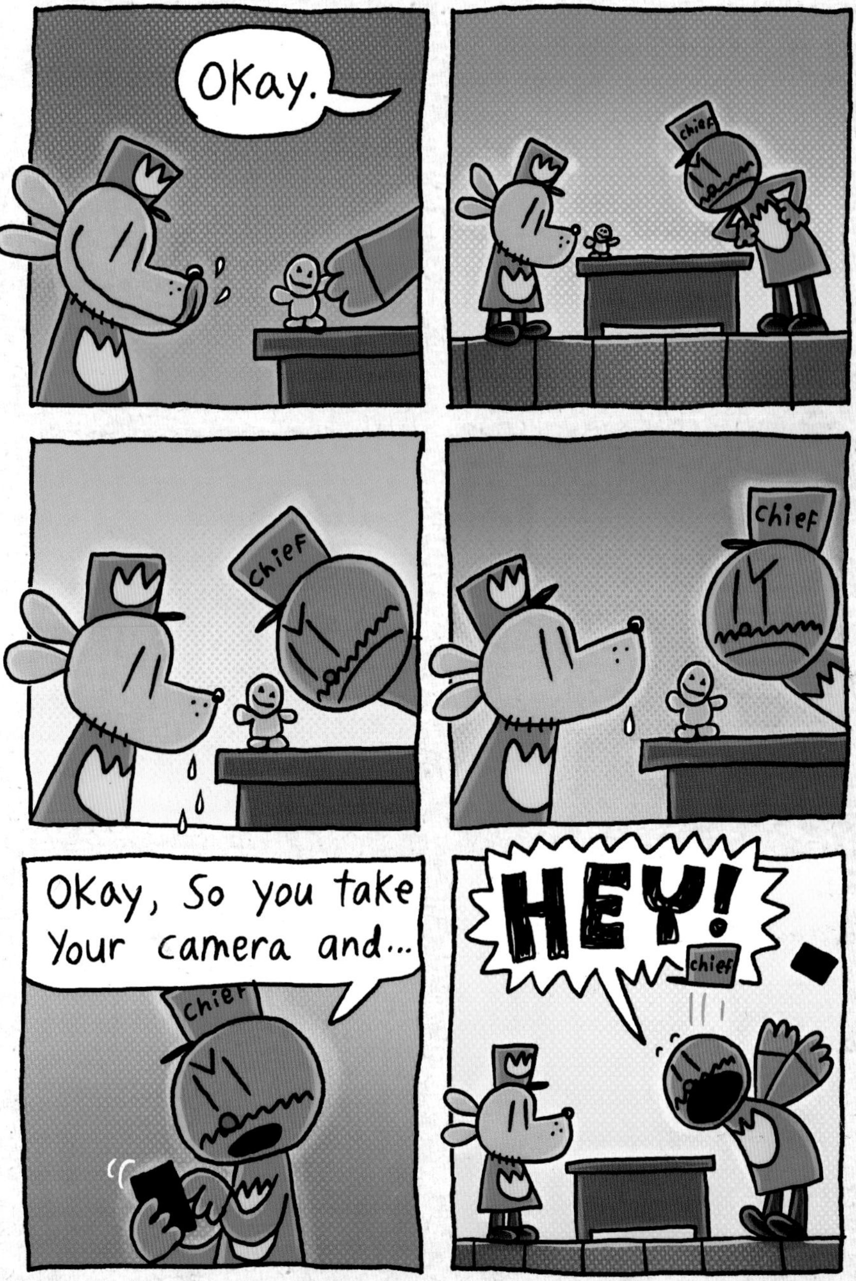
Okay.
chief
chief
chief
Okay, So you take Your camera and...
chief
HEY!
chief

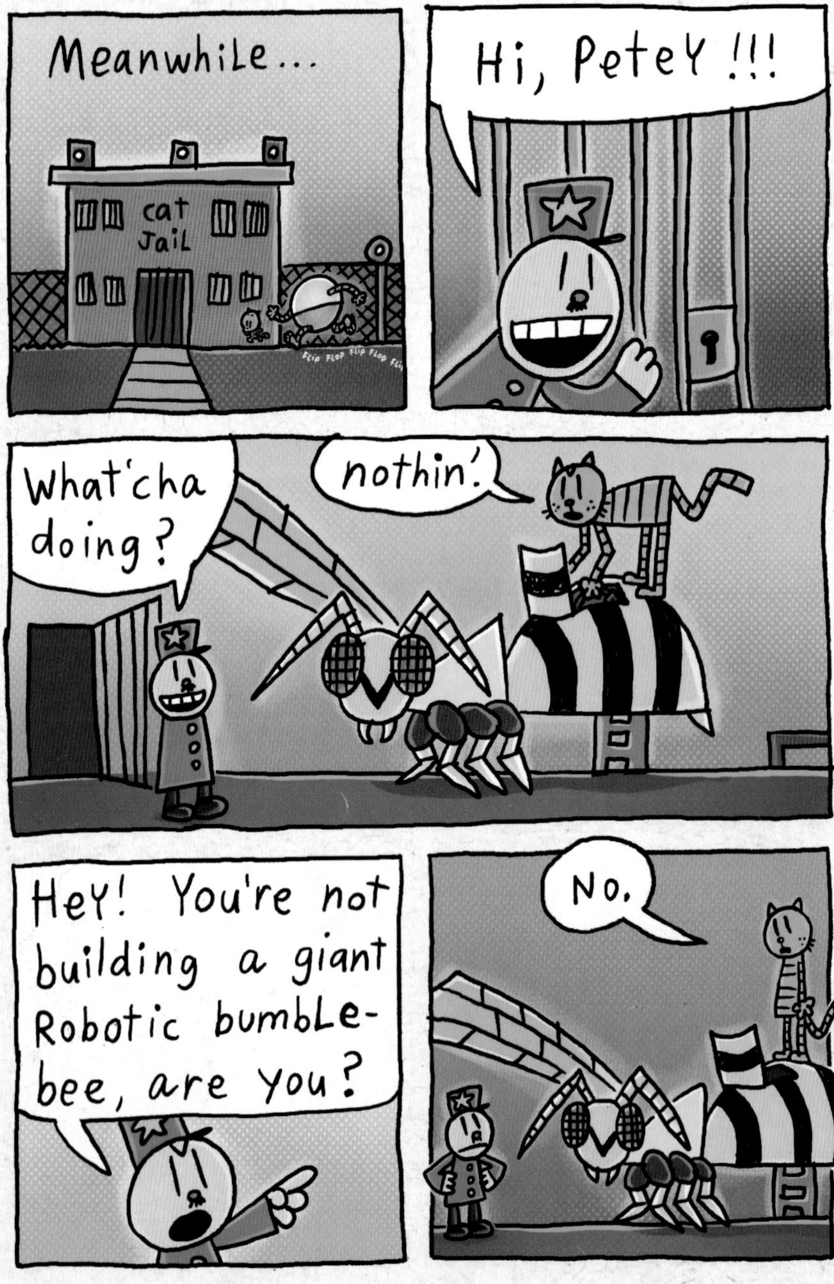
Meanwhile...
Cat Jail
Flip Flop Flip Flop Flip
Hi, Petey!!!
What'cha doing?
nothin'.
Hey! You're not building a giant Robotic bumble-bee, are you?
No.

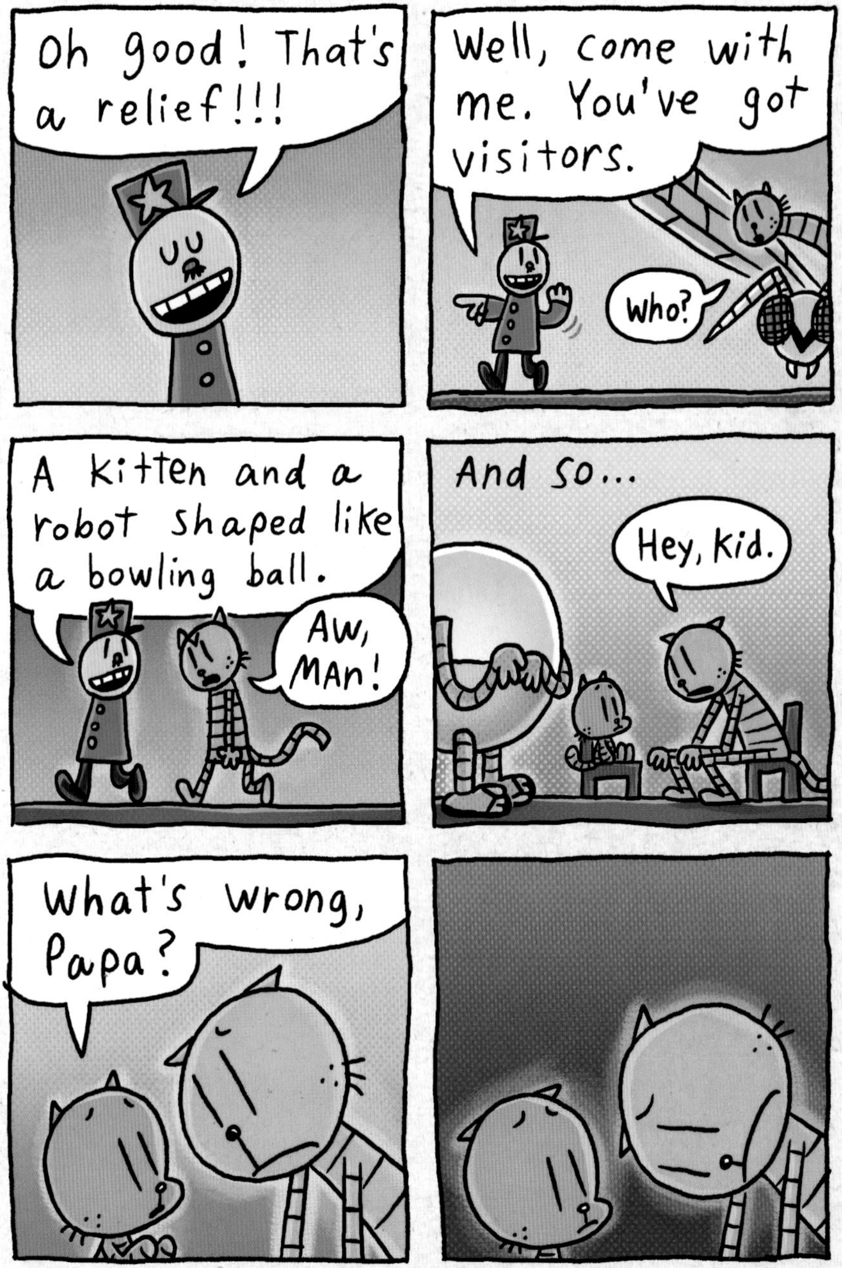
Oh good! That's a relief!!!
Well, come with me. You've got visitors.
Who?
A kitten and a robot shaped like a bowling ball.
AW, MAN!
And so...
Hey, kid.
What's wrong, Papa?

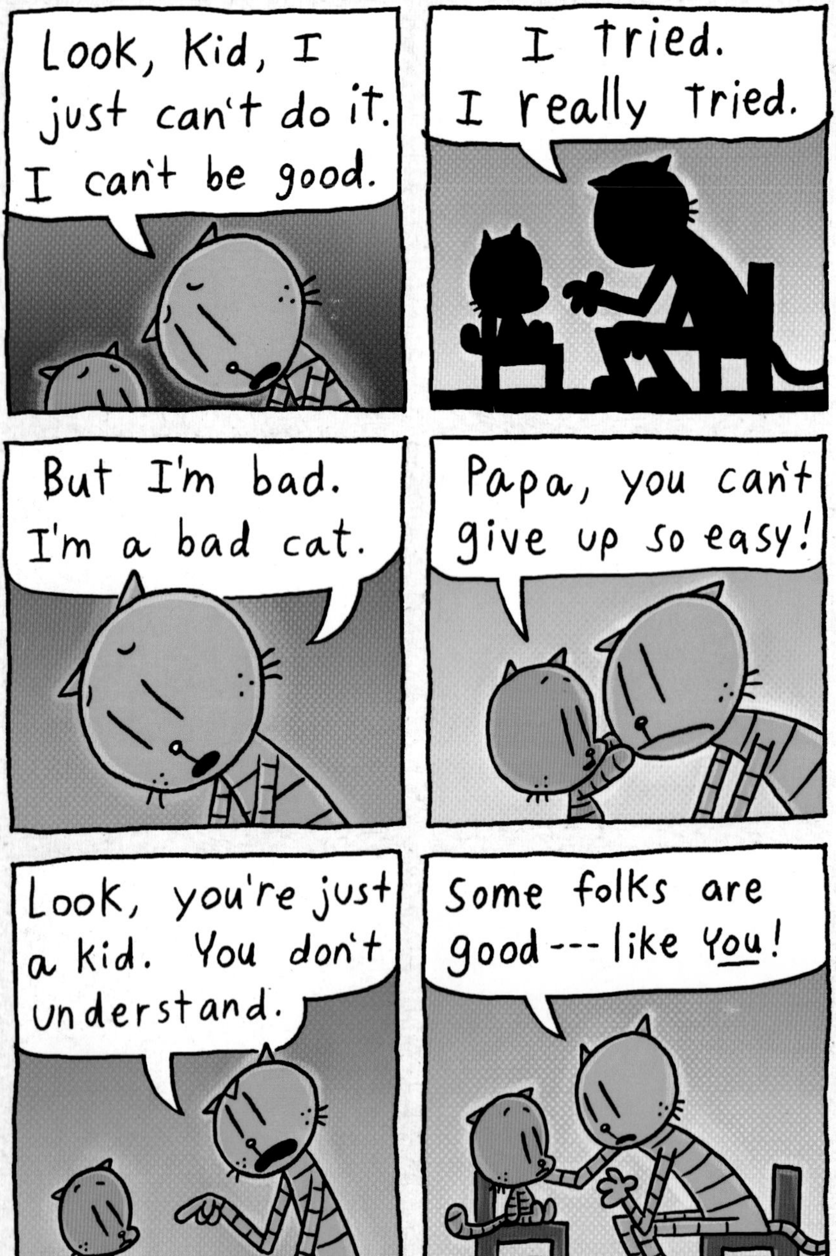
Look, Kid, I just can't do it. I can't be good.
I tried. I really tried.
But I'm bad. I'm a bad cat.
Papa, you can't give up so easy!
Look, you're just a kid. You don't understand.
Some folks are good---like you!

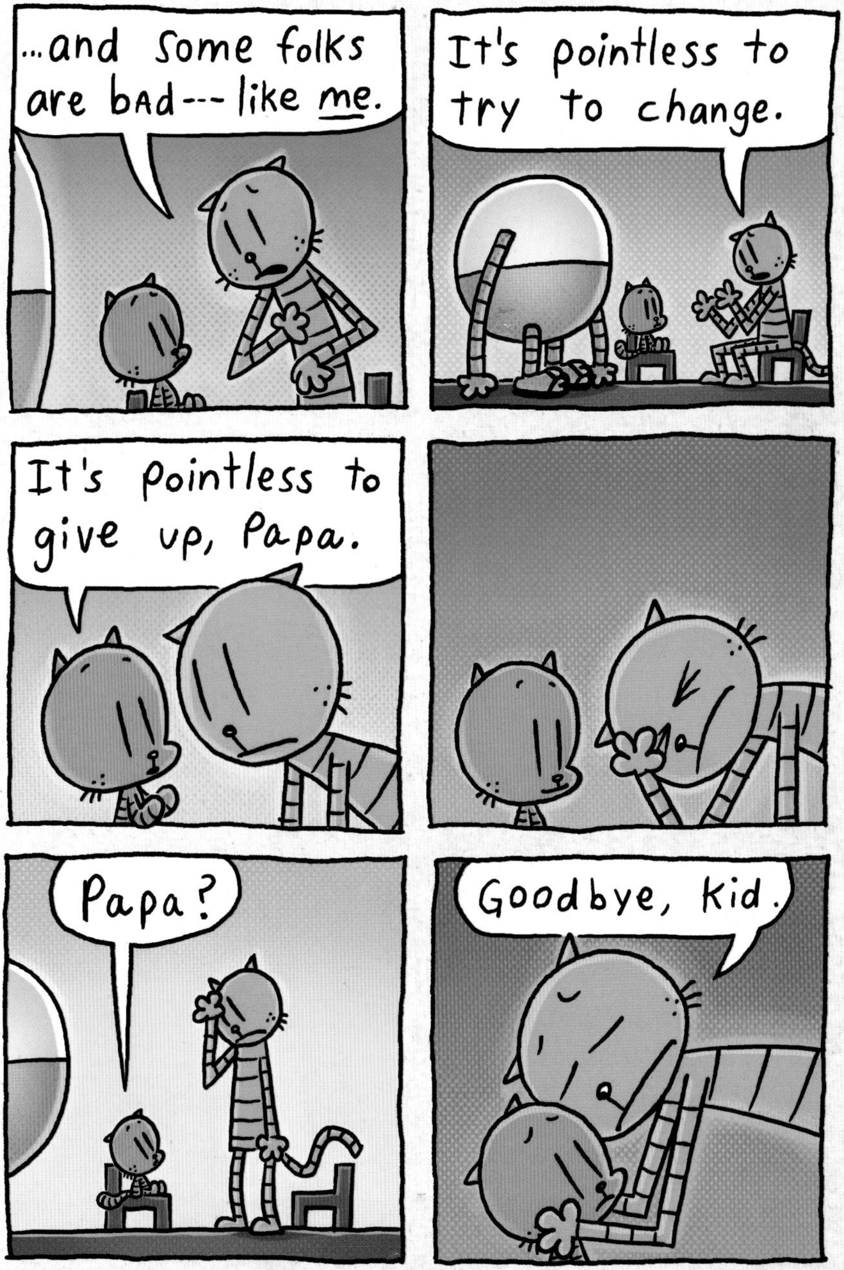
...and some folks are BAD--- like me.
It's pointless to try to change.
It's pointless to give up, Papa.
Papa?
Goodbye, kid.

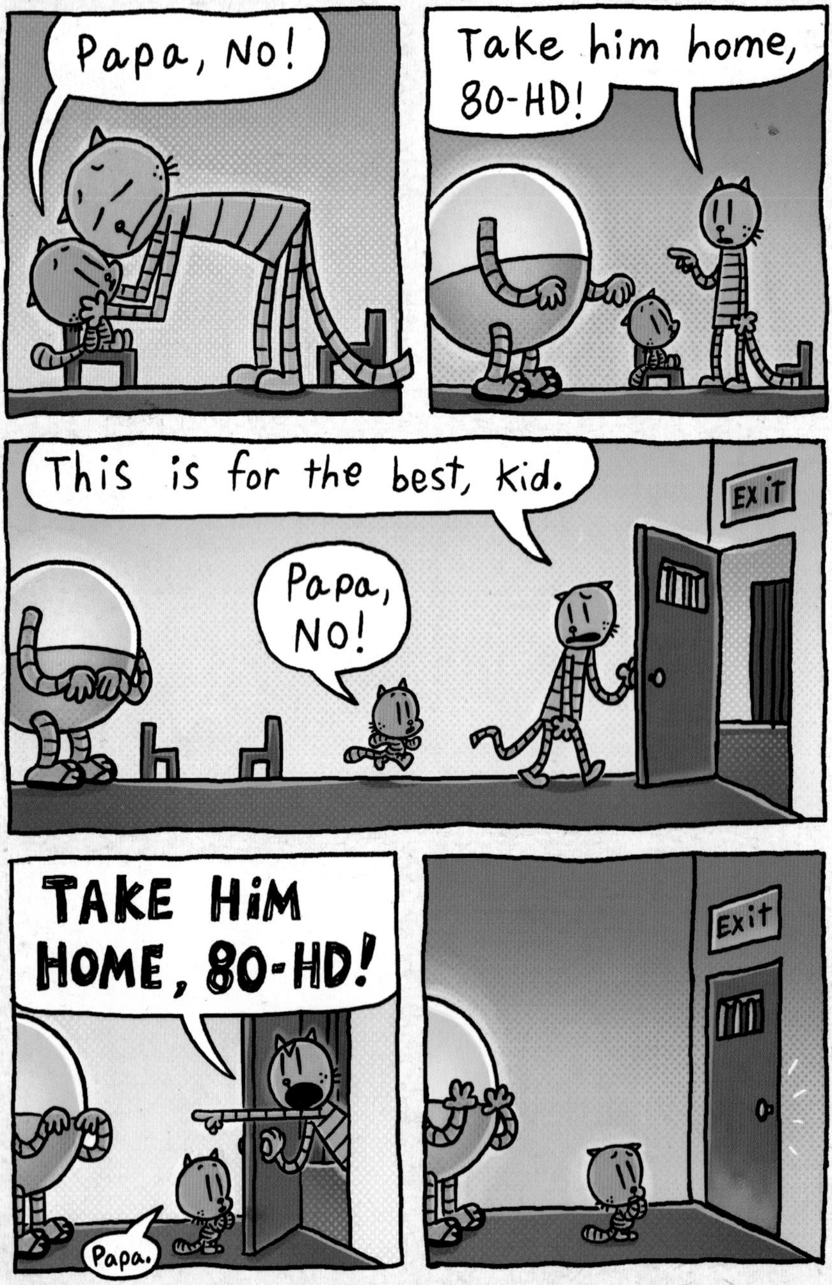
Papa, No!
Take him home, 80-HD!
This is for the best, kid.
EXIT
Papa, NO!
TAKE HiM HOME, 80-HD!
Papa.
Exit

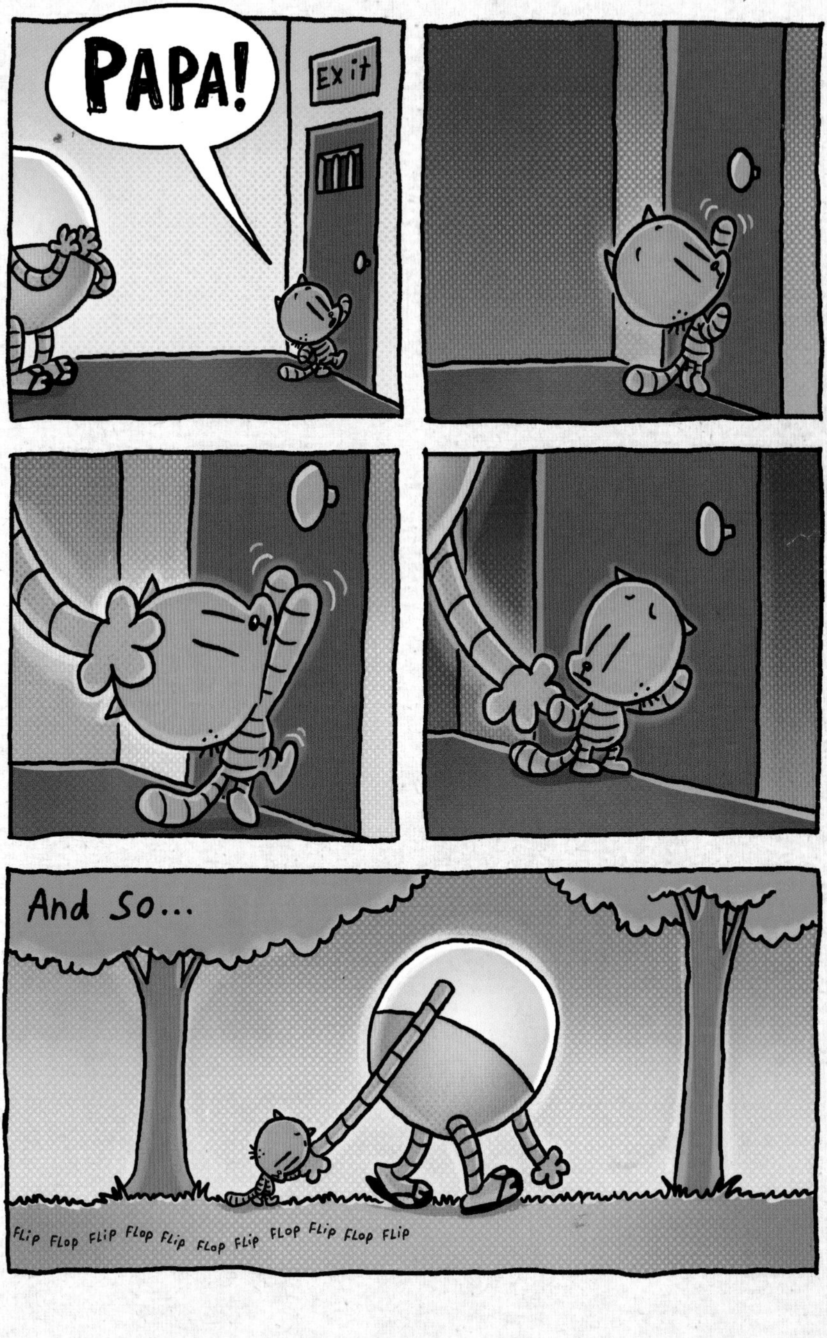
PAPA!
Exit
And so...
FLip FLop FLip FLop FLip FLop FLip FLop FLip FLop FLip

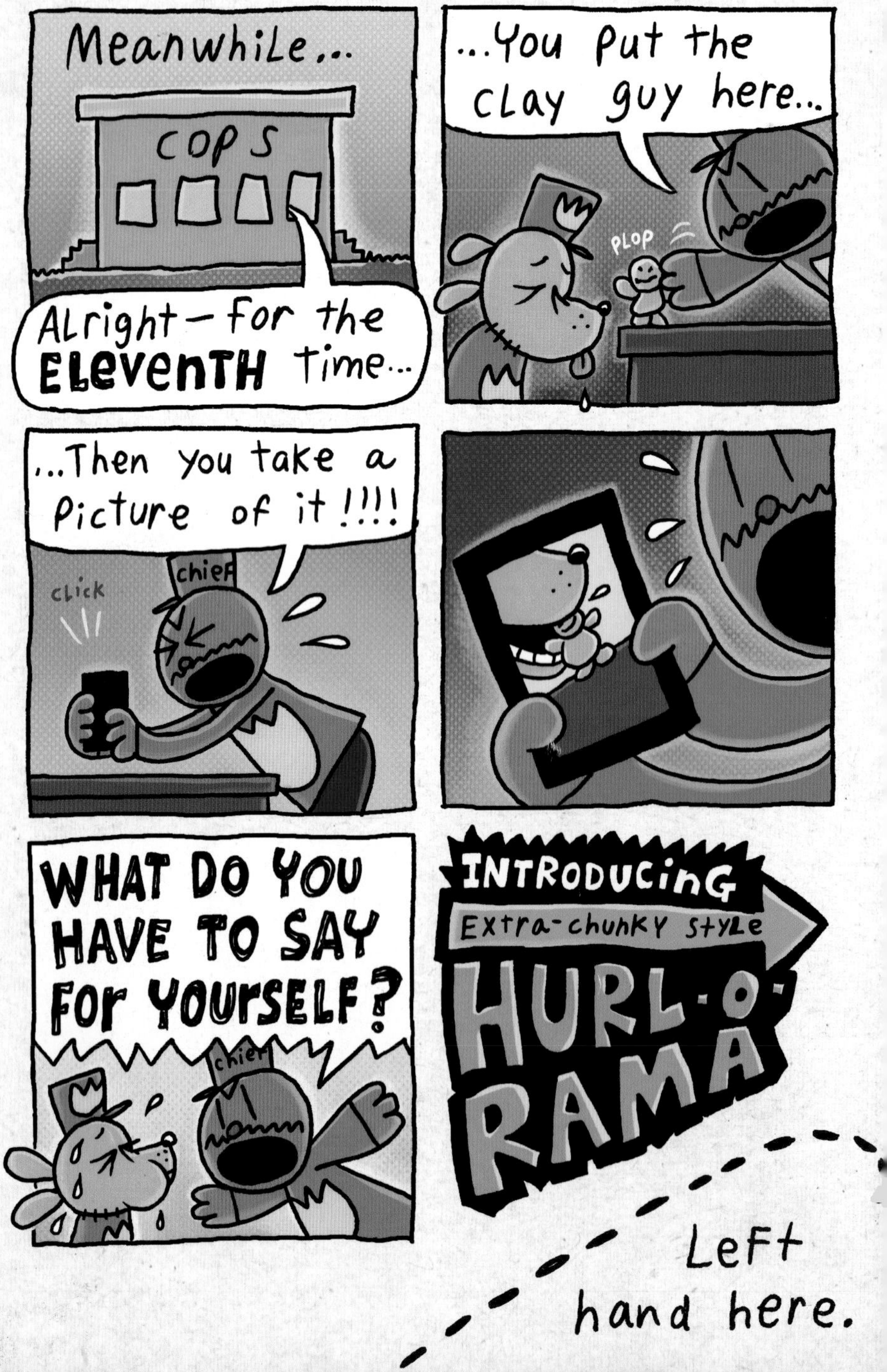
Meanwhile...
COPS
Alright—for the ELEVENTH time...
...You put the clay guy here...
PLOP
...Then you take a picture of it!!!!
chief
CLICK
WHAT DO YOU HAVE TO SAY FOR YOURSELF?
chief
INTRODUCING
Extra-chunky style
HURL-O-RAMA
Left hand here.

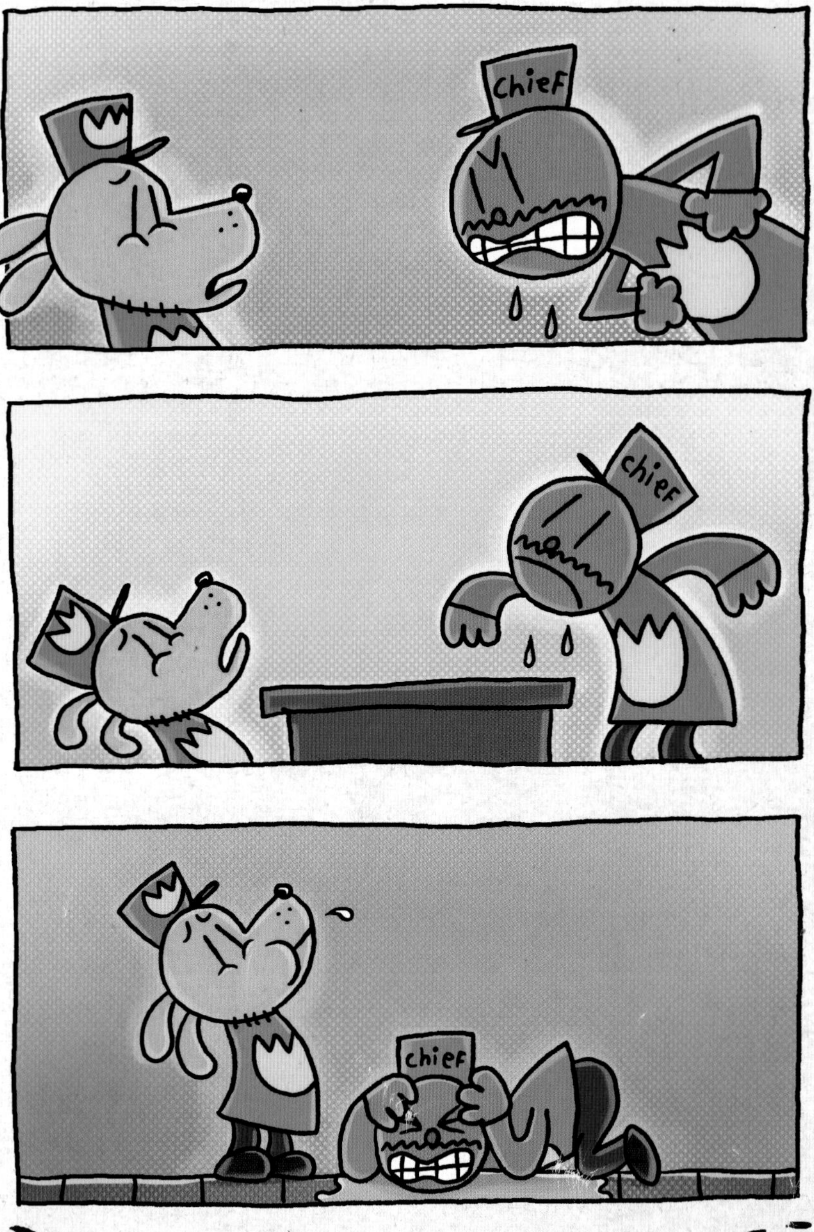
Chief
chief
chief

Right Thumb here.

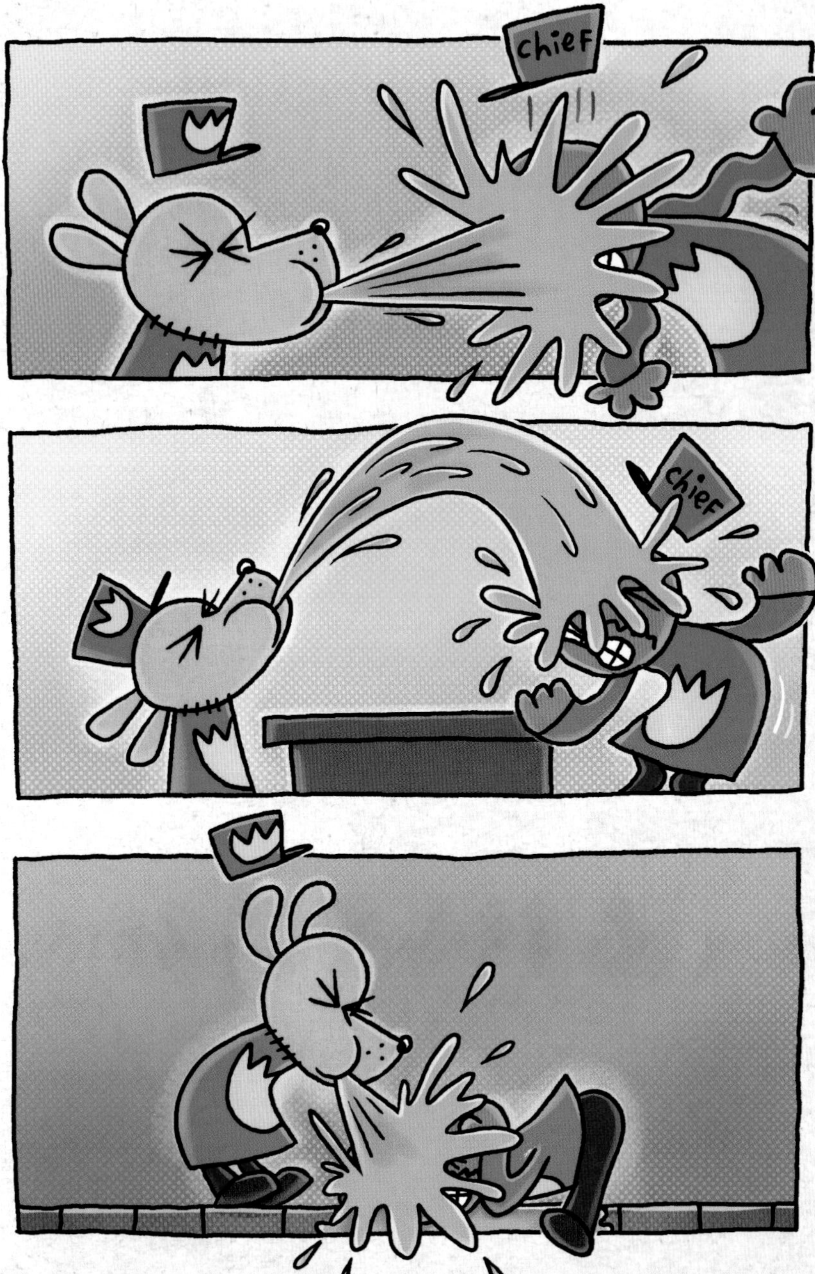
chief
chief

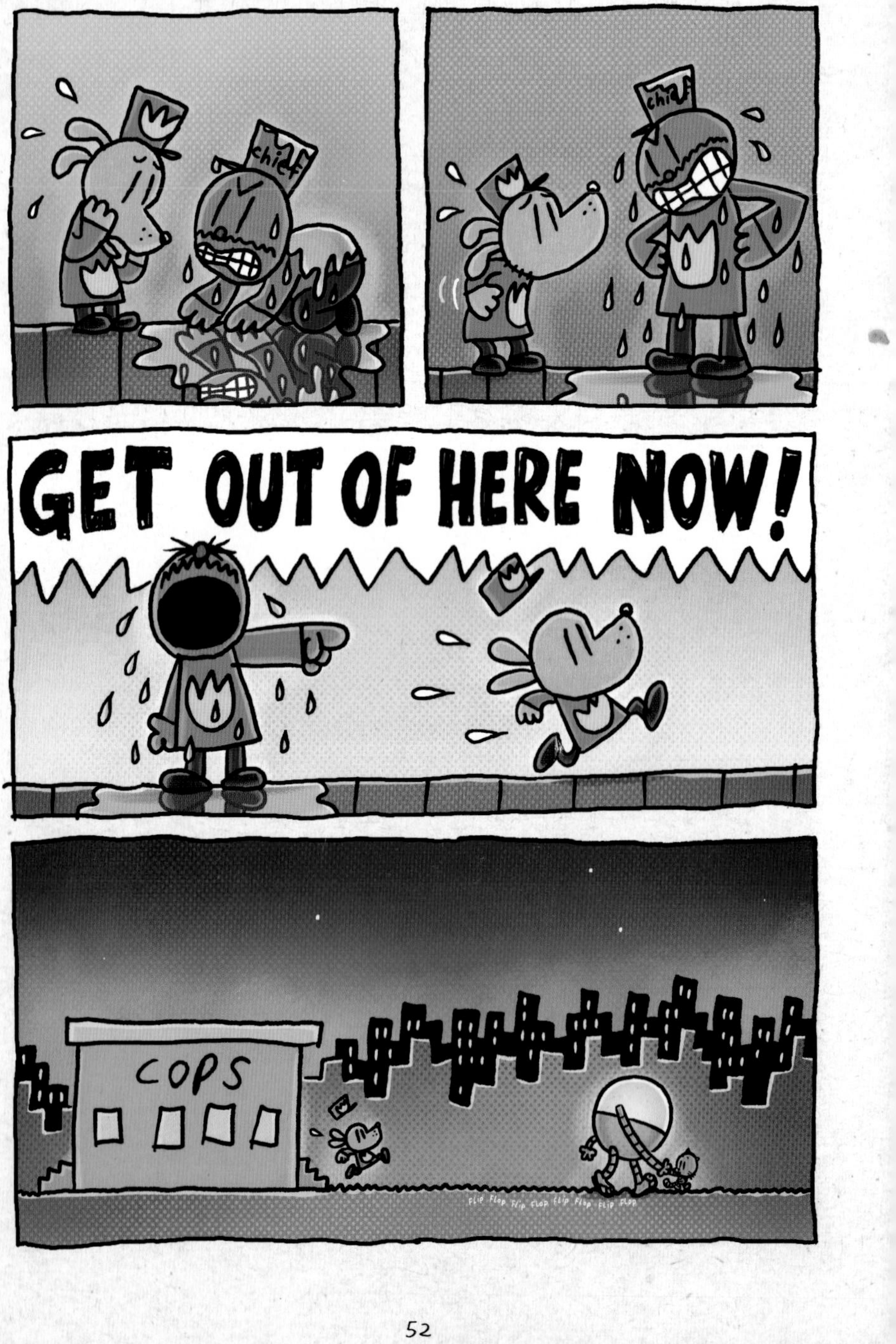
chief
chief
GET OUT OF HERE NOW!
COPS
FLIP FLOP FLIP FLOP FLIP FLOP FLIP FLOP

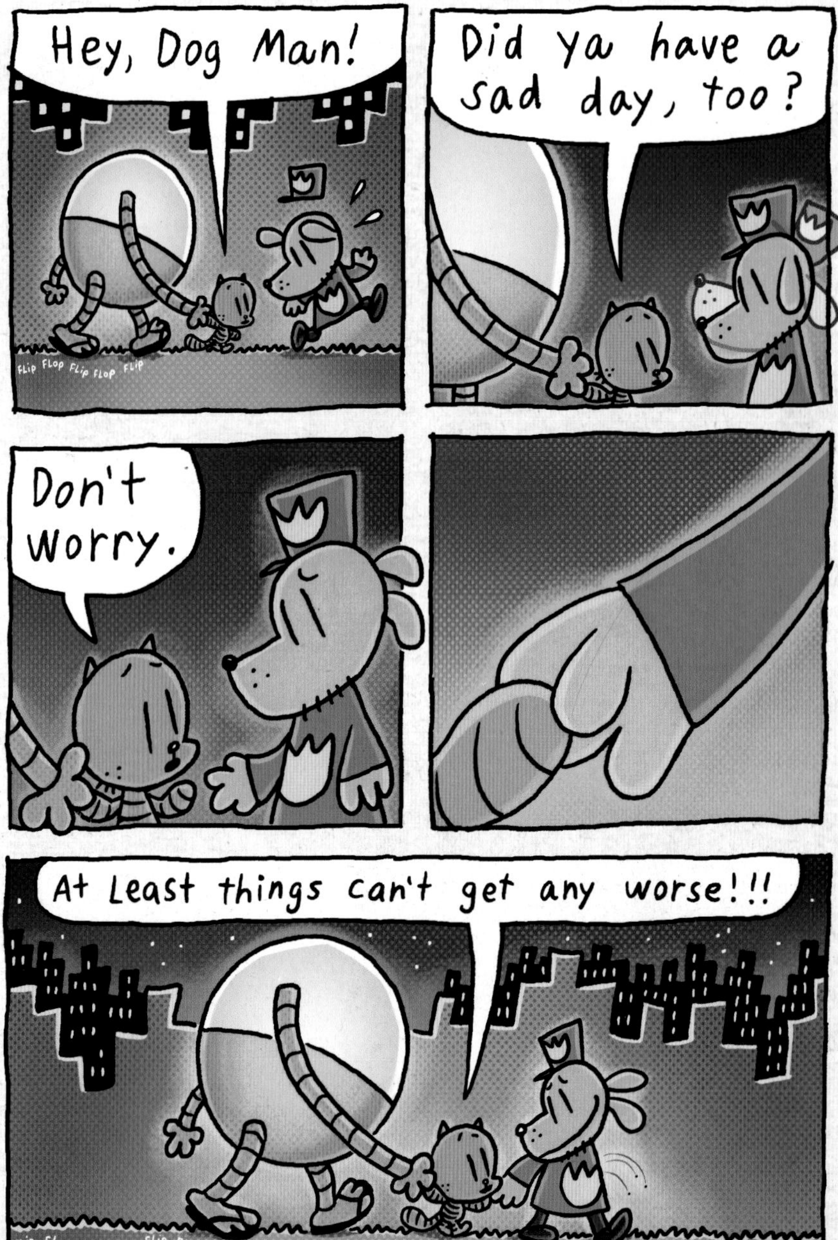
Hey, Dog Man!
FLIP FLOP FLIP FLOP FLIP
Did ya have a sad day, too?
Don't worry.
At Least things can't get any worse!!!
FLIP FLOP FLIP FLOP FLIP FLOP FLIP

Chapter 3

Things Get Worse!

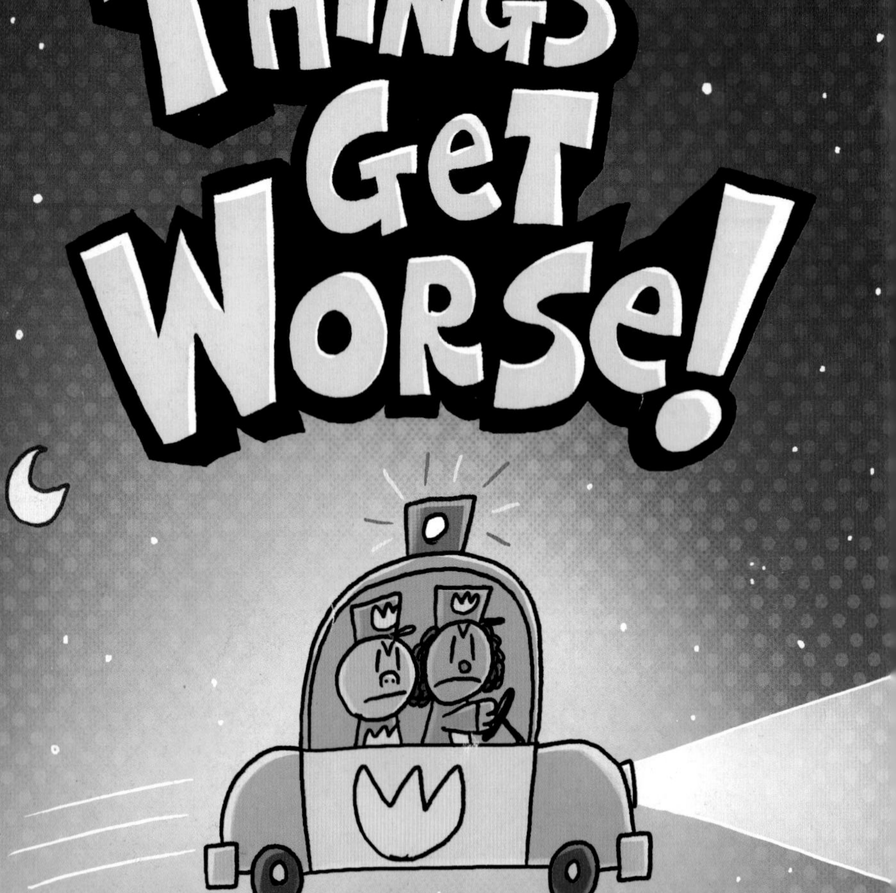

By George Beard and Harold Hutchins

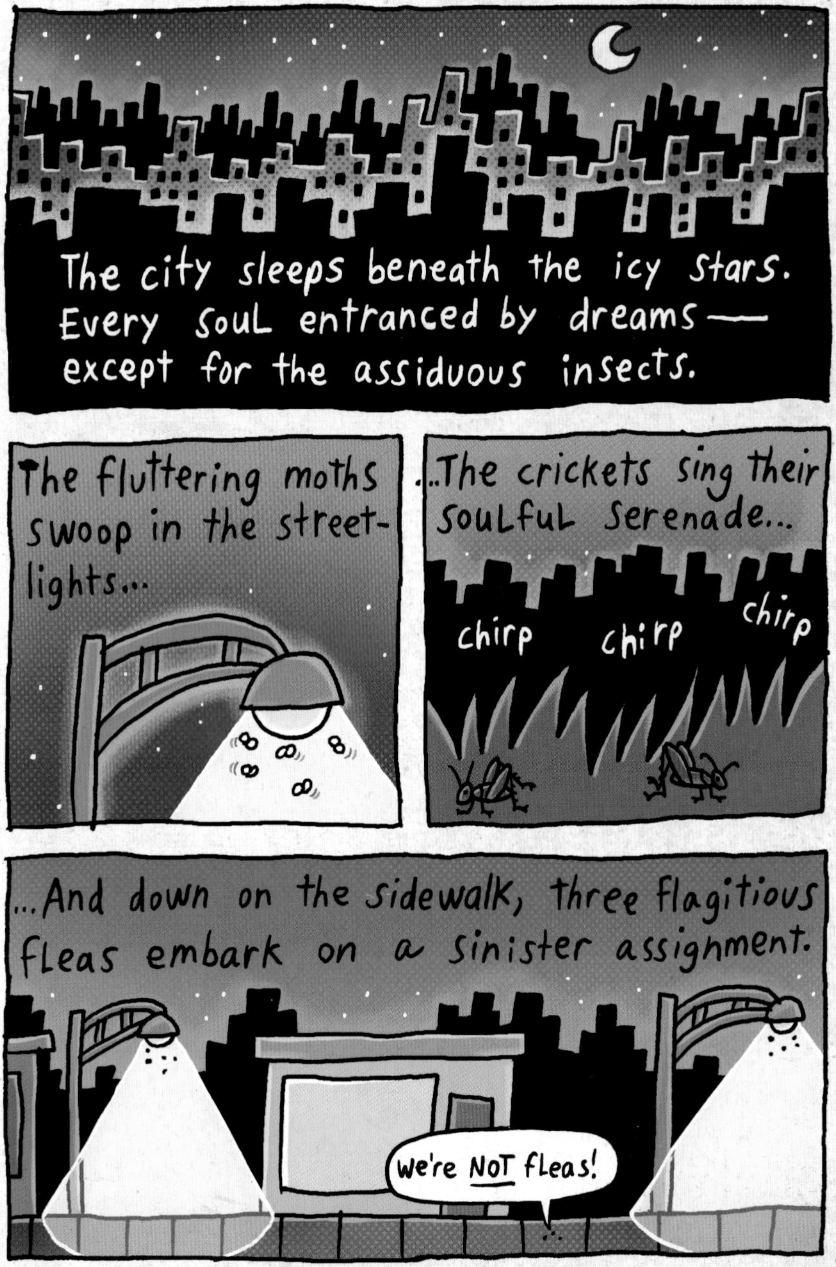

The city sleeps beneath the icy stars. Every soul entranced by dreams— except for the assiduous insects.
The fluttering moths swoop in the street-lights...
...The crickets sing their soulful serenade...
chirp
chirp
chirp
...And down on the sidewalk, three flagitious fleas embark on a sinister assignment.
We're NOT fleas!

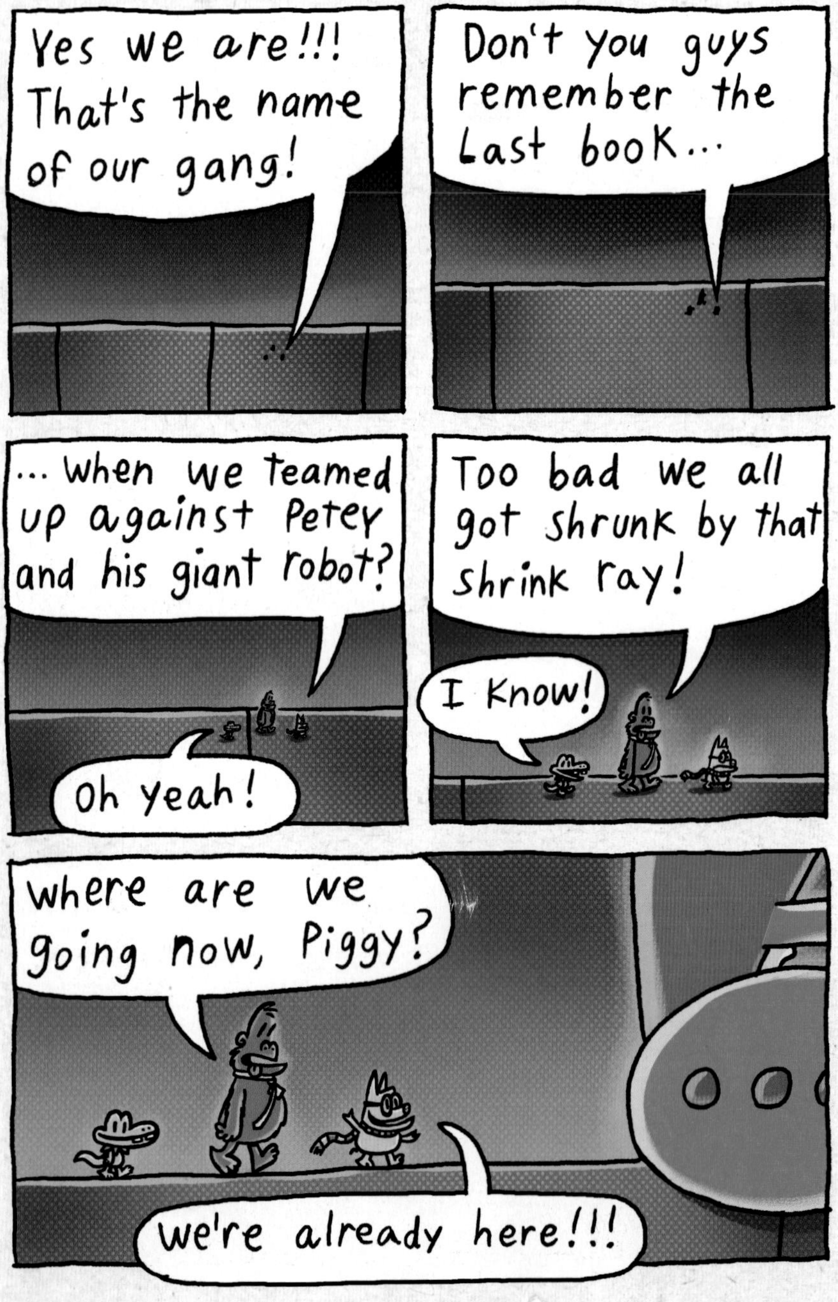
Yes we are!!! That's the name of our gang!
Don't you guys remember the Last book...
... when we teamed up against Petey and his giant robot?
Oh yeah!
Too bad we all got shrunk by that shrink ray!
I Know!
Where are we going now, Piggy?
We're already here!!!

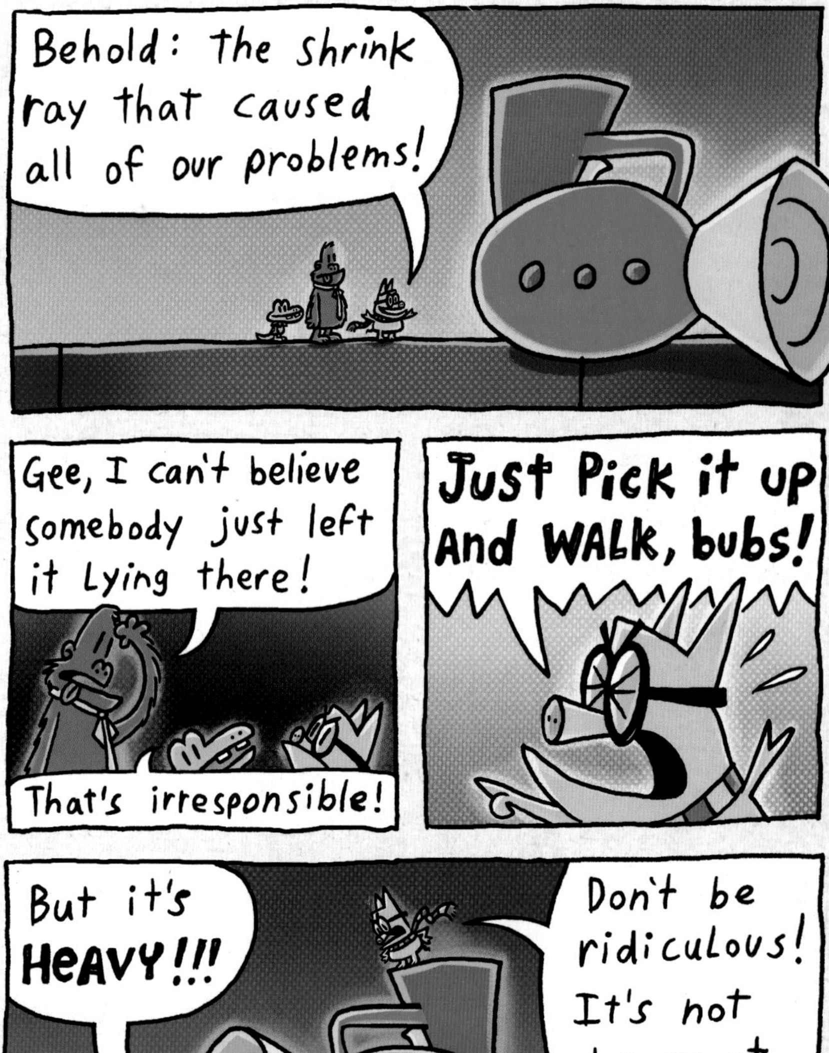
Behold: the shrink ray that caused all of our problems!
Gee, I can't believe somebody just left it Lying there!
That's irresponsible!
Just Pick it up And WALK, bubs!
But it's HEAVY!!!
Don't be ridiculous! It's not heavy at all!!!

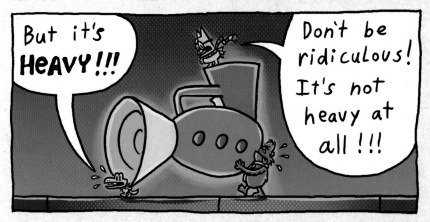

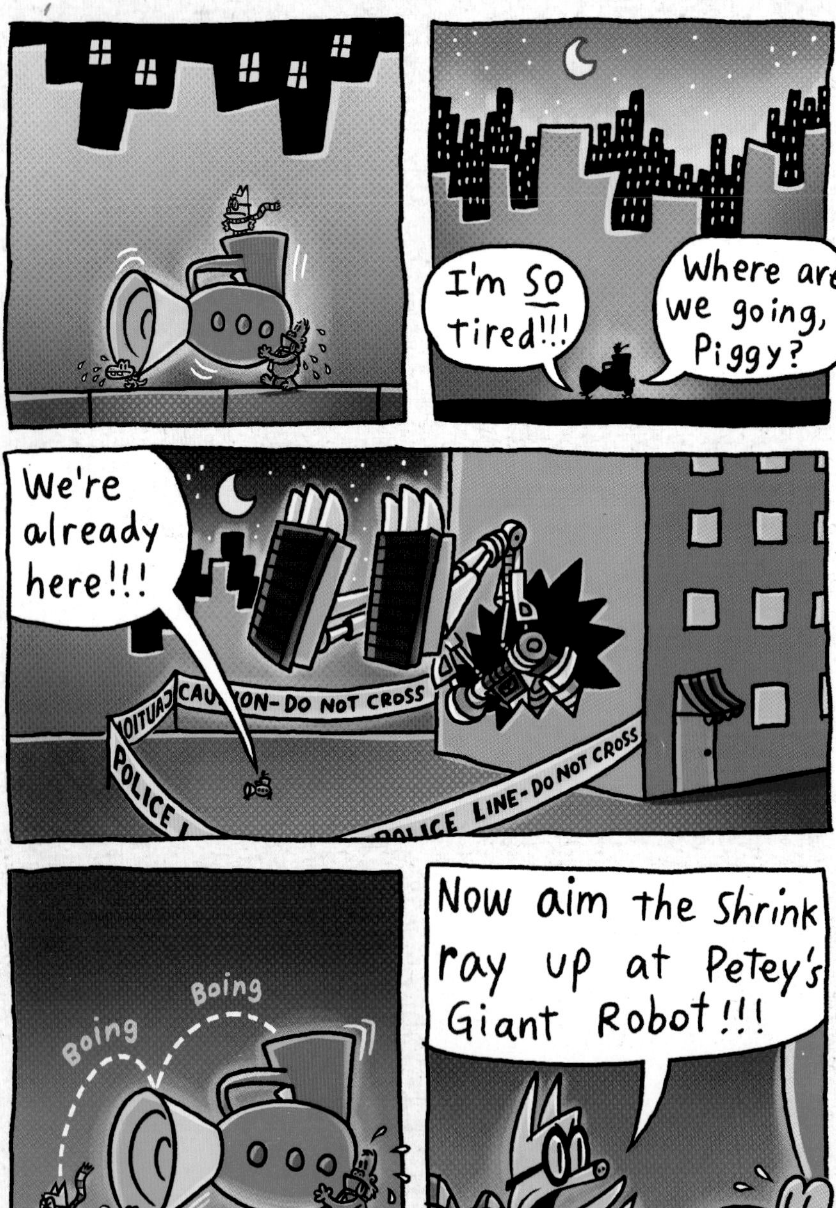
I'm SO tired!!!
Where are we going, Piggy?
We're already here!!!
CAUTION
CAU ON-DO NOT CROSS
POLICE L
POLICE LINE-DO NOT CROSS
Boing
Boing
Now aim the Shrink ray up at Petey's Giant Robot!!!

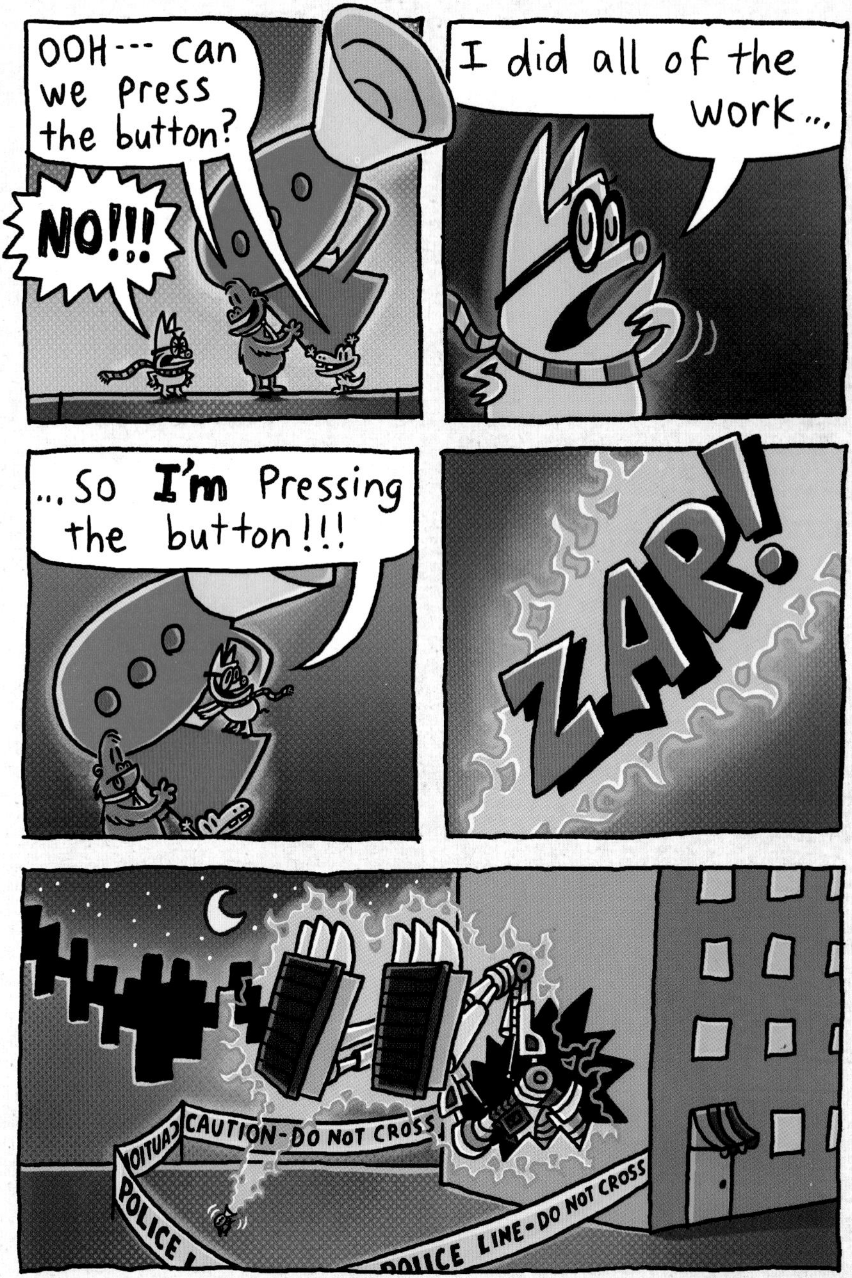
OOH--- can we press the button?
NO!!!
I did all of the work...
...So I'm Pressing the button!!!
ZAP!
CAUTION-DO NOT CROSS
POLICE LINE-DO NOT CROSS

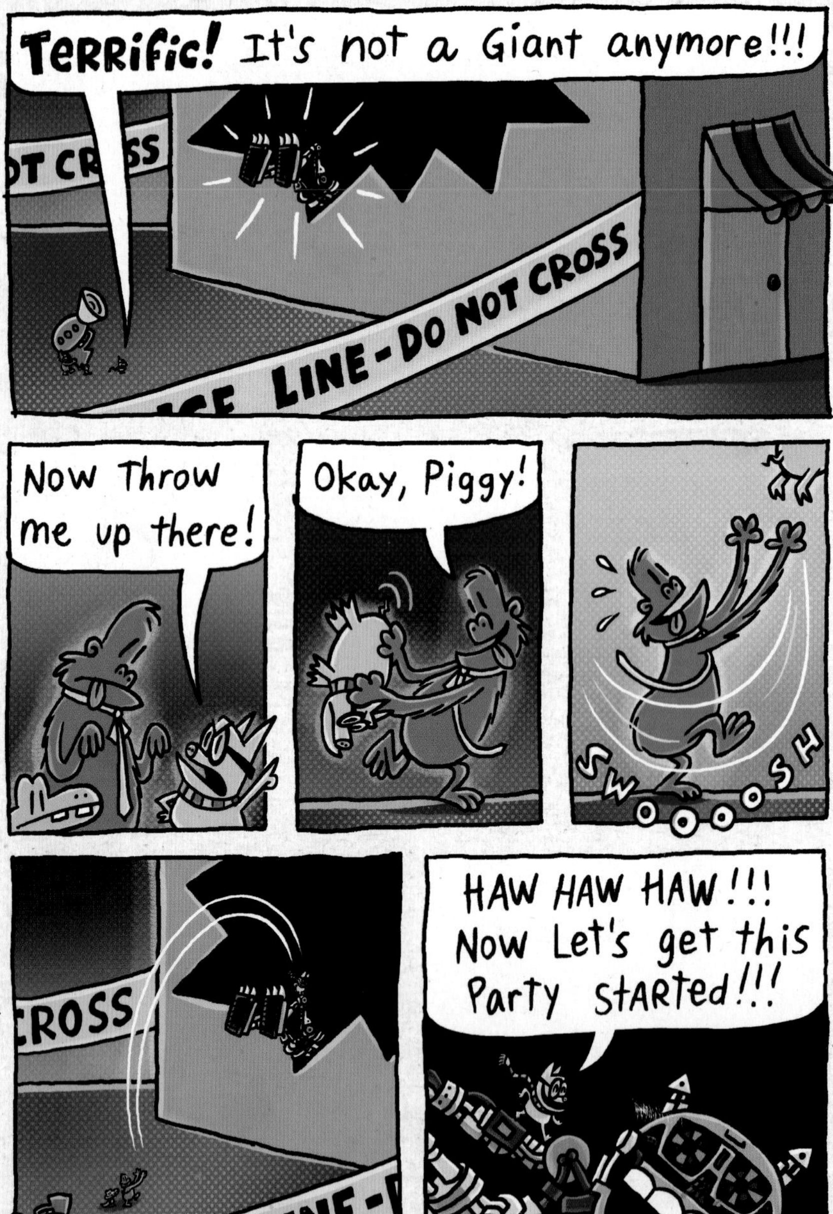
TERRIFIC! It's not a Giant anymore!!!
OT CROSS
LINE-DO NOT CROSS
Now Throw me up there!
Okay, Piggy!
SWOOOOSH
CROSS
LINE-
HAW HAW HAW!!! Now Let's get this Party STARTED!!!

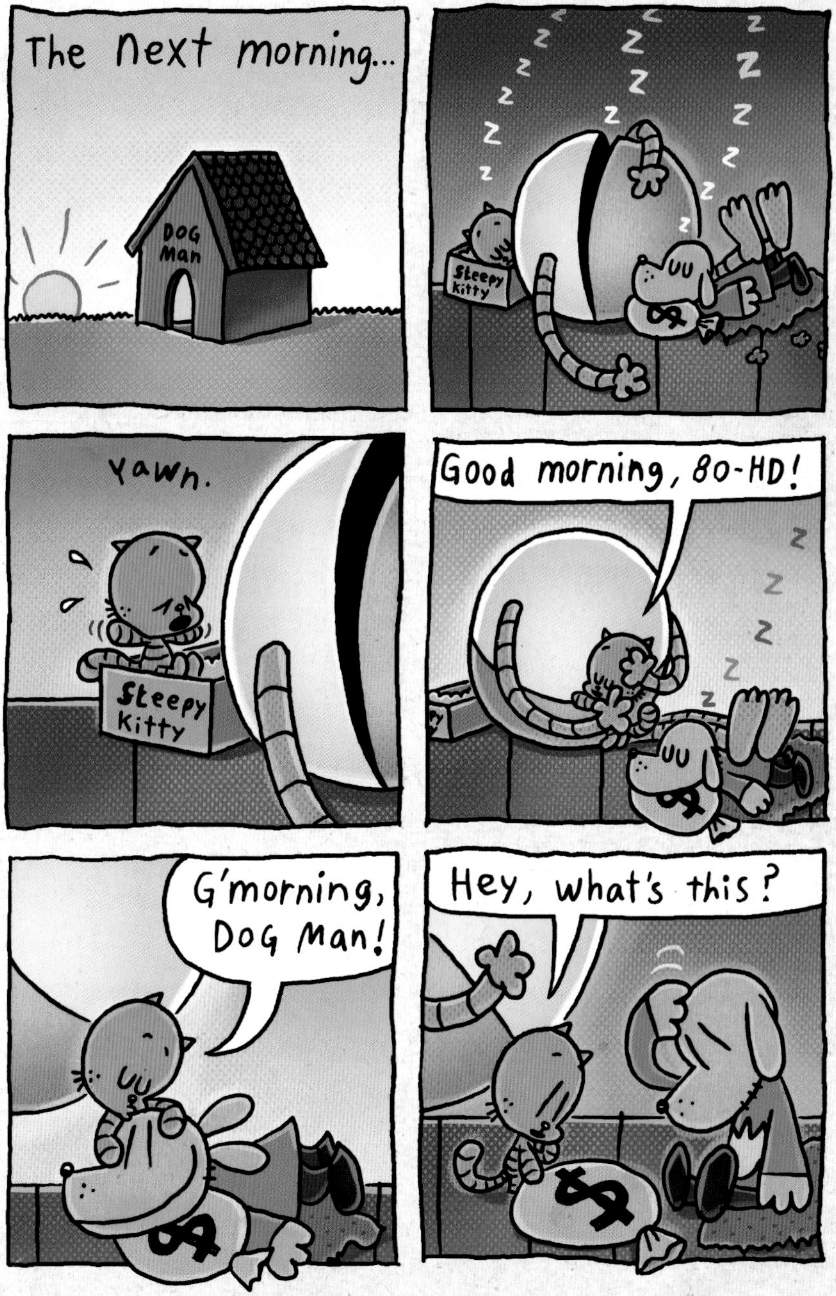
The next morning...
DOG Man
z z z z z z z z z z z z z
Steepy Kitty
Yawn.
Steepy Kitty
Good morning, 80-HD!
z z z z z
G'morning, DOG Man!
Hey, what's this?

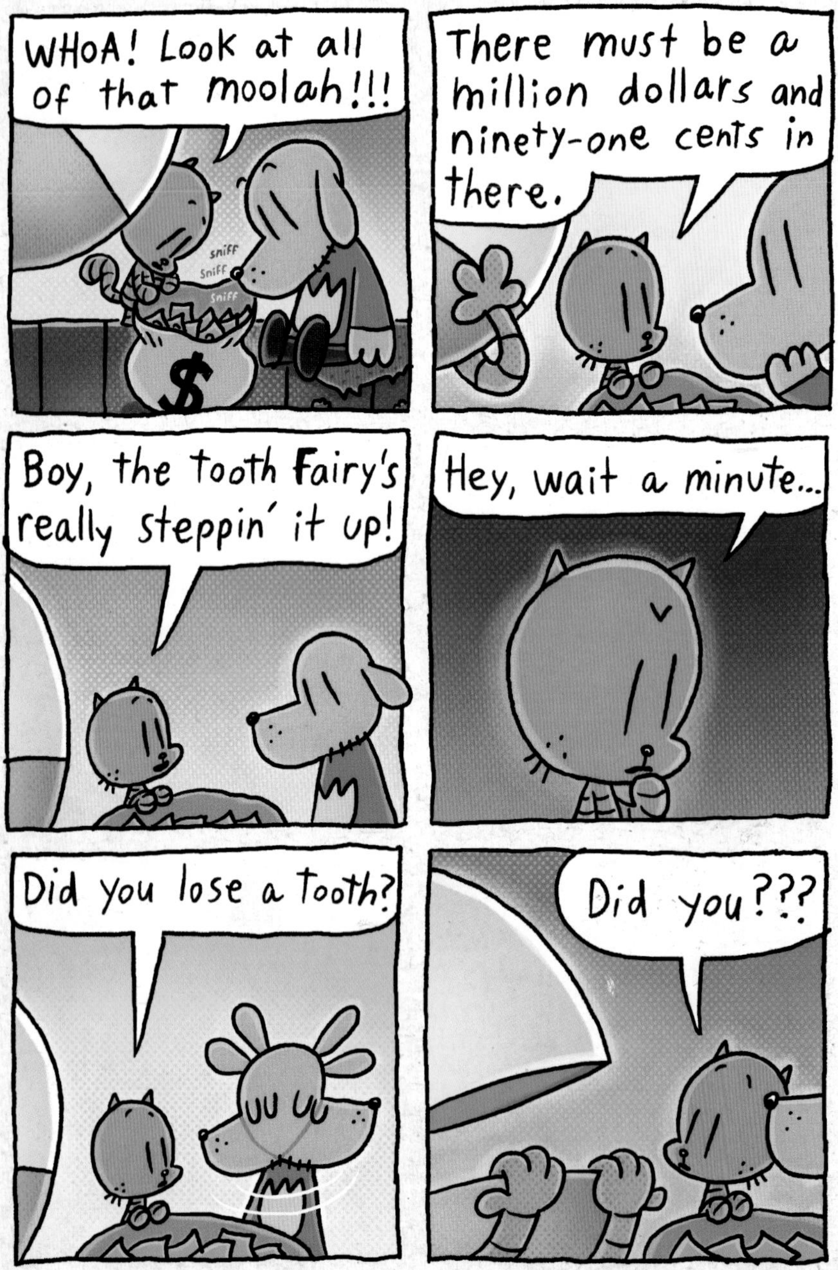
WHOA! Look at all of that moolah!!!
sniff
sniff
sniff
There must be a million dollars and ninety-one cents in there.
Boy, the tooth Fairy's really steppin' it up!
Hey, wait a minute...
Did you lose a tooth?
Did you???

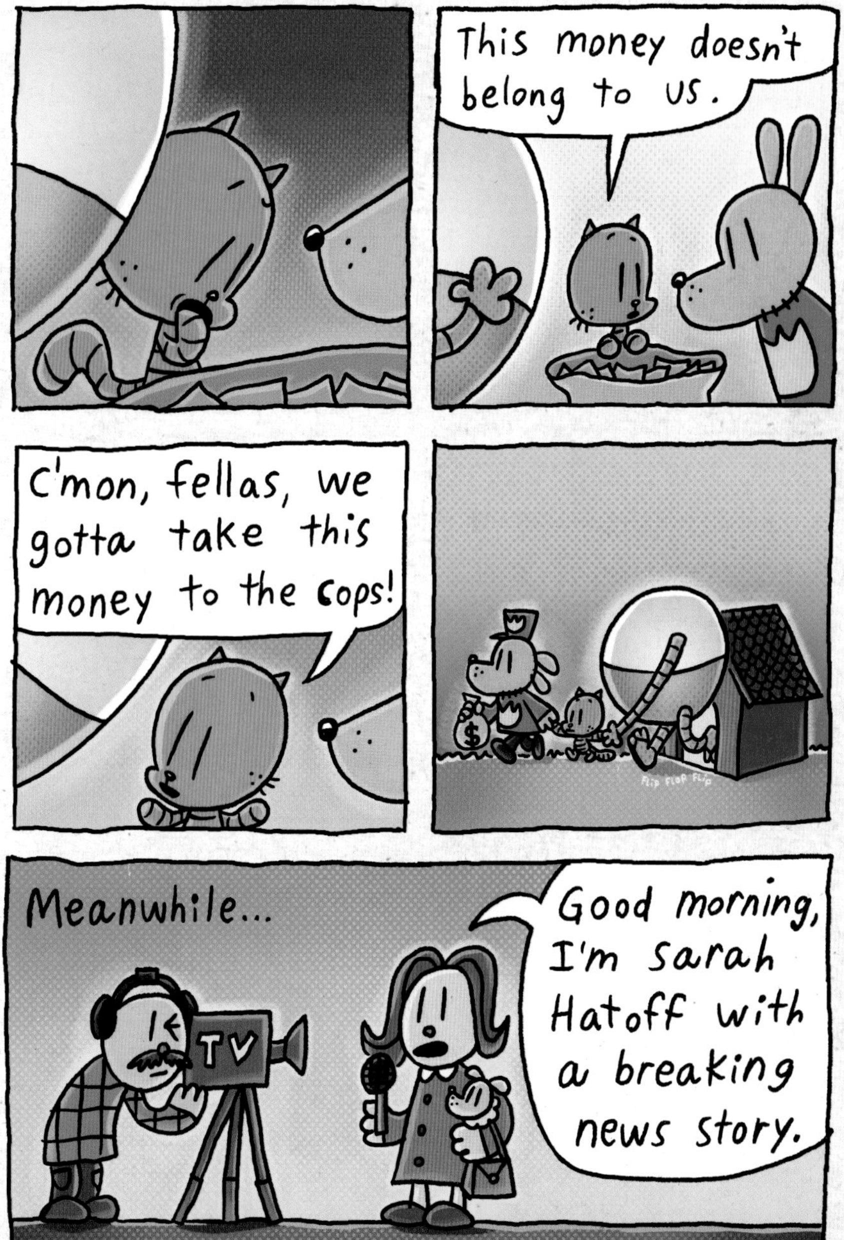
This money doesn't belong to us.
C'mon, fellas, we gotta take this money to the cops!
Flip Flop Flip
Meanwhile...
Good morning, I'm Sarah Hatoff with a breaking news story.

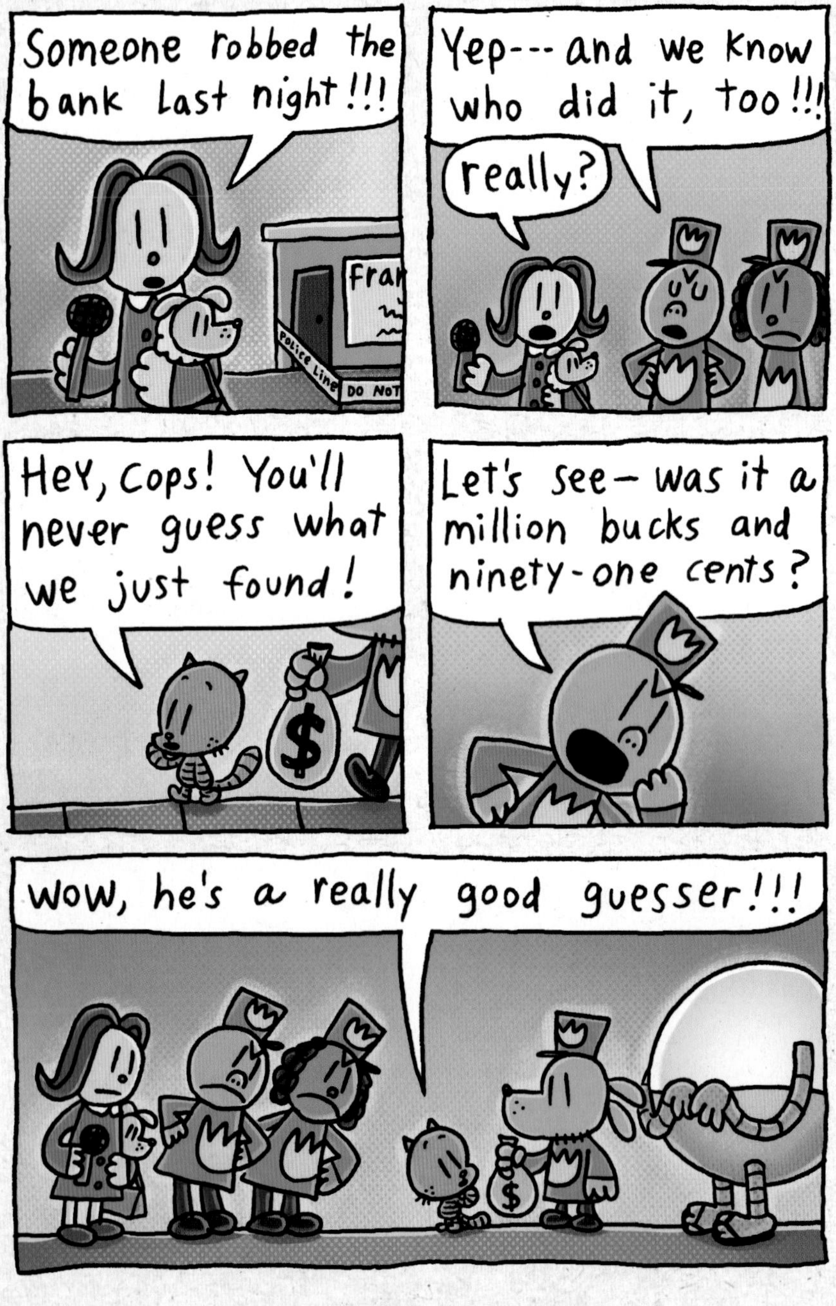
Someone robbed the bank last night!!!
Fran
POLICE LINE
DO NOT
Yep---and we know who did it, too!!!
really?
Hey, Cops! You'll never guess what we just found!
$
Let's see—was it a million bucks and ninety-one cents?
wow, he's a really good guesser!!!
$

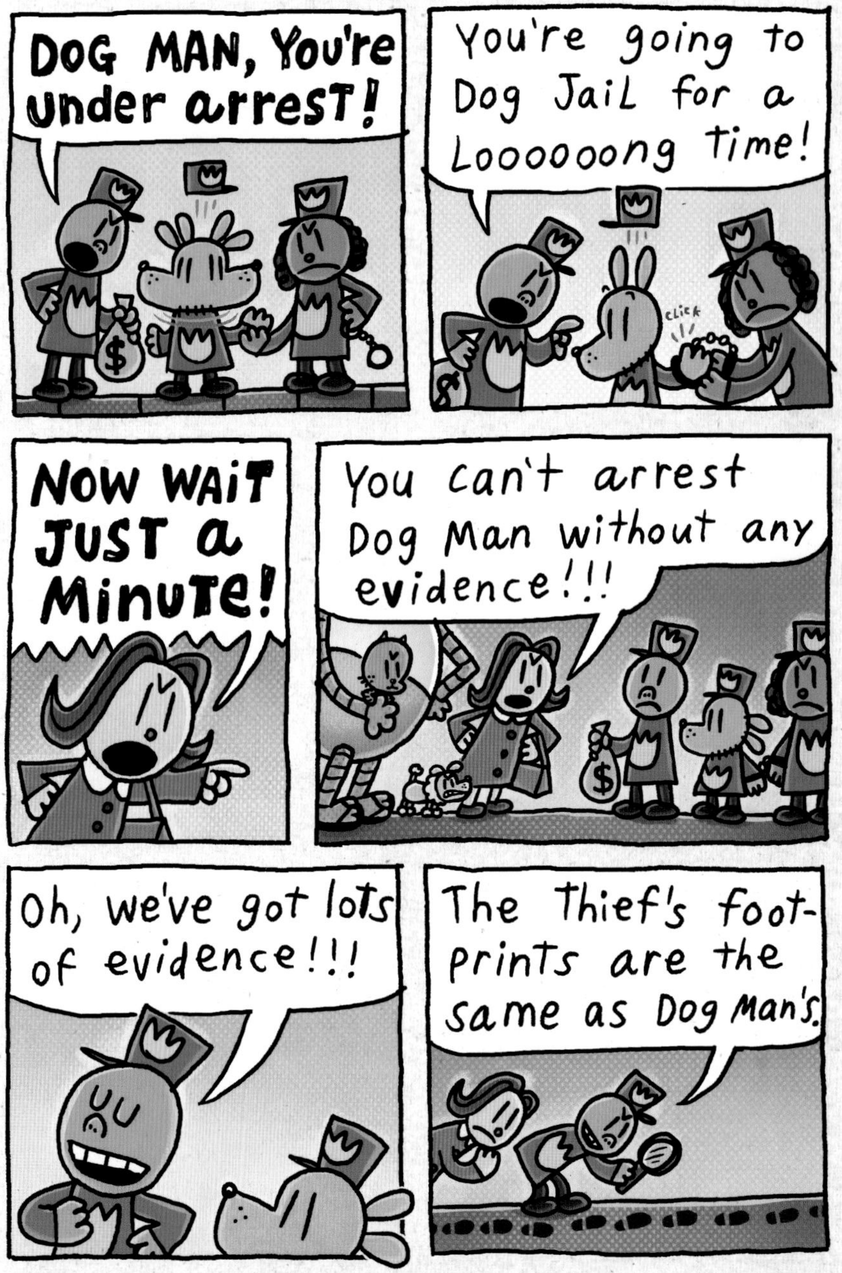
DOG MAN, You're under arrest!
You're going to Dog Jail for a Loooooong time!
click
NOW WAIT JUST a MinuTe!
You can't arrest Dog Man without any evidence!!!
Oh, we've got lots of evidence!!!
The Thief's foot-prints are the same as Dog Man's.

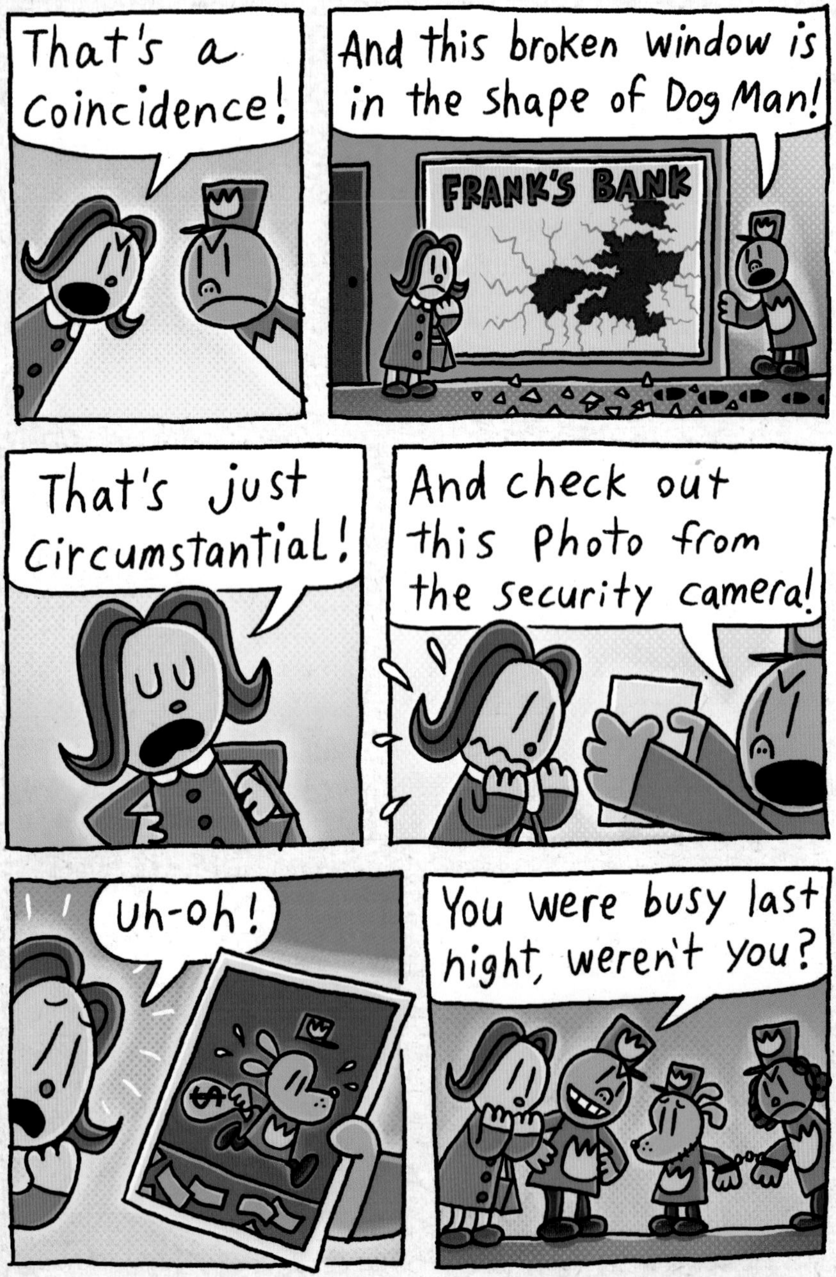
That's a Coincidence!
And this broken window is in the shape of Dog Man!
FRANK'S BANK
That's just Circumstantial!
And check out this Photo from the security camera!
Uh-oh!
You were busy last night, weren't you?

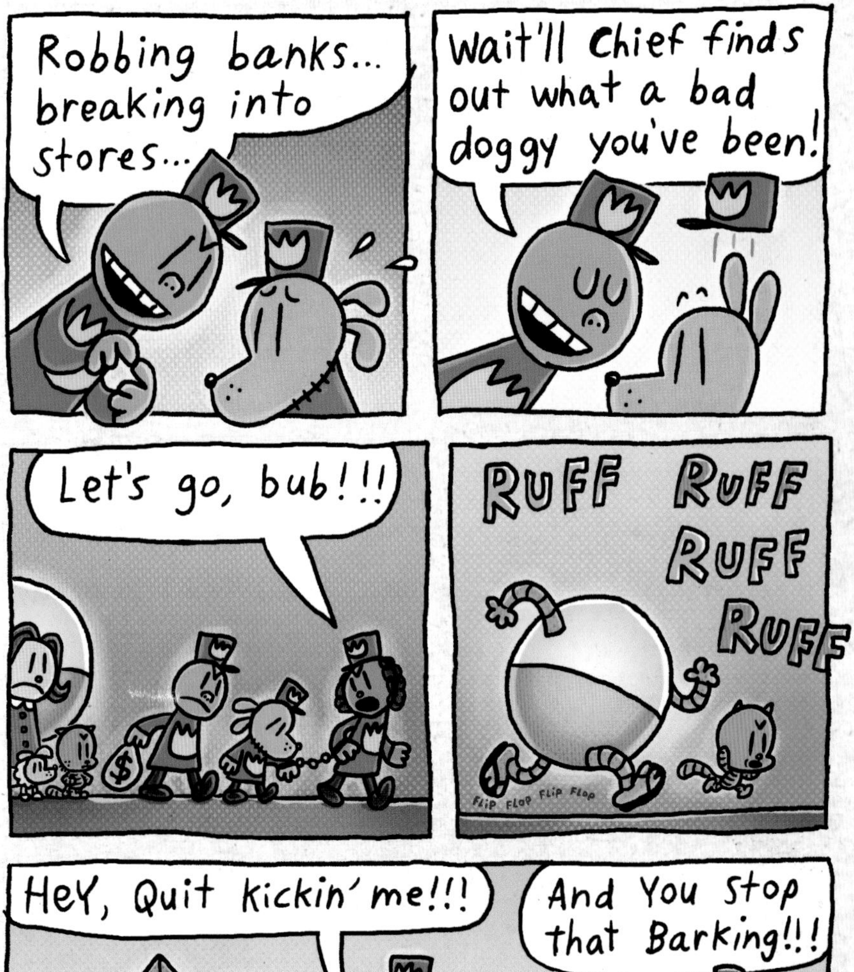
Robbing banks... breaking into stores...
Wait'll Chief finds out what a bad doggy you've been!
Let's go, bub!!!
RUFF RUFF RUFF RUFF
FLIP FLOP FLIP FLOP
HEY, Quit kickin' me!!!
And You stop that Barking!!!
RUFF RUFF RUFF

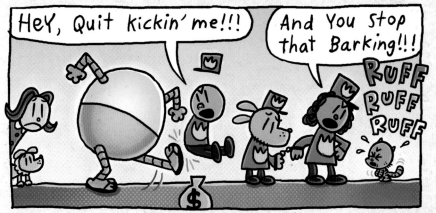

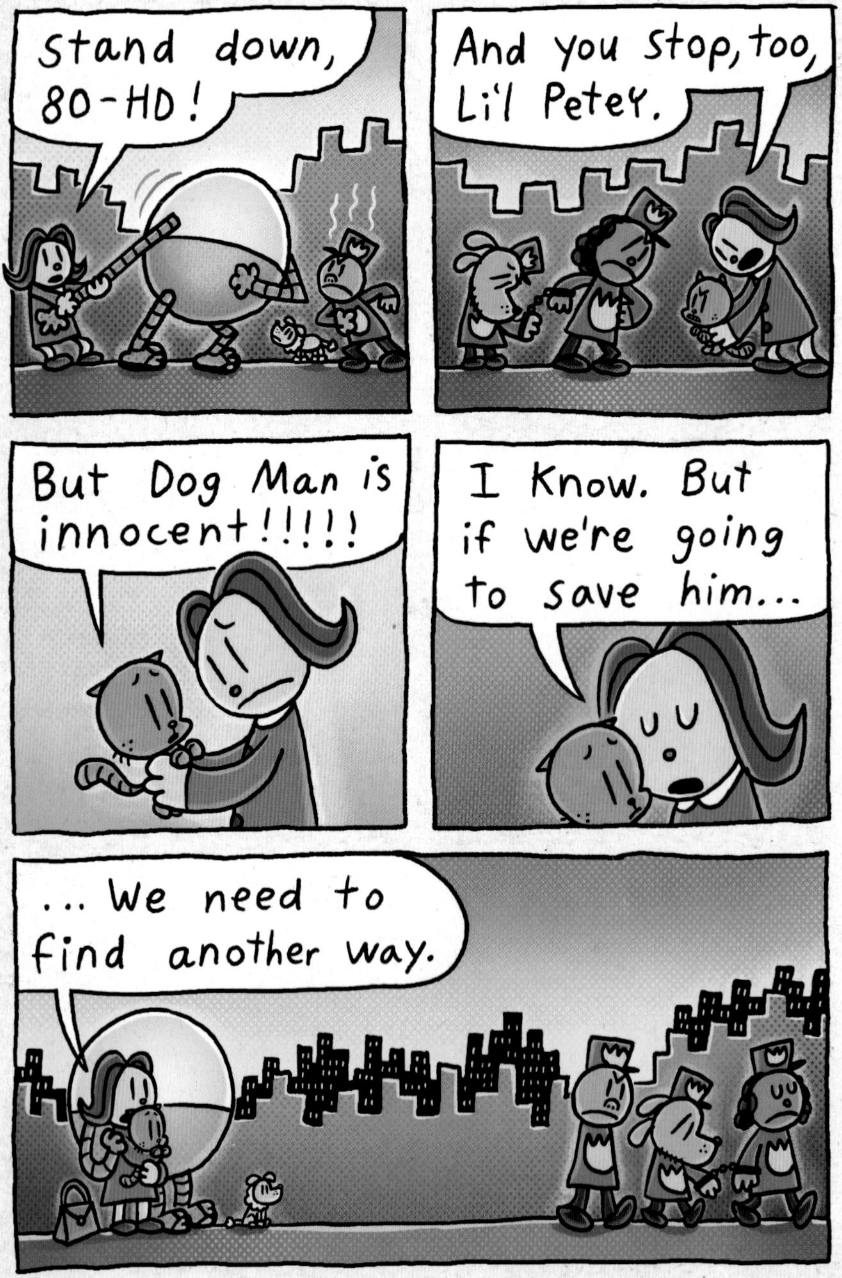
Stand down, 80-HD!
And you stop, too, Li'l Petey.
But Dog Man is innocent!!!!!
I Know. But if we're going to save him...
...We need to find another way.

CHAPTER 4

A Buncha Stuff That Happened Next

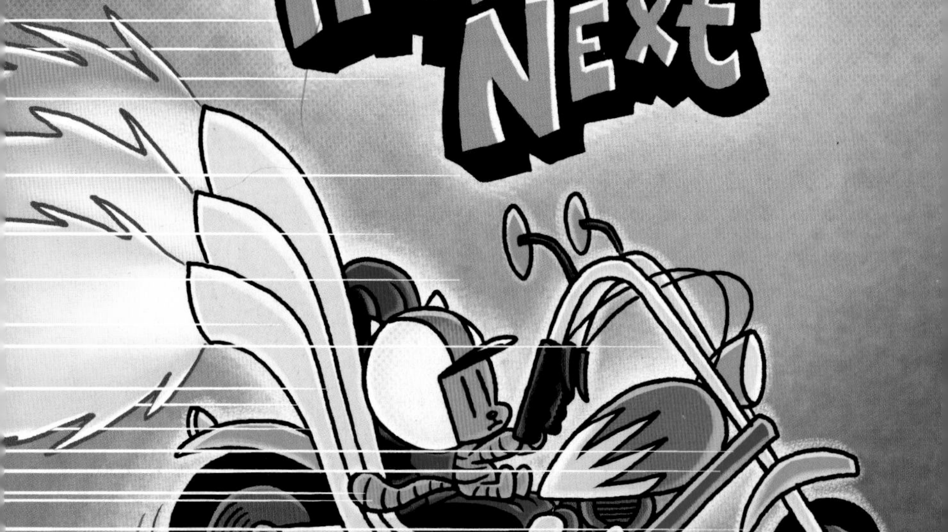

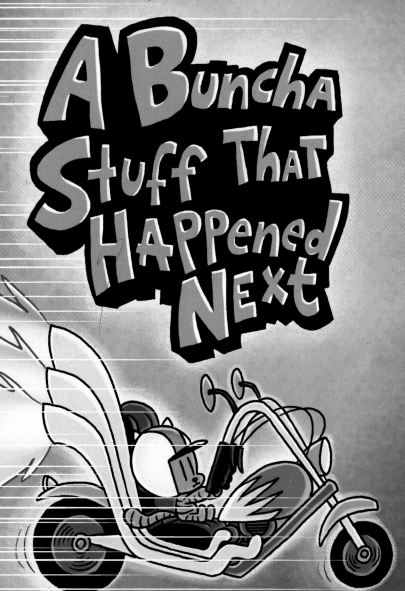

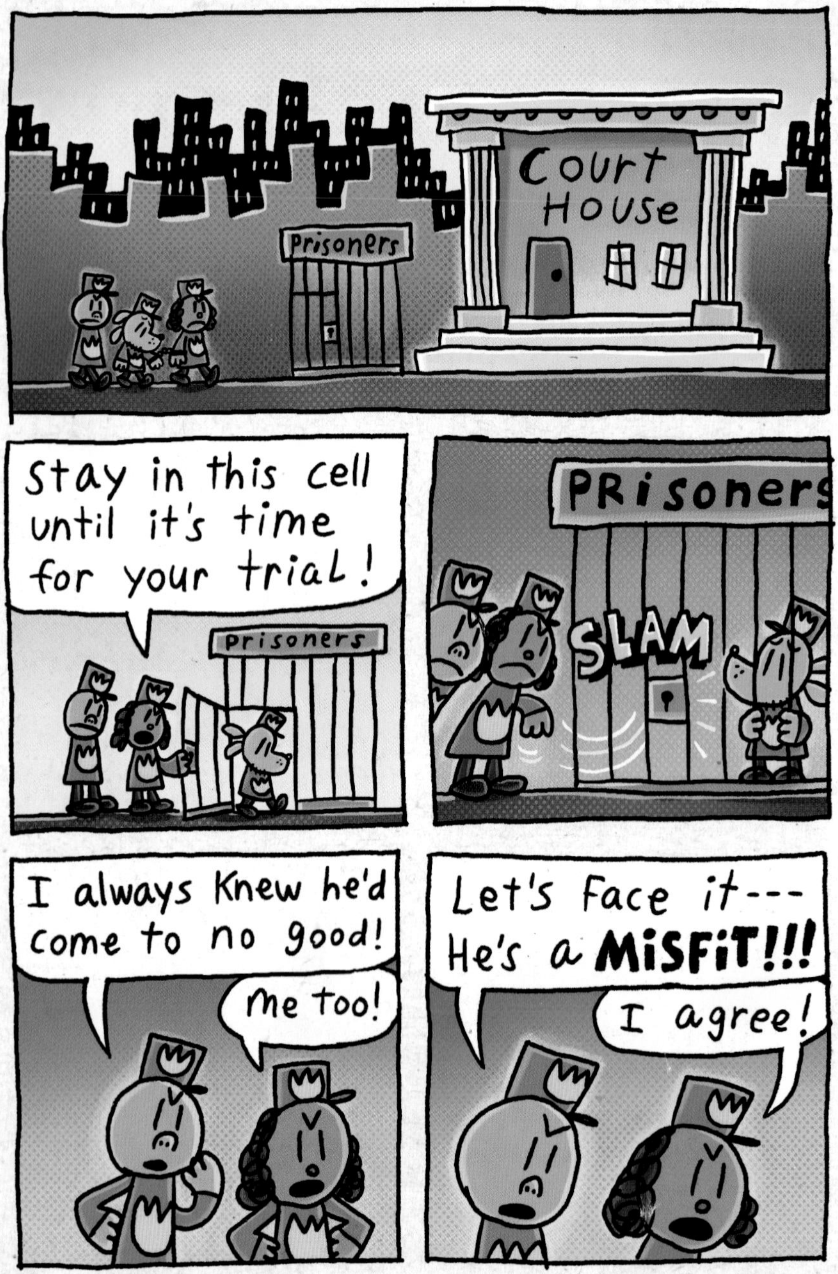
Prisoners
Court House
Stay in this cell until it's time for your trial!
Prisoners
PRisoners
SLAM
I always Knew he'd come to no good!
Me too!
Let's Face it--- He's a MiSFiT!!!
I agree!

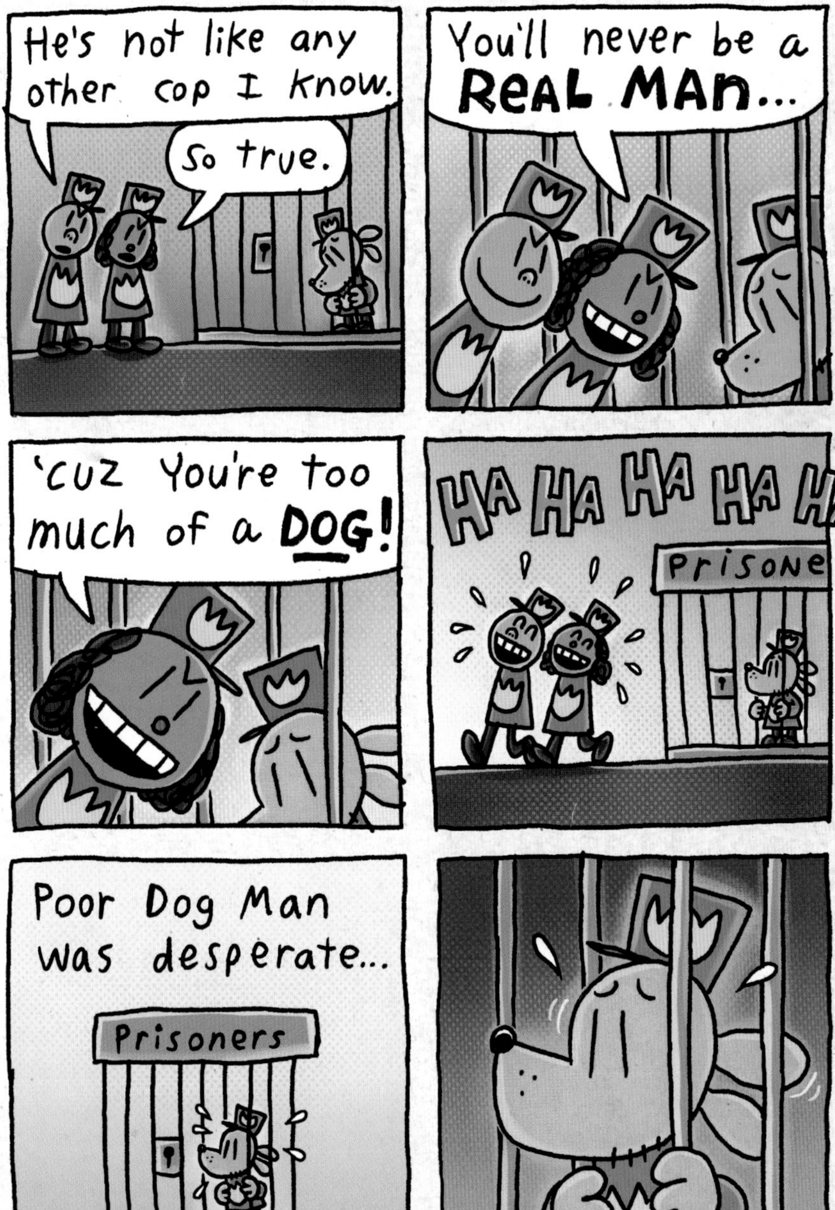
He's not like any other cop I know.
So true.
You'll never be a REAL MAN...
'cuz you're too much of a DOG!
HA HA HA HA HA
Prisone
Poor Dog Man was desperate...
Prisoners

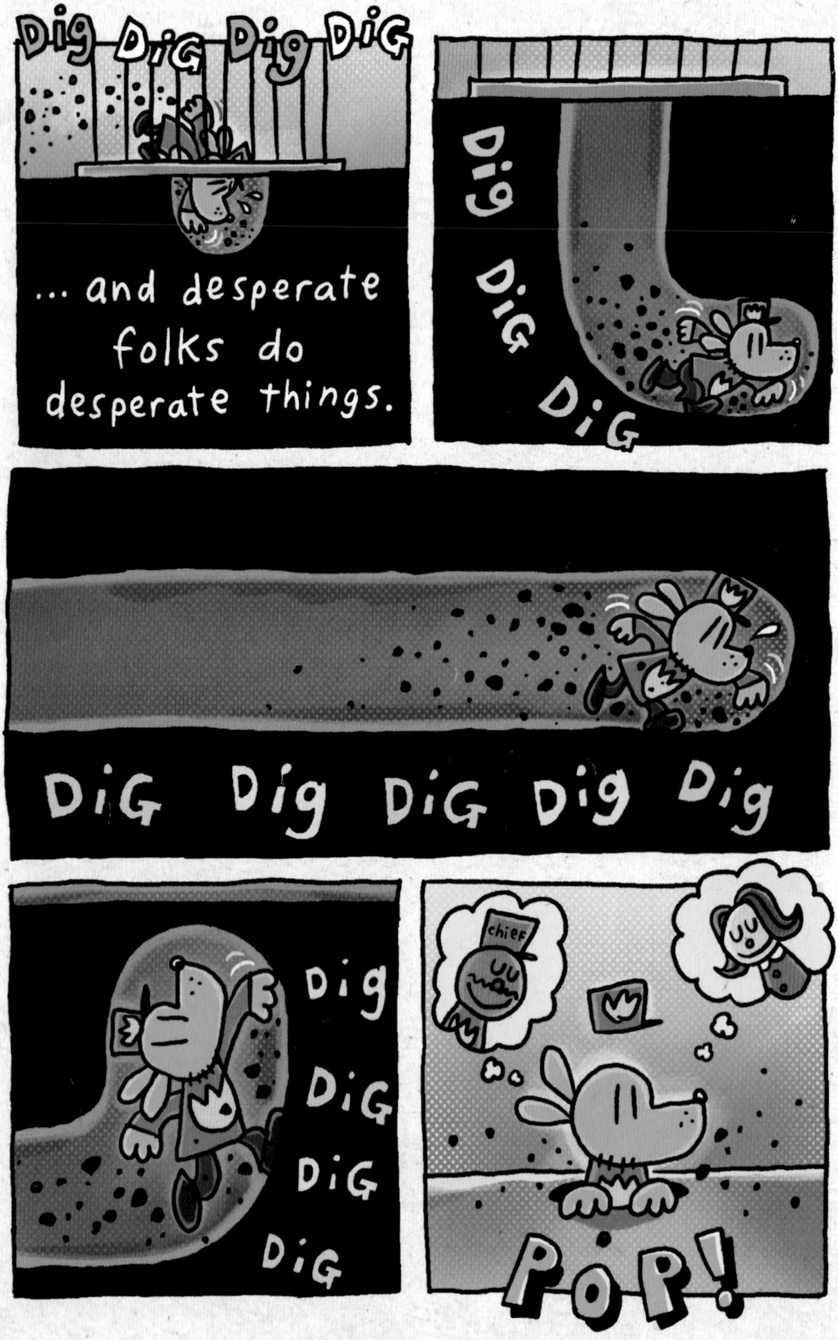
Dig DiG Dig DiG
... and desperate folks do desperate things.
Dig DiG DiG
DiG Dig DiG Dig Dig
Dig DiG DiG DiG
chief
POP!

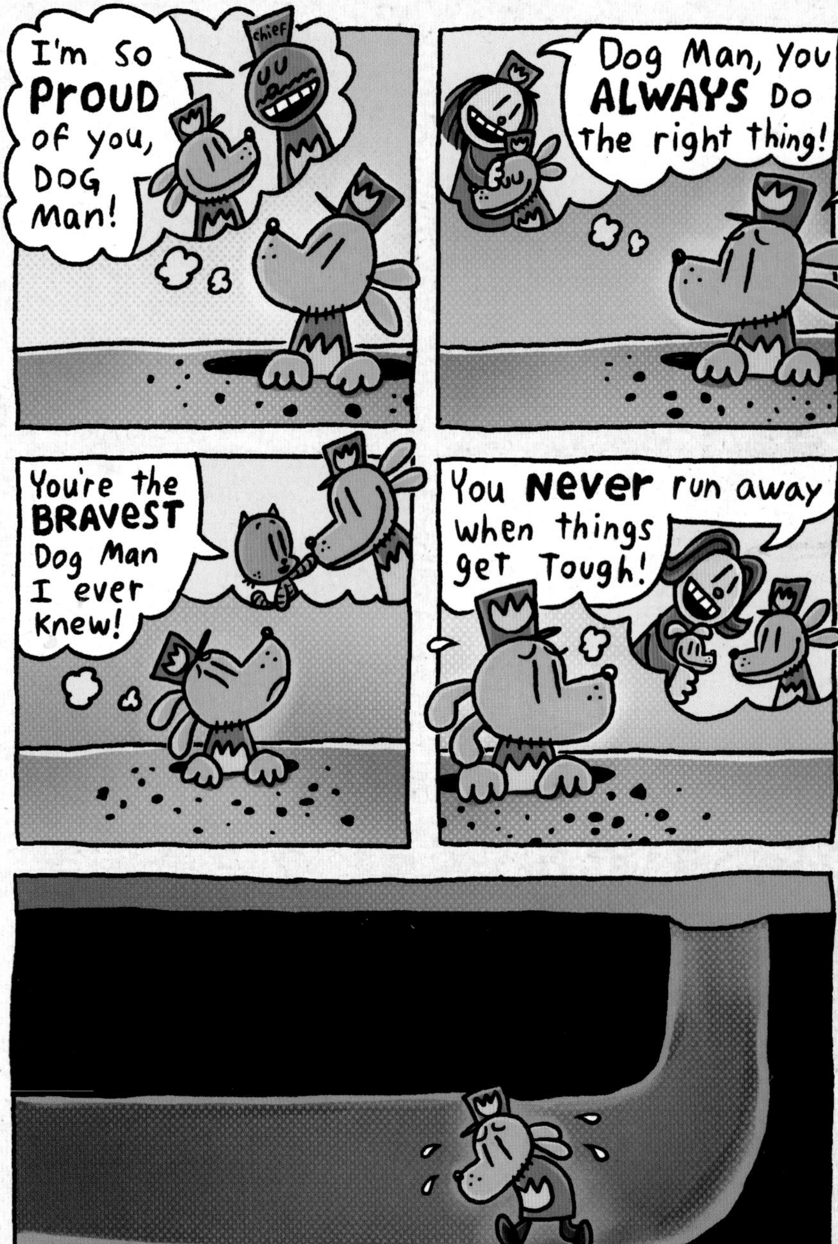
I'm so PROUD of you, DOG Man!
chief
Dog Man, you ALWAYS do the right thing!
You're the BRAVEST Dog Man I ever knew!
You NEVER run away when things get Tough!

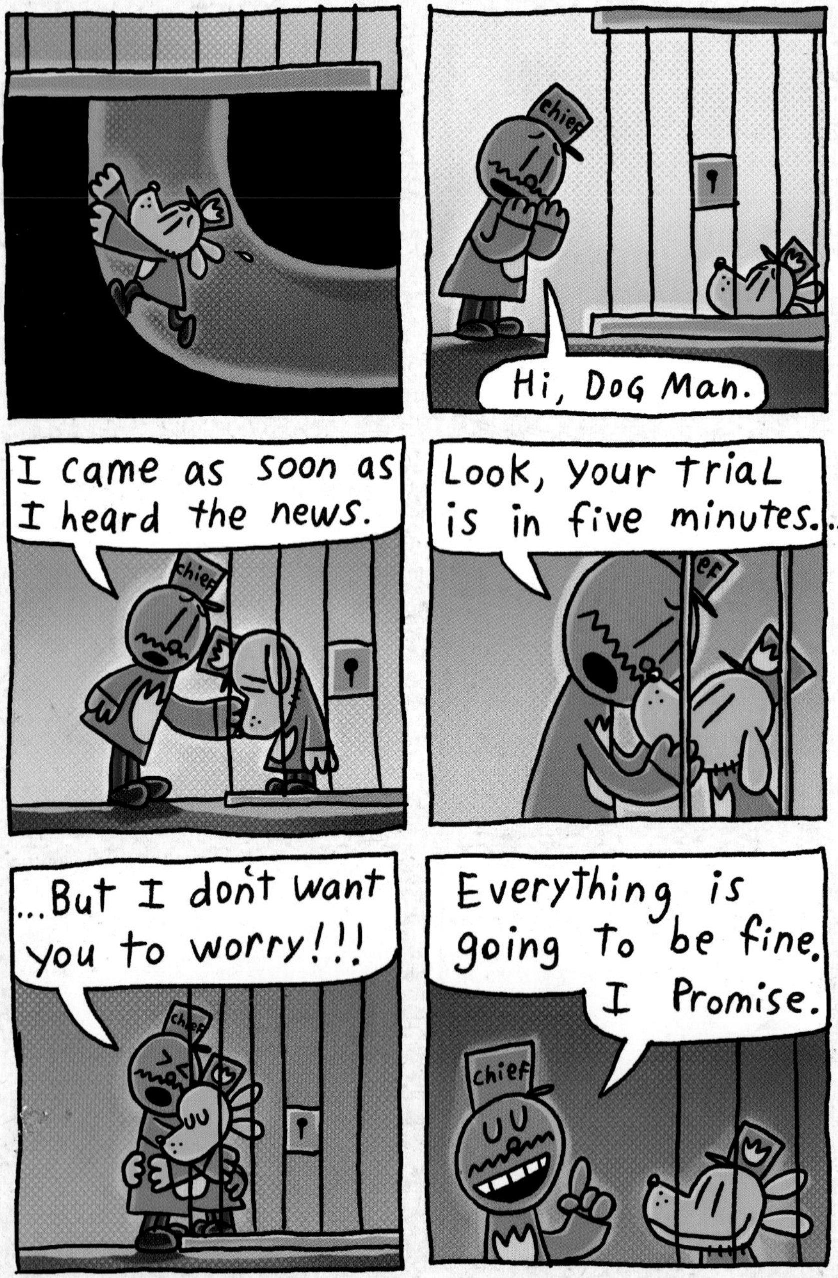

Hi, Dog Man.
I came as soon as I heard the news.
Look, your trial is in five minutes...
...But I don't want you to worry!!!
Everything is going to be fine. I Promise.

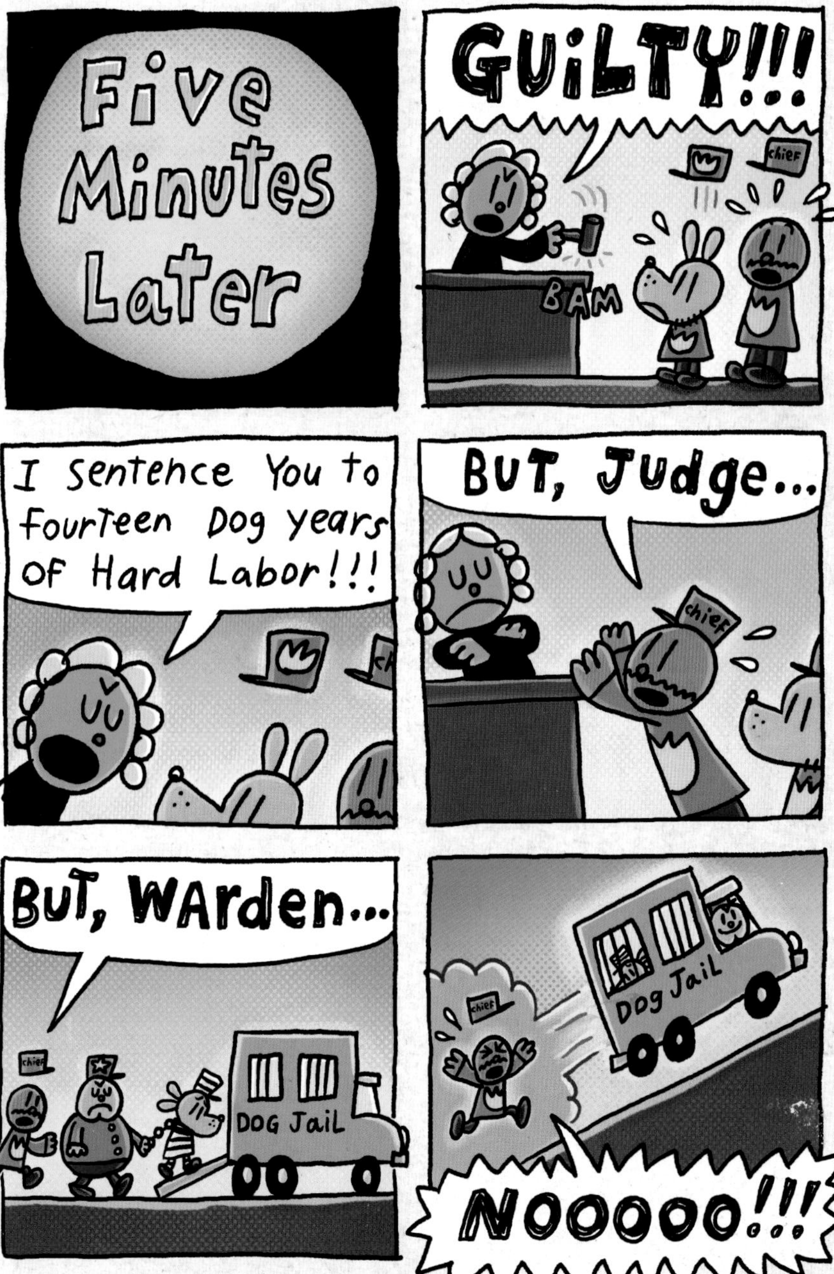
Five Minutes Later
GUILTY!!!
BAM
chief
I sentence You to Fourteen Dog years of Hard Labor!!!
BUT, Judge...
chief
BUT, WArden...
chief
DOG JaiL
chief
Dog JaiL
NOOOOO!!!

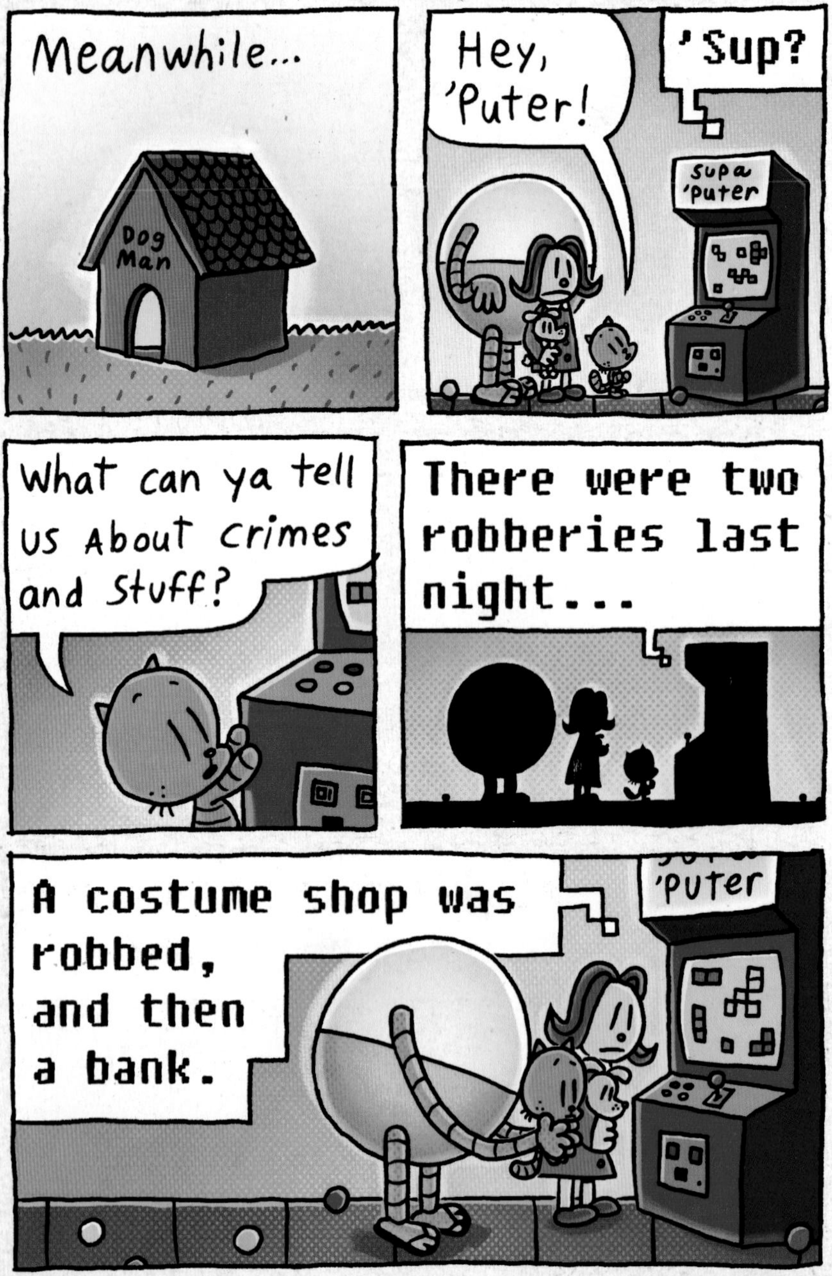
Meanwhile...
Dog Man
Hey, 'Puter!
'Sup?
Supa 'Puter
What can ya tell us About crimes and Stuff?
There were two robberies last night...
A costume shop was robbed, and then a bank.
'Puter

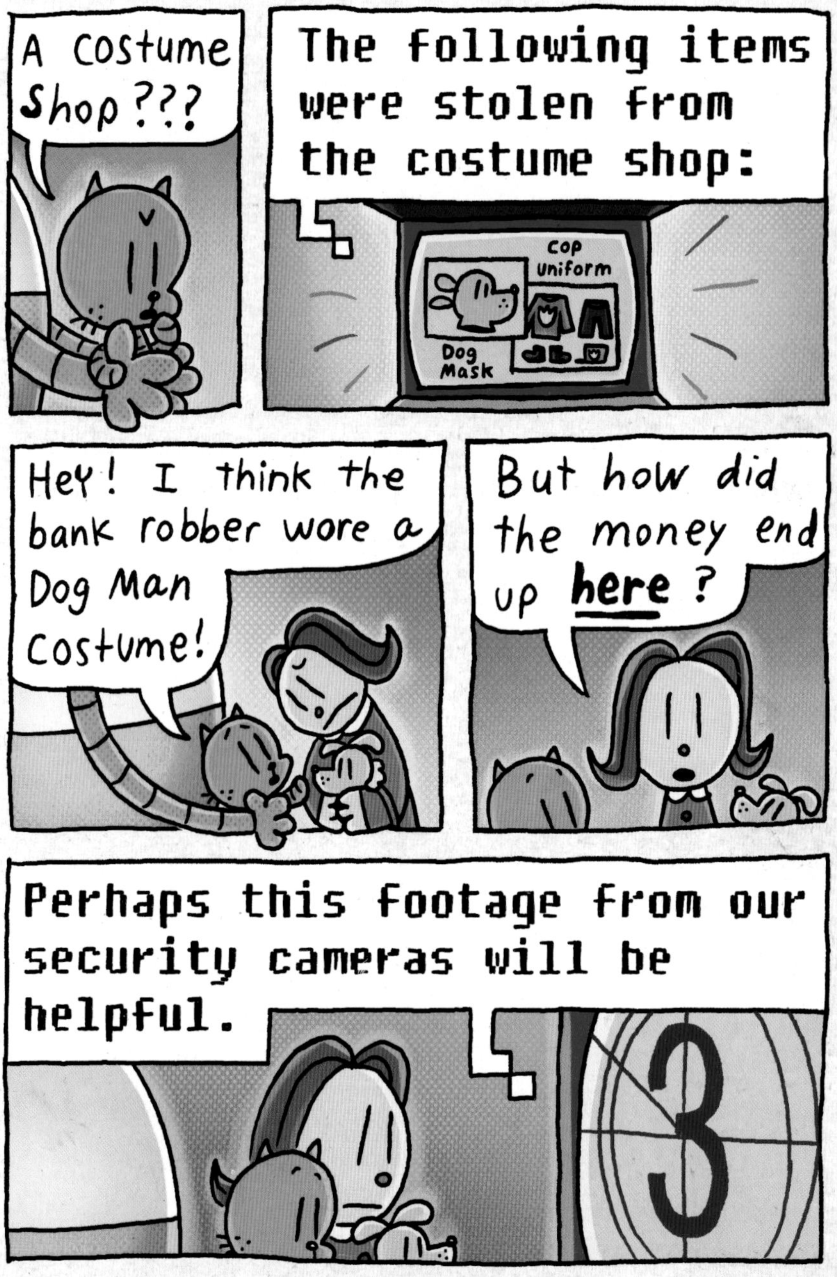
A costume Shop???
The following items were stolen from the costume shop:
Cop Uniform
Dog Mask
Hey! I think the bank robber wore a Dog Man costume!
But how did the money end up **here**?
Perhaps this footage from our security cameras will be helpful.
3

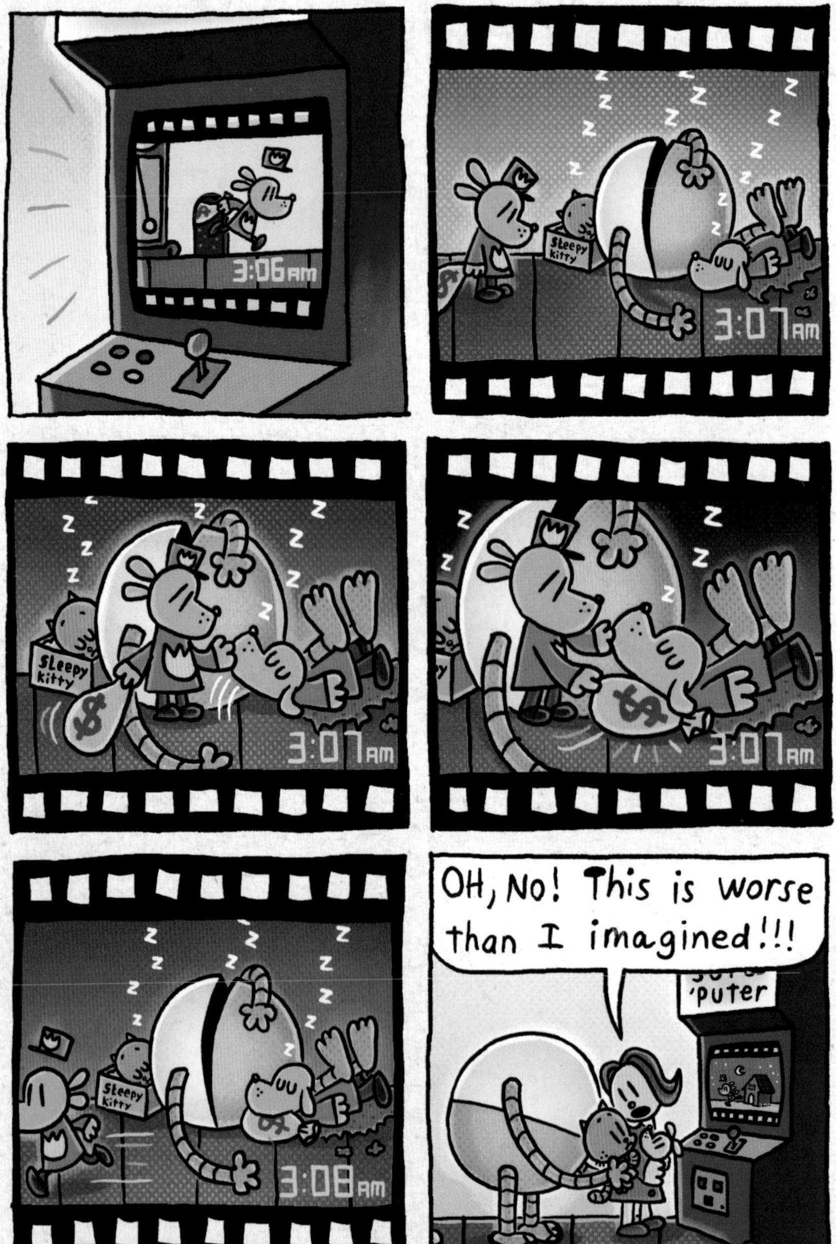

3:06AM
Sleepy Kitty
3:07AM
Sleepy Kitty
3:07AM
3:07AM
Sleepy Kitty
3:08AM
OH, No! This is worse than I imagined!!!
'puter

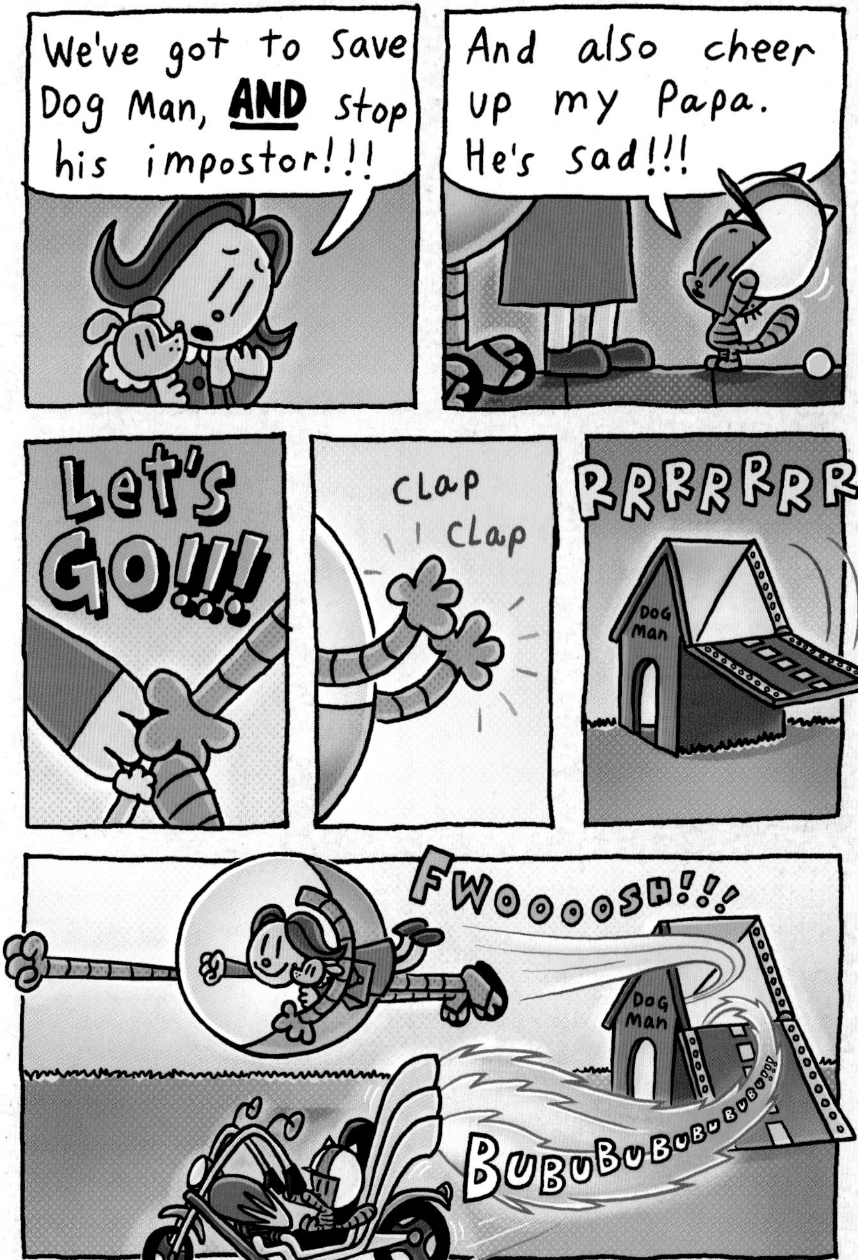
We've got to save Dog Man, **AND** stop his impostor!!!
And also cheer up my Papa. He's sad!!!
Let's GO!!!
Clap
Clap
RRRRRRR
DOG Man
FWOOOOOSH!!!
DOG Man
BUBUBUBUBUBUBUBUBU!!!

Meanwhile...

HEY!

So Dog Man's up to his old tricks, eh?

SCReeeech

*Ciao! Come Stai?

Hey! You're Yolay Caprese, the world's greatest actress!

Si*

* Italian for: Yo! What up?   * Italian for: You Betcha!

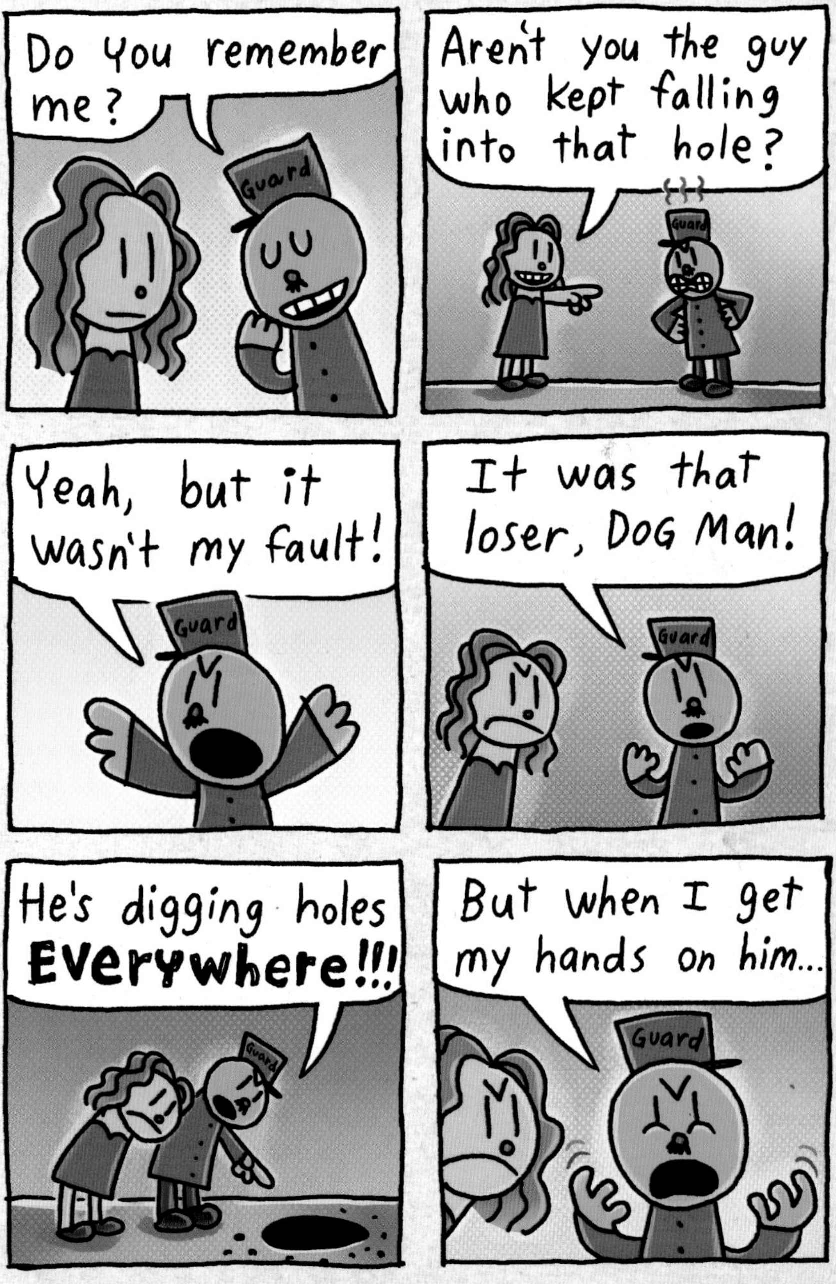
Do you remember me?
Aren't you the guy who kept falling into that hole?
Guard
Yeah, but it wasn't my fault!
It was that loser, DOG MAN!
He's digging holes **Everywhere!!!**
But when I get my hands on him...

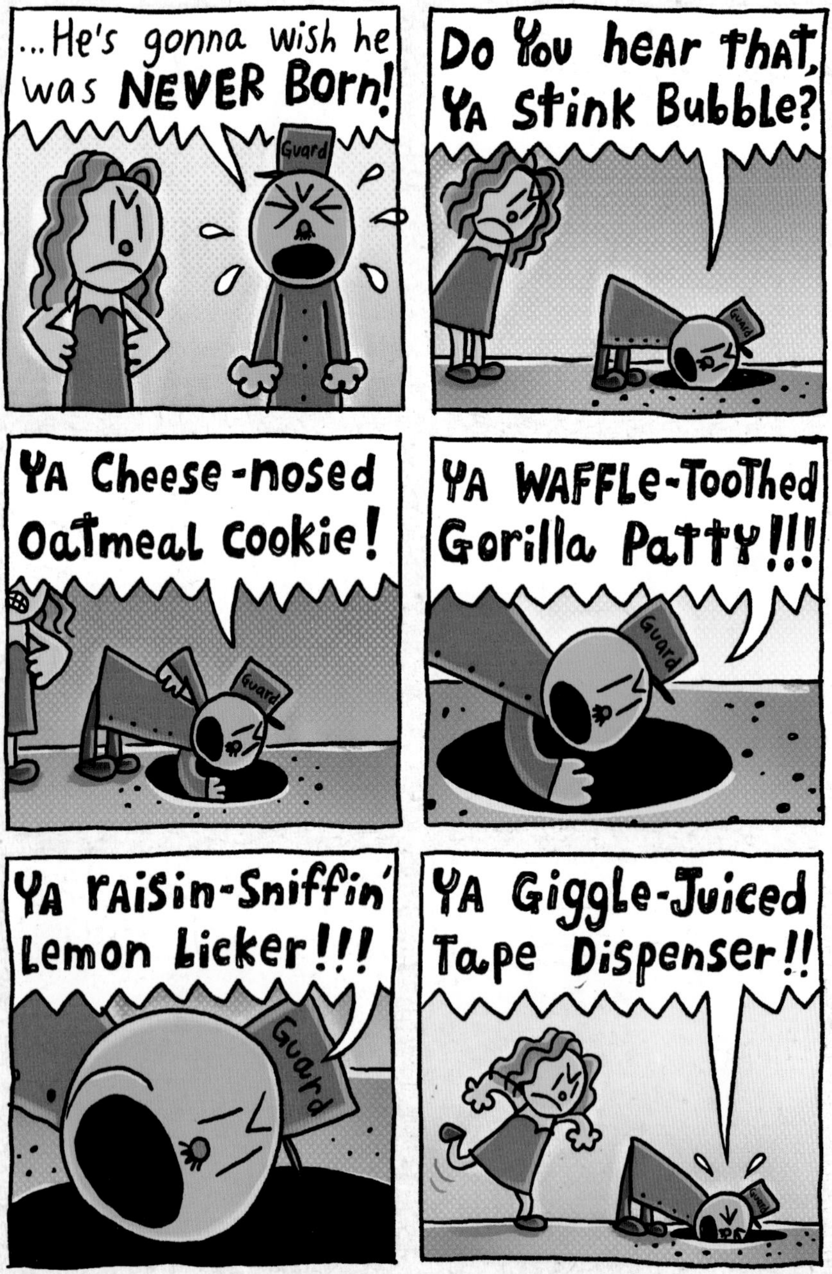
...He's gonna wish he was NEVER Born!
Guard
Do You hear THAT, YA Stink Bubble?
Guard
YA Cheese-nosed Oatmeal Cookie!
Guard
YA WAFFLE-TooThed Gorilla PaTTY!!!
Guard
YA raisin-Sniffin' Lemon Licker!!!
Guard
YA Giggle-Juiced Tape Dispenser!!
Guard

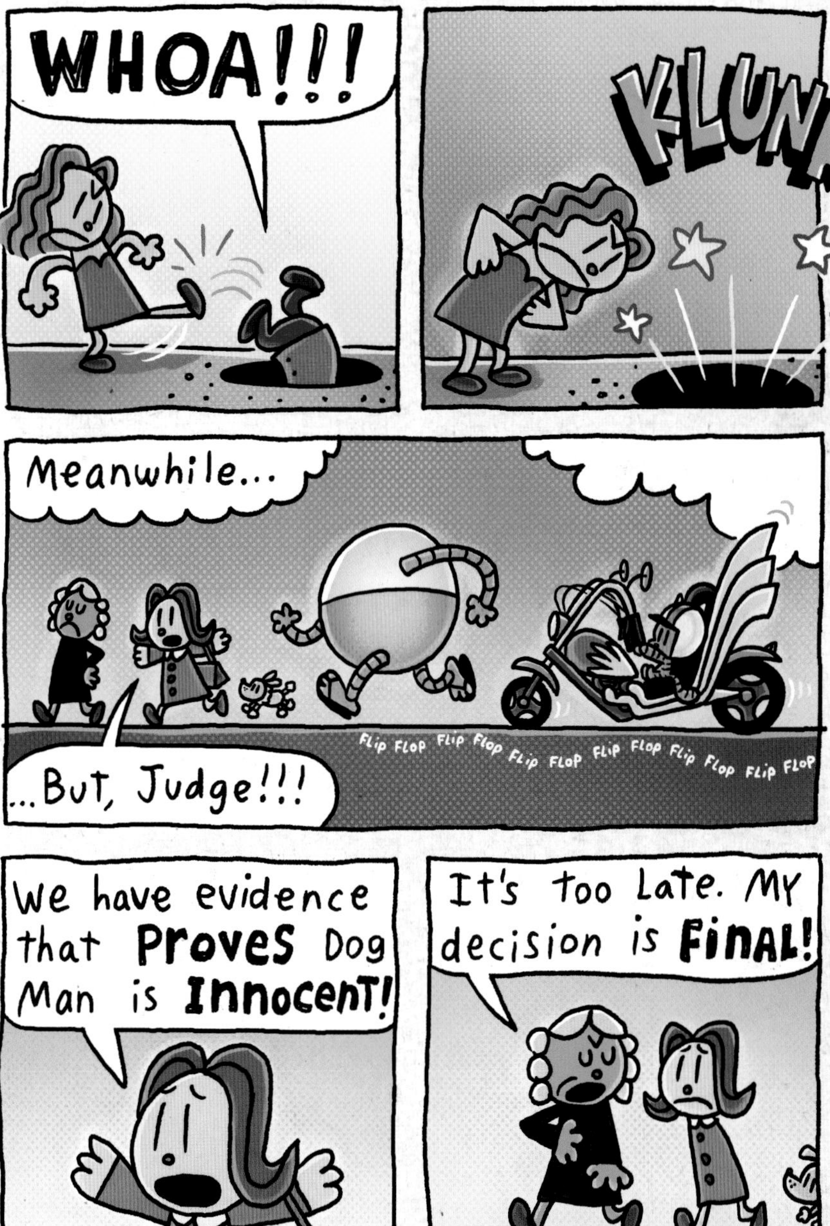
WHOA!!!
KLUNK
Meanwhile...
...But, Judge!!!
FLIP FLOP FLIP FLOP FLIP FLOP FLIP FLOP FLIP FLOP FLIP FLOP
We have evidence that PROVES Dog Man is INNOCENT!
It's too Late. My decision is FINAL!

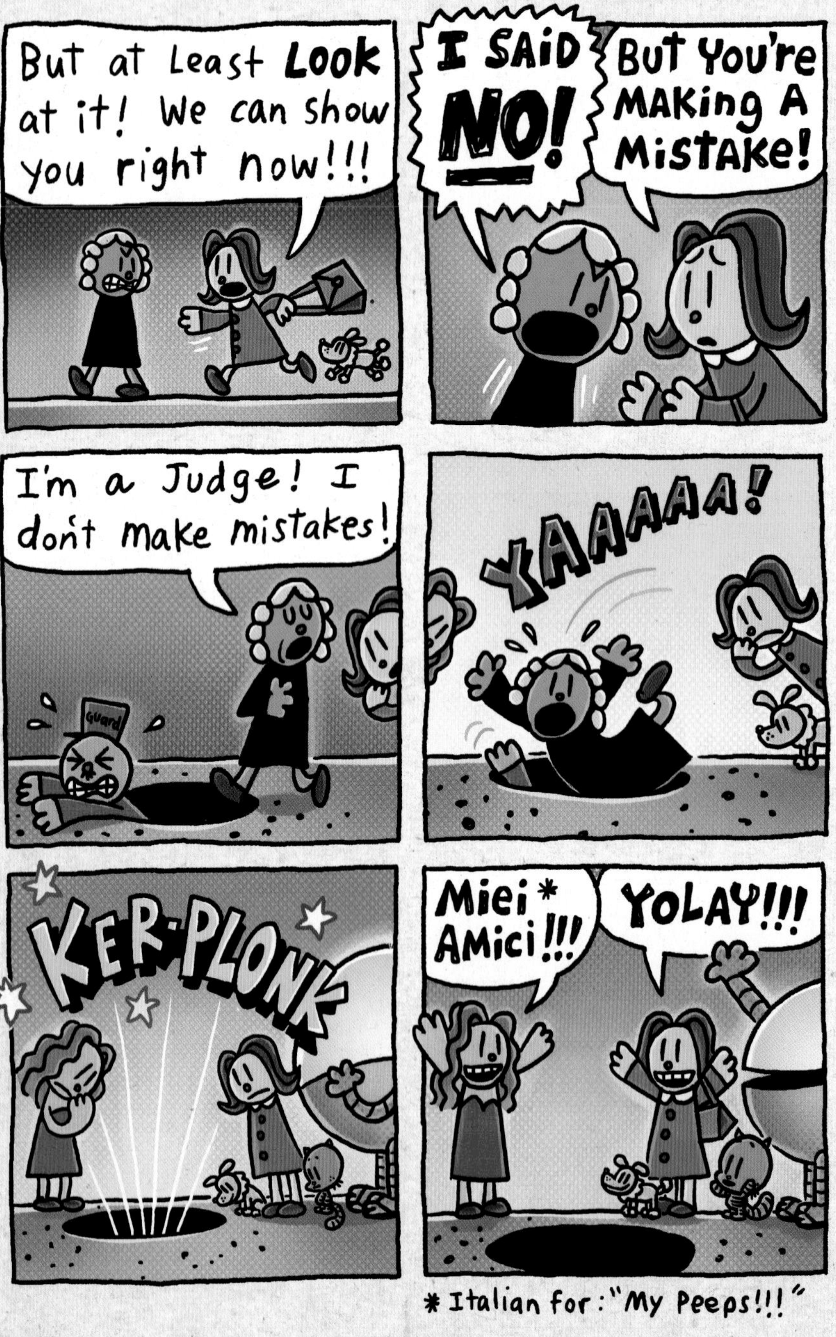
But at Least LOOK at it! We can show you right now!!!
I SAID NO!
But You're MAKING A MISTAKE!
I'm a Judge! I don't make mistakes!
GUARD
YAAAAAA!
KER-PLONK
Miei* AMici!!!
YOLAY!!!

* Italian for: "My Peeps!!!"

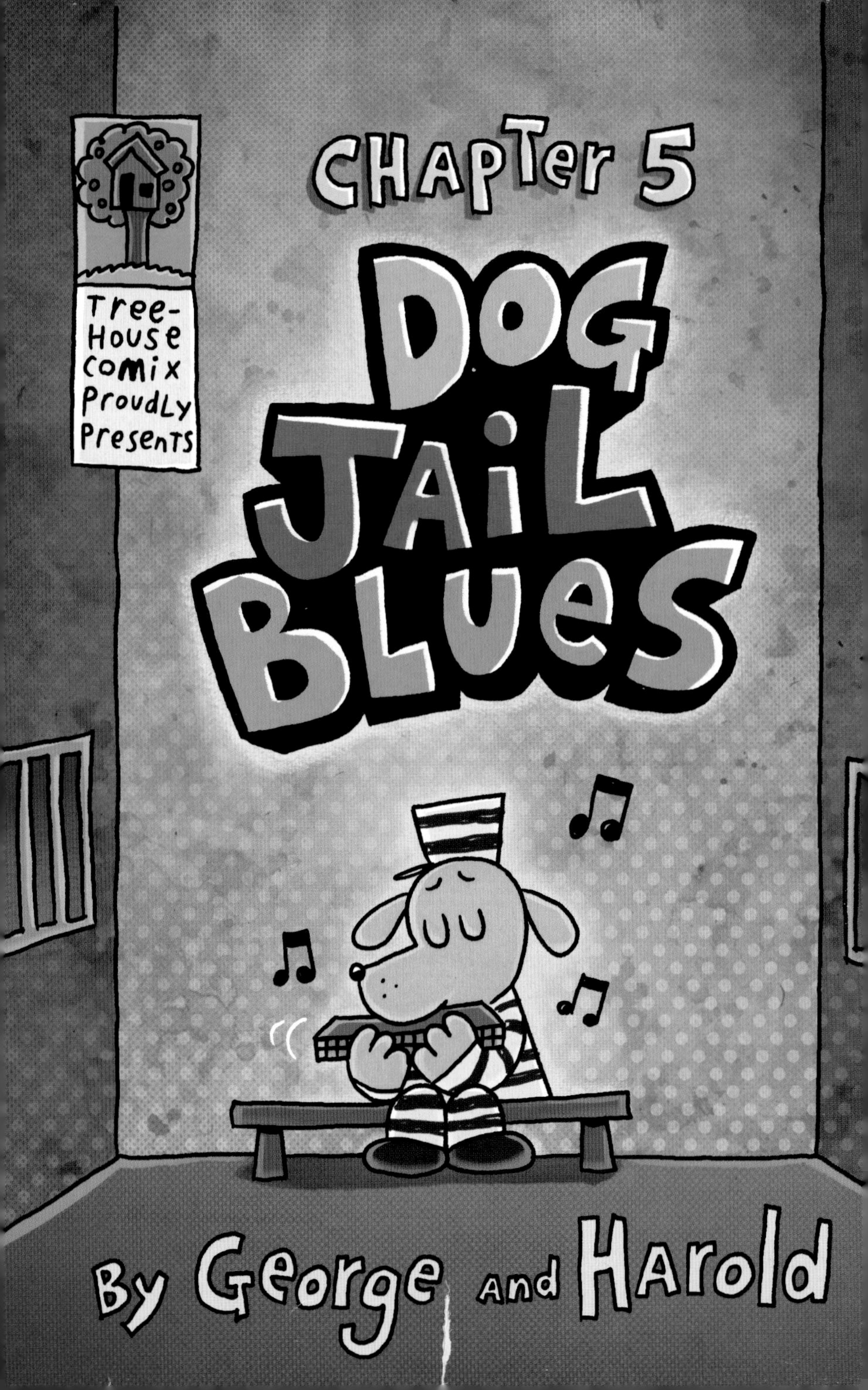
Tree-House Comix Proudly Presents
Chapter 5
Dog Jail Blues
By George and Harold

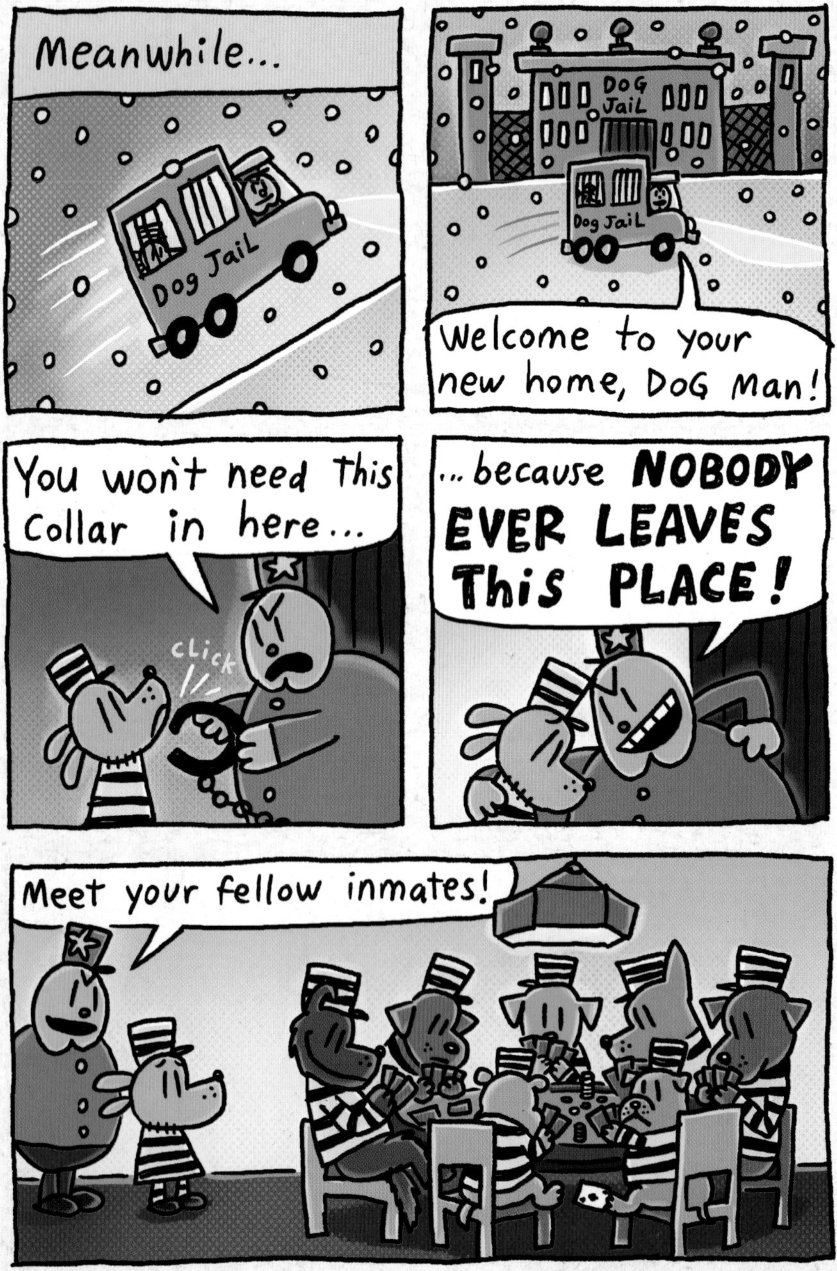
Meanwhile...
Dog Jail
DOG JaiL
Dog JaiL
Welcome to your new home, DoG Man!
You won't need this collar in here...
CLick
...because NOBODY EVER LEAVES This PLACE!
Meet your fellow inmates!

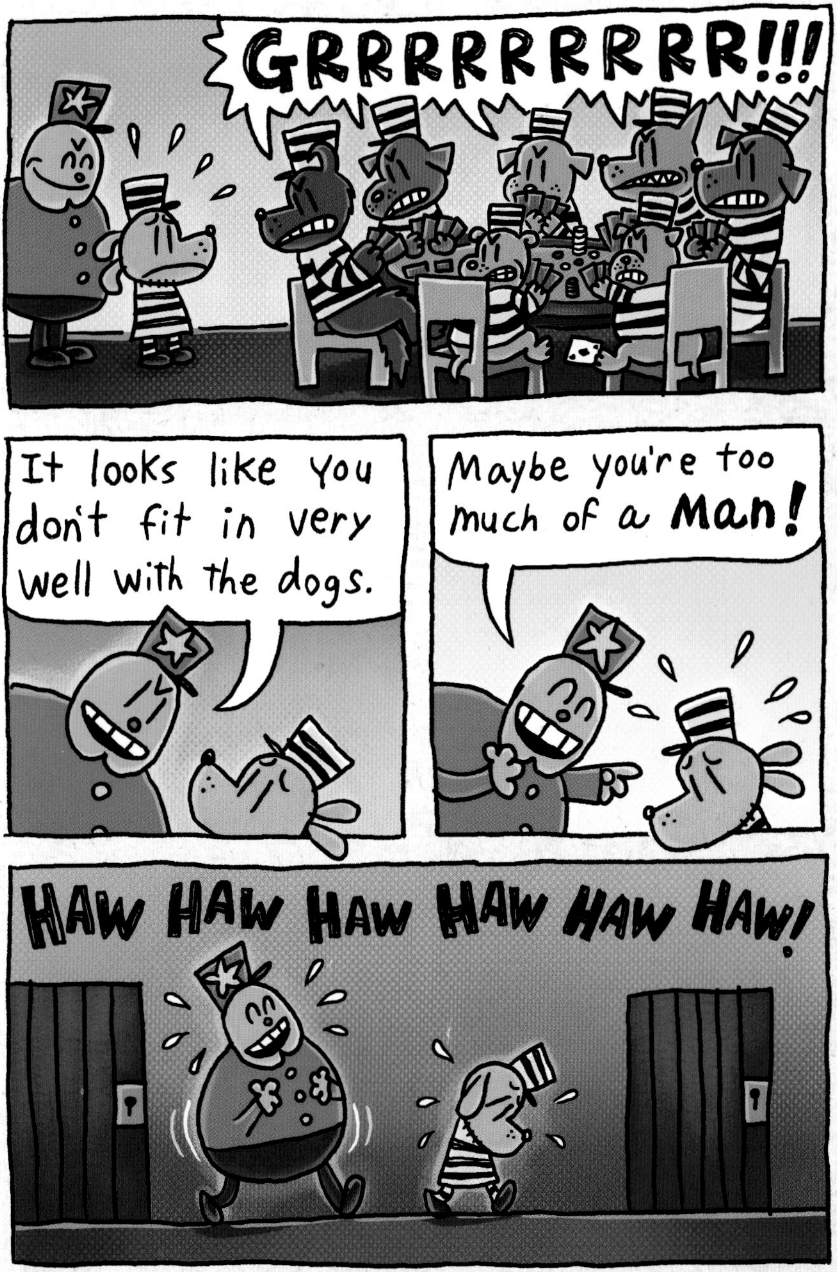

GRRRRRRRRR!!!
It looks like you don't fit in very well with the dogs.
Maybe you're too much of a Man!
HAW HAW HAW HAW HAW HAW!

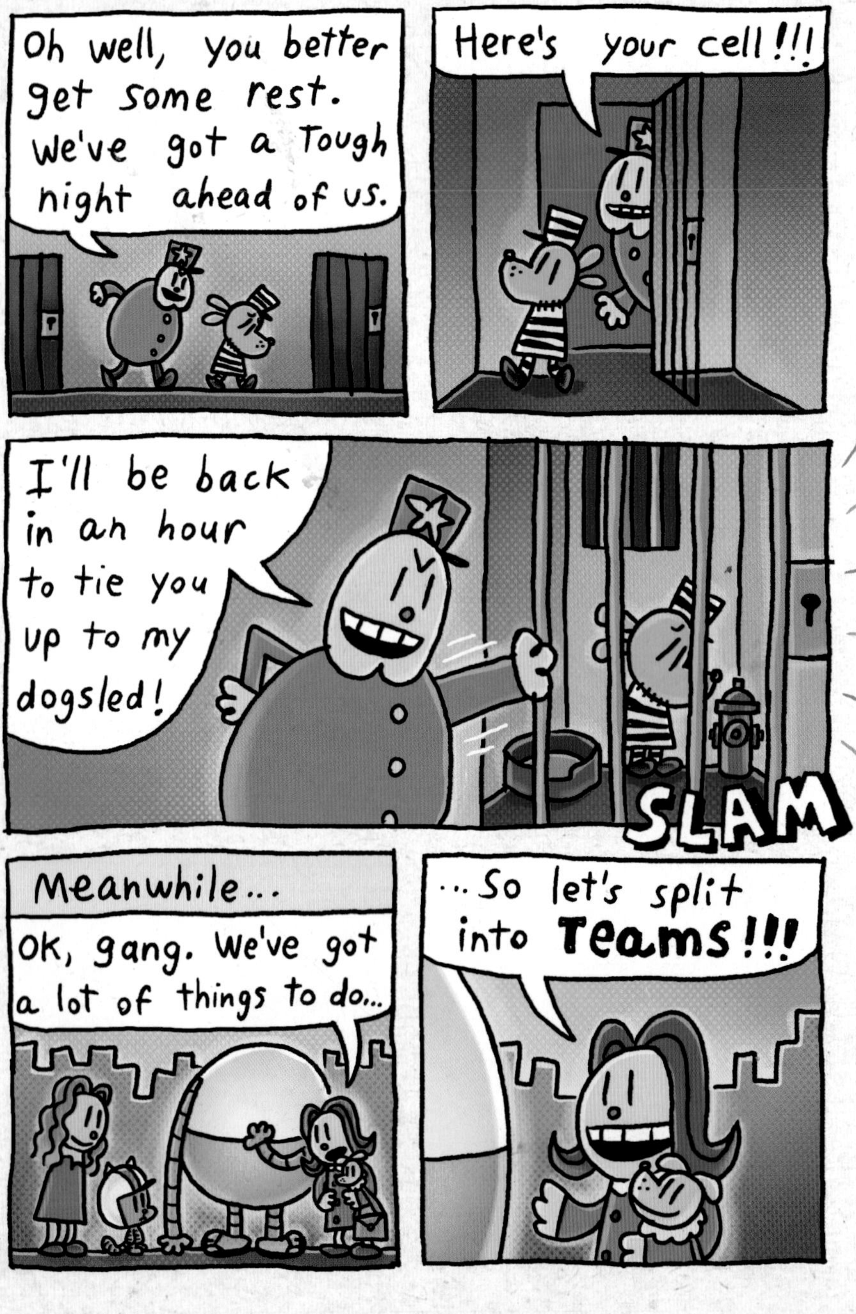
Oh well, you better get some rest. We've got a tough night ahead of us.
Here's your cell!!!
I'll be back in an hour to tie you up to my dogsled!
SLAM
Meanwhile...
Ok, gang. We've got a lot of things to do...
...So let's split into Teams!!!

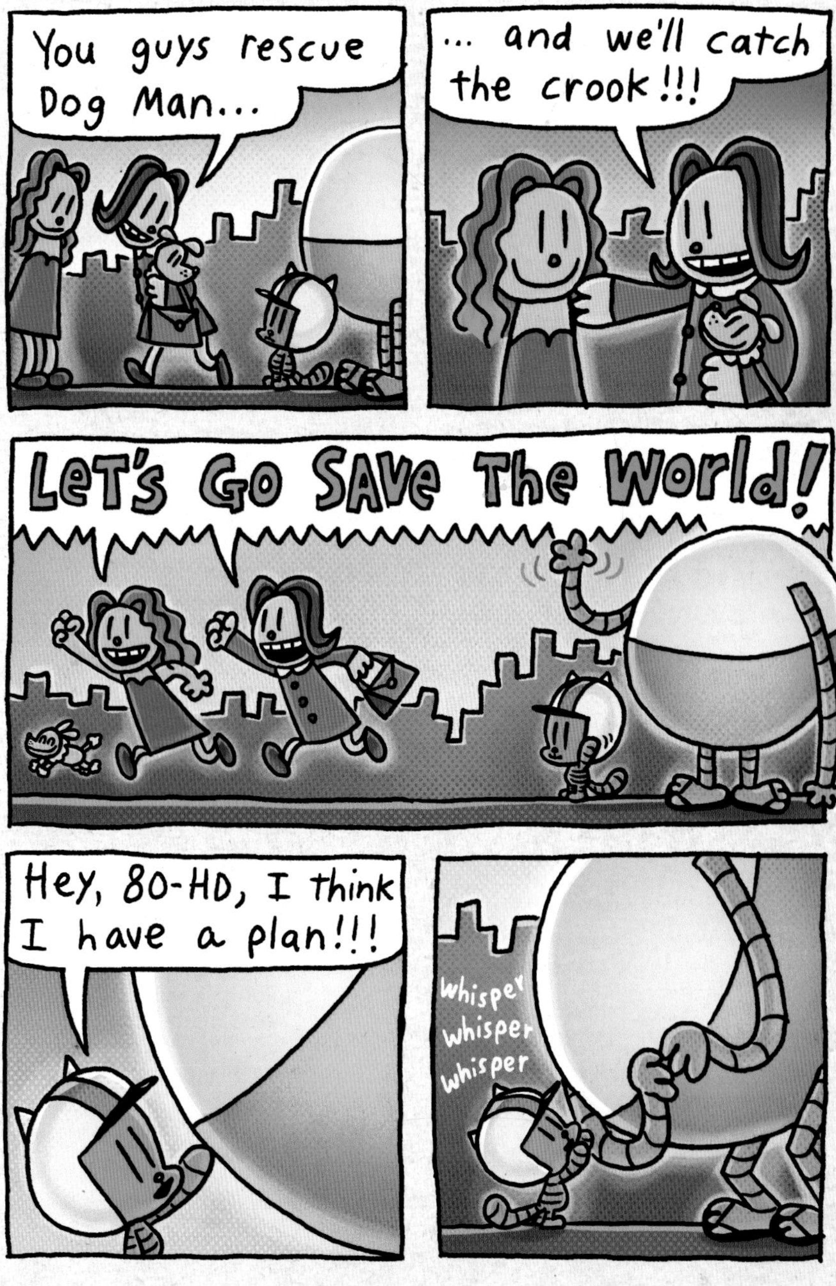
You guys rescue Dog Man...
... and we'll catch the crook!!!
LeT's Go SAVe The World!
Hey, 80-HD, I think I have a plan!!!
whisper
whisper
whisper

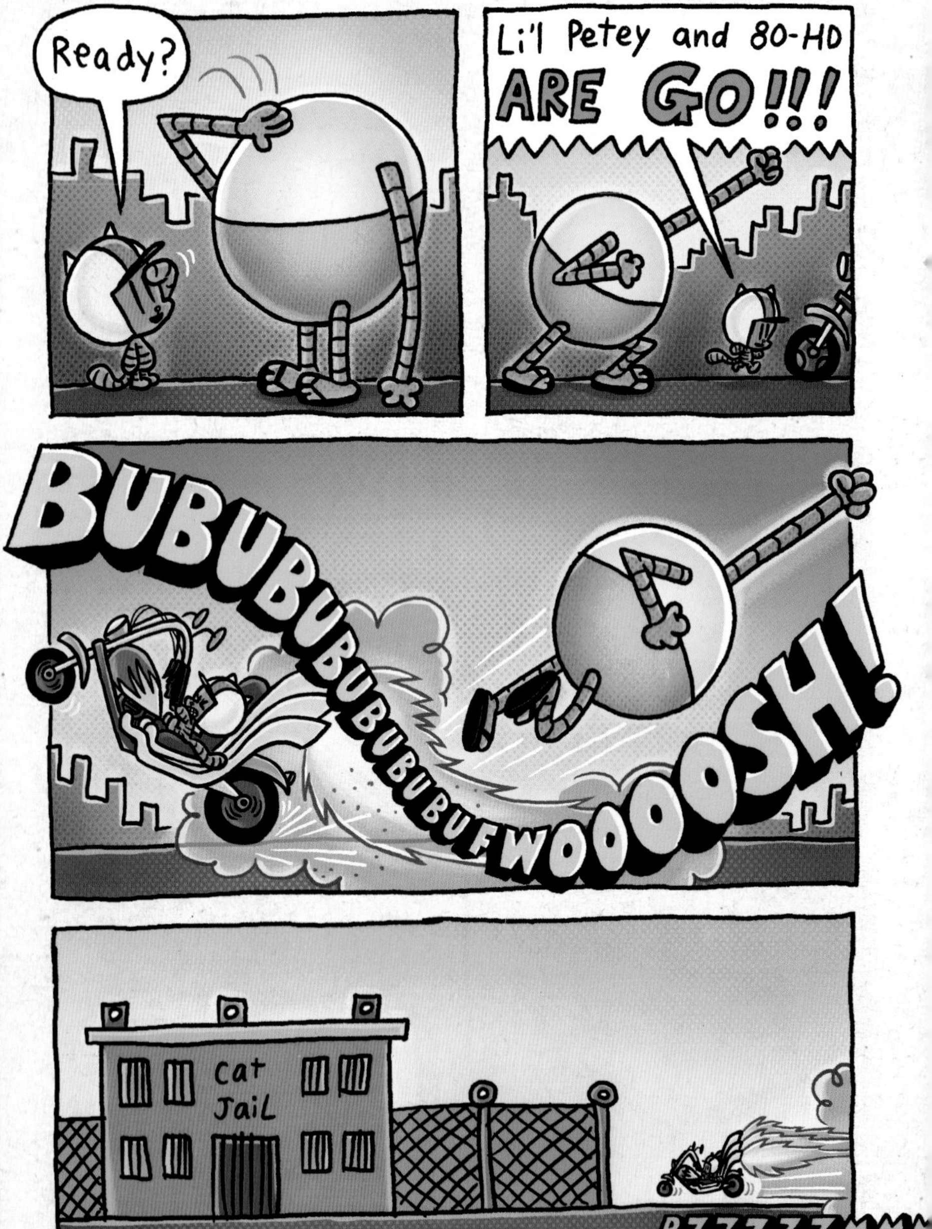
Ready?
Li'l Petey and 80-HD ARE GO!!!
BUBUBUBUBUBUBUFWOOOOOSH!
Cat Jail
BZZZZZMMM

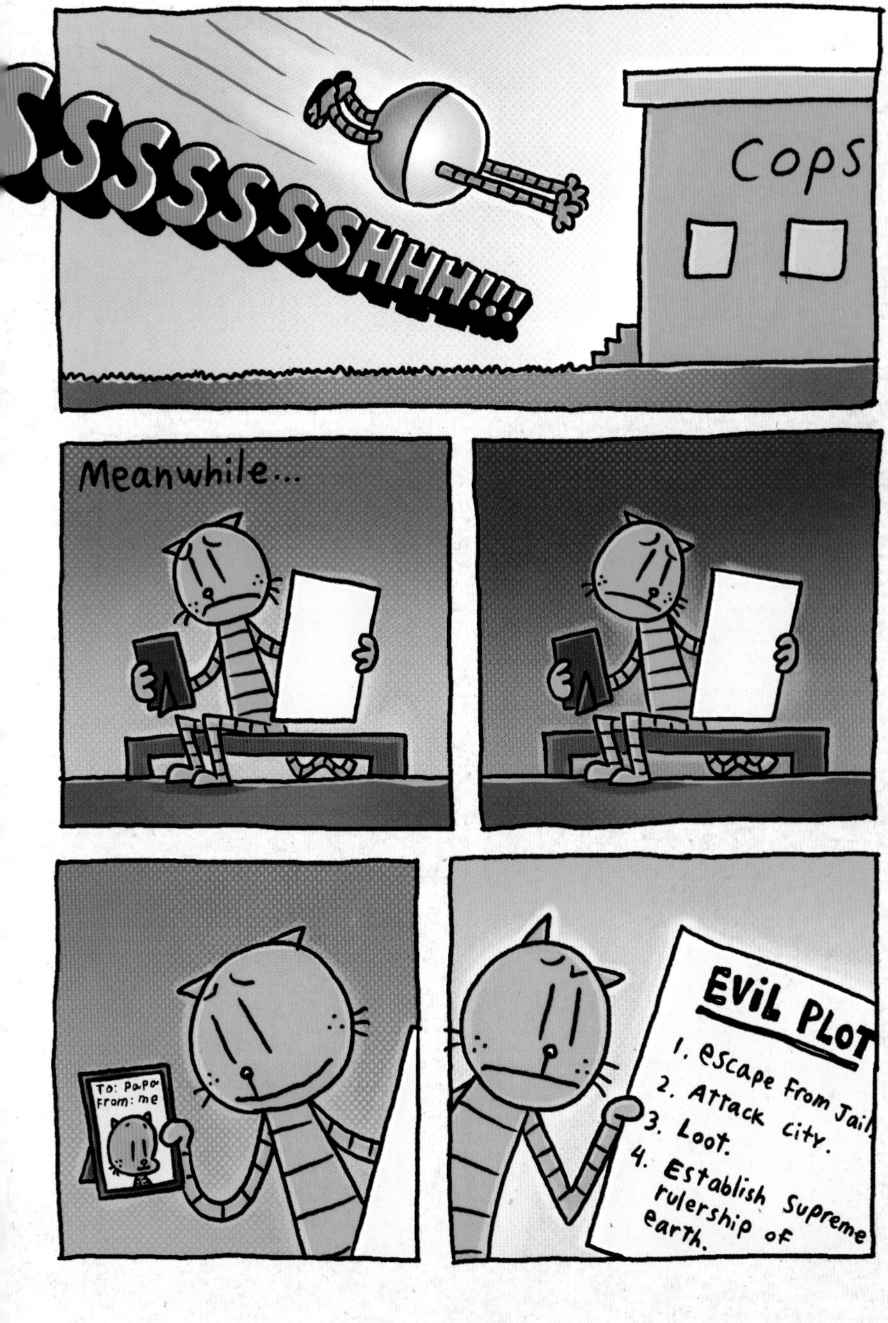
SSSSSSSSHHH!!!
COPS
Meanwhile...
To: Papa
From: me
EVIL PLOT
1. escape from Jail
2. Attack city.
3. Loot.
4. Establish Supreme rulership of earth.

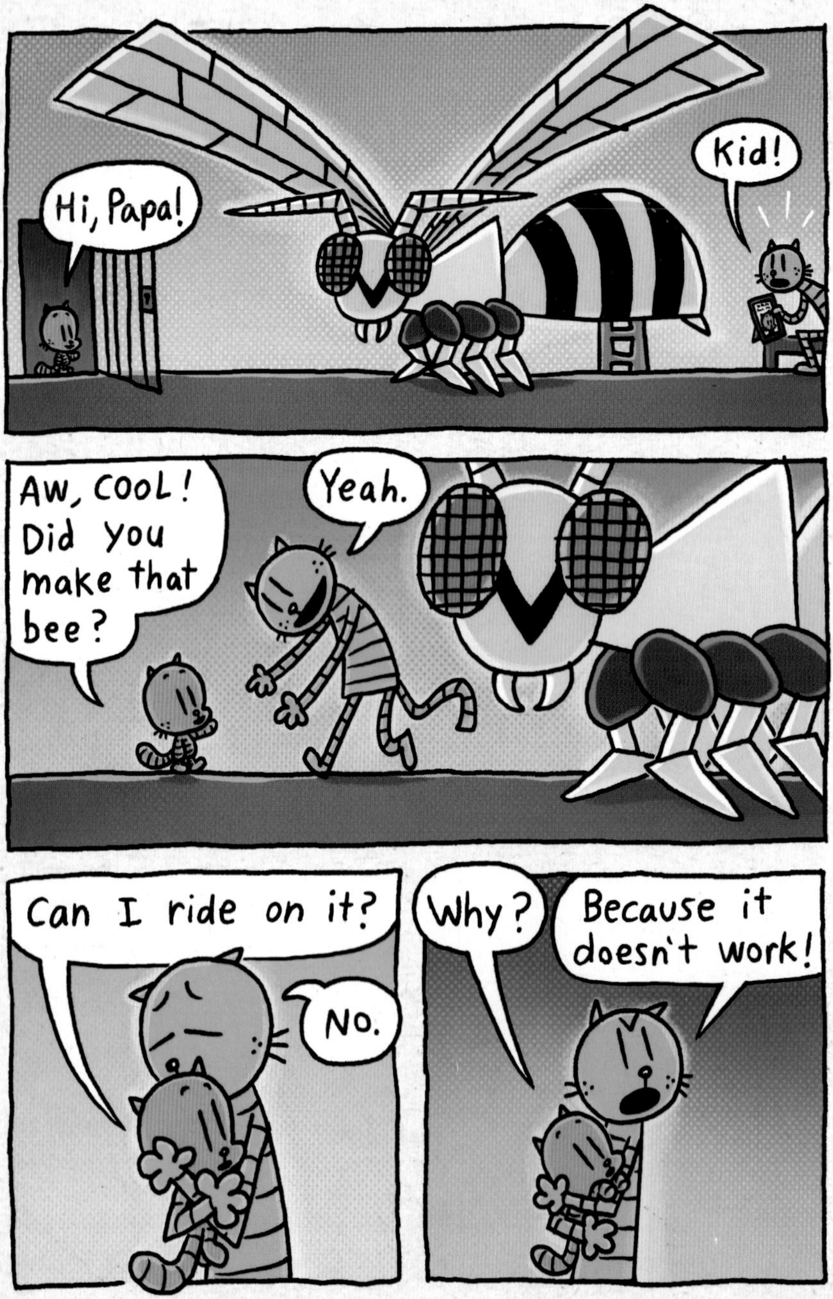
Hi, Papa!
Kid!
AW, COOL! Did you make that bee?
Yeah.
Can I ride on it?
No.
Why?
Because it doesn't work!

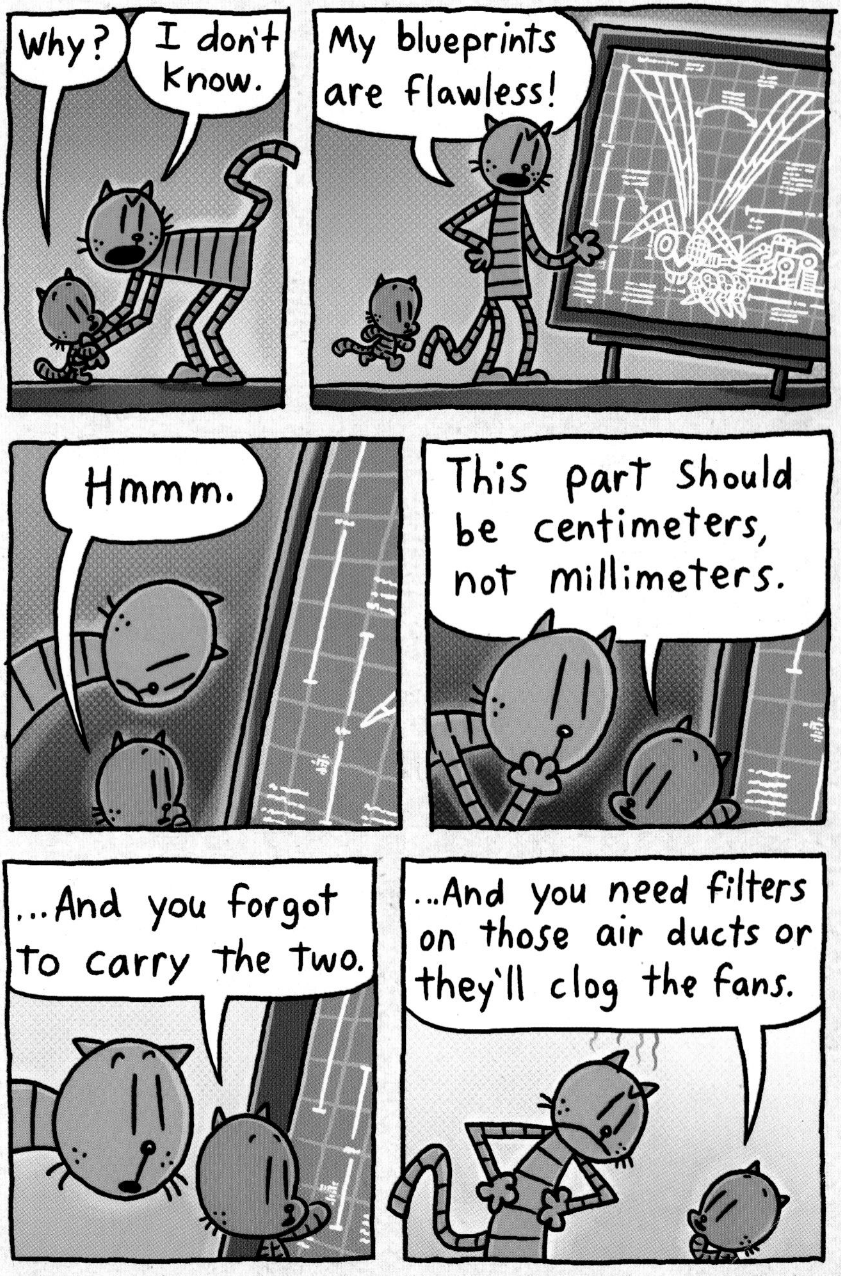
Why?
I don't know.
My blueprints are flawless!
Hmmm.
This part should be centimeters, not millimeters.
...And you forgot to carry the two.
...And you need filters on those air ducts or they'll clog the fans.

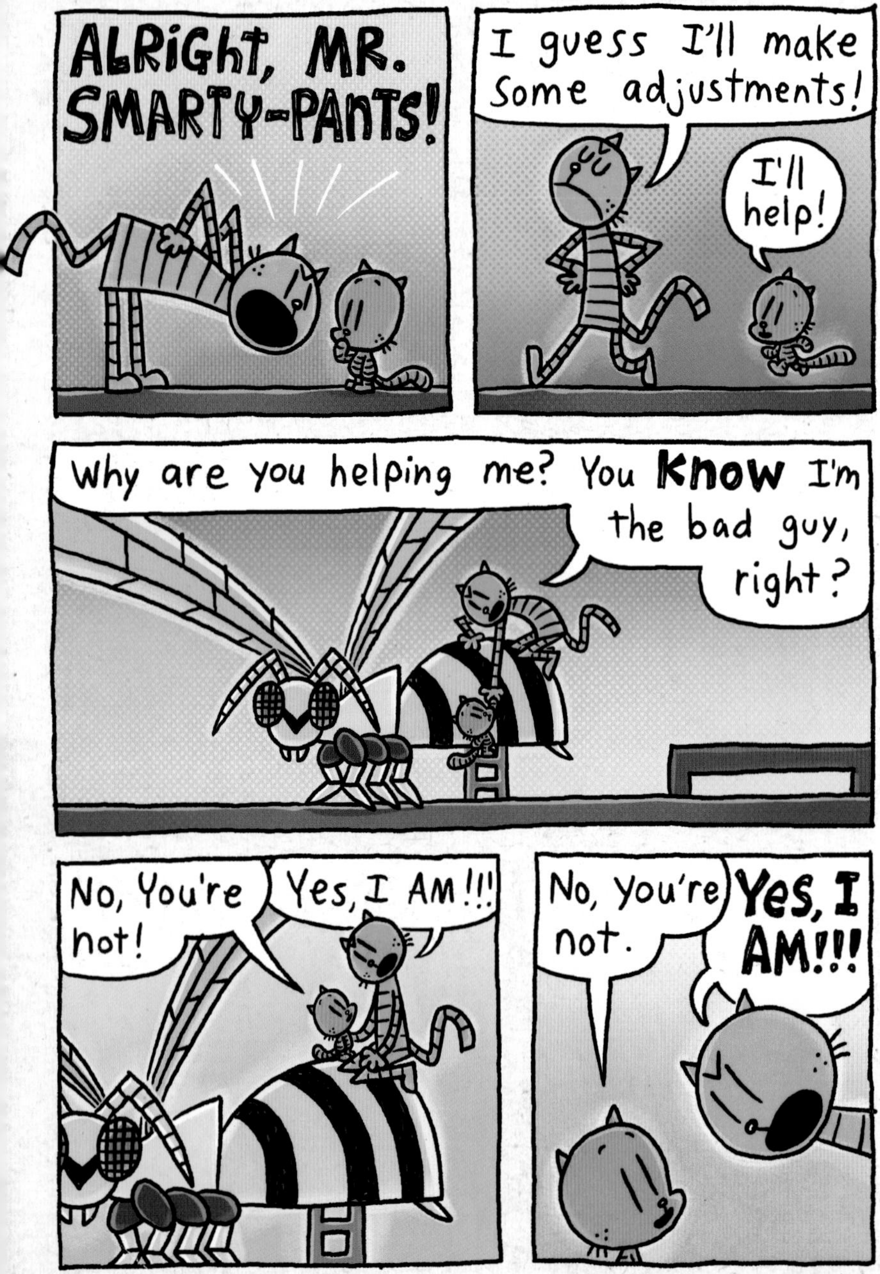
ALRIGHT, MR. SMARTY-PANTS!
I guess I'll make Some adjustments!
I'll help!
Why are you helping me? You KNOW I'm the bad guy, right?
No, You're not!
Yes, I AM!!!
No, you're not.
Yes, I AM!!!

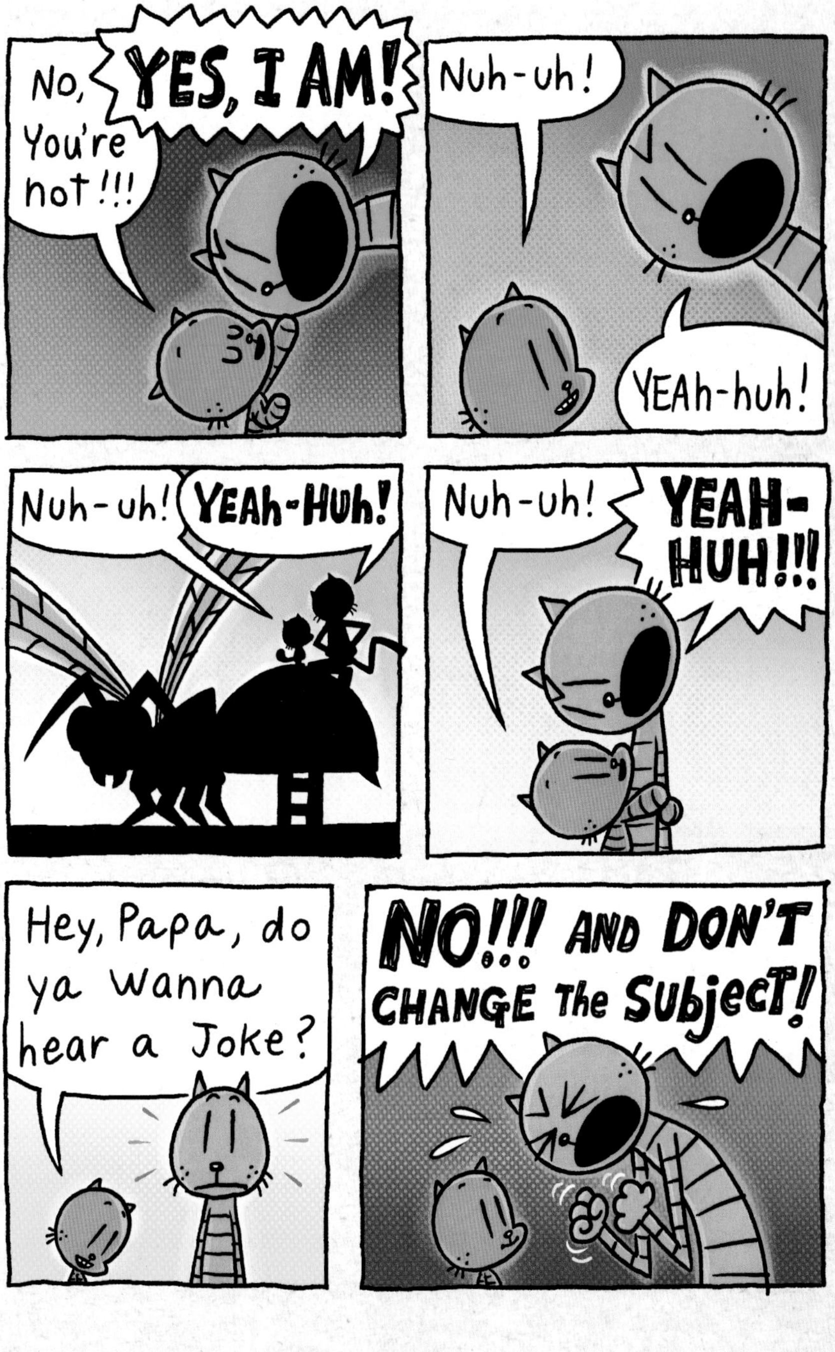
No, You're not!!!
YES, I AM!
Nuh-uh!
YEAh-huh!
Nuh-uh!
YEAh-HUh!
Nuh-uh!
YEAH-HUH!!!
Hey, Papa, do ya wanna hear a Joke?
NO!!! AND DON'T CHANGE The SubjecT!

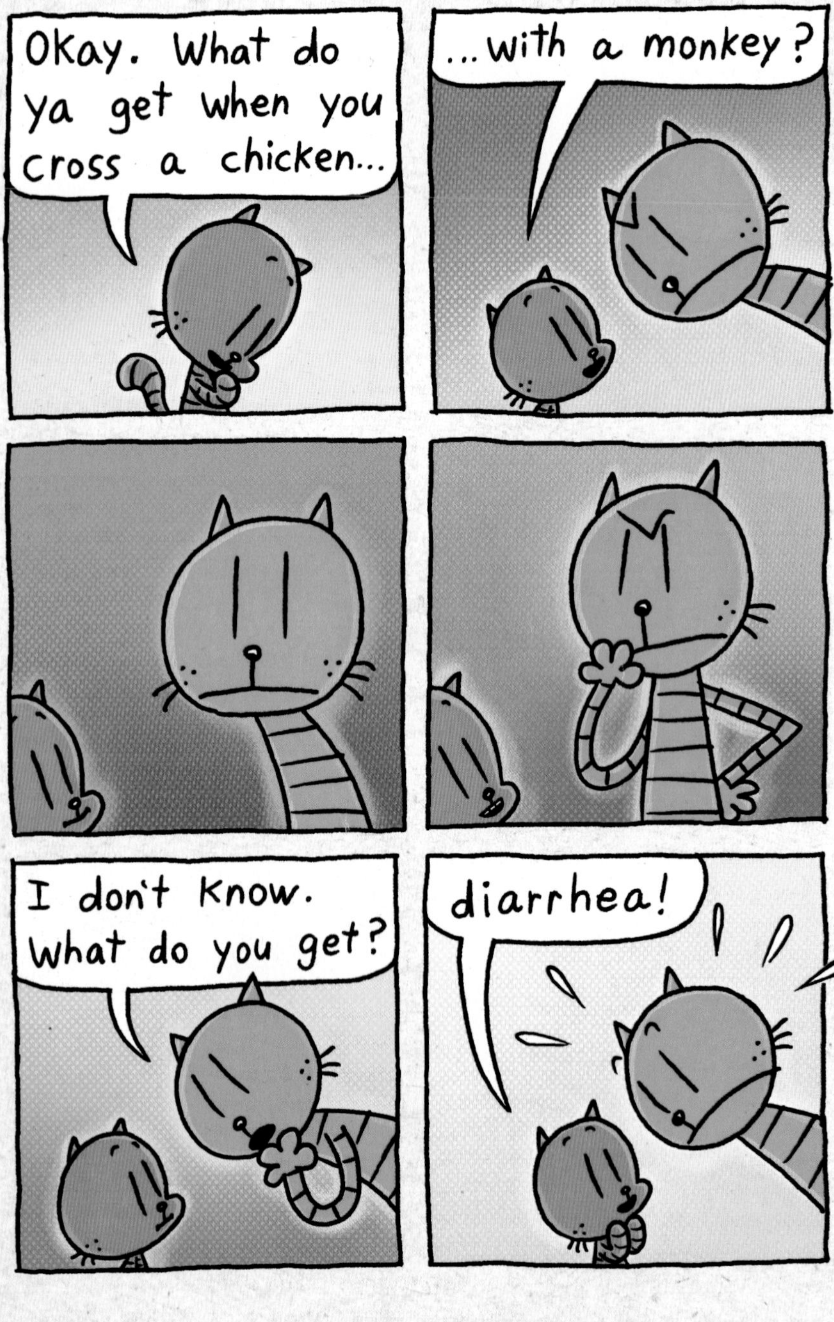
Okay. What do ya get when you cross a chicken...
...with a monkey?
I don't know. What do you get?
diarrhea!

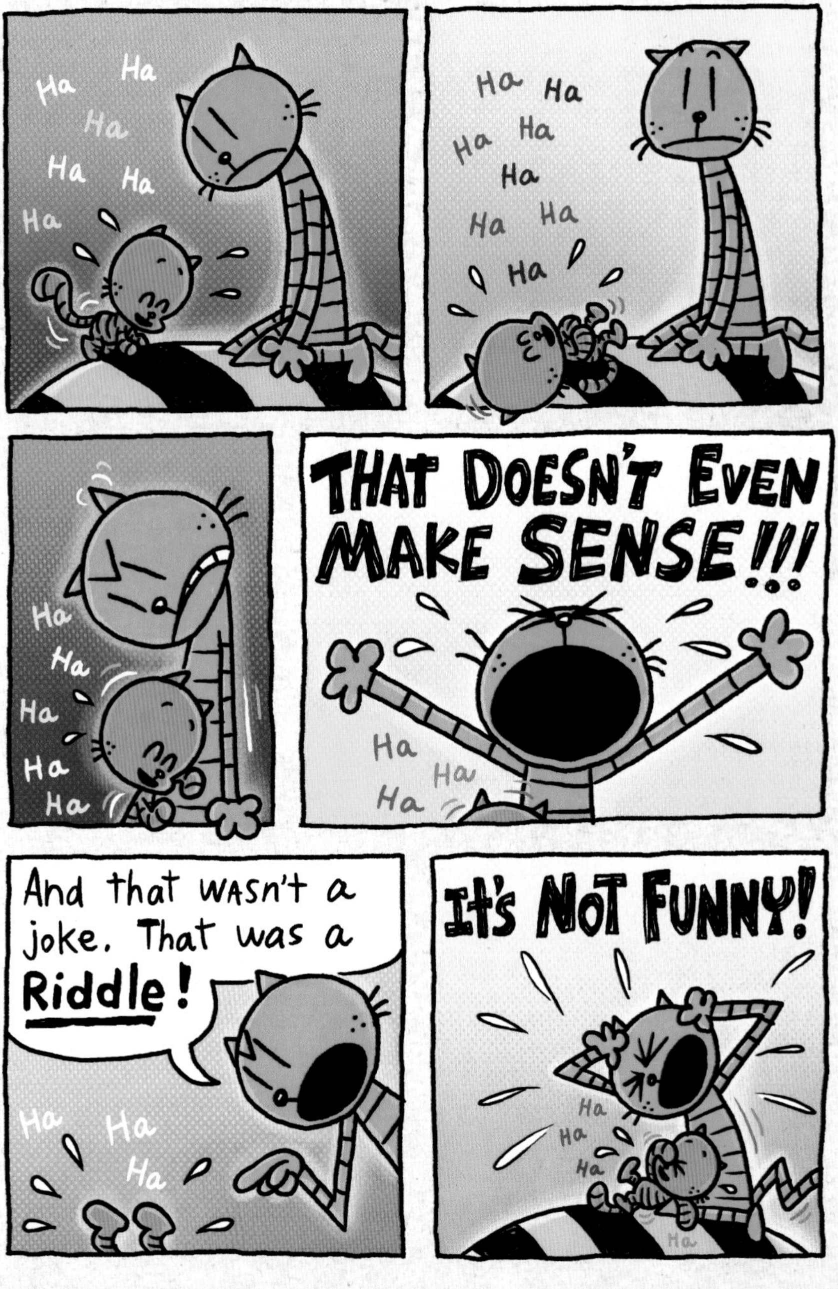
Ha Ha Ha Ha Ha Ha
Ha Ha Ha Ha Ha Ha Ha Ha
Ha Ha Ha Ha Ha
THAT DOESN'T EVEN MAKE SENSE!!!
Ha Ha Ha
And that WASN'T a joke. That was a Riddle!
Ha Ha Ha
It's NOT FUNNY!
Ha Ha Ha Ha

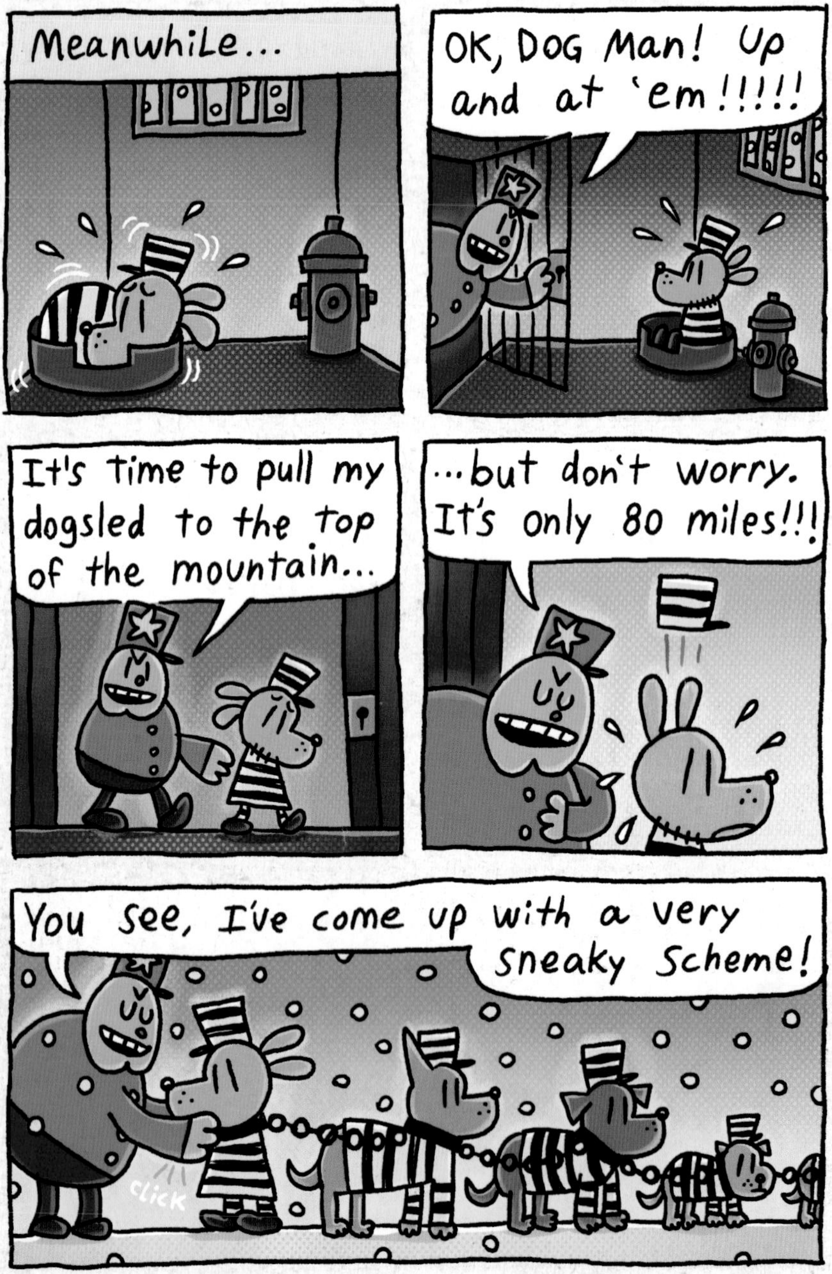
Meanwhile...
OK, DOG Man! Up and at 'em!!!!!
It's time to pull my dogsled to the top of the mountain...
...but don't worry. It's only 80 miles!!!
You see, I've come up with a very sneaky Scheme!
CLICK

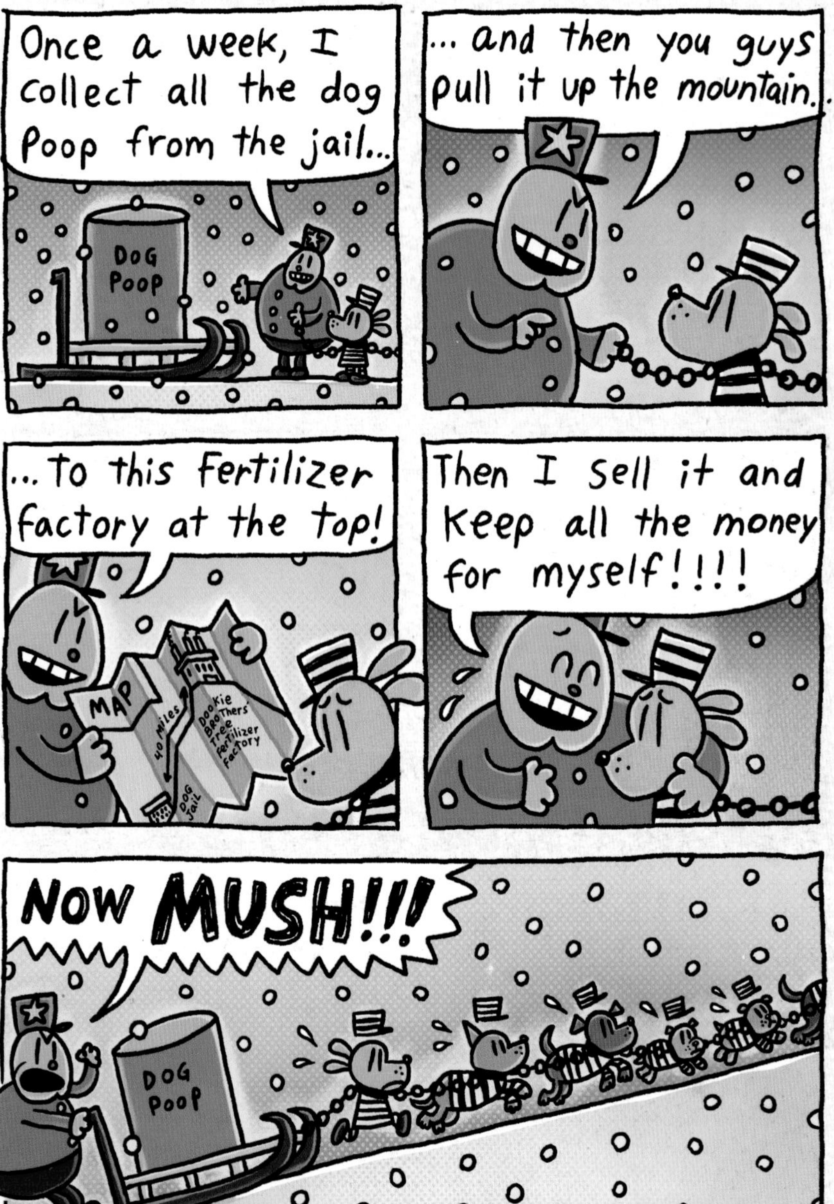
Once a week, I collect all the dog poop from the jail...
DOG POOP
... and then you guys pull it up the mountain...
... to this fertilizer factory at the top!
MAP
40 miles
Dookie Brothers' Tree Fertilizer Factory
DOG JAIL
Then I sell it and keep all the money for myself!!!!
NOW MUSH!!!
DOG POOP

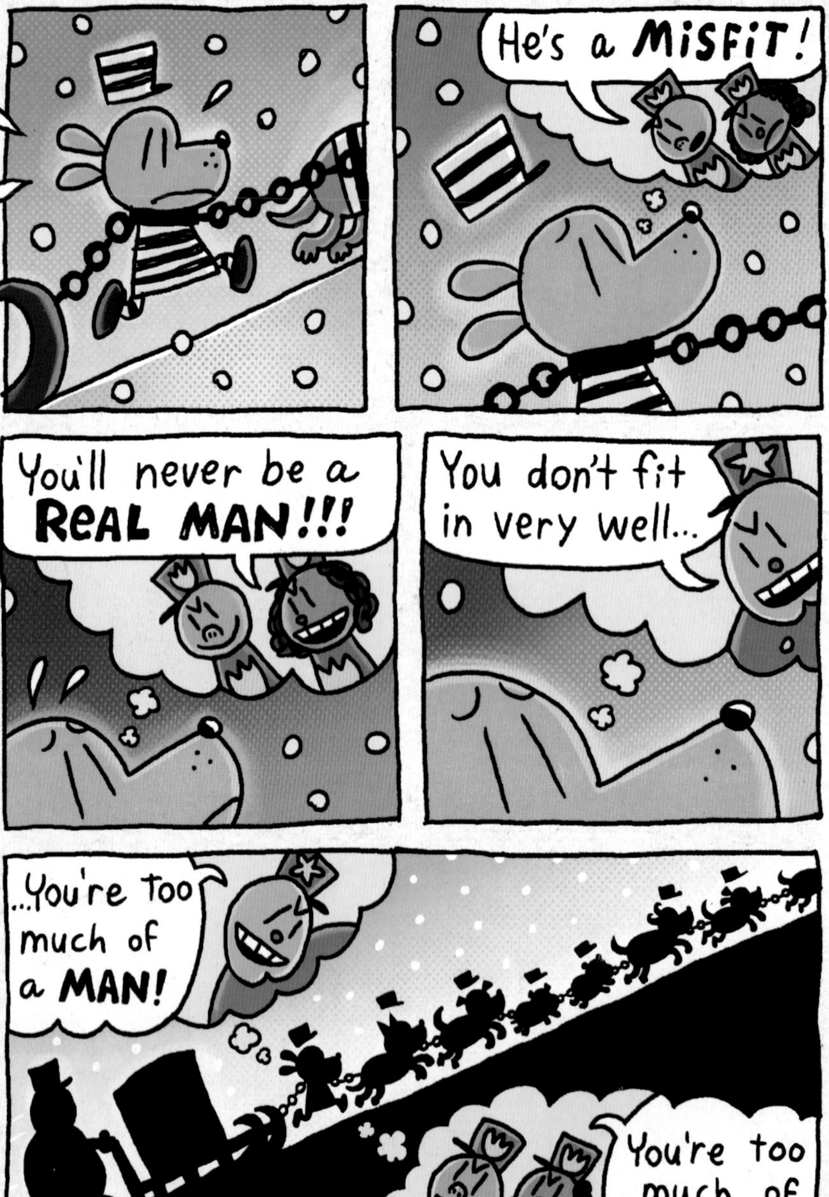

He's a MISFIT!
You'll never be a REAL MAN!!!
You don't fit in very well...
...You're too much of a MAN!
You're too much of a DOG!

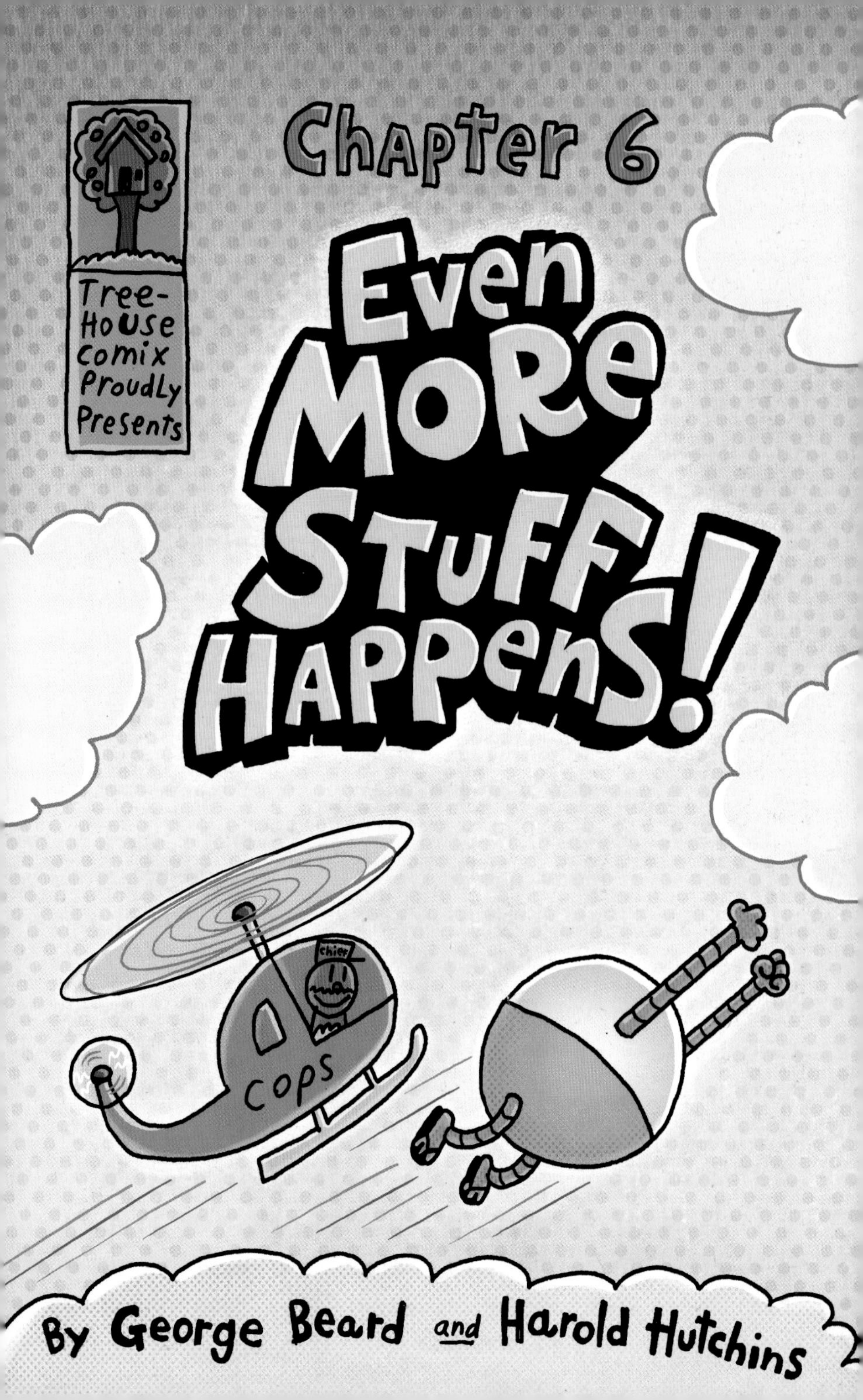
Tree-House Comix Proudly Presents
Chapter 6
Even MORE STUFF HAPPENS!
chief
cops
By George Beard and Harold Hutchins

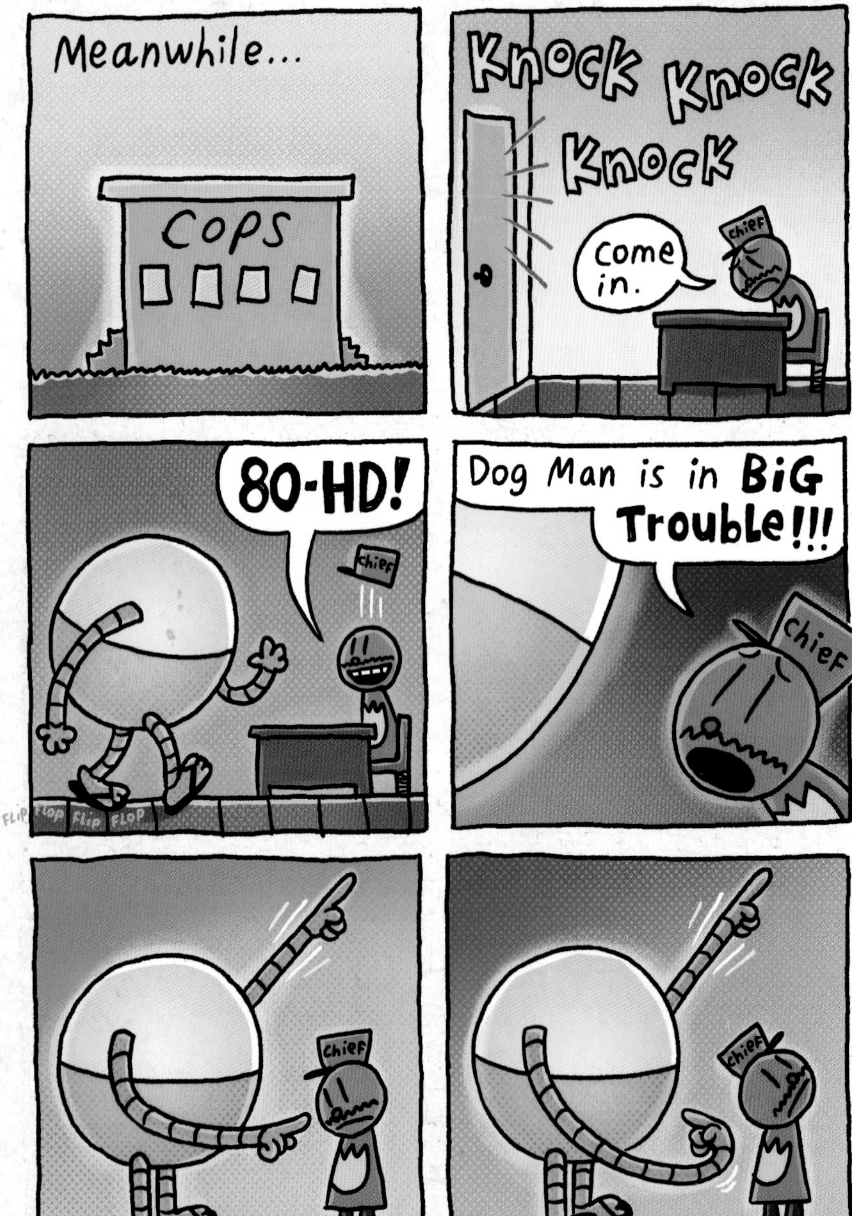
Meanwhile...
COPS
Knock Knock
Knock
come in.
chief
80-HD!
chief
FLIP FLOP FLIP FLOP
Dog Man is in BiG Trouble!!!
Chief
chief
chief

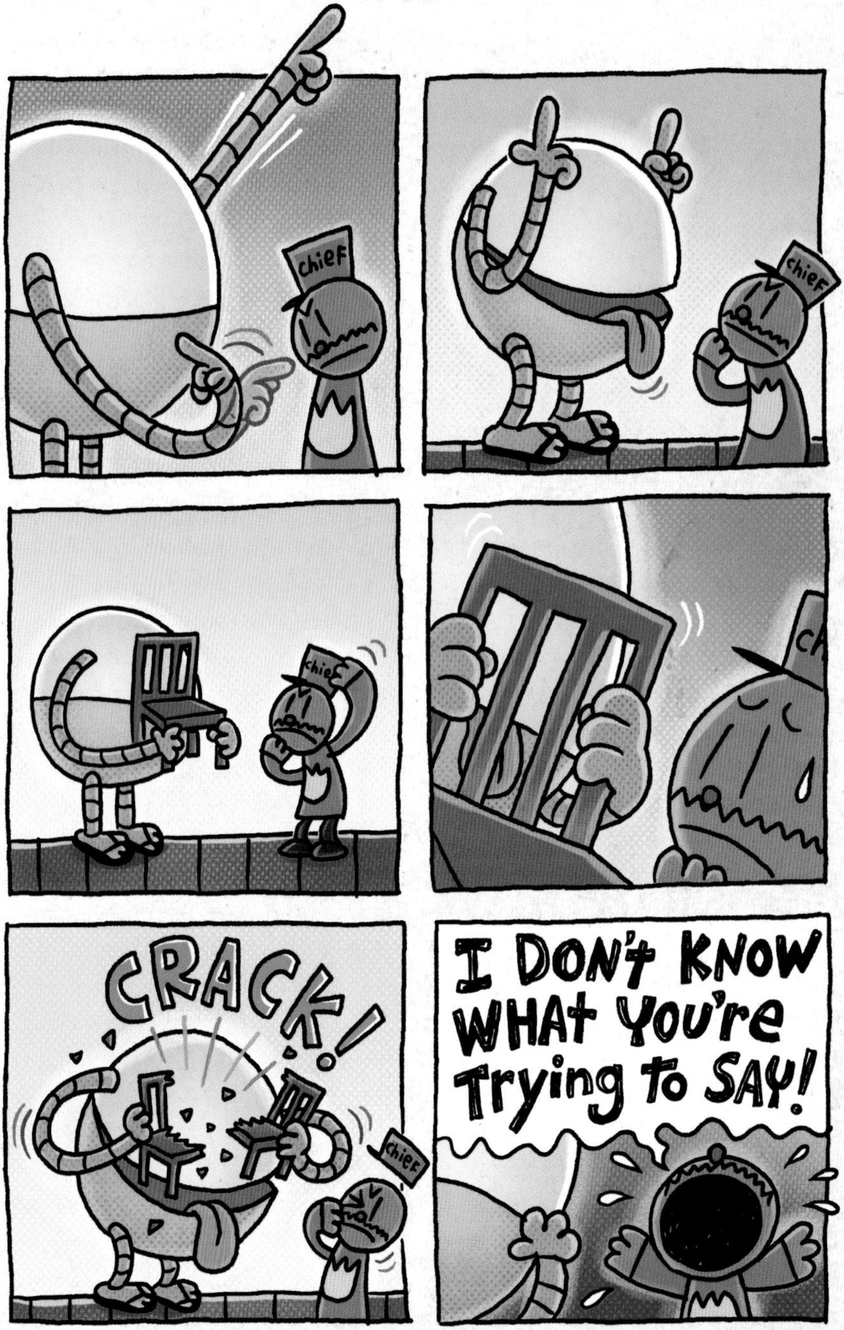
chief
chief
chief
CRACK!
chief
I DON'T KNOW WHAT YOU'RE TRYING TO SAY!

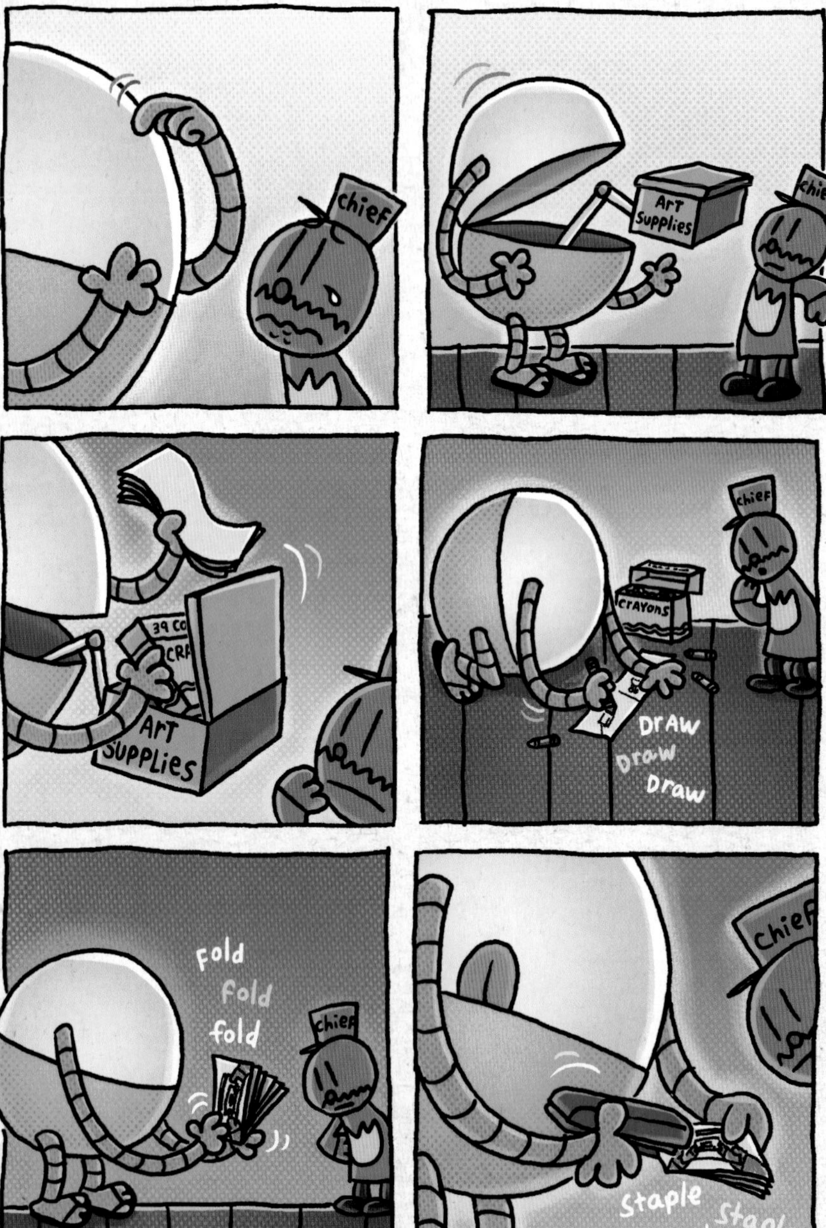
chief
chief
ArT Supplies
ArT SUPPLies
39 Co
CRA
chief
CRAYONS
DrAW
Draw
Draw
Fold
Fold
fold
chieF
chieF
staple
staple
staple

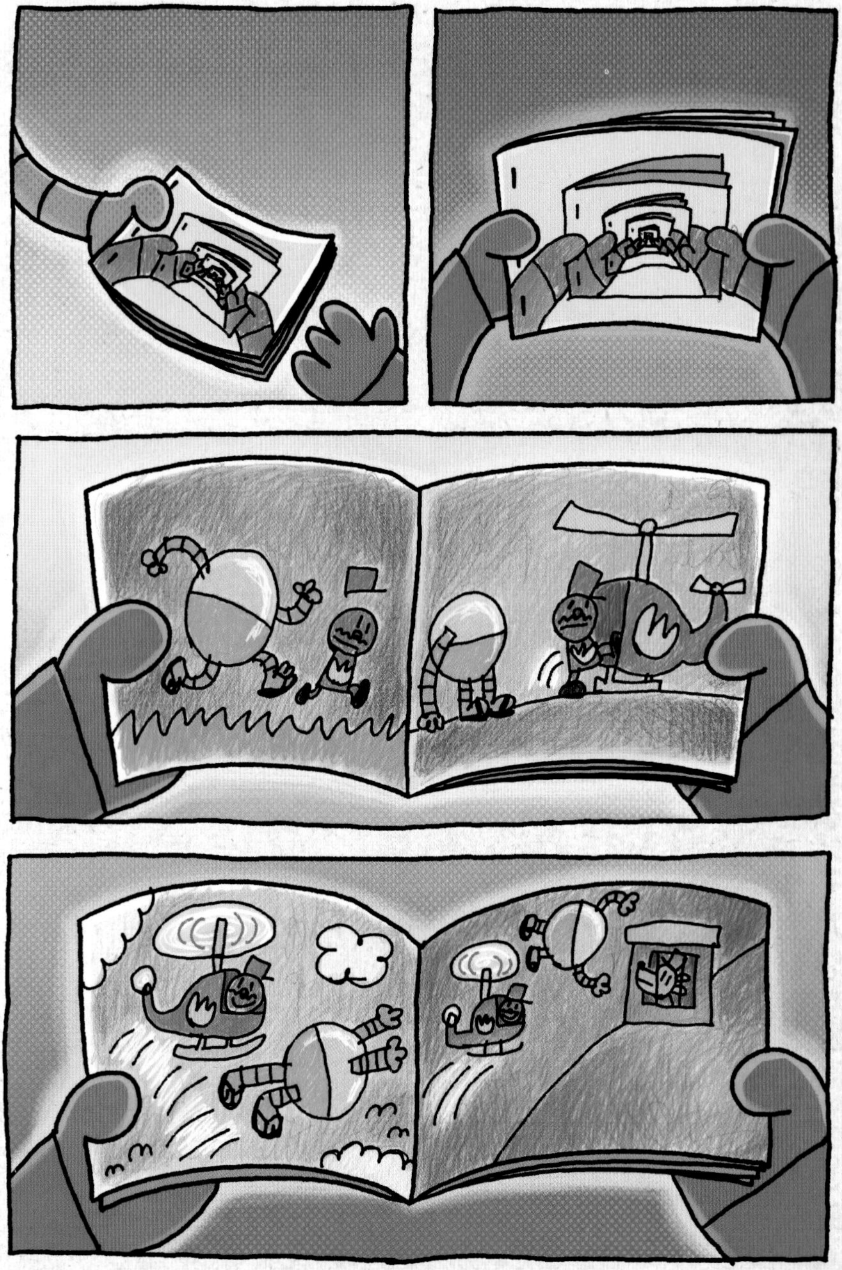

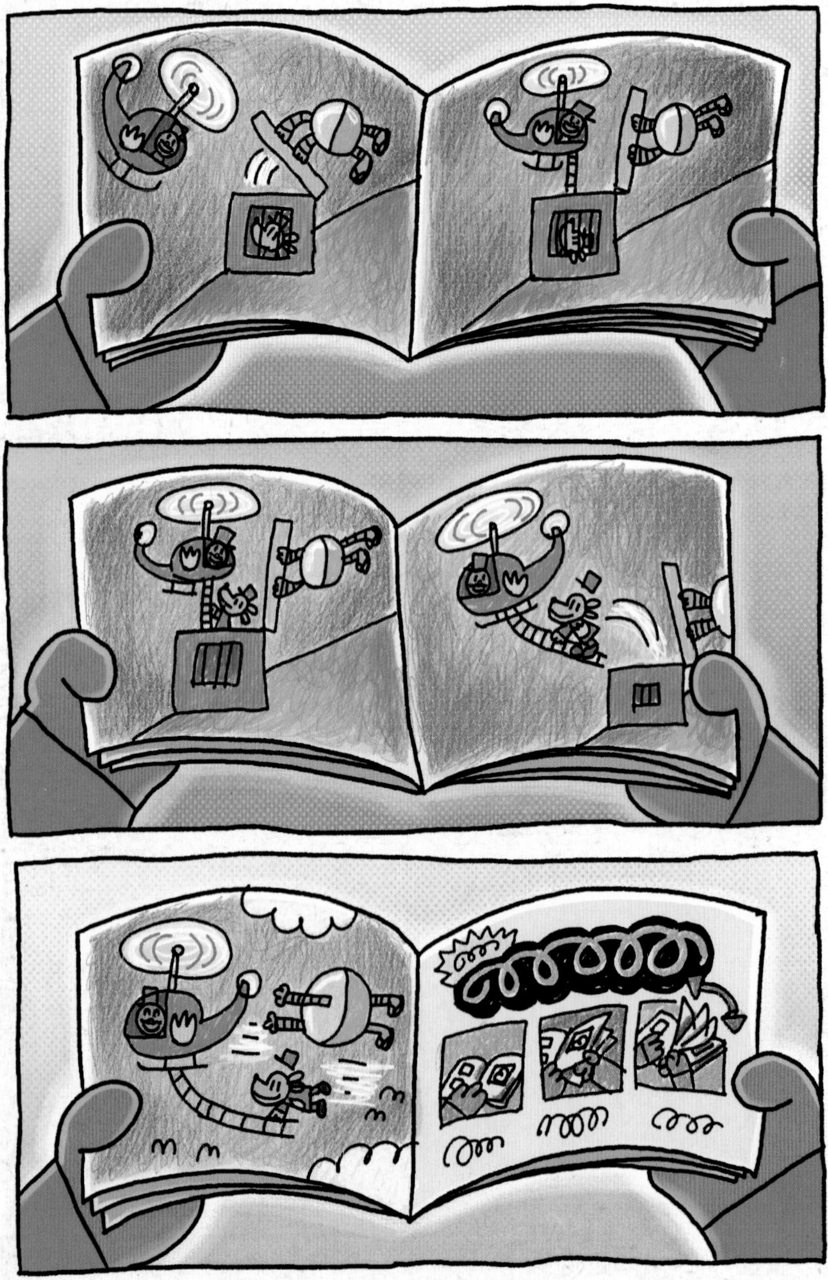

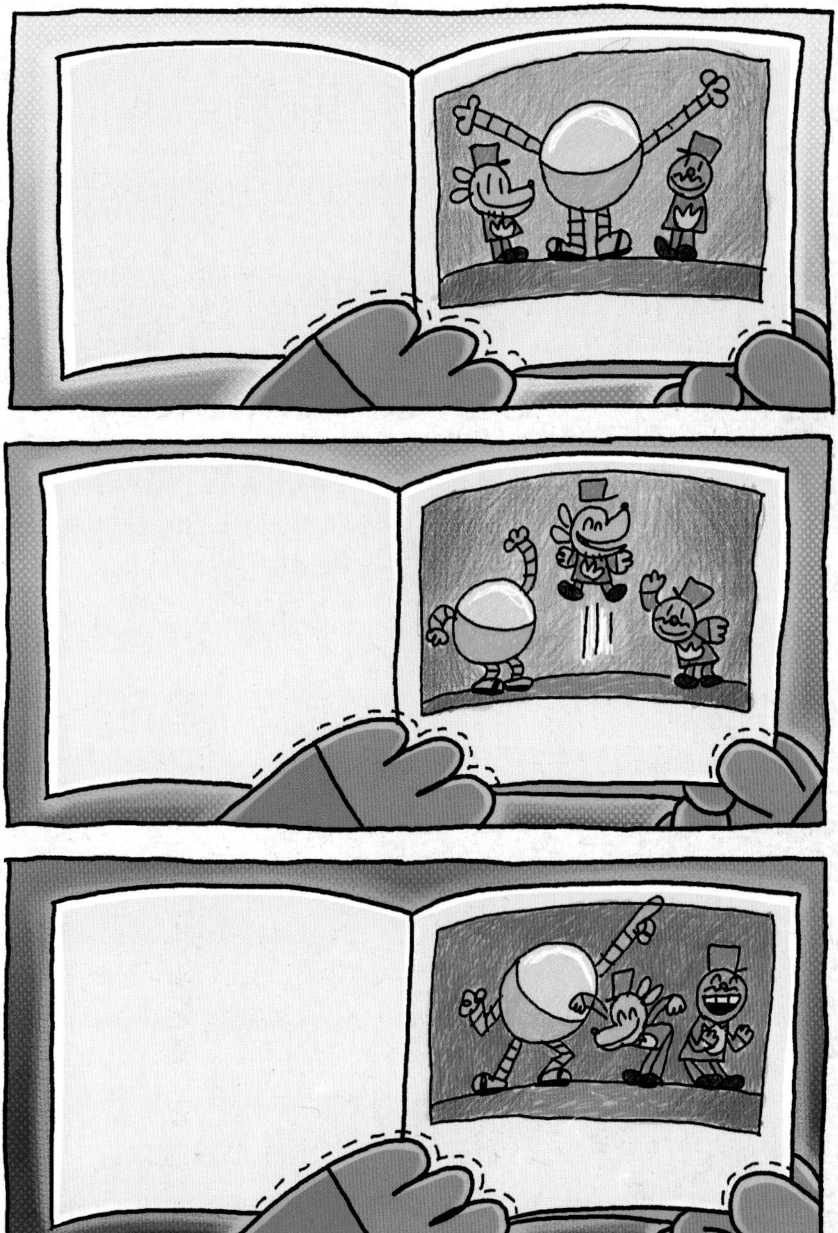

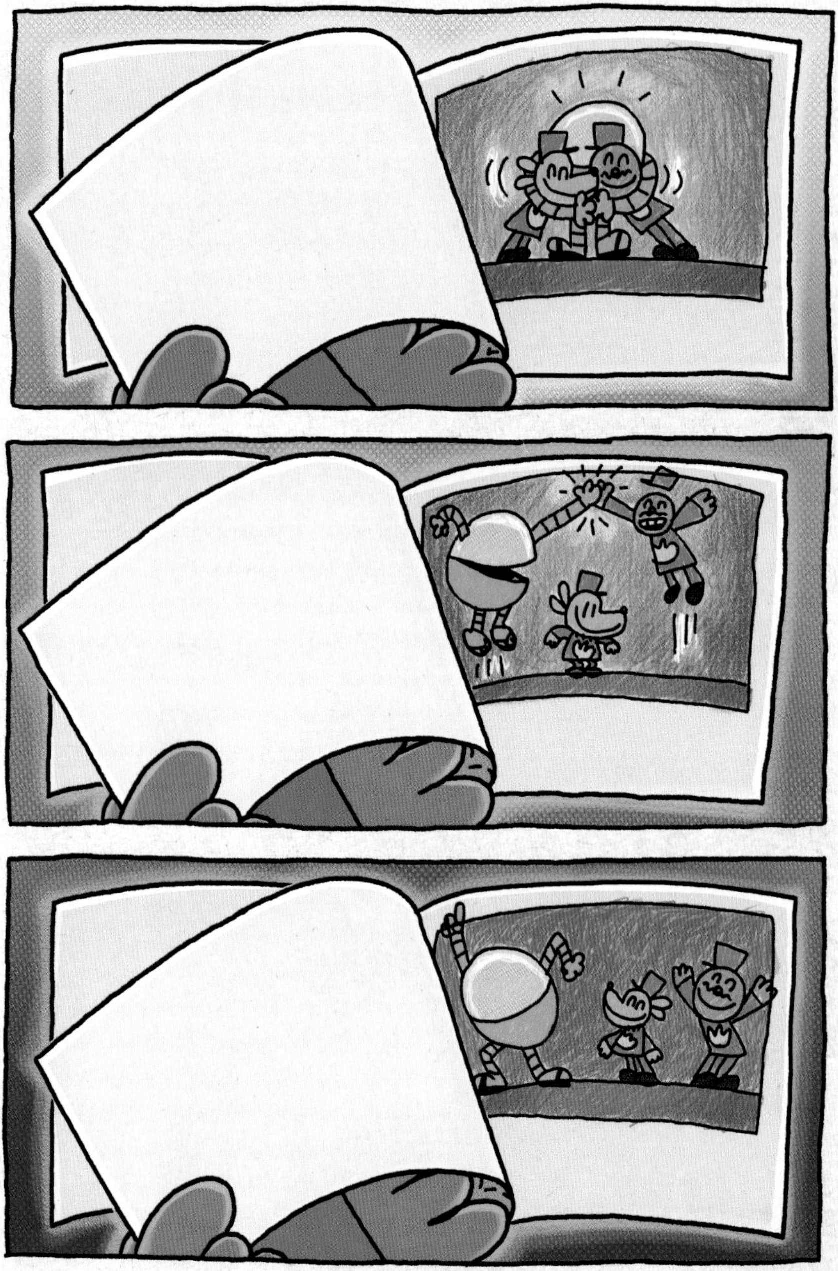

So you want me to help ya bust Dog Man out of Jail?

That's **ILLegal!** **THaT's Dangerous!** **THaT's Irresponsible!**

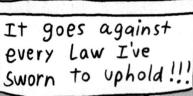

It goes against every Law I've sworn to uphold!!!

Let's DO it!!!

FLiP FLoP FLiP FLoP FLiP

Oh boy, This is gonna be **GREAT!!!**

COPS

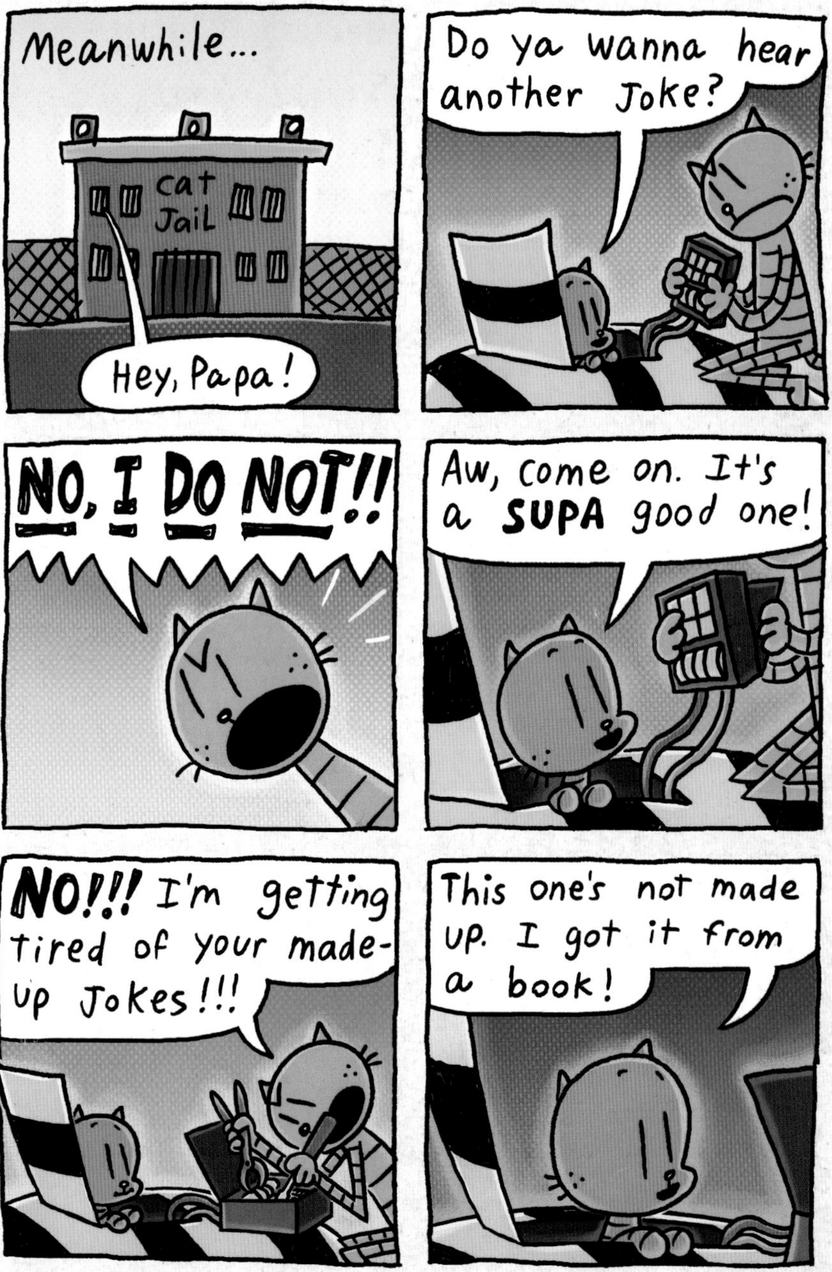
Meanwhile...
Cat Jail
Hey, Papa!
Do ya wanna hear another Joke?
NO, I DO NOT!!
Aw, come on. It's a SUPA good one!
NO!!! I'm getting tired of your made-up Jokes!!!
This one's not made up. I got it from a book!

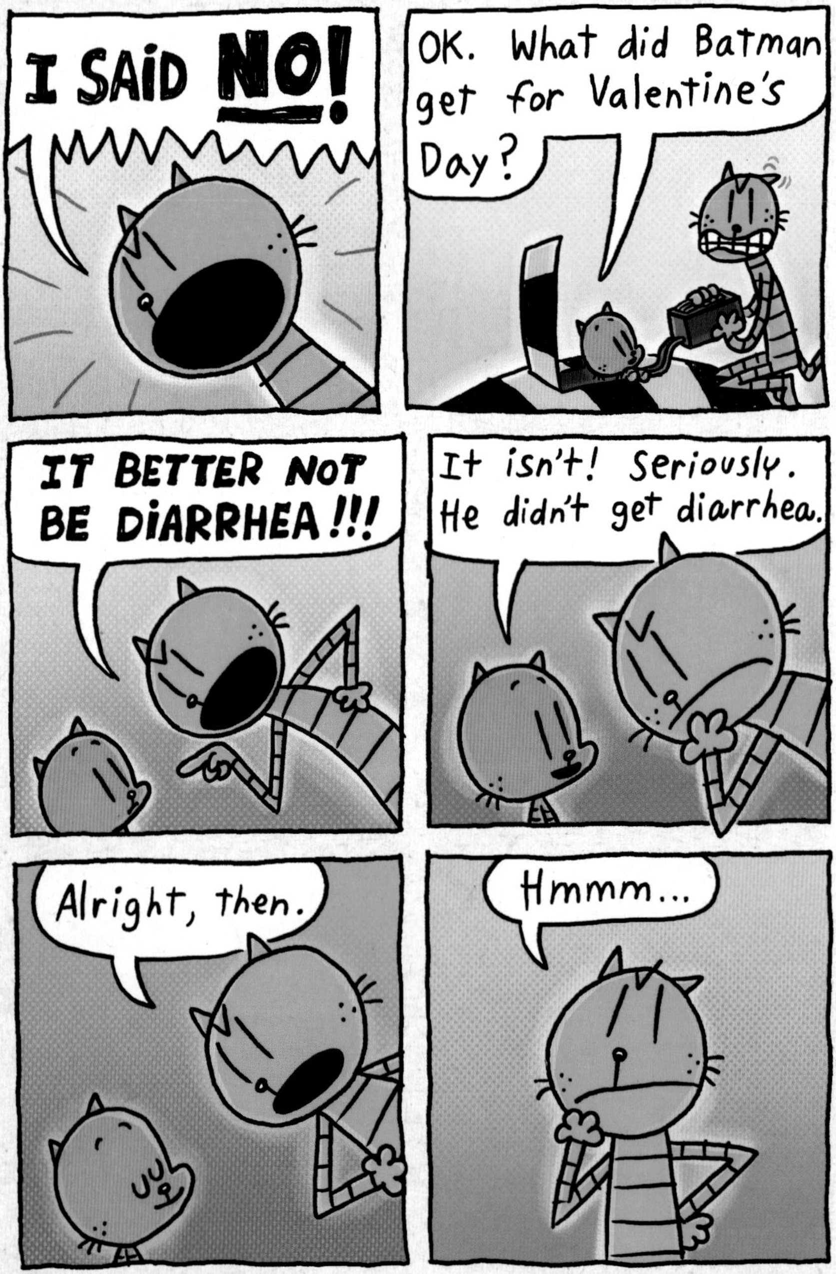
I SAID NO!
OK. What did Batman get for Valentine's Day?
IT BETTER NOT BE DIARRHEA!!!
It isn't! Seriously. He didn't get diarrhea.
Alright, then.
Hmmm...

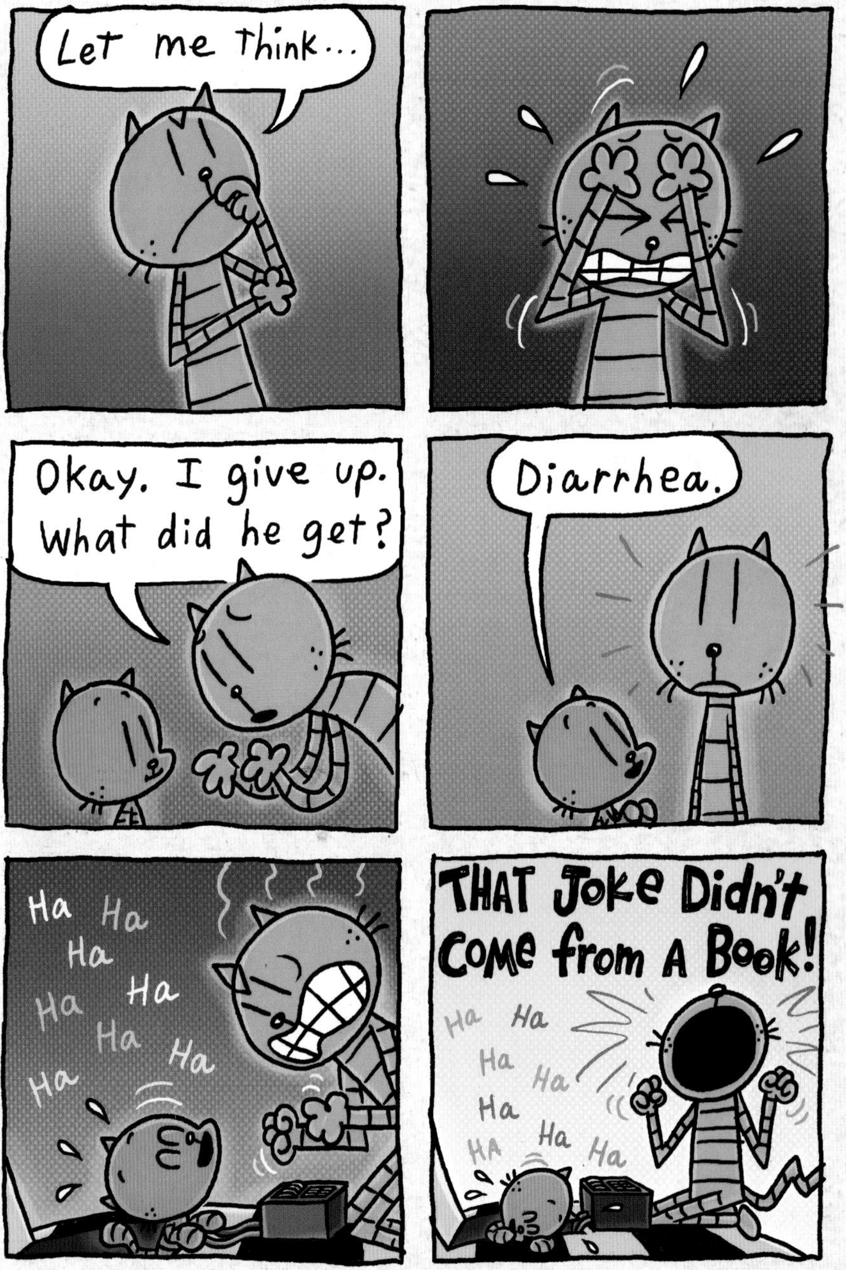
Let me think...
Okay. I give up. What did he get?
Diarrhea.
Ha Ha Ha Ha Ha Ha Ha Ha
THAT JOKE DIDN'T COME FROM A BOOK!
Ha Ha Ha Ha Ha HA Ha Ha

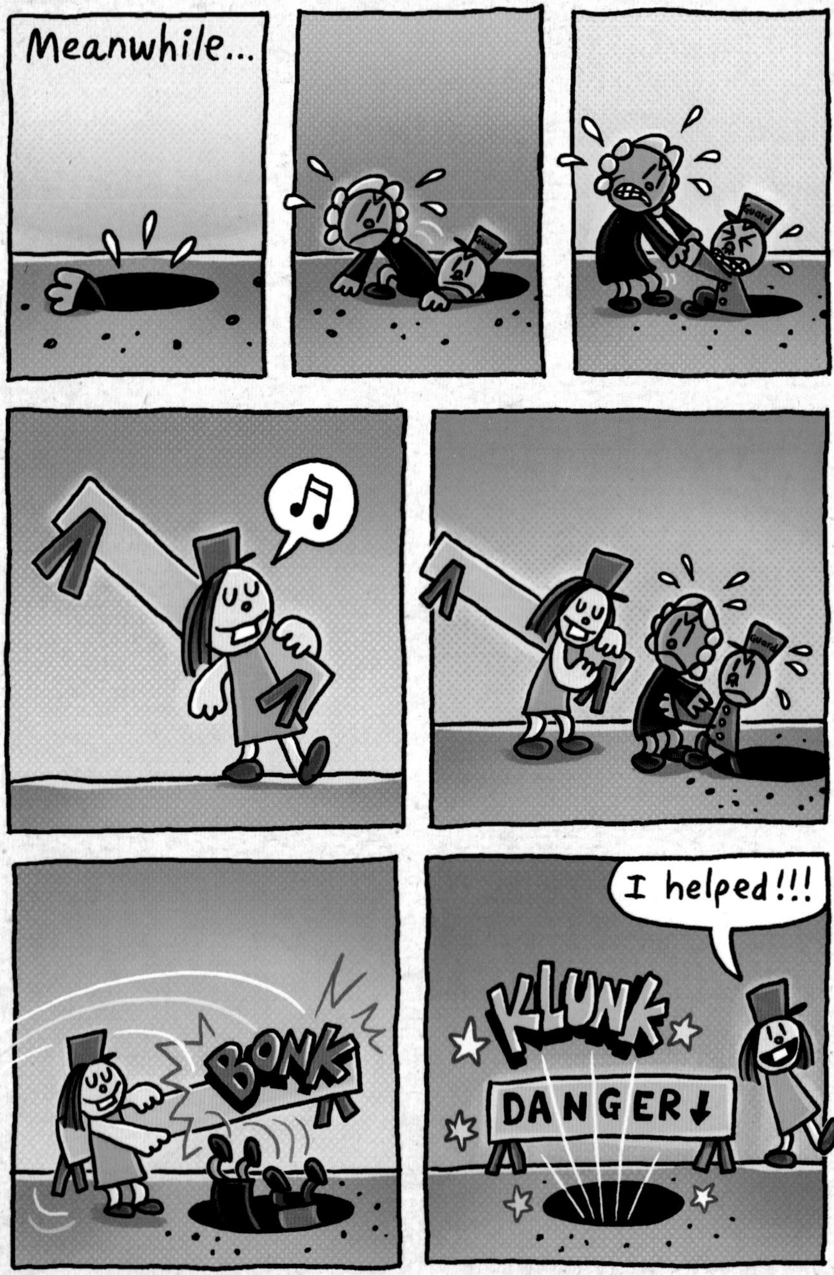
Meanwhile...
Guard
Guard
Guard
♫
I helped!!!
BONK
KLUNK
DANGER↓

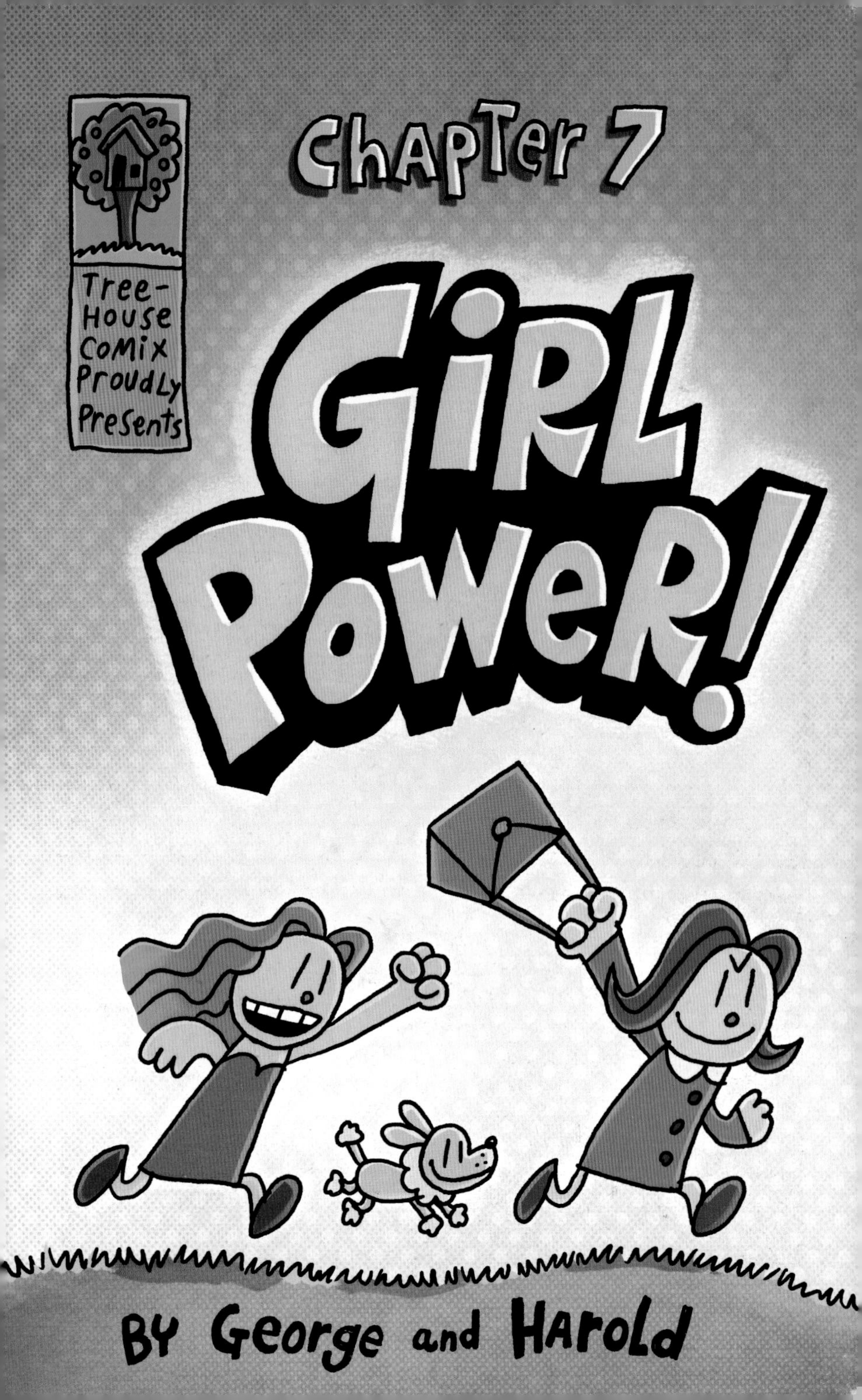
Tree-House Comix Proudly Presents
Chapter 7
Girl Power!
By George and Harold

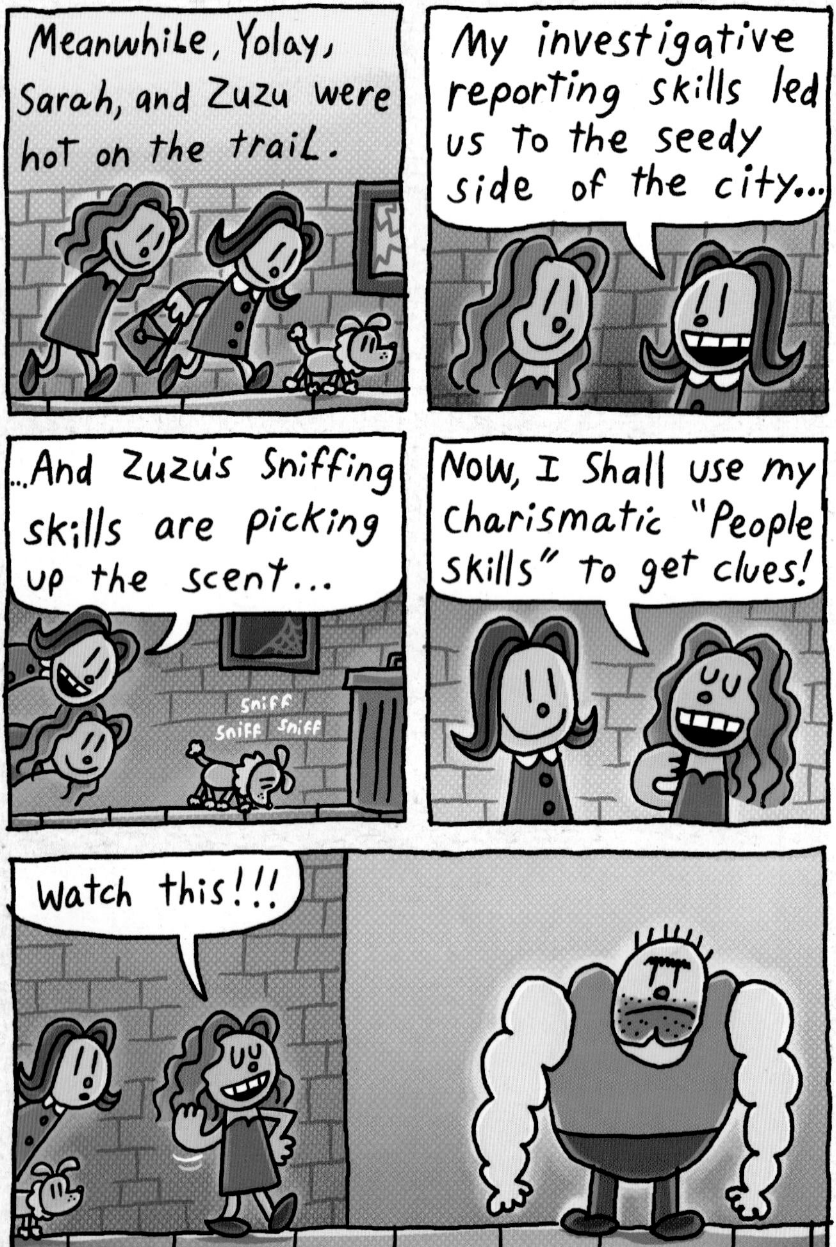
Meanwhile, Yolay, Sarah, and Zuzu were hot on the trail.
My investigative reporting skills led us to the seedy side of the city...
...And Zuzu's sniffing skills are picking up the scent...
sniff
sniff sniff
Now, I shall use my charismatic "People skills" to get clues!
Watch this!!!

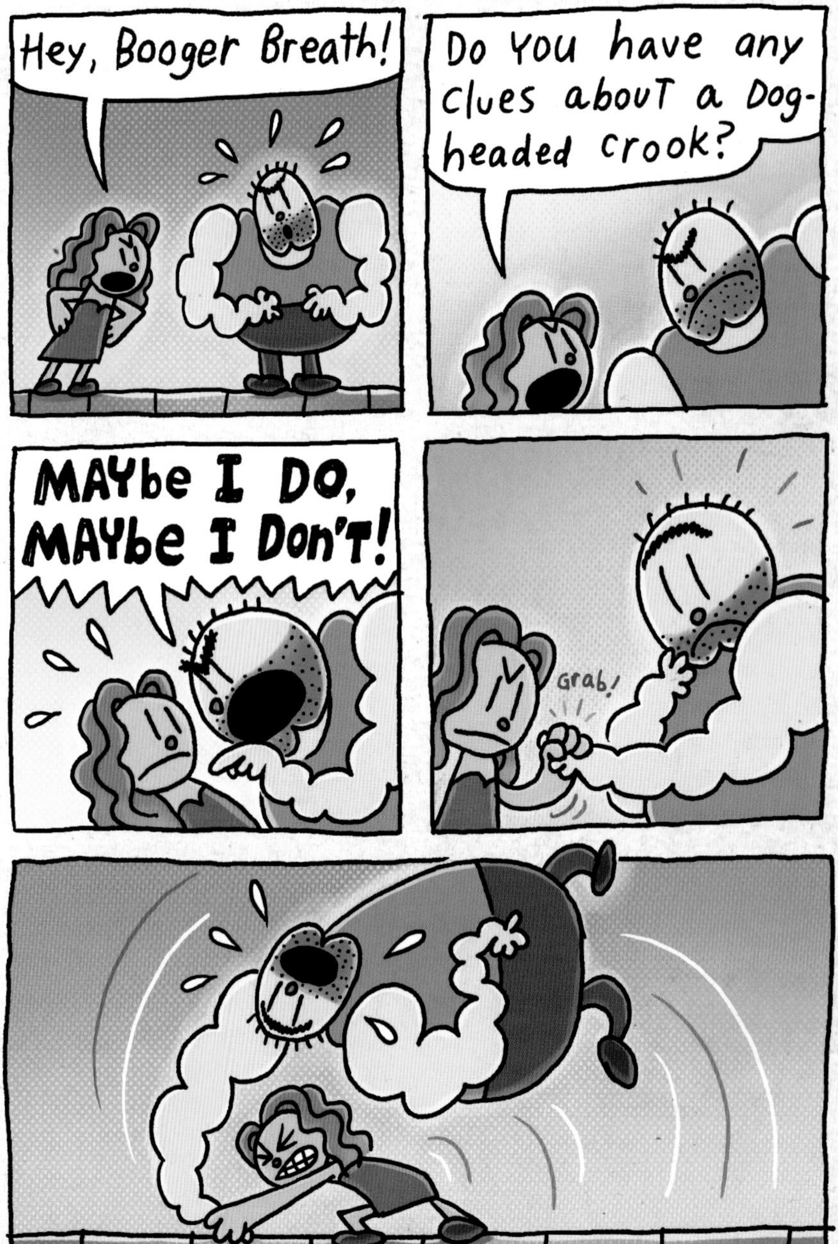
Hey, Booger Breath!
Do you have any clues about a Dog-headed crook?
MAYbe I DO, MAYbe I Don'T!
Grab!

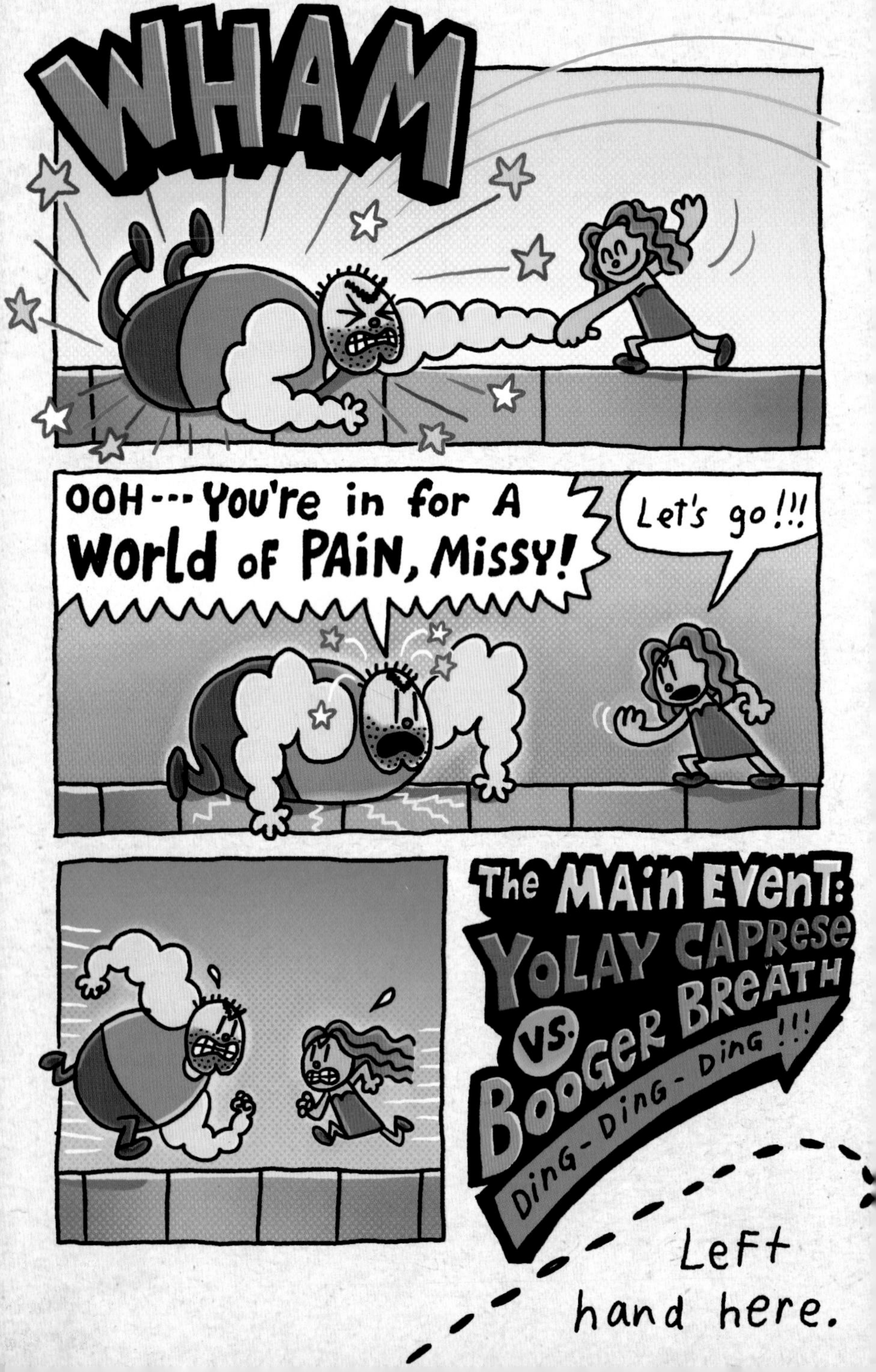
WHAM
OOH--- You're in for A World of PAIN, Missy!
Let's go!!!
The MAin EVenT:
YOLAY CAPRese
VS.
BOOGeR BReATH
DinG- DinG- DinG!!!
LeFt hand here.

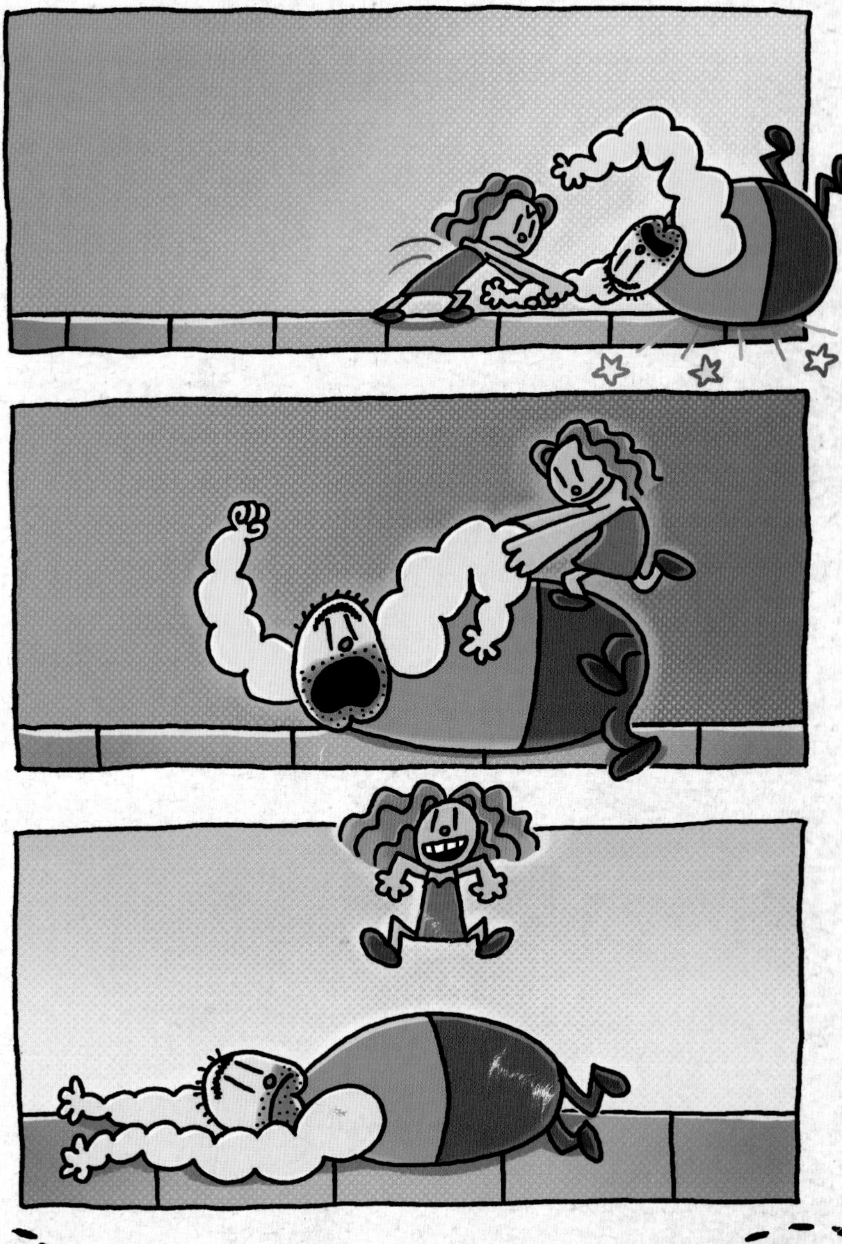

Right Thumb here.

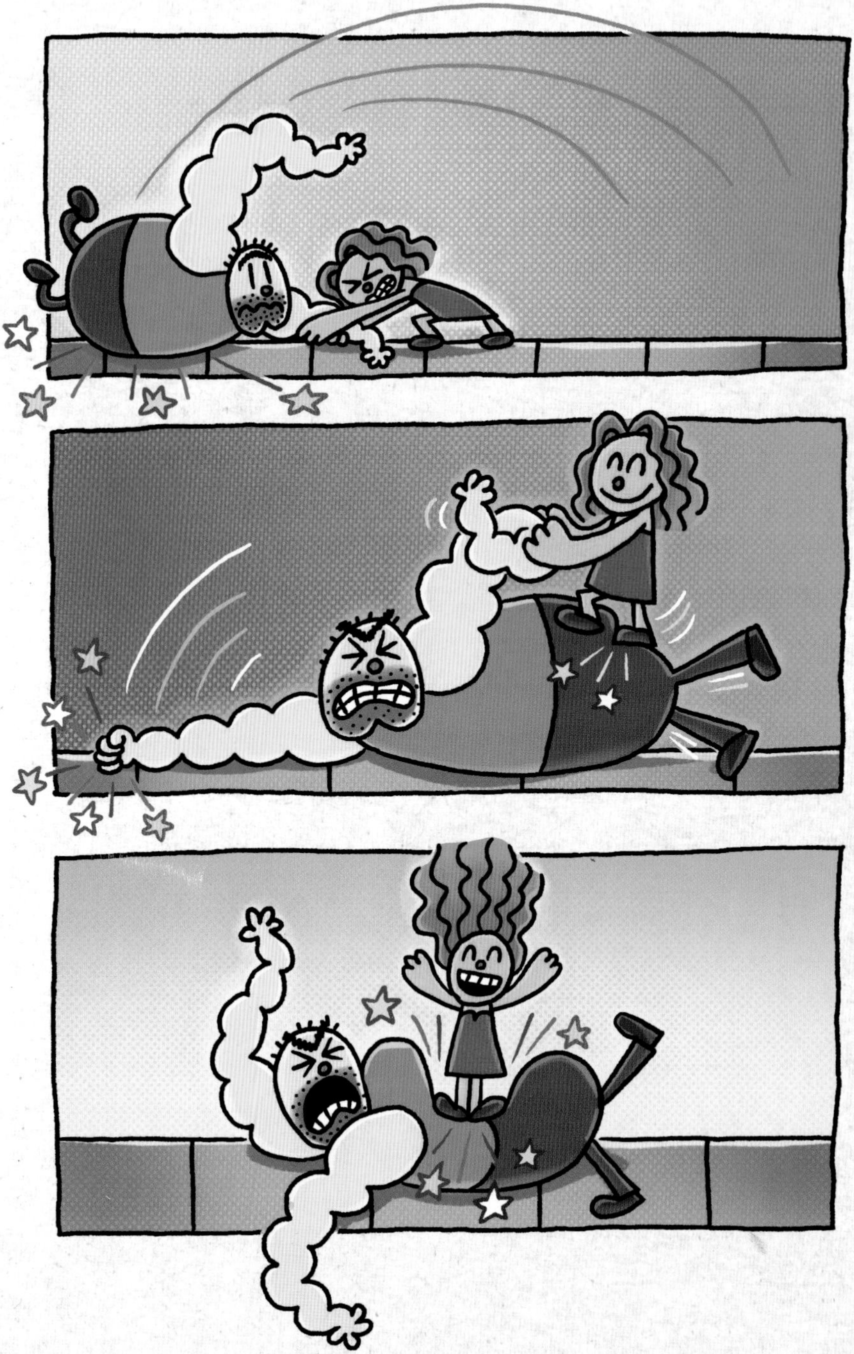

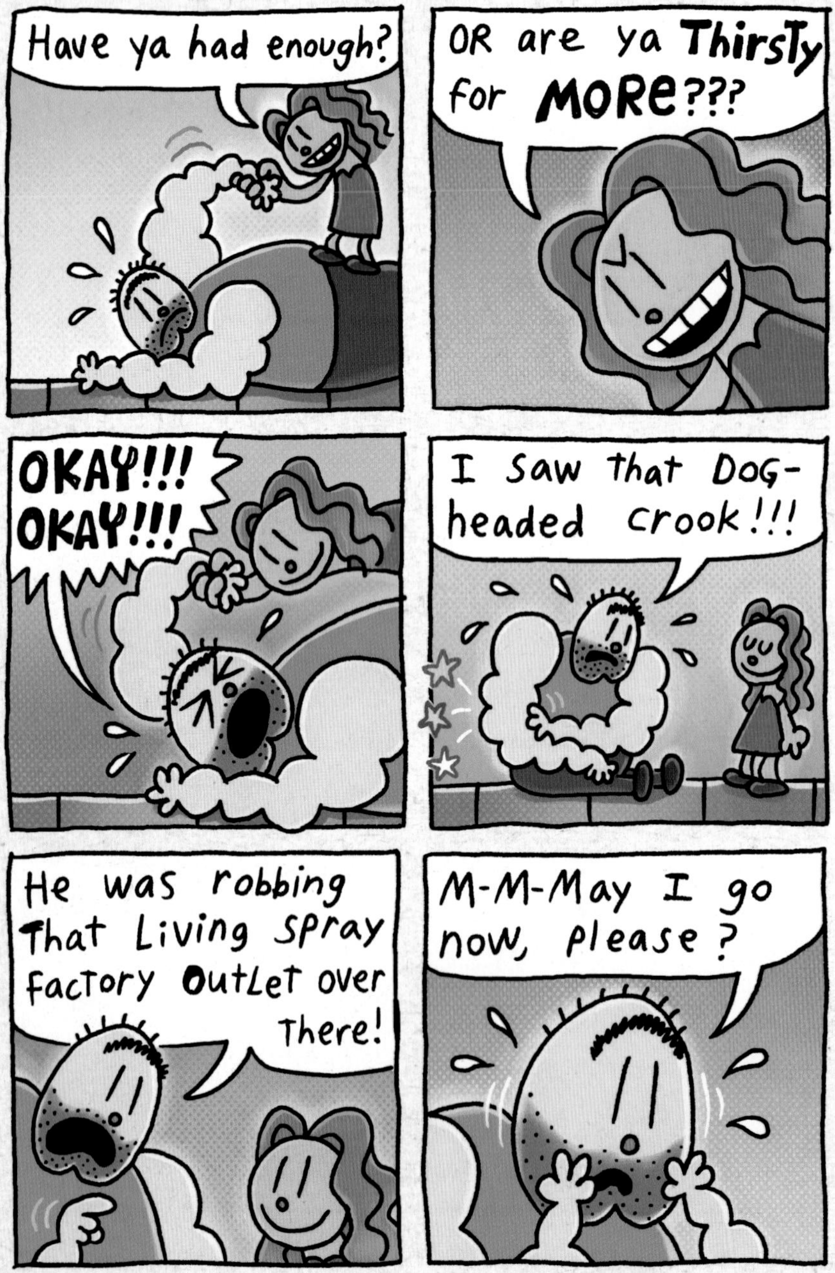
Have ya had enough?
OR are ya ThirsTy for MORE???
OKAY!!! OKAY!!!
I saw that DOG-headed crook!!!
He was robbing That Living Spray Factory OutLet over There!
M-M-May I go now, please?

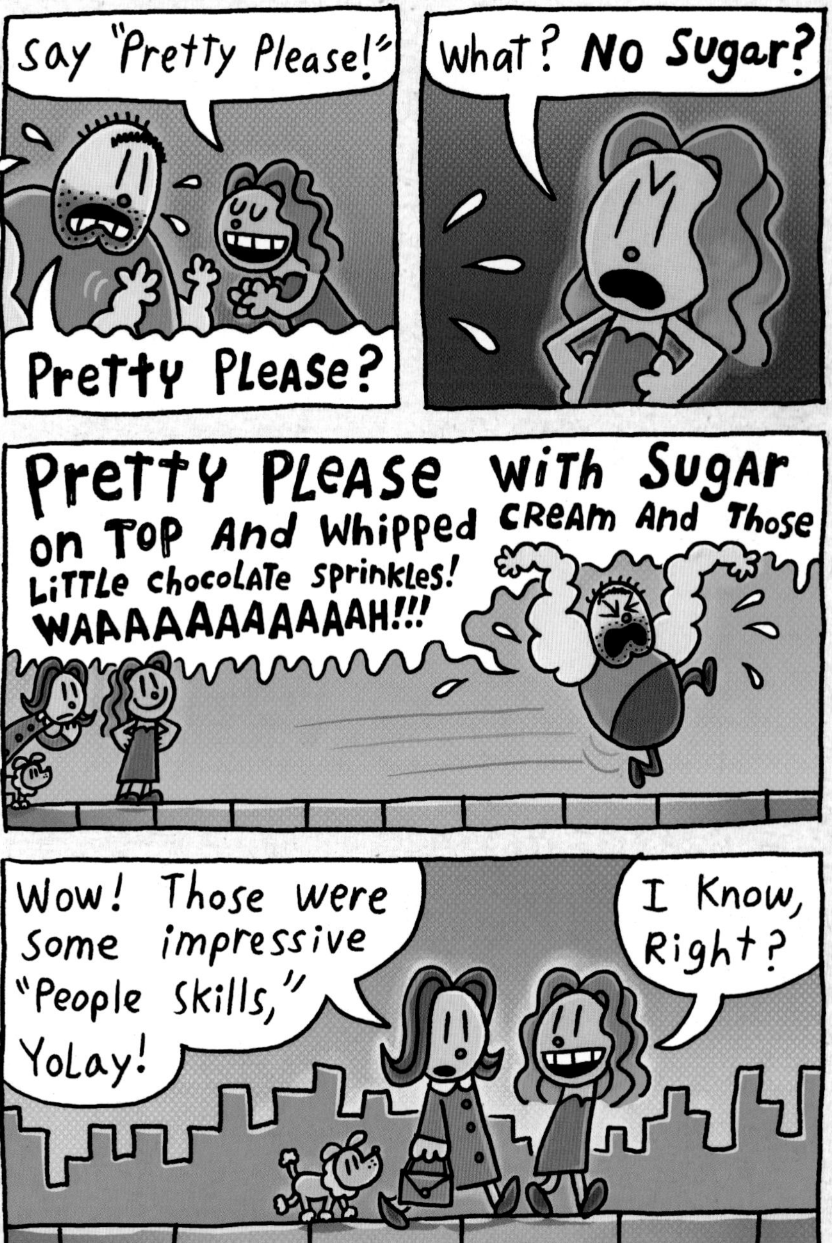
Say "Pretty Please!"
Pretty Please?
What? No Sugar?
Pretty Please with Sugar on Top And Whipped Cream And Those Little chocolate sprinkles! WAAAAAAAAAAAH!!!
Wow! Those were some impressive "People Skills," YoLay!
I Know, Right?

Chapter 8

Help is on the Way

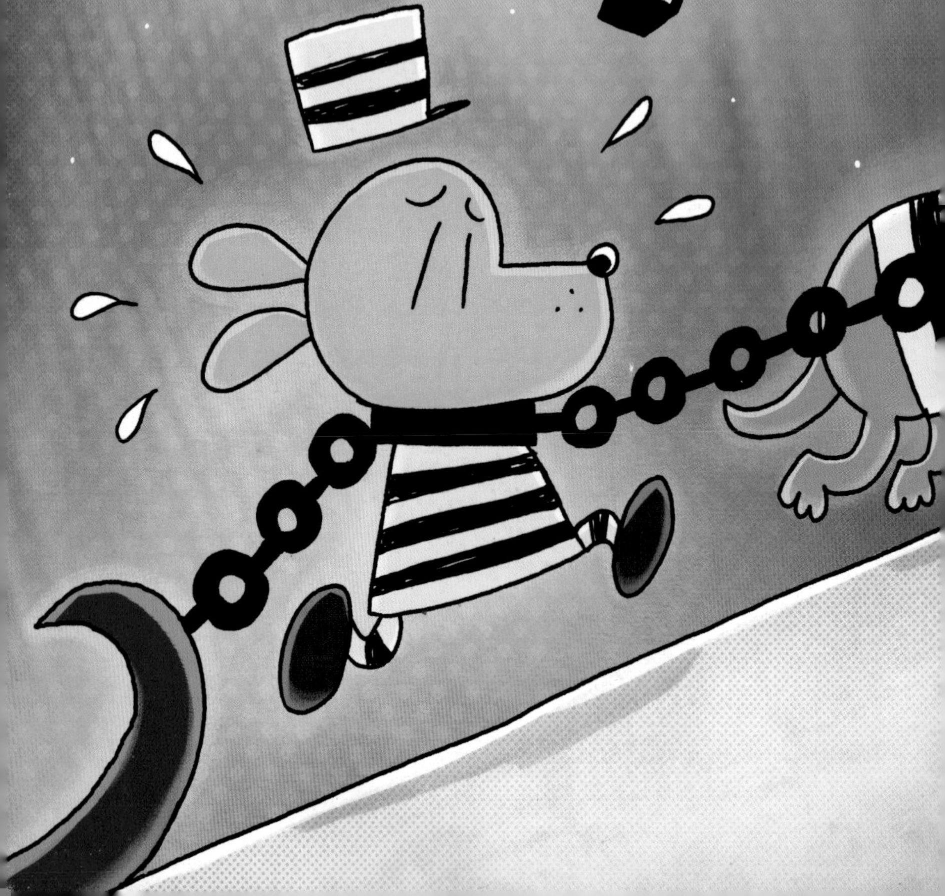

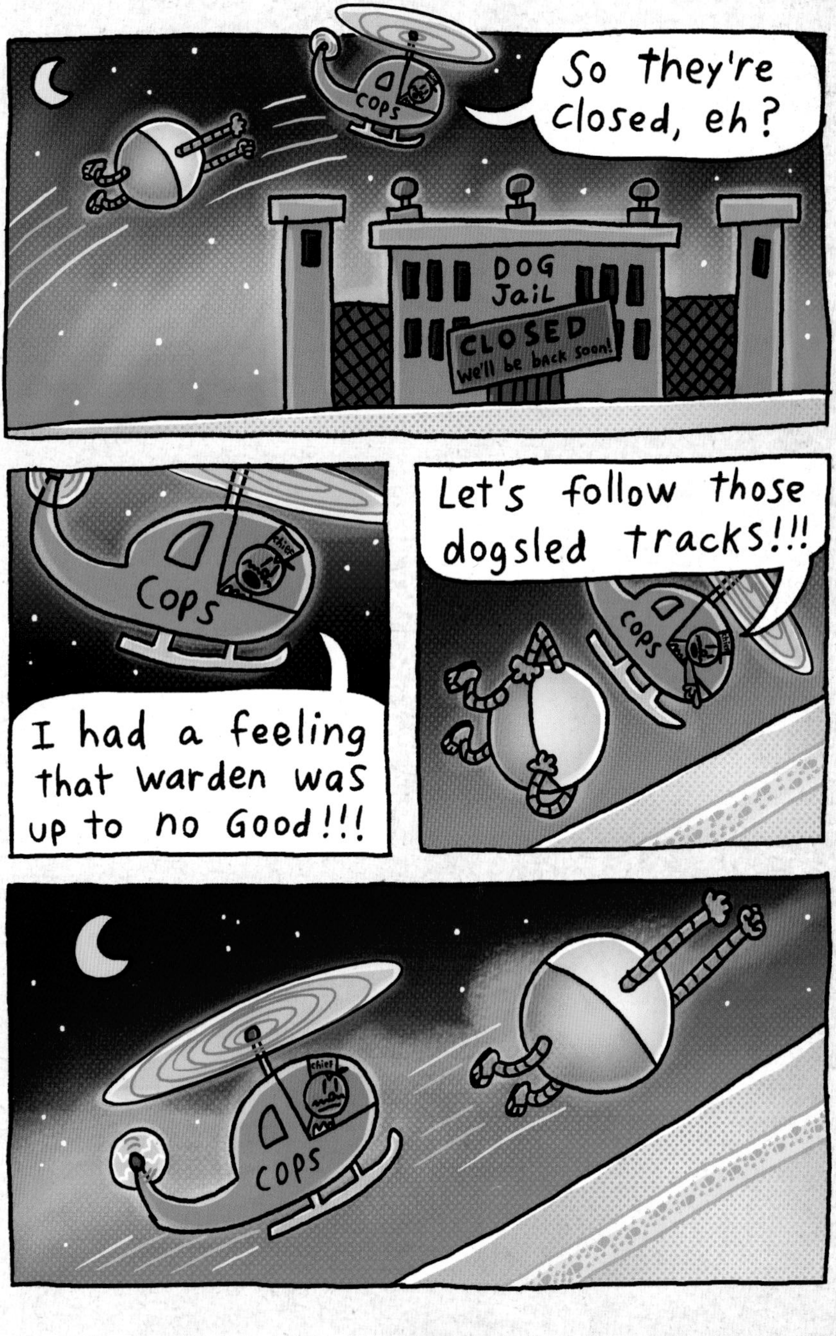
So they're closed, eh?
COPS
DOG Jail
CLOSED We'll be back soon!
COPS
Chief
I had a feeling that warden was up to no Good!!!
Let's follow those dogsled tracks!!!
COPS
Chief
COPS

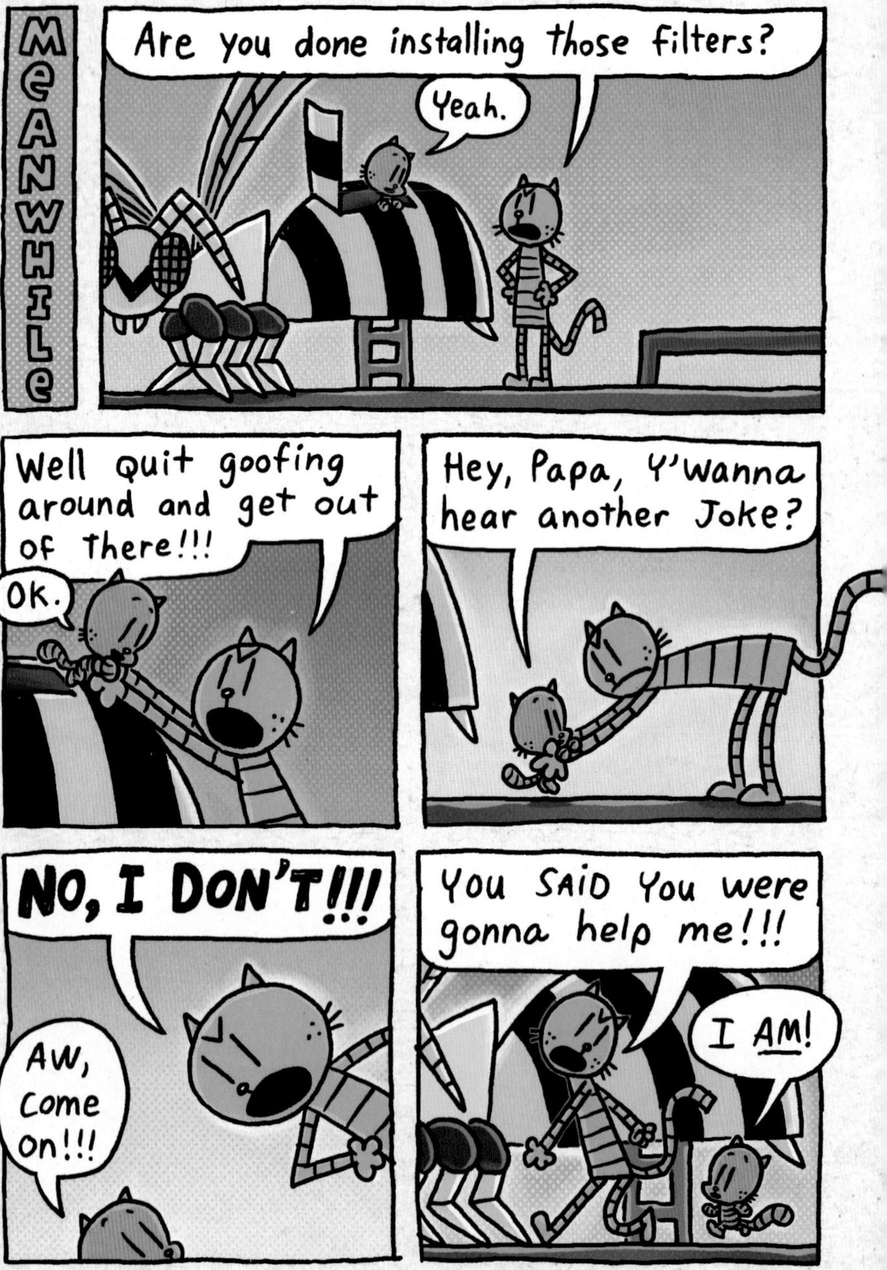
MEANWHILE
Are you done installing those filters?
Yeah.
Well quit goofing around and get out of there!!!
OK.
Hey, Papa, Y'wanna hear another Joke?
NO, I DON'T!!!
AW, come on!!!
You SAID You were gonna help me!!!
I AM!

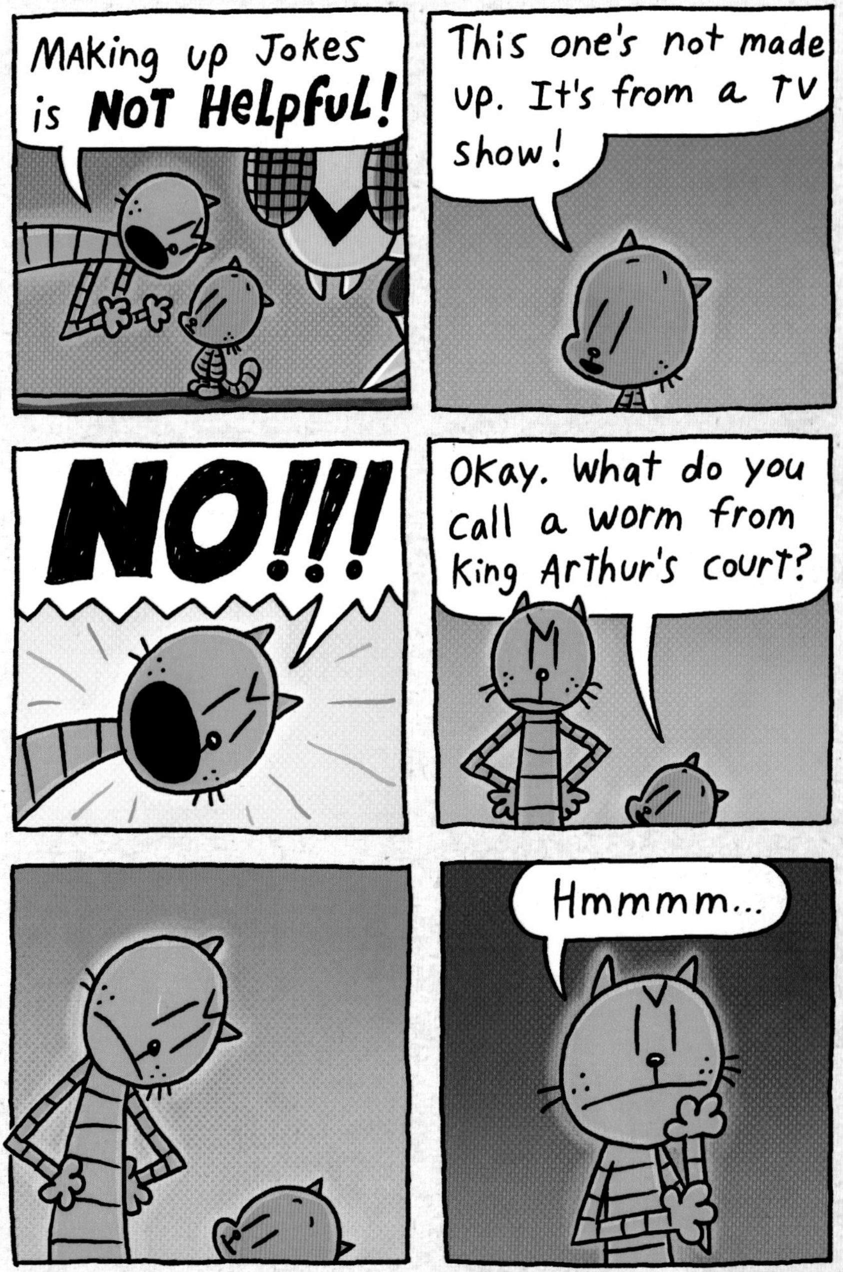
MAking up Jokes is NOT HeLpfuL!
This one's not made up. It's from a TV show!
NO!!!
OKay. What do you call a worm from King Arthur's court?
Hmmmm...

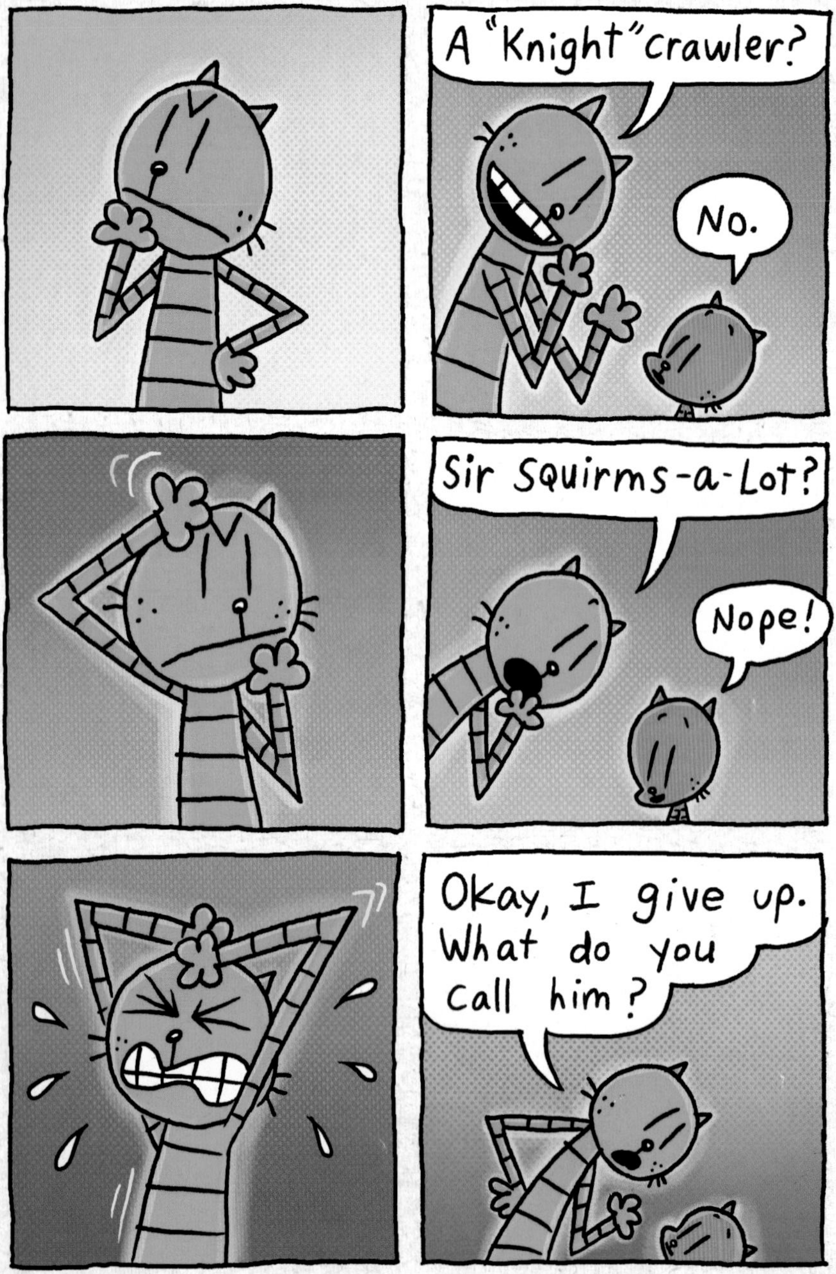
A "Knight" crawler?
No.
Sir Squirms-a-Lot?
Nope!
Okay, I give up. What do you call him?

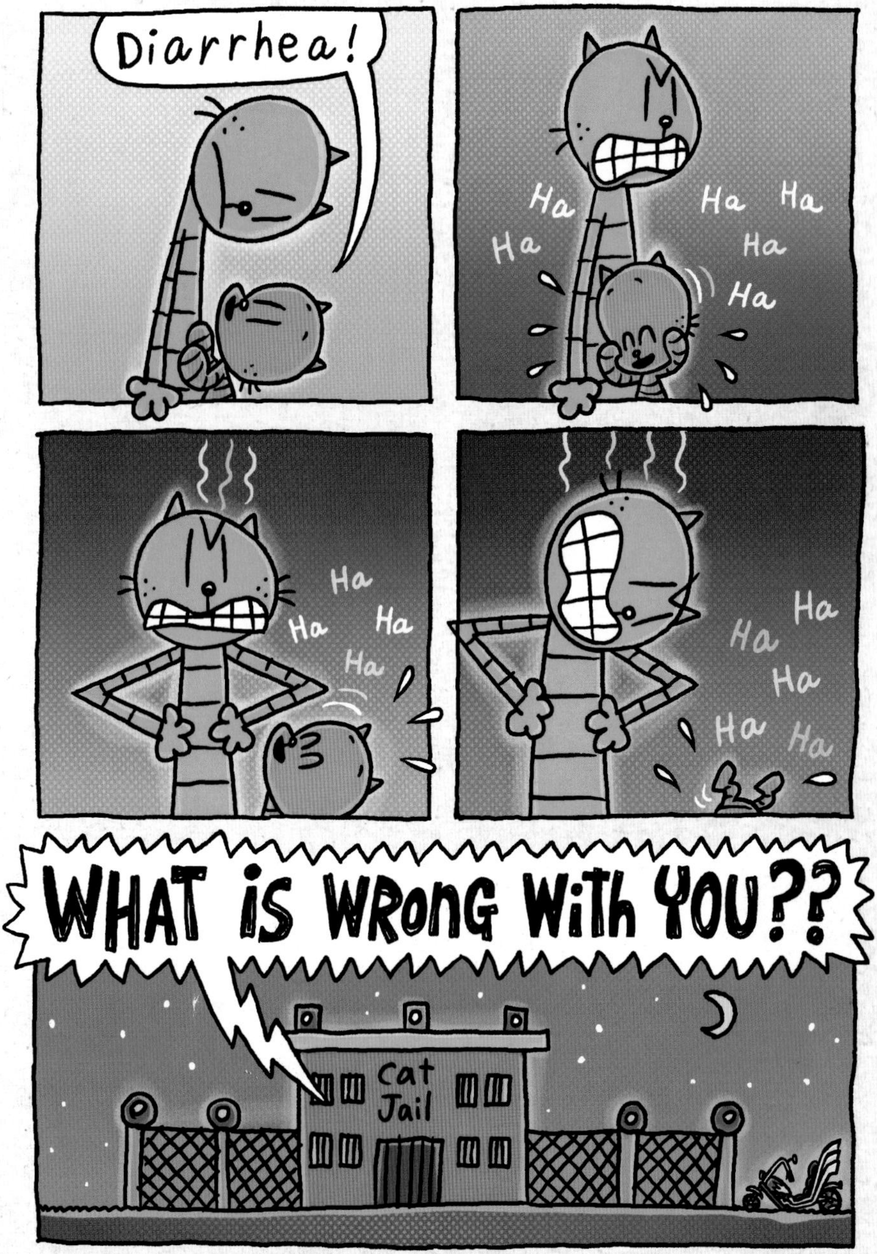
Diarrhea!
Ha Ha Ha Ha Ha Ha
Ha Ha Ha Ha
Ha Ha Ha Ha Ha Ha
WHAT is WRONG With YOU??
Cat Jail

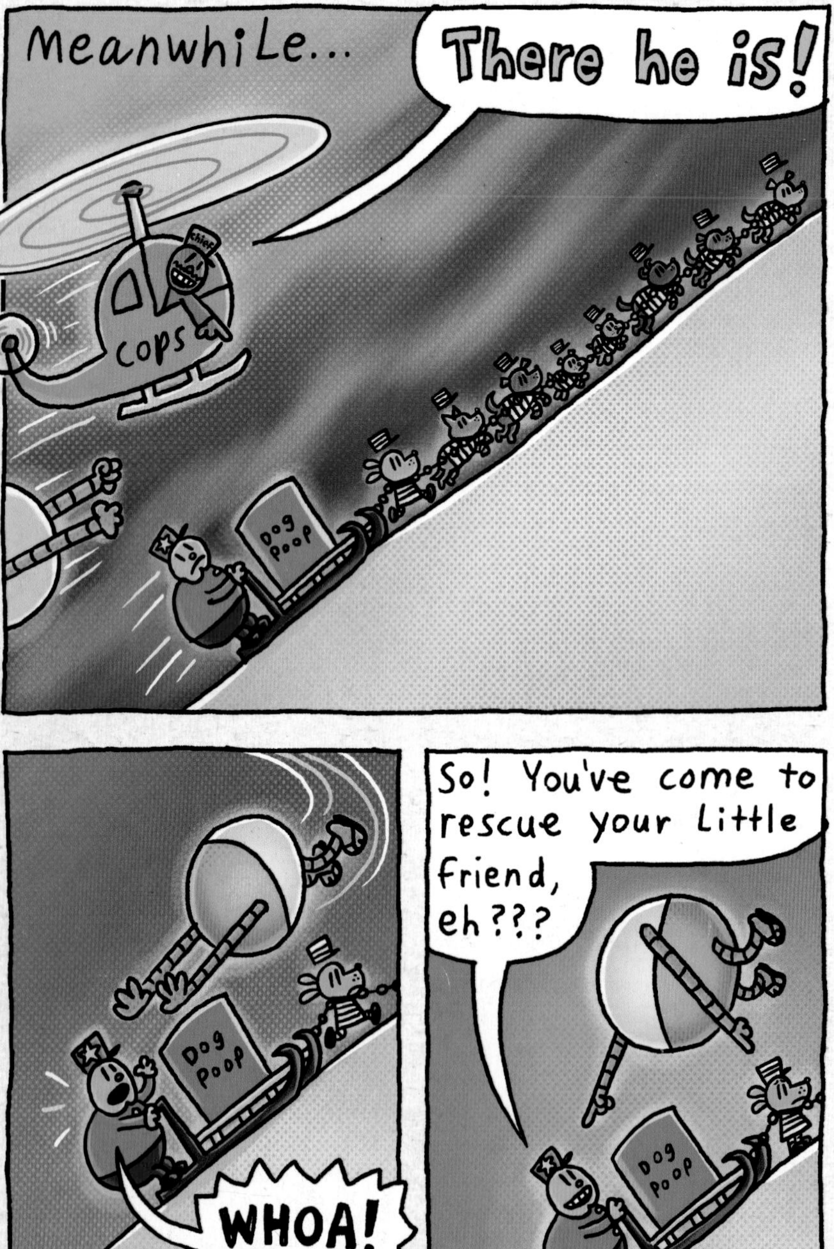
Meanwhile...
There he is!
chief
COPS
DOG POOP
DOG POOP
WHOA!
So! You've come to rescue your little friend, eh???
DOG POOP

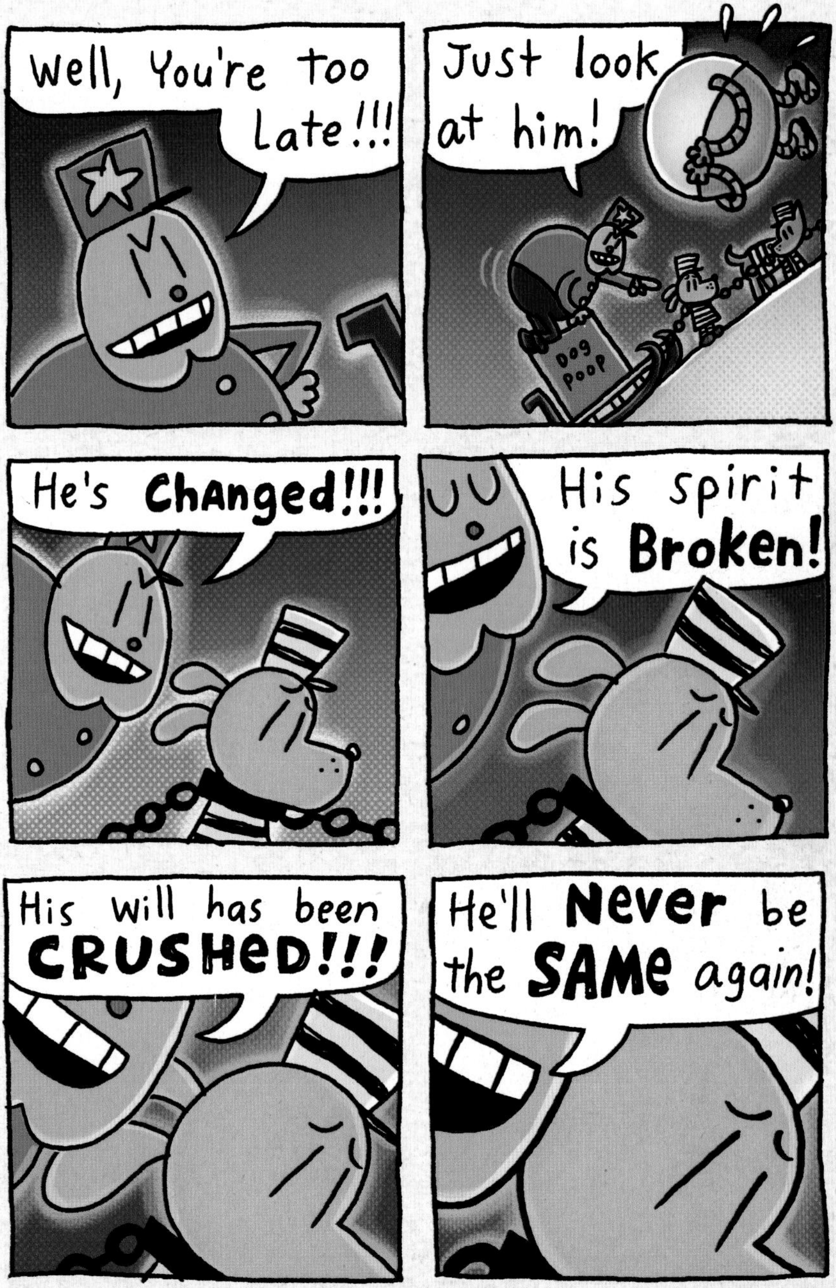
Well, You're too Late!!!
Just look at him!
DOG POOP
He's Changed!!!
His spirit is Broken!
His will has been CRUSHED!!!
He'll Never be the SAME again!

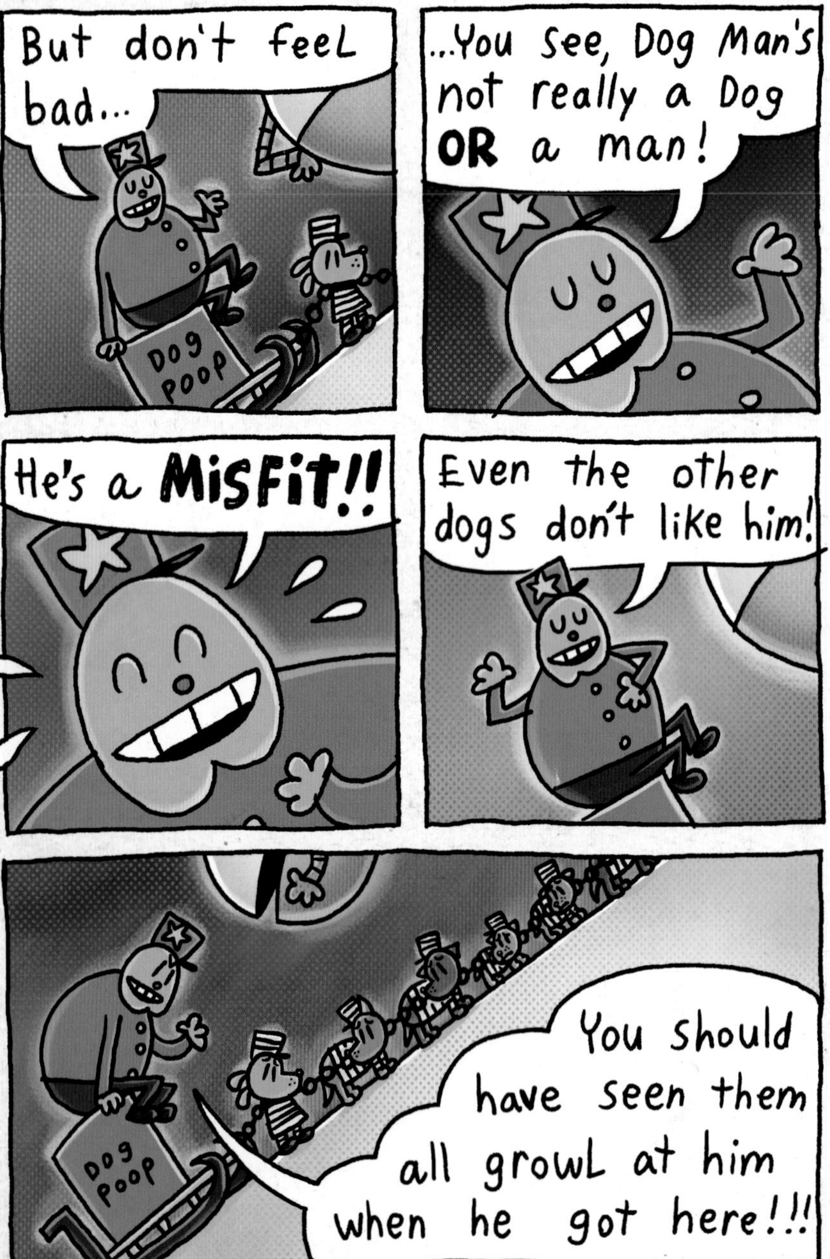
But don't feeL bad...
...You see, Dog Man's not really a Dog OR a man!
DOG POOP
He's a MISFIT!!
Even the other dogs don't like him!
DOG POOP
You should have seen them all growL at him when he got here!!!

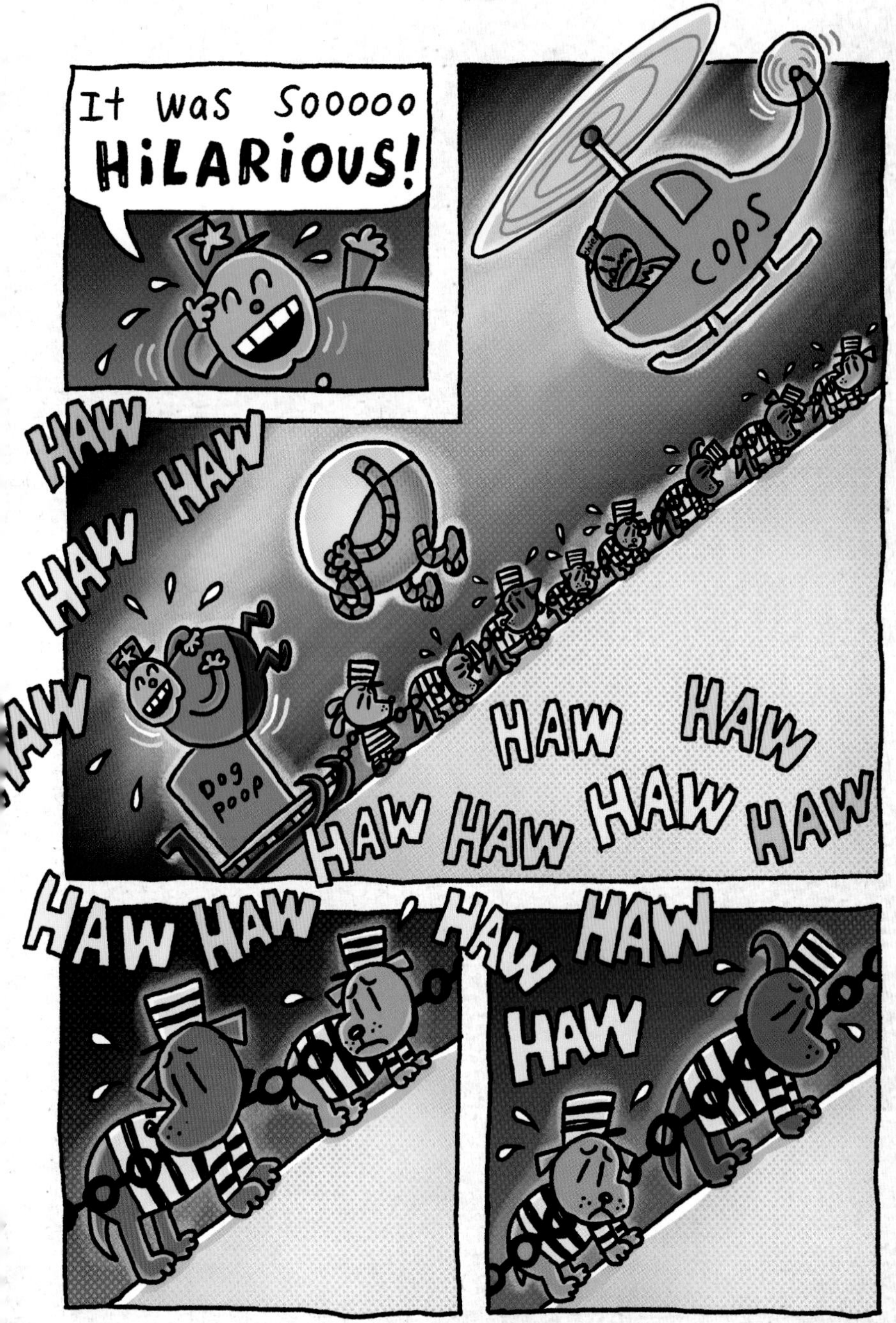

It was Sooooo HILARIOUS!
COPS
HAW
HAW HAW
HAW
Dog Poop
HAW HAW
HAW HAW HAW HAW
HAW HAW
HAW HAW
HAW

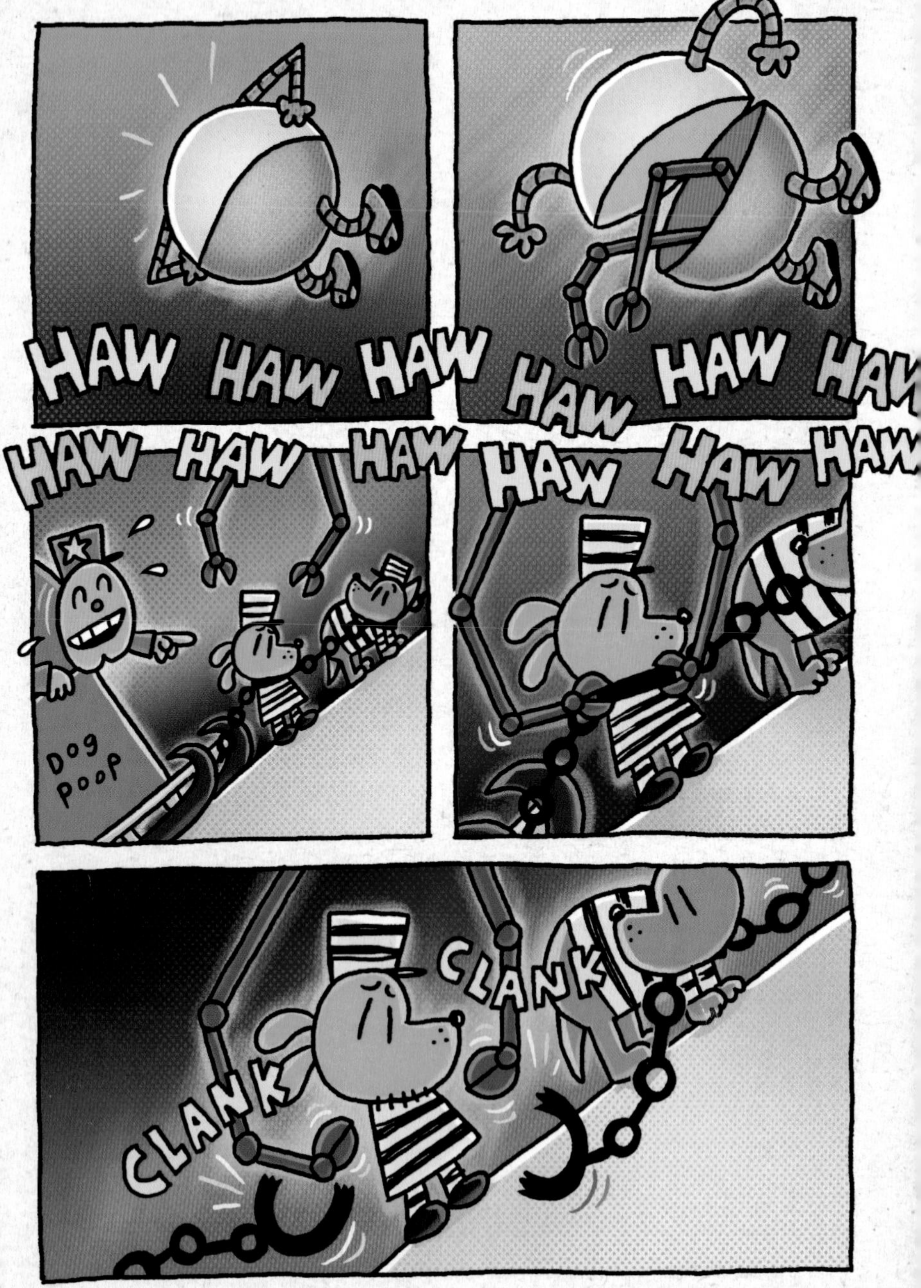
HAW HAW HAW HAW HAW HAW
HAW HAW HAW HAW HAW HAW
DOG POOP
CLANK
CLANK

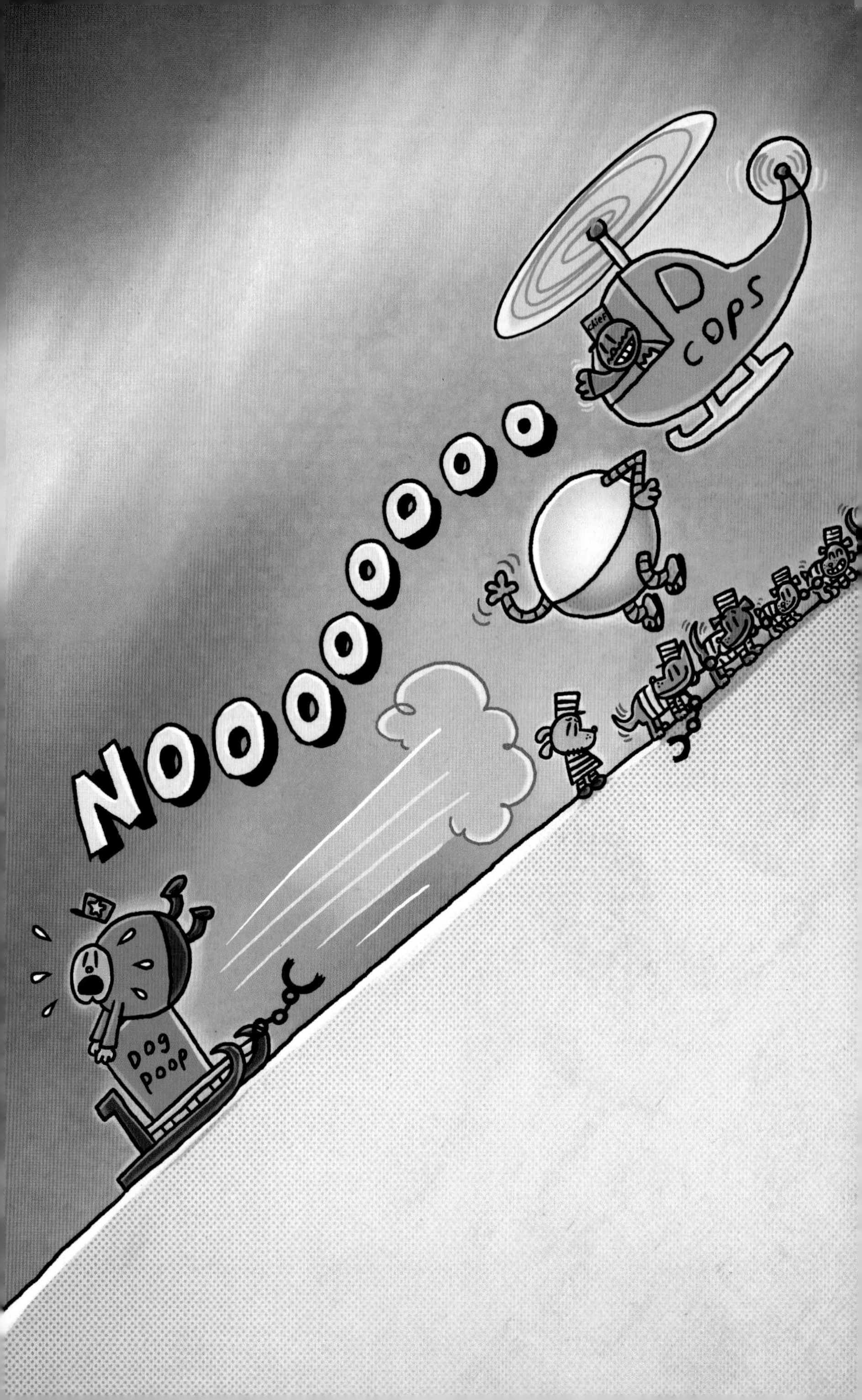

NOOOOOOOOO
CHIEF
D
COPS
DOG POOP

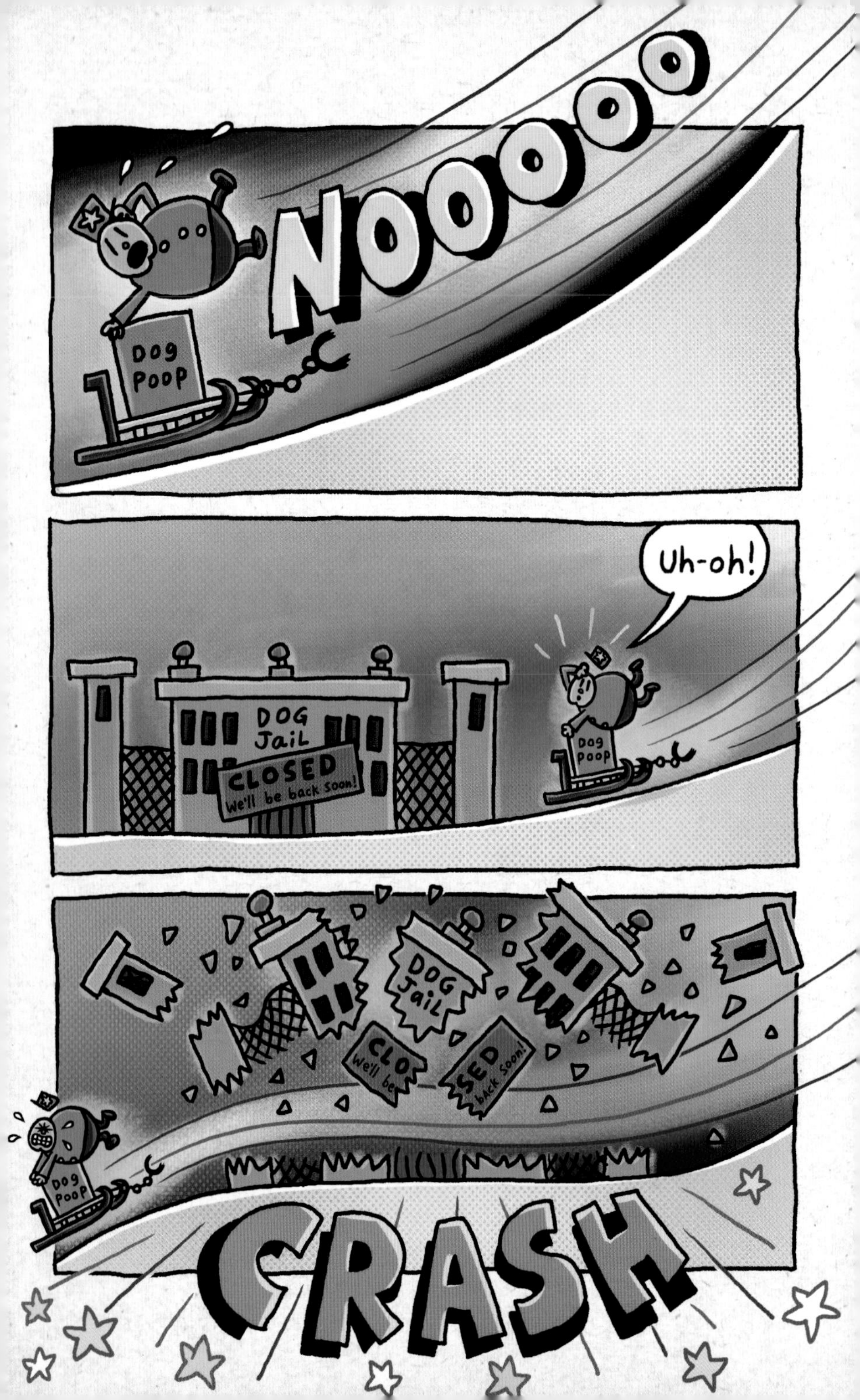
NOOOOOOO
DOG POOP
Uh-oh!
DOG JaiL
CLOSED
We'll be back soon!
Dog Poop
DOG JaiL
CLO We'll be
SED back soon!
Dog Poop
CRASH

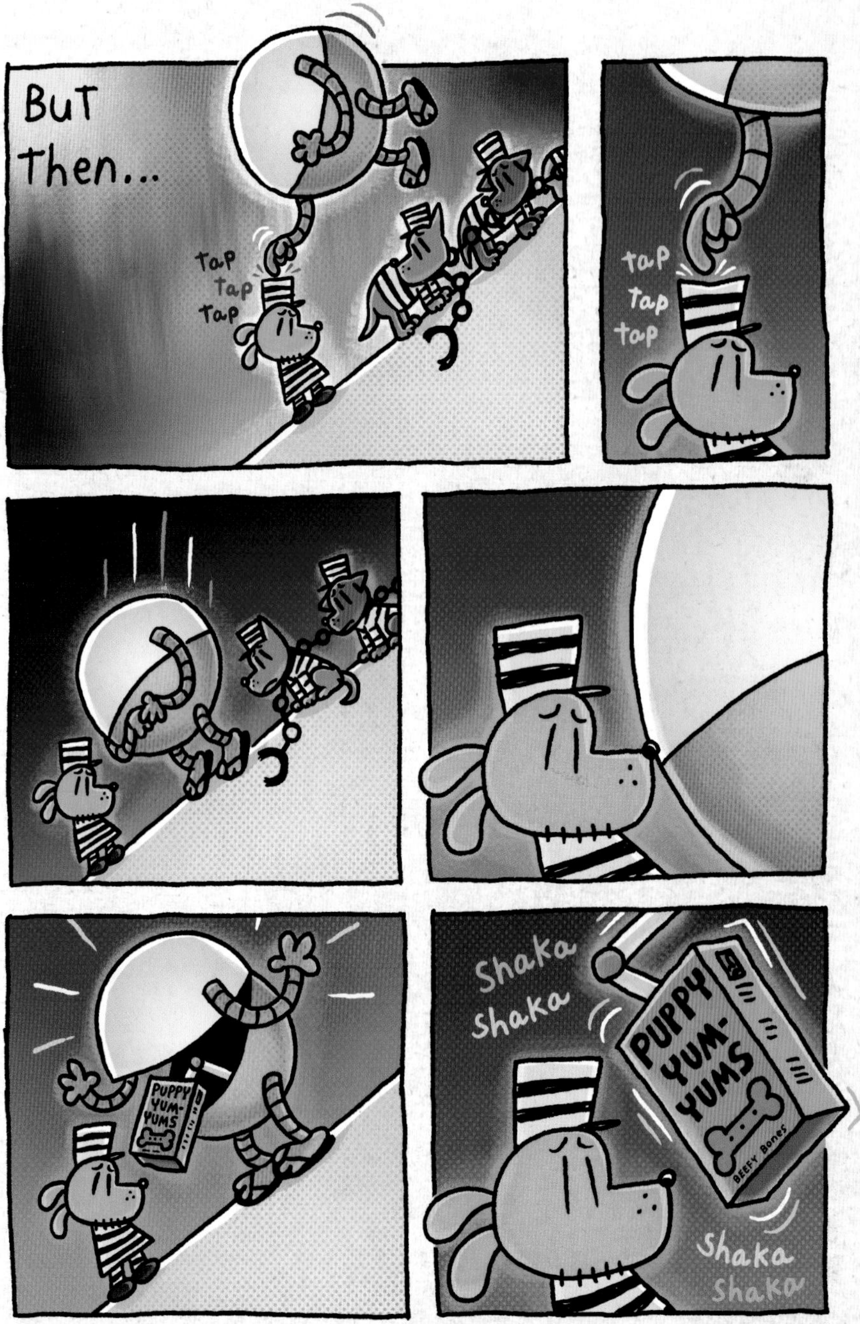
But Then...
Tap
Tap
Tap
tap
tap
tap
PUPPY YUM-YUMS
Shaka
Shaka
PUPPY YUM-YUMS
BEEFY Bones
Shaka
Shaka

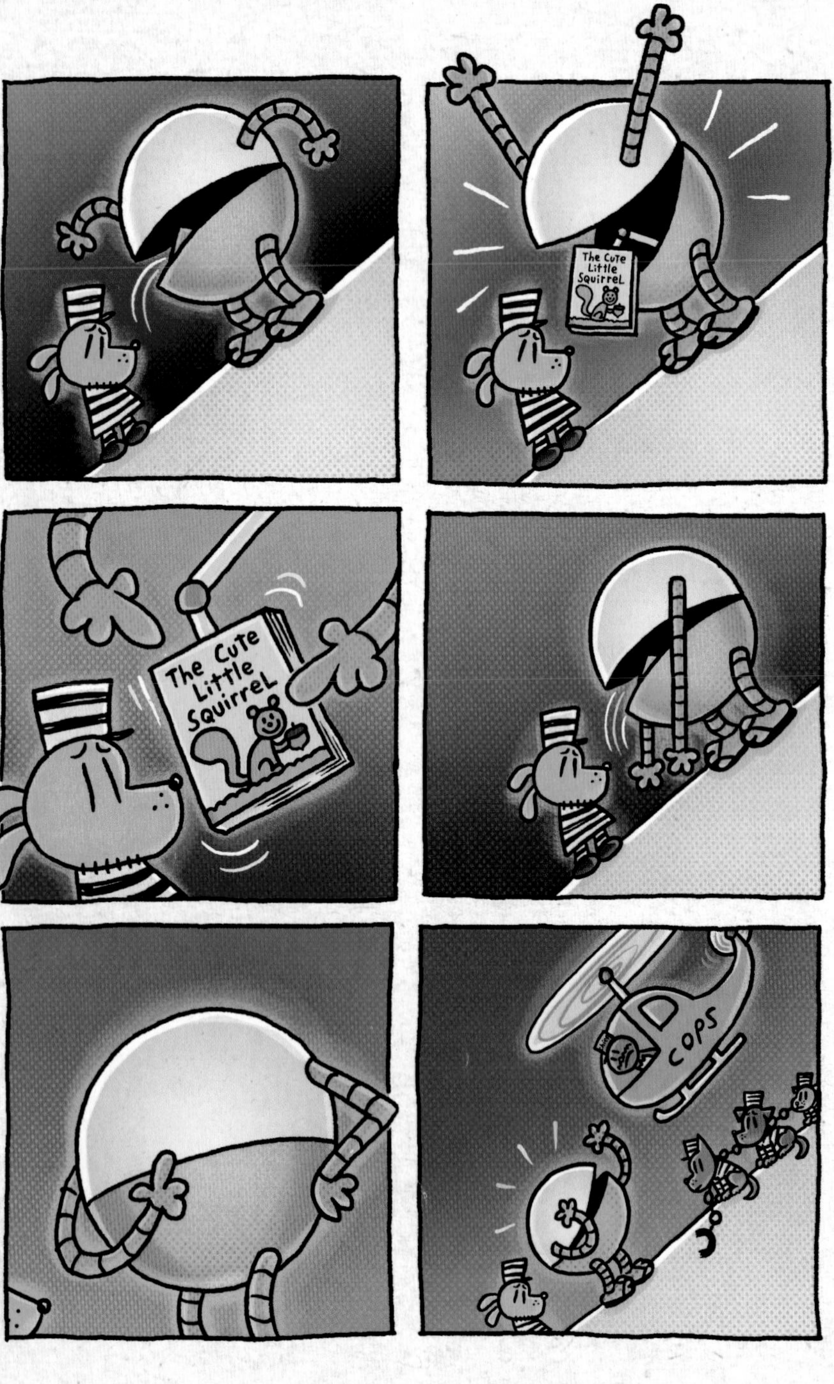
The Cute Little Squirrel
The Cute Little Squirrel
COPS

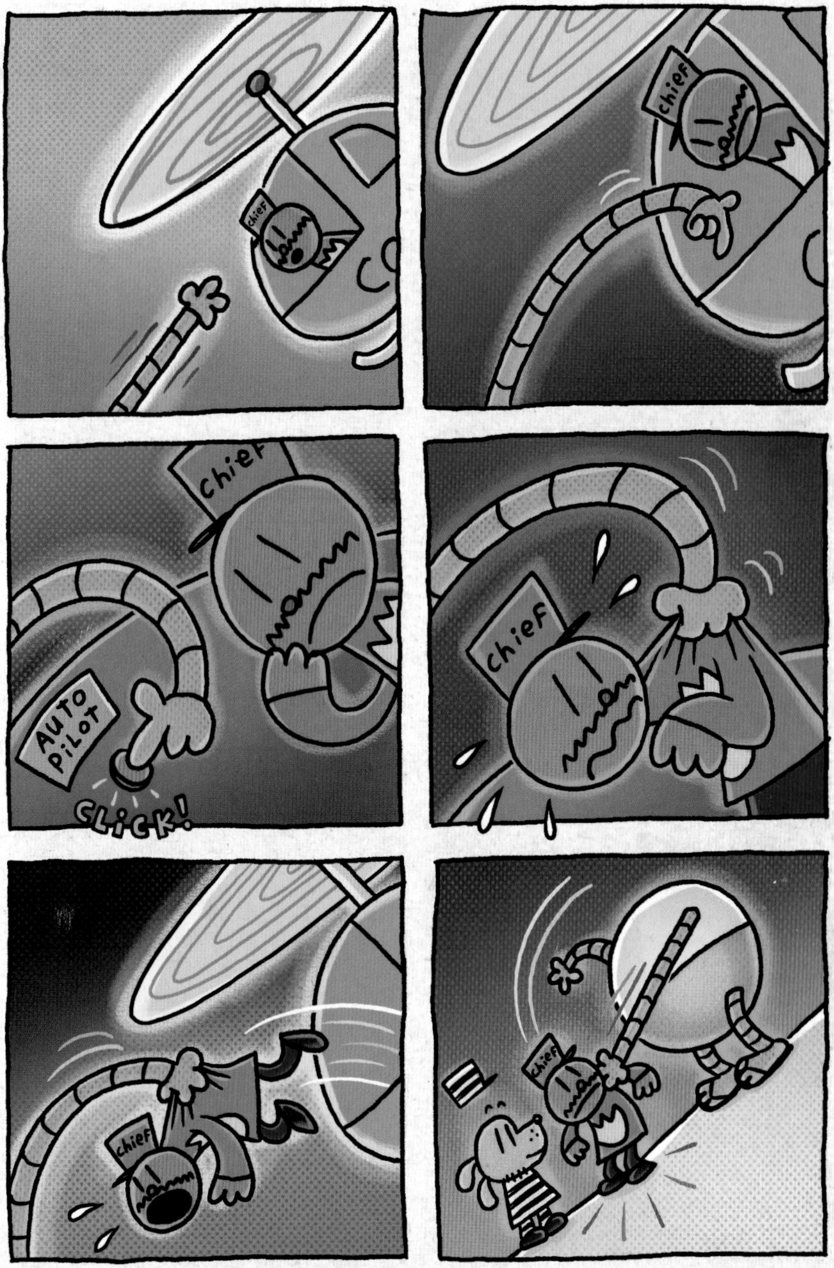
chief
chief
chief
AUTO PILOT
CLICK!
chief
chief
chief

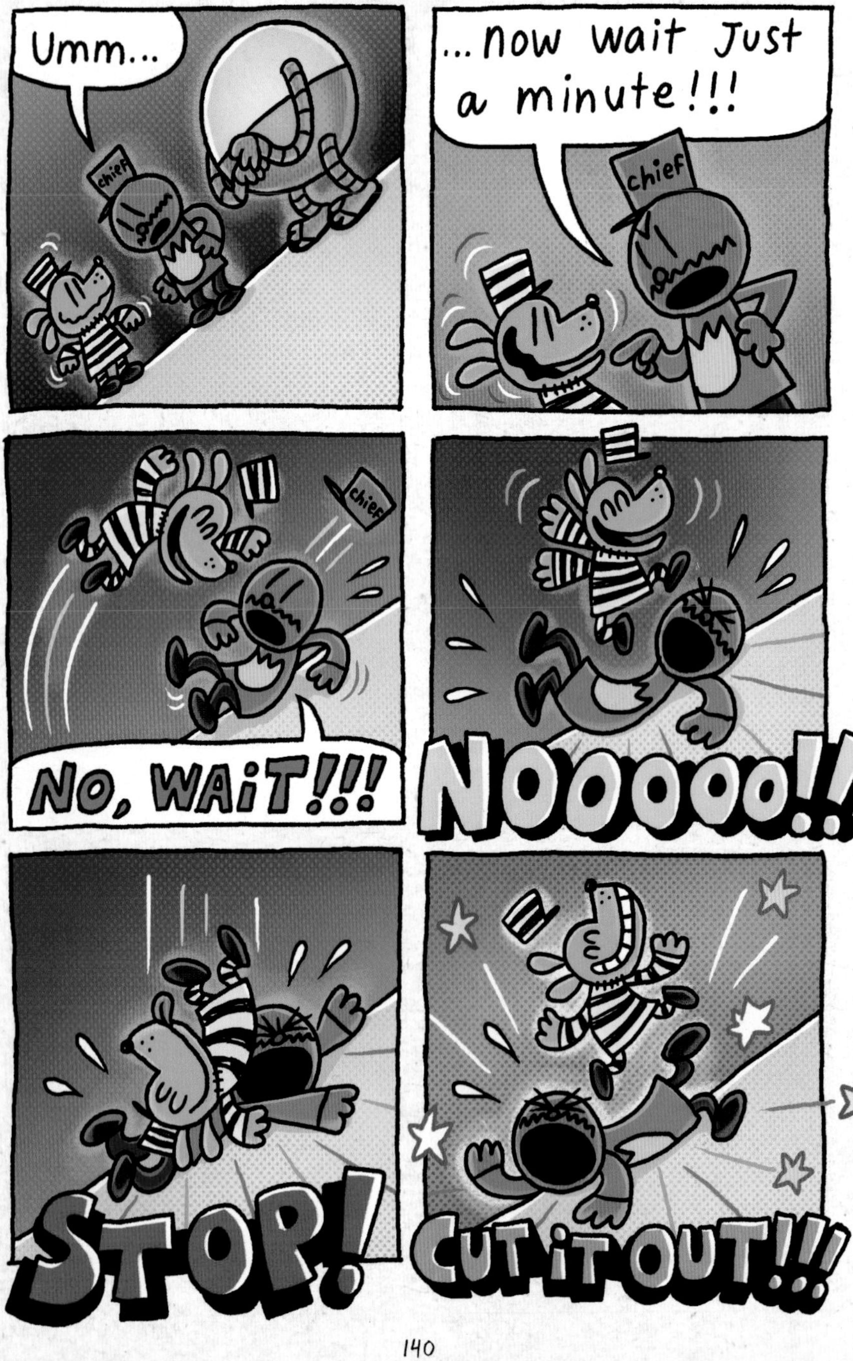
Umm...
chief
...now wait Just a minute!!!
chief
chief
NO, WAiT!!!
NOOOOO!!
STOP!
CUT iT OUT!!!

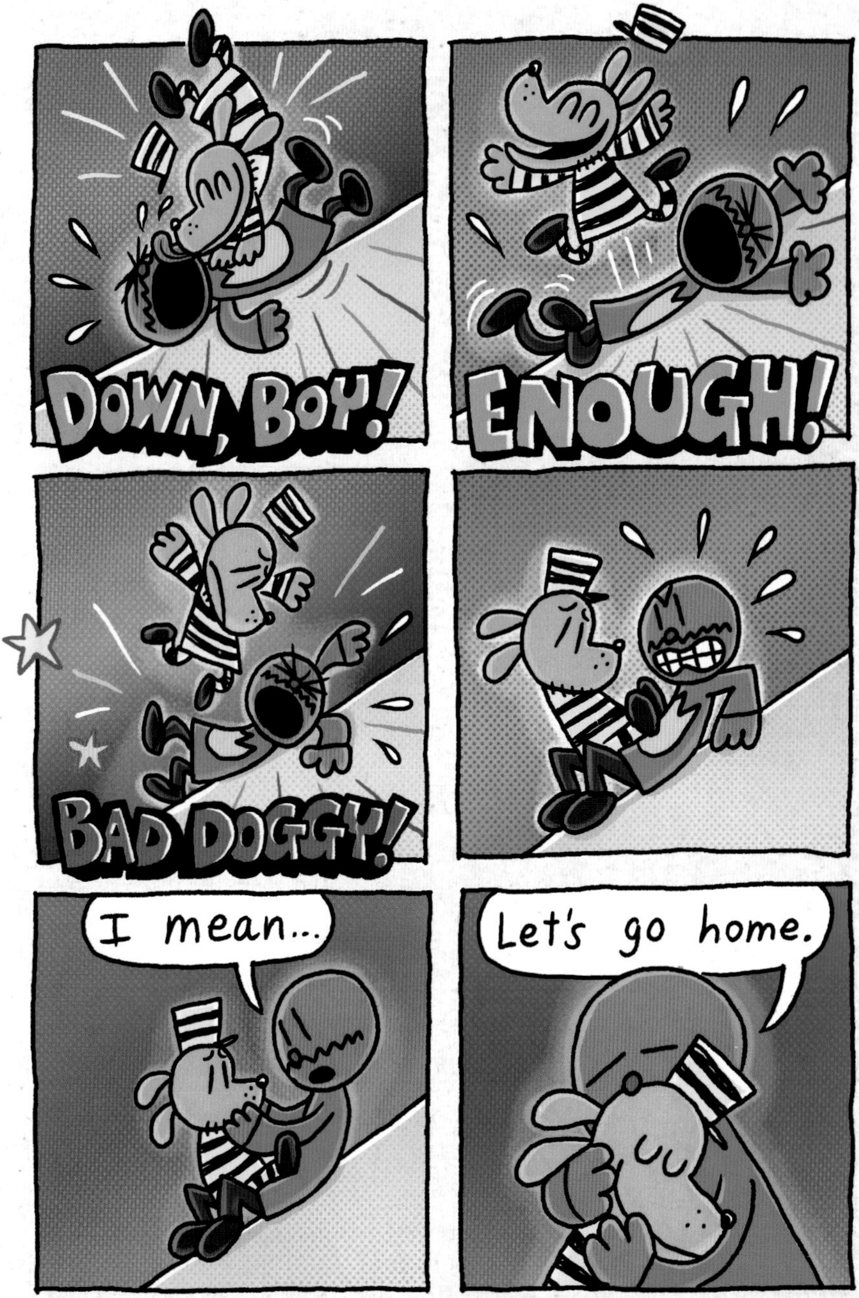
DOWN, BOY!
ENOUGH!
BAD DOGGY!
I mean...
Let's go home.

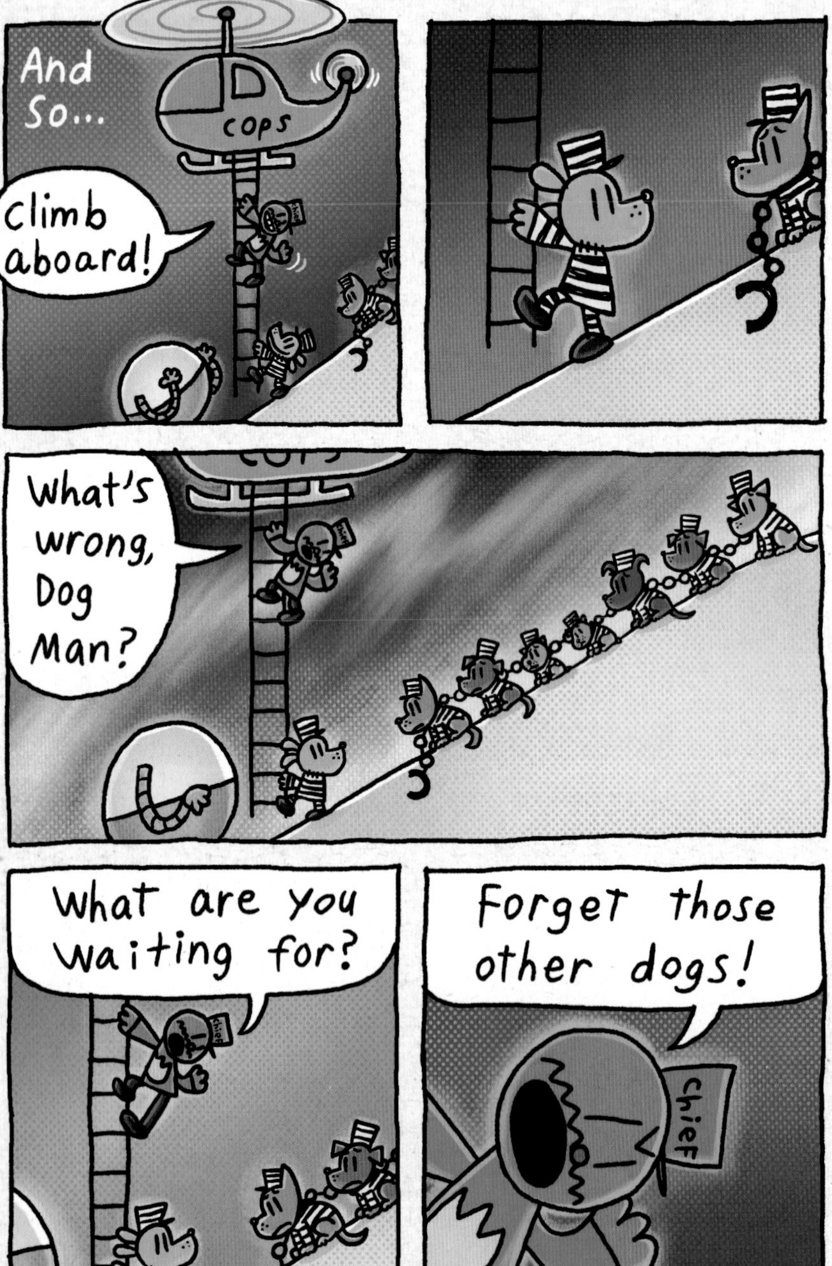
And So...
COPS
Climb aboard!
What's wrong, Dog Man?
What are you waiting for?
Chief
Forget those other dogs!
Chief

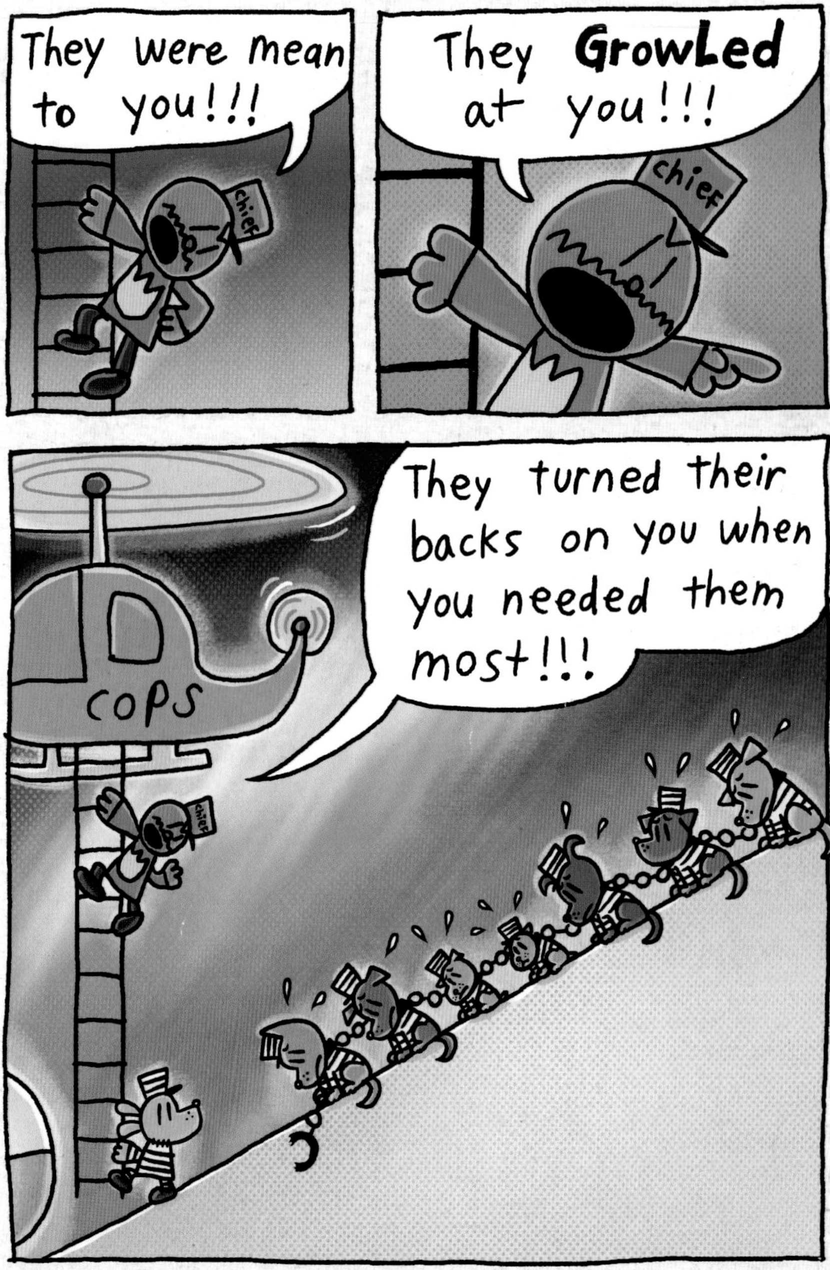
They were mean to you!!!
They GrowLed at you!!!
chief
chief
They turned their backs on you when you needed them most!!!
COPS
chief

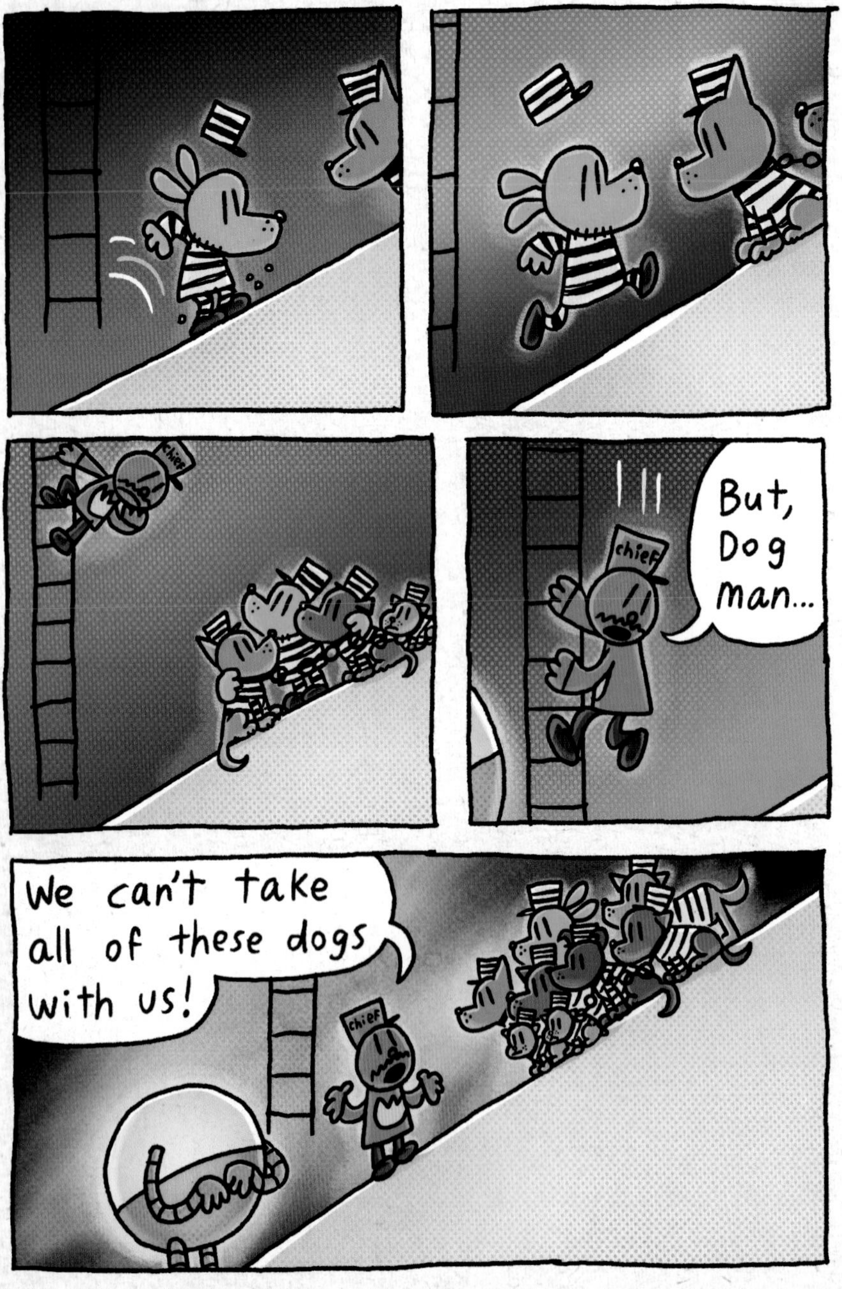
chief
chief
But, Dog man...
chief
We can't take all of these dogs with us!

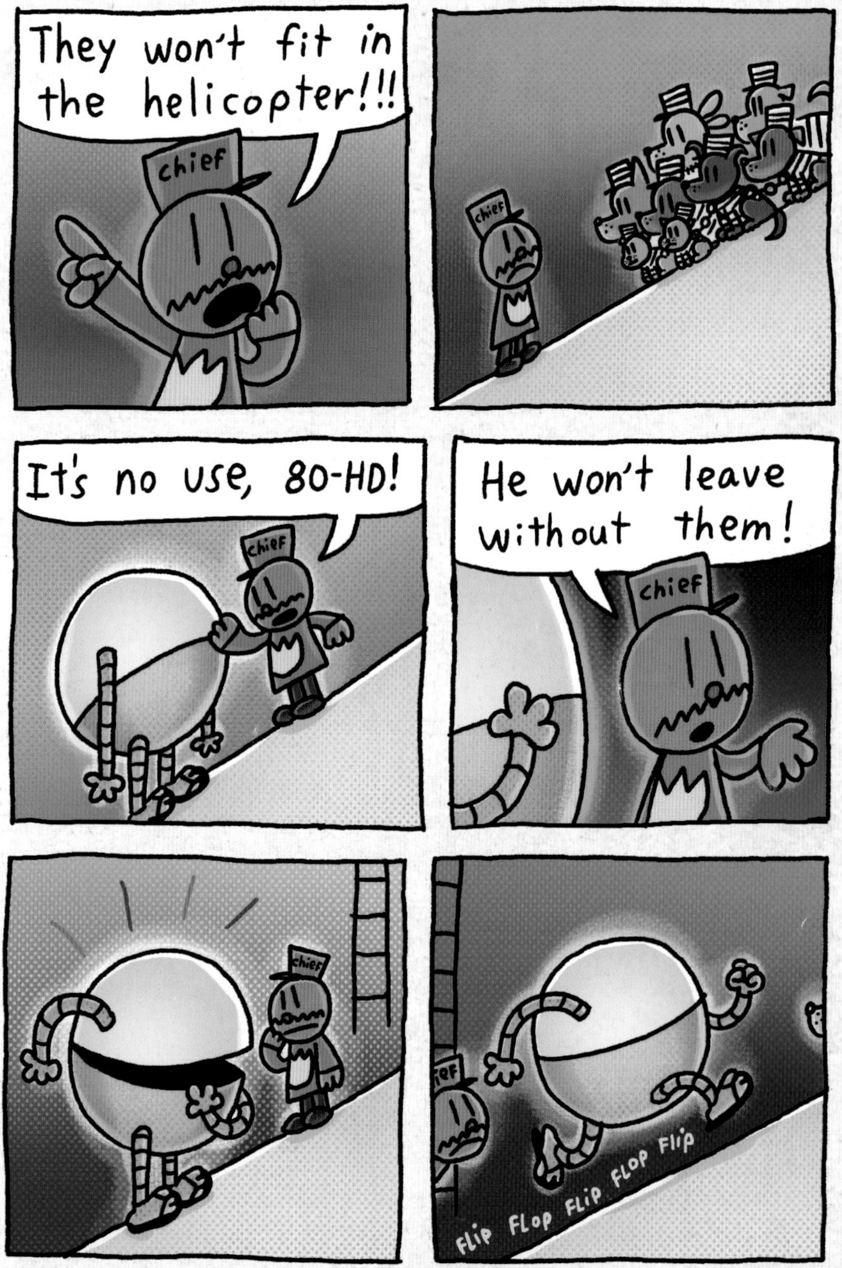
They won't fit in the helicopter!!!
chief
chief
It's no use, 80-HD!
chief
He won't leave without them!
chief
chief
FLIP FLOP FLIP FLOP FLIP

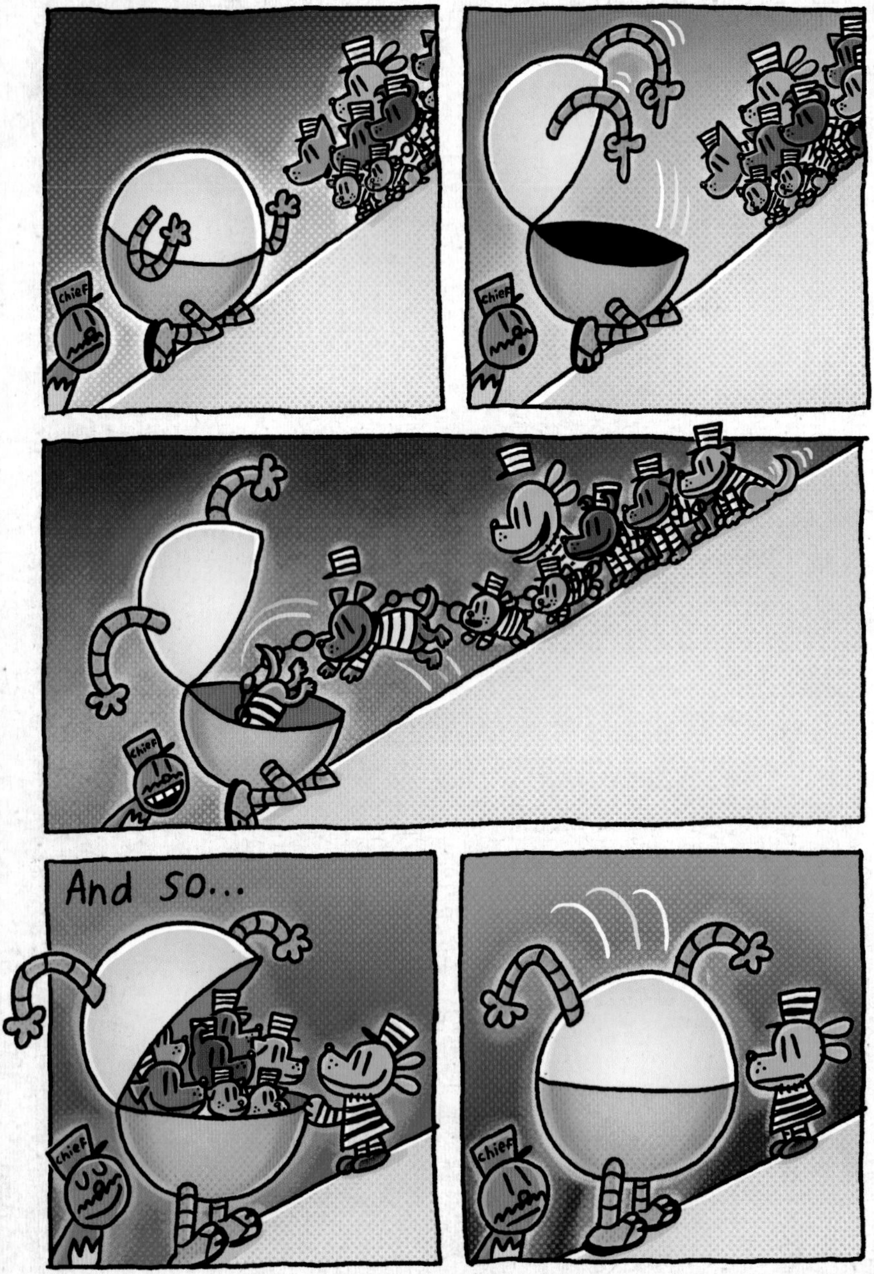
And so...

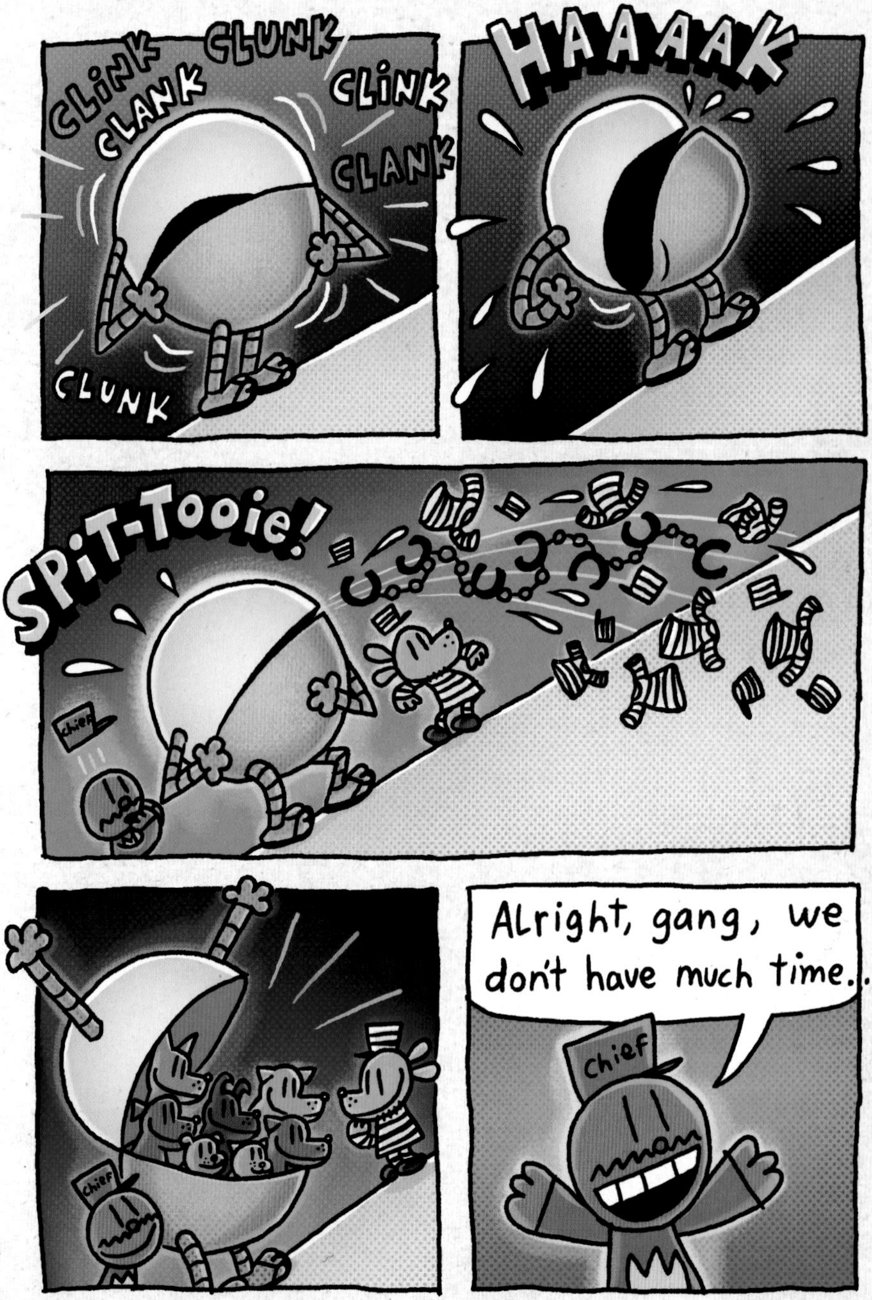
CLINK
CLANK
CLUNK
CLINK
CLANK
CLUNK
HAAAAK
SPIT-TOOIE!
CHIEF
CHIEF
Alright, gang, we don't have much time....
CHIEF

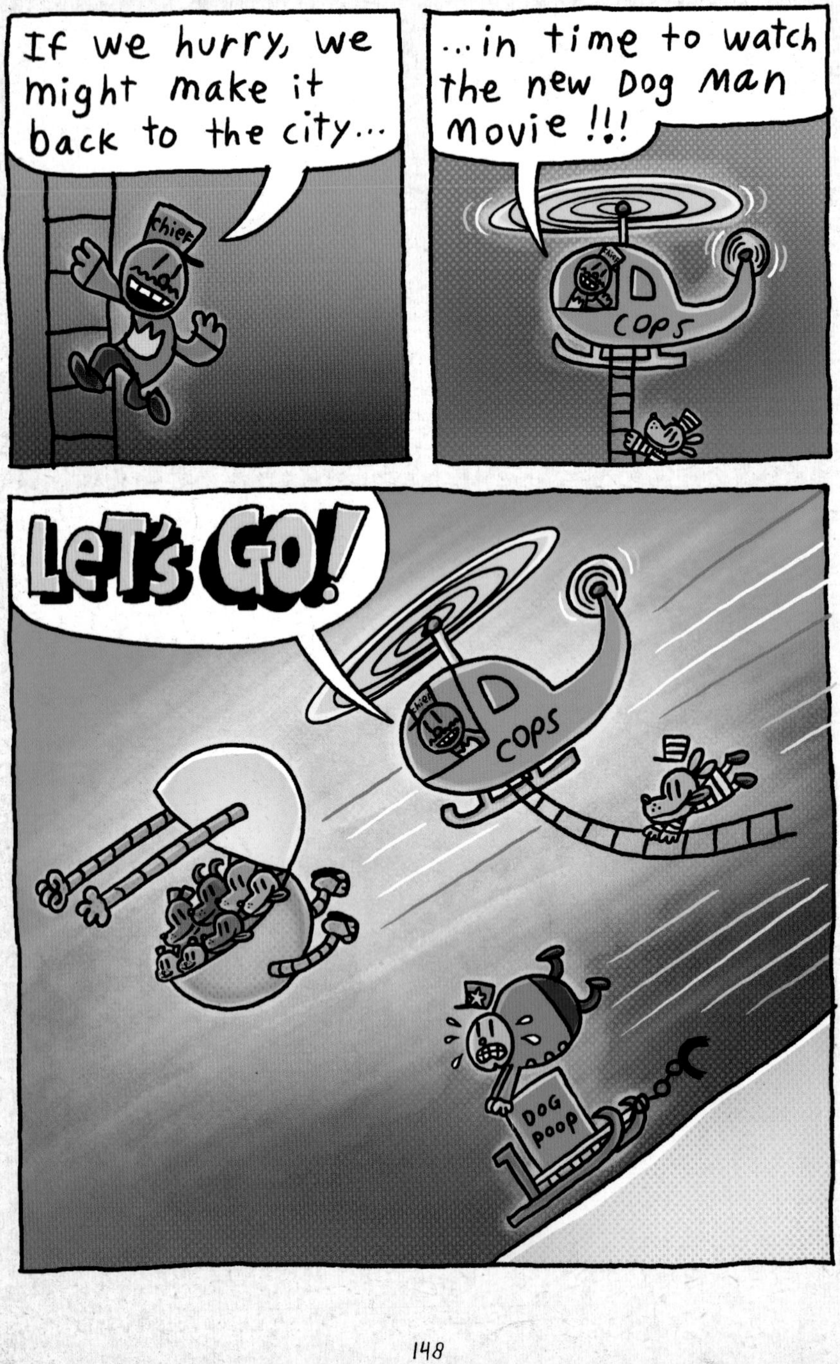
If we hurry, we might make it back to the city...
CHIEF
...in time to watch the new Dog Man movie!!!
COPS
LET'S GO!
COPS
DOG POOP

CHAPTER 9

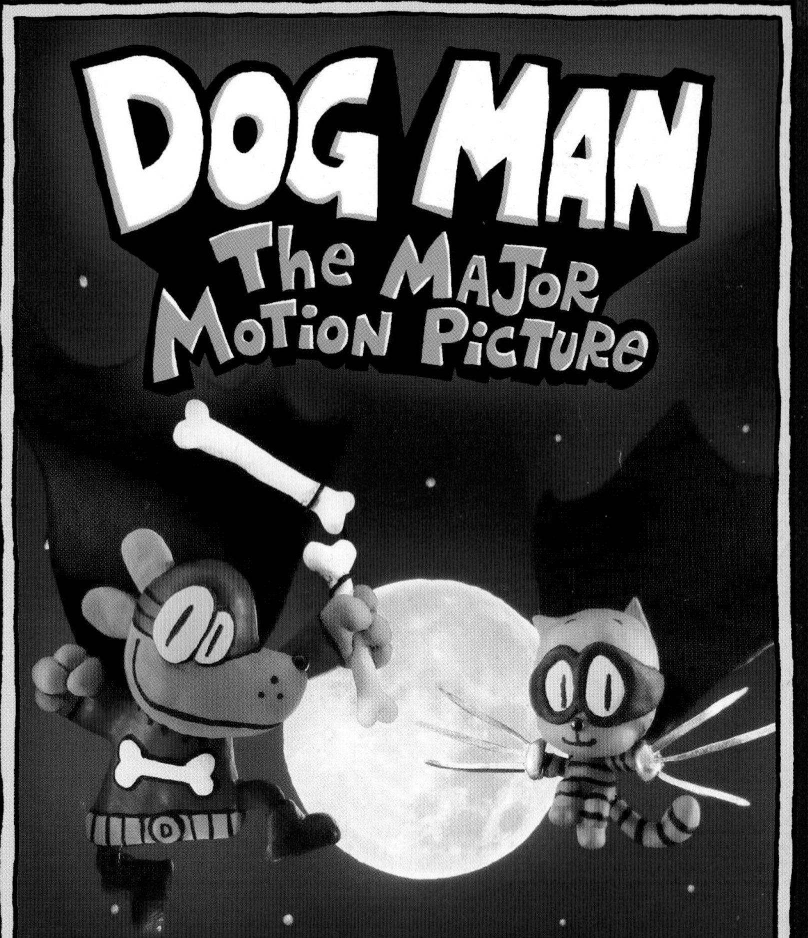
DOG MAN
The MAJOR Motion Picture
Sam E. Hamilton Presents
A GASSY Behemoth Animation Production
DOG Man: The MAJOR Motion Picture
Featuring the vocal talents of: YoLay Caprese • Scooter McRibs
Ding-Dong Magoo • And Samson J. Johnson as "Chief"
Soundtrack available on Gassy Behemoth 8-Tracks
DOGGY Surround Sound
K-9 Suitable for canines
Some material may be too intense for humans

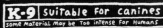

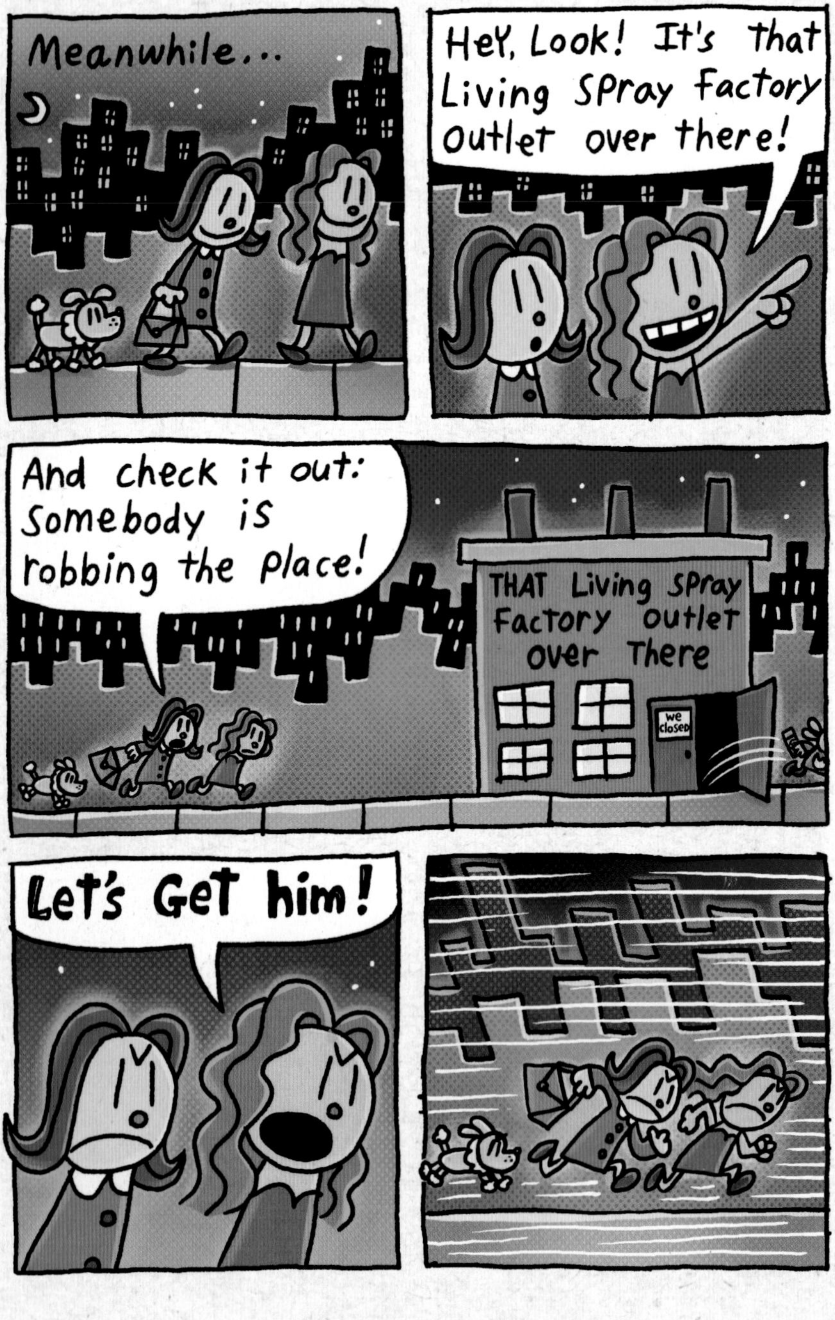
Meanwhile...
HeY, Look! It's that Living SPray Factory Outlet over there!
And check it out: Somebody is robbing the Place!
THAT Living SPray Factory outlet over There
we closed
Let's Get him!

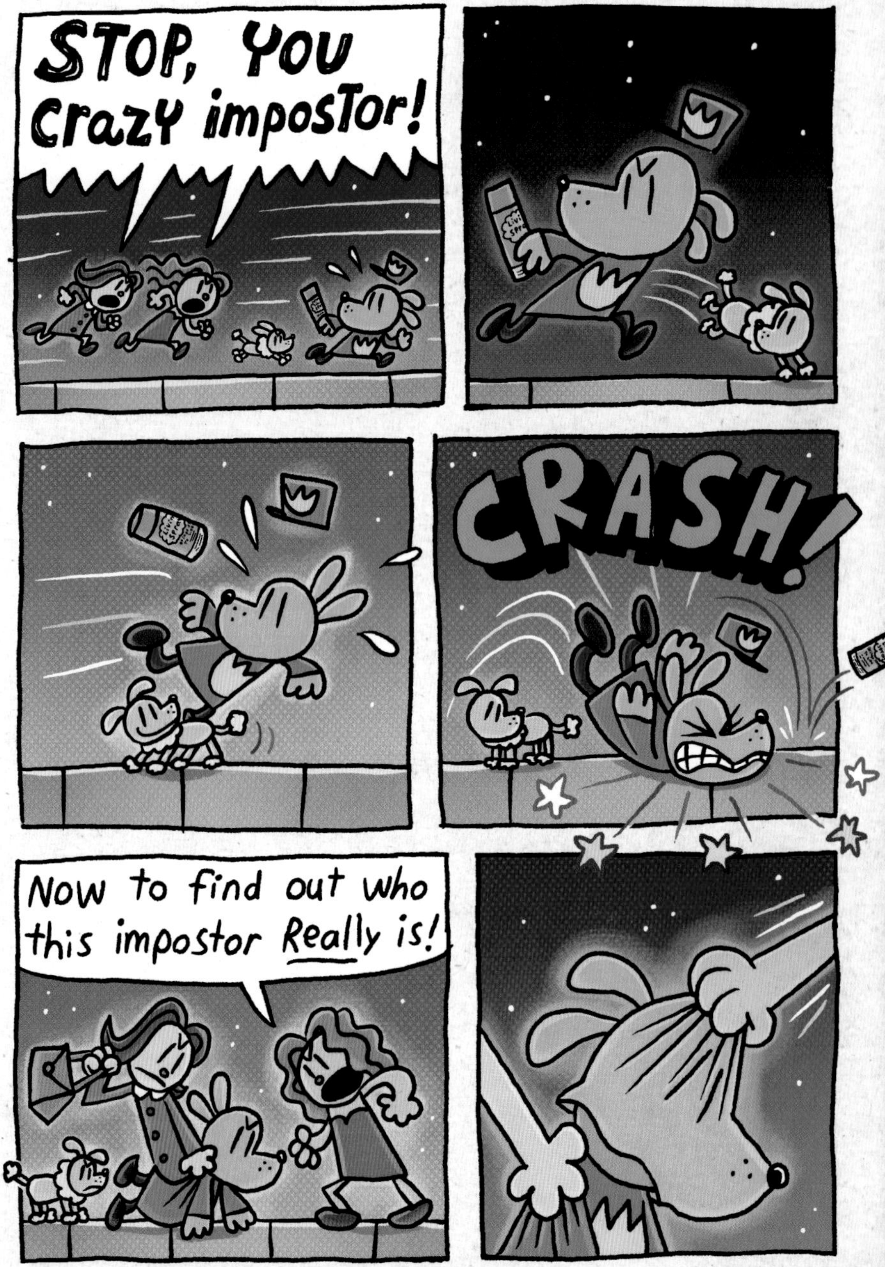
STOP, YOU Crazy impostor!
CRASH!
Now to find out who this impostor Really is!

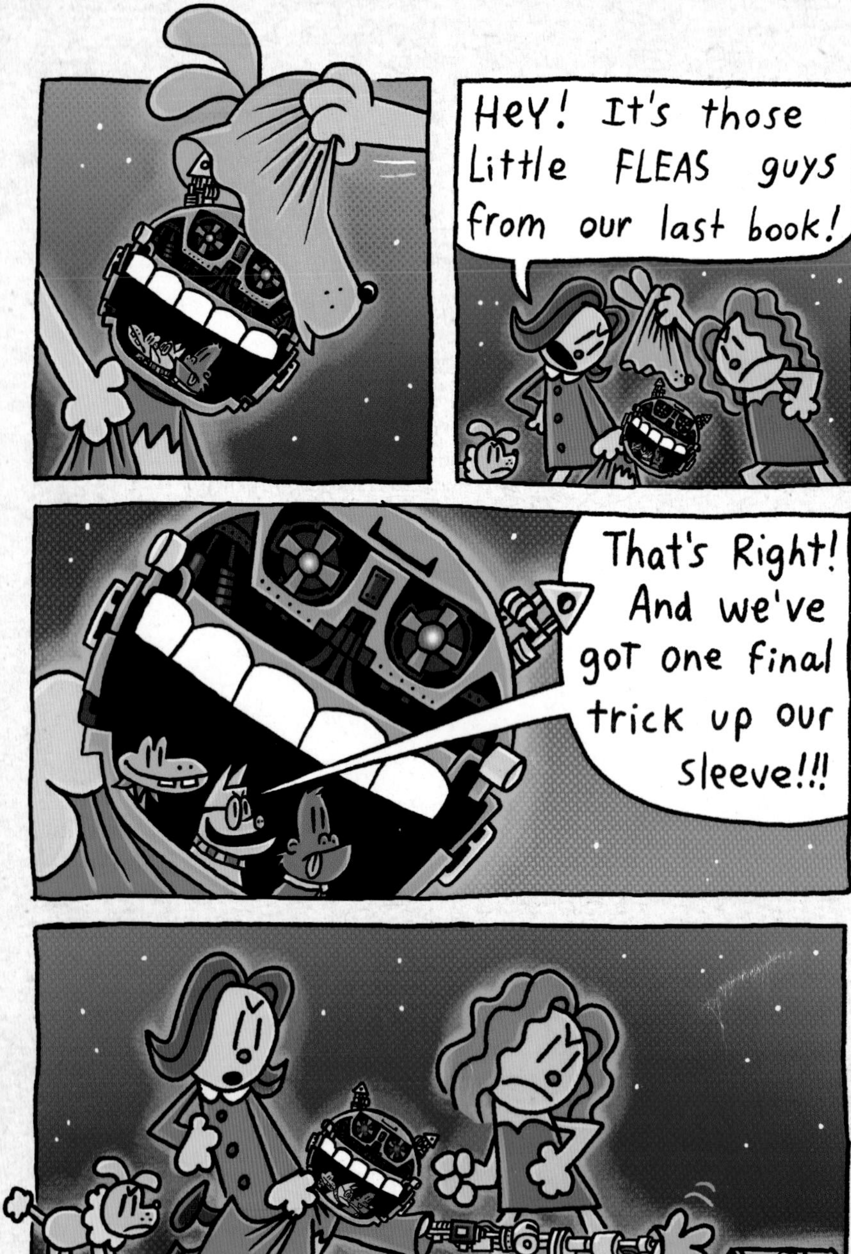
HEY! It's those Little FLEAS guys from our last book!
That's Right! And we've got one final trick up our sleeve!!!
Living Spray

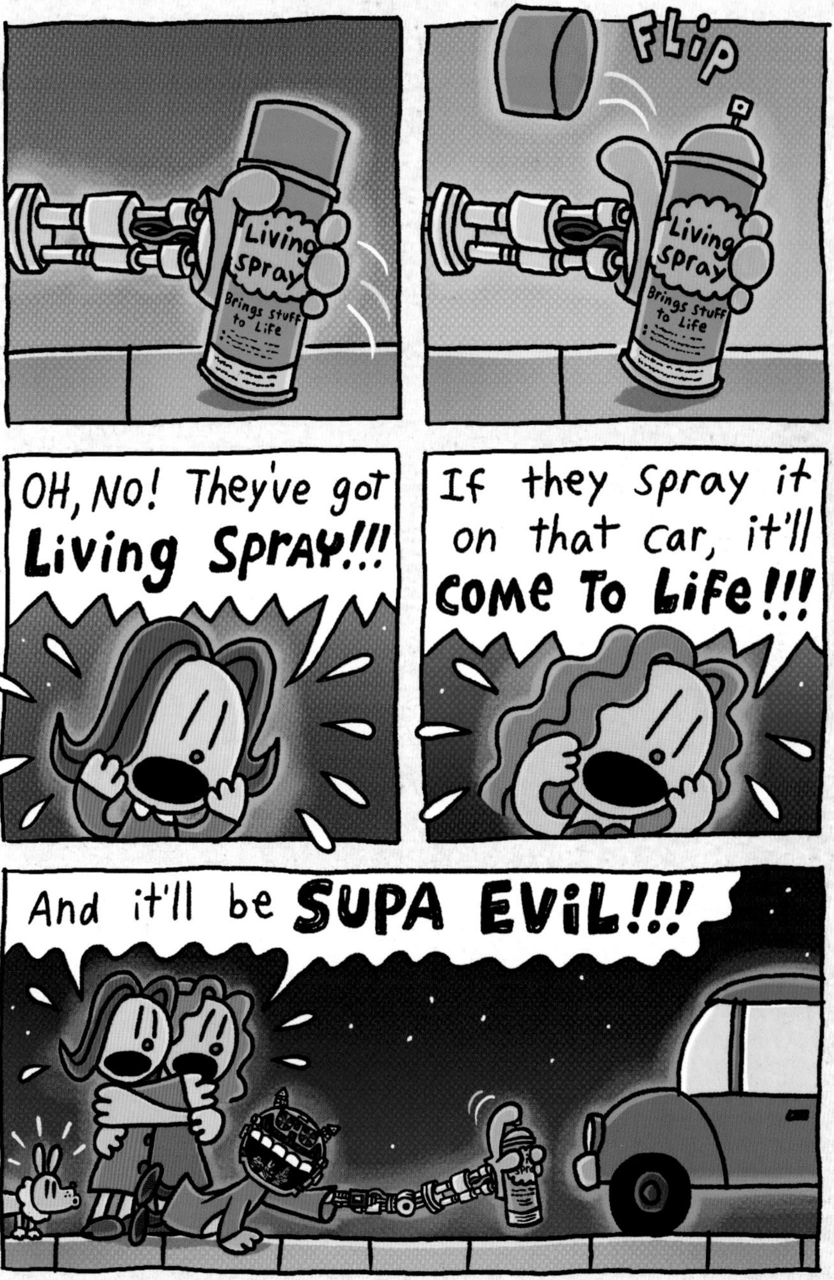

Living spray
Brings stuff to Life
FLIP
Living spray
Brings stuff to Life
OH, NO! They've got Living SPRAY!!!
If they spray it on that car, it'll COME TO LIFE!!!
And it'll be SUPA EVIL!!!

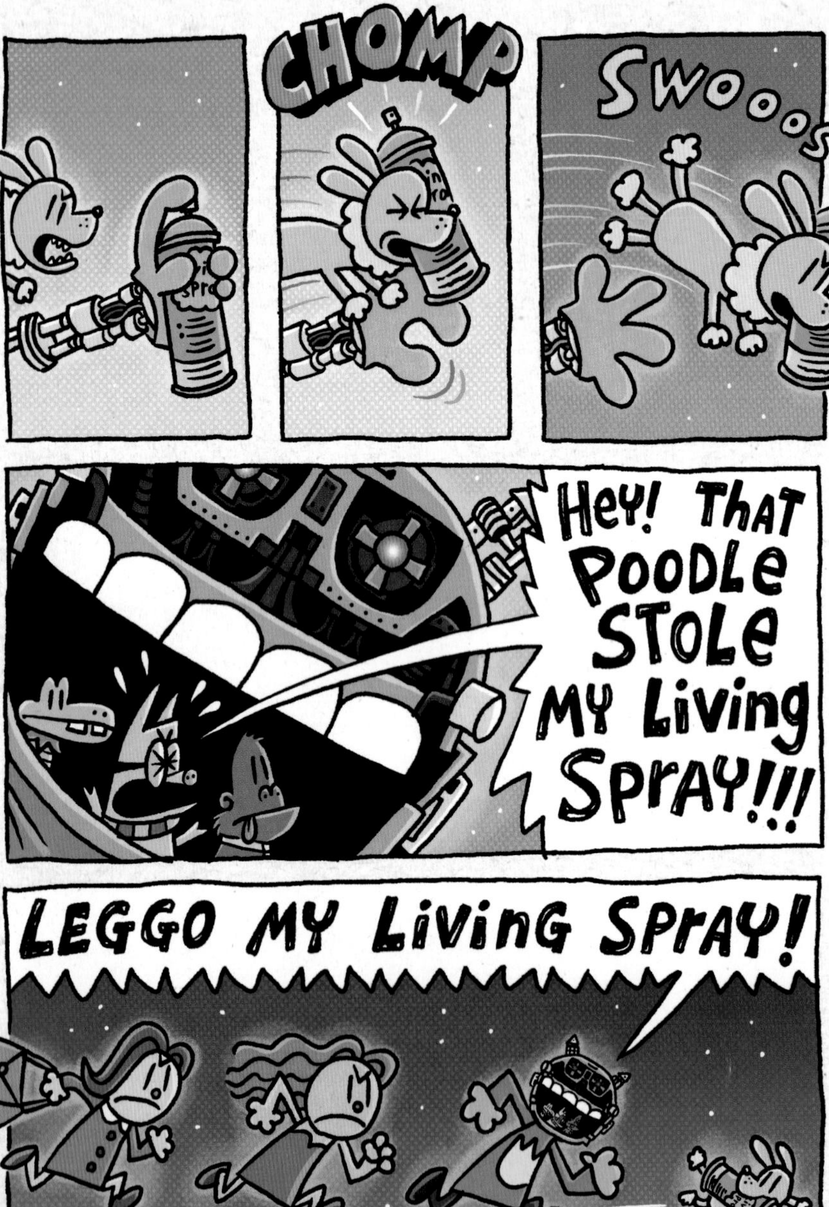
CHOMP
SWOOOOSH
Hey! That Poodle Stole My Living Spray!!!
LEGGO MY LIVING SPRAY!

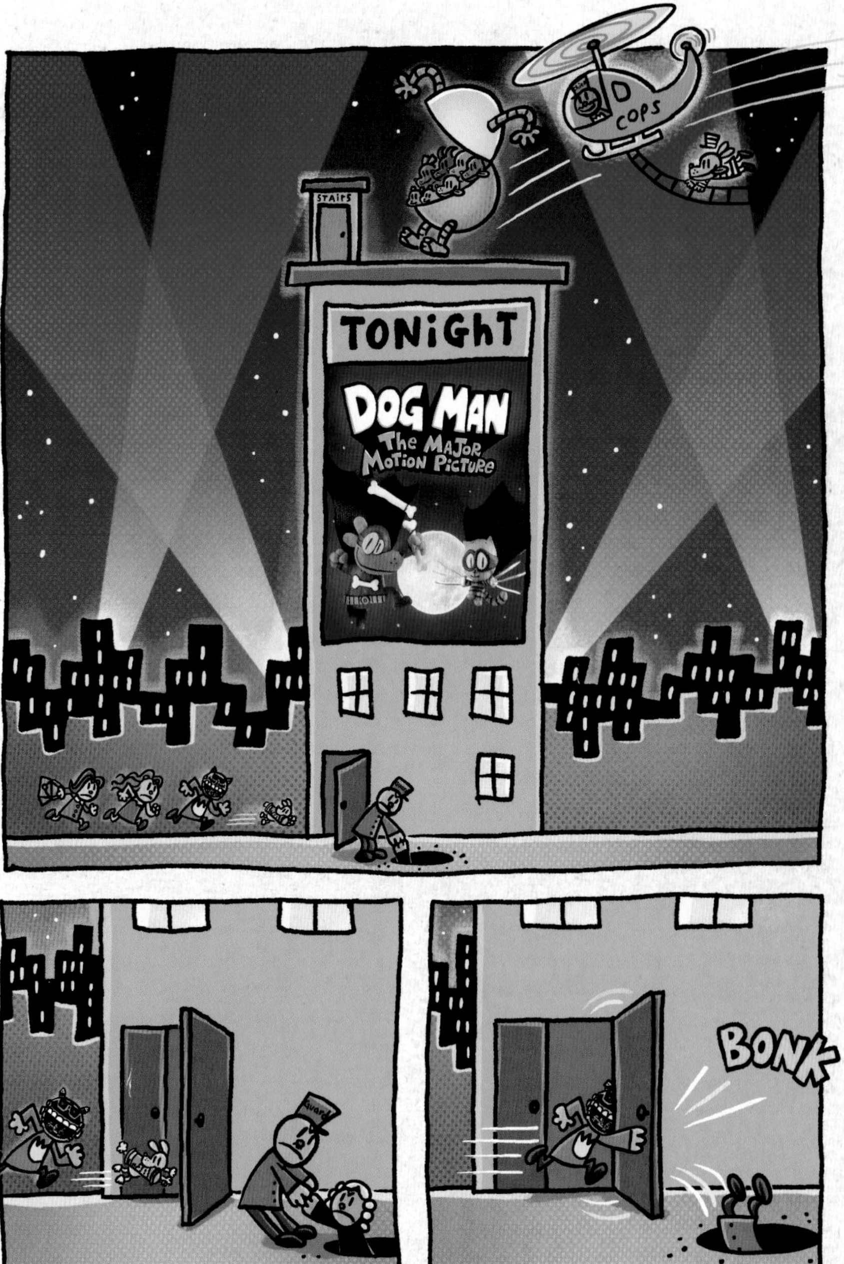
STAIRS
COPS
TONIGHT
DOG MAN
The MAJOR Motion Picture
Guard
BONK

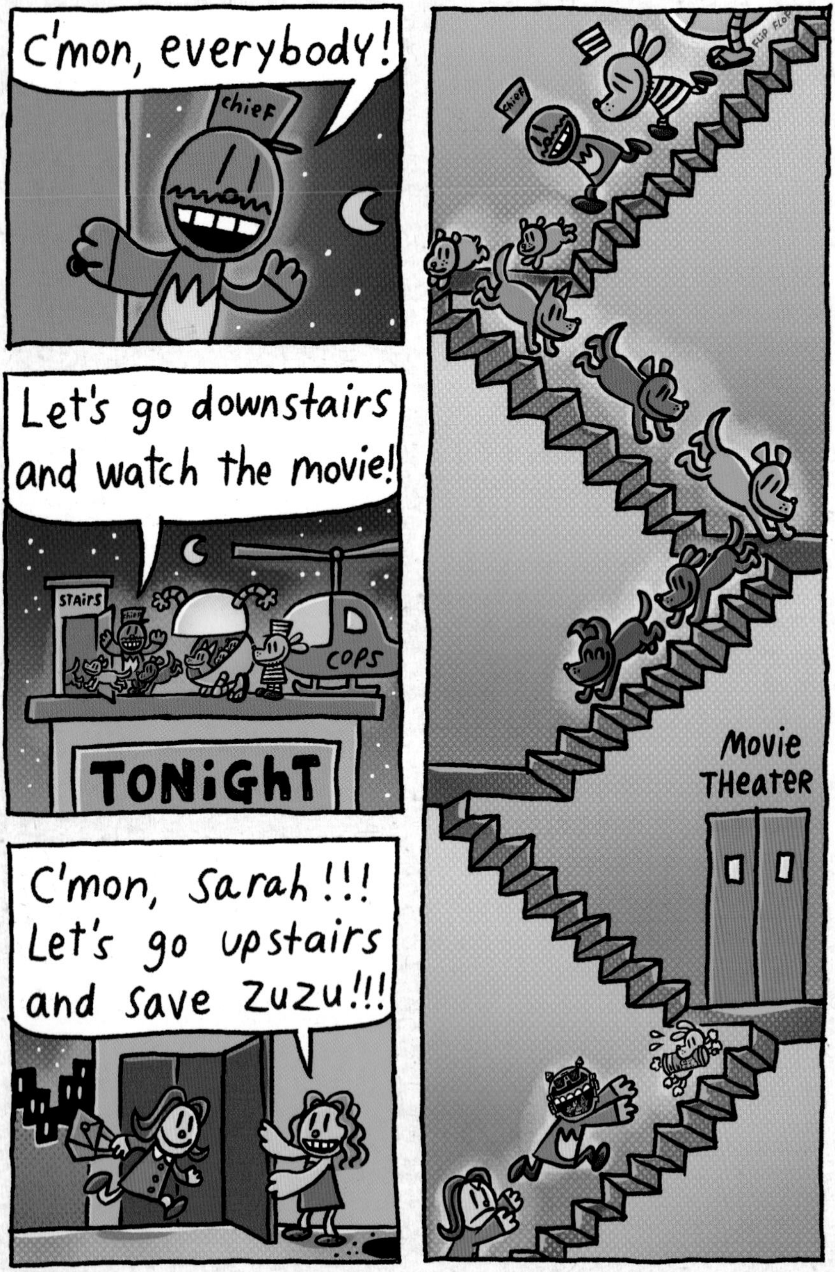
C'mon, everybody!
chief
Let's go downstairs and watch the movie!
STAIRS
COPS
TONIGHT
C'mon, Sarah!!! Let's go upstairs and save Zuzu!!!
chief
FLIP FLOP
MOVIE THEATER

EXIT
Living Spray
GRAB
Living Spray
Brings Stuff To Life
HAW HAW HAW! We've got you Now!!!

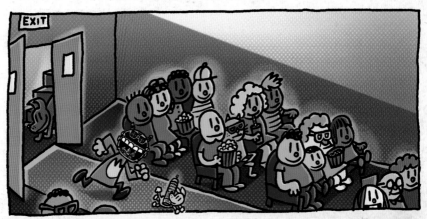

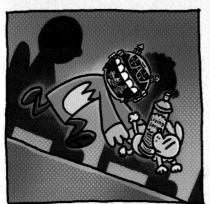

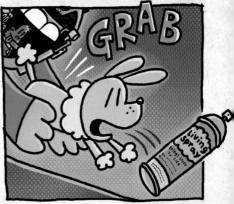

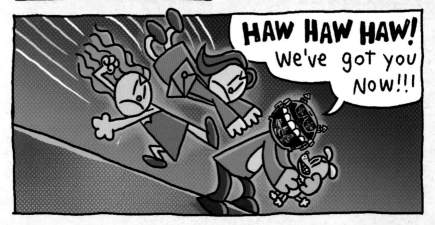

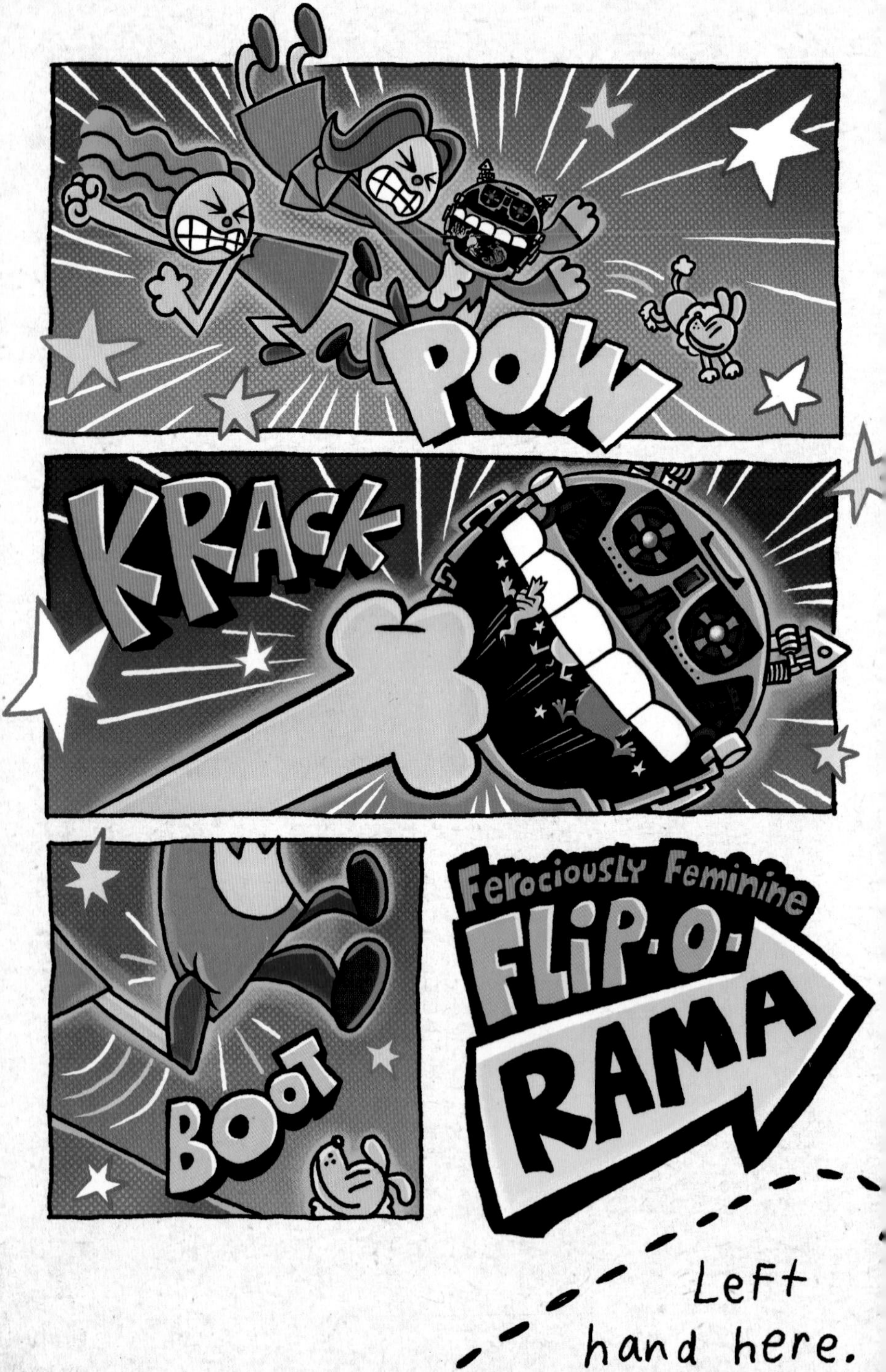
POW
KRACK
BOOT
Ferociously Feminine
FLIP-O-RAMA
Left hand here.

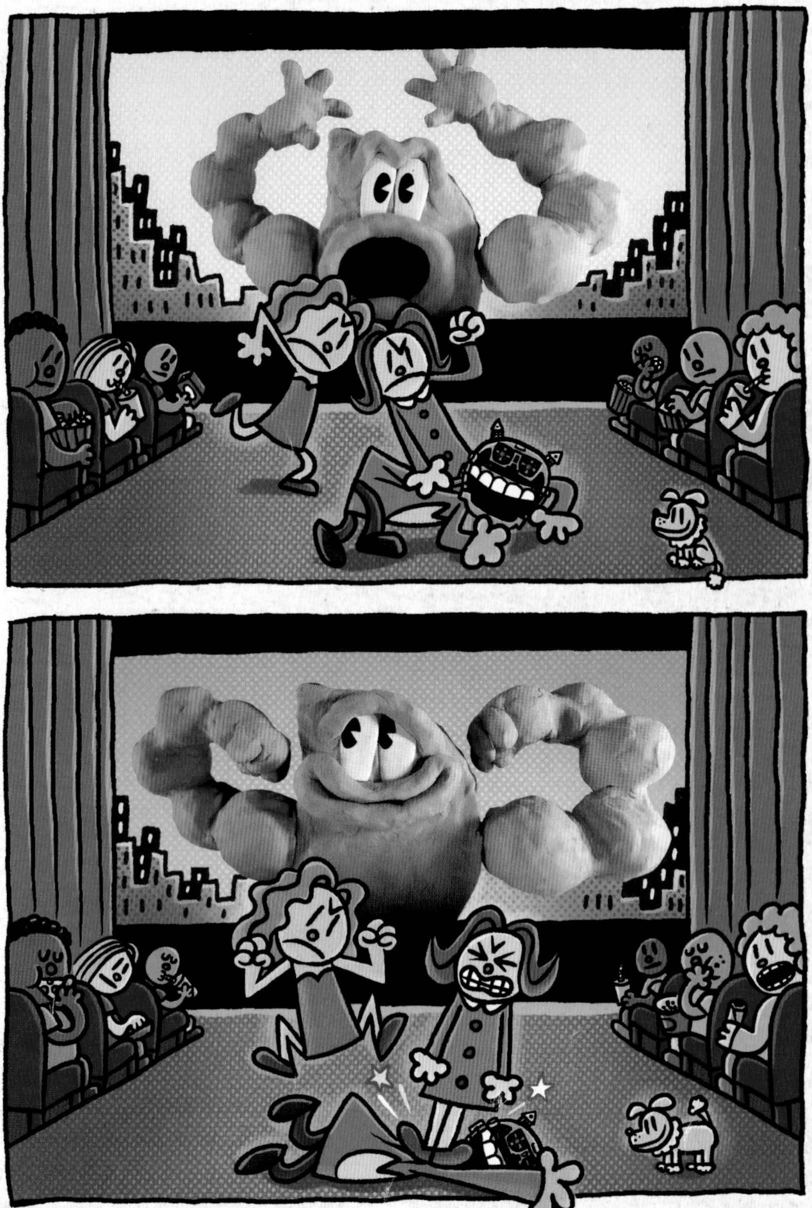

Right Thumb here.

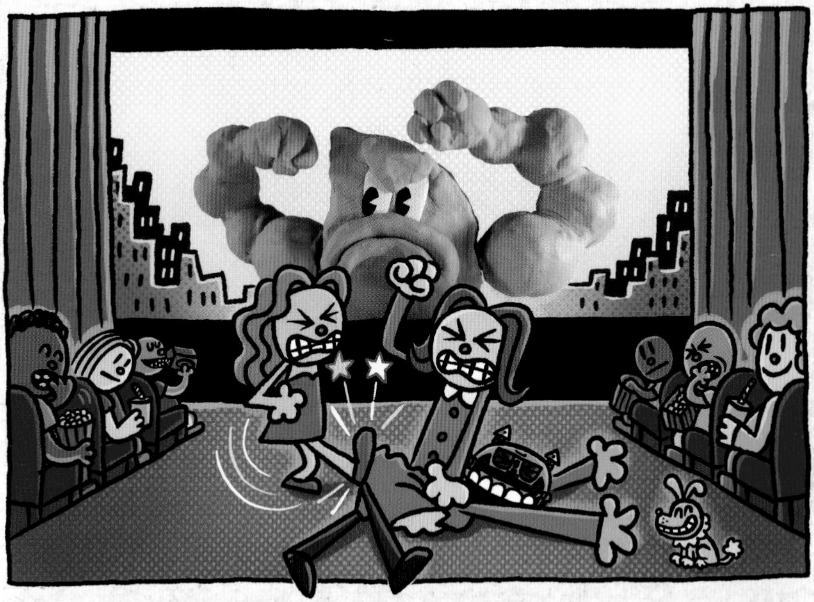

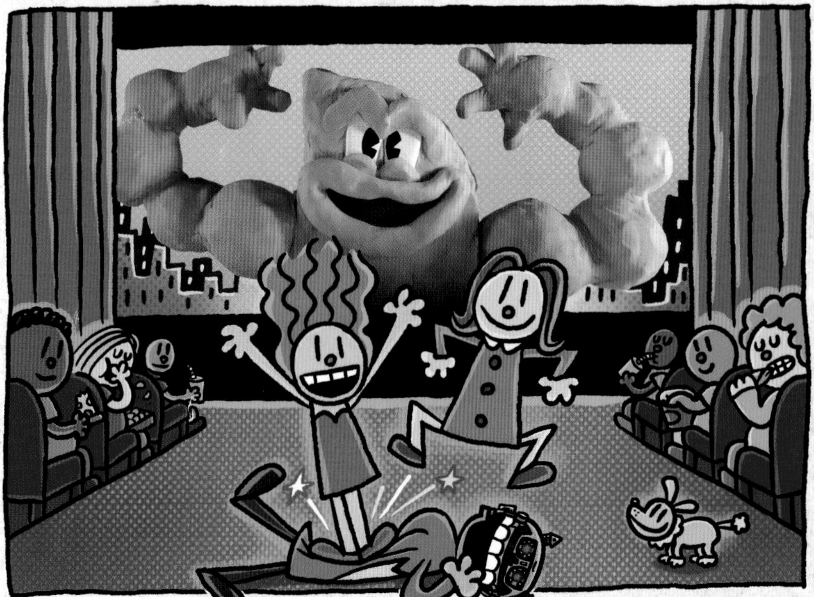

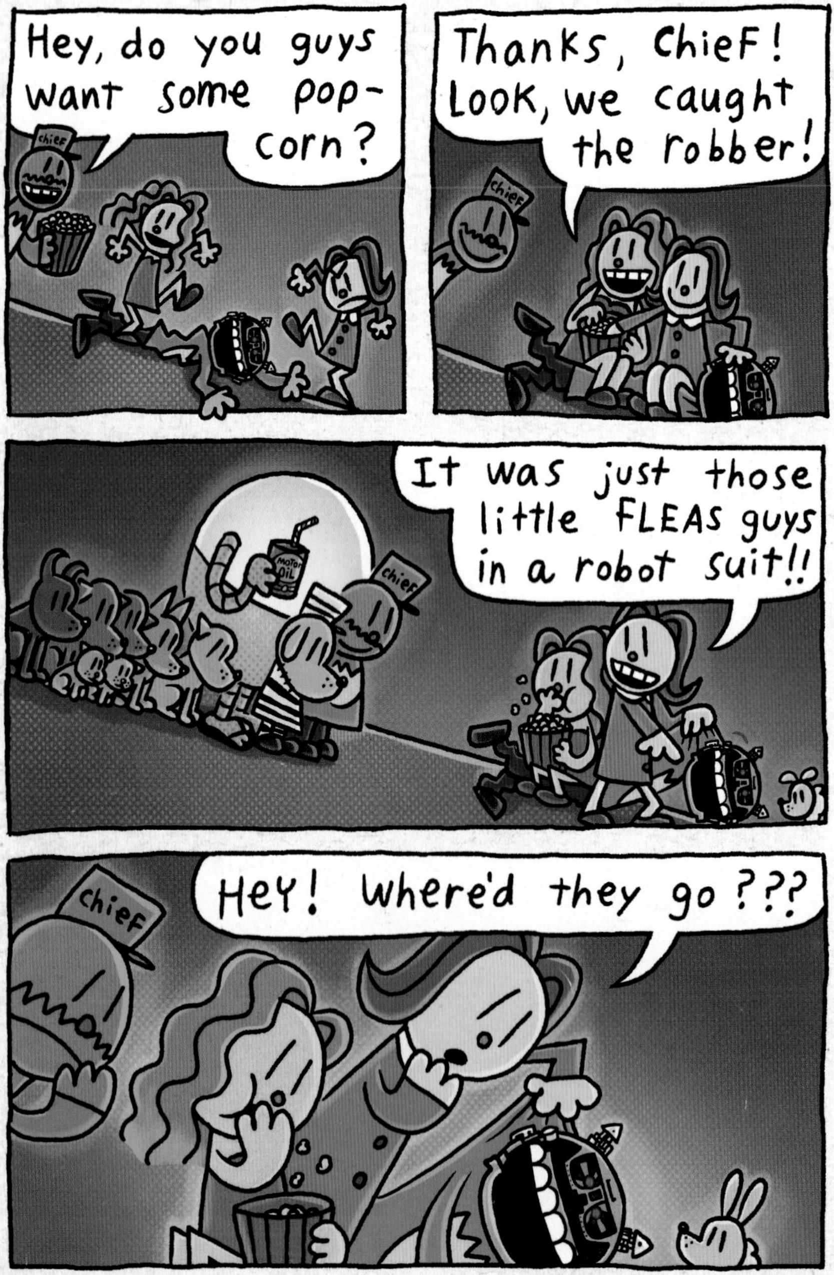
Hey, do you guys want some pop-corn?
Thanks, Chief! Look, we caught the robber!
It was just those little FLEAS guys in a robot suit!!
Hey! Where'd they go???

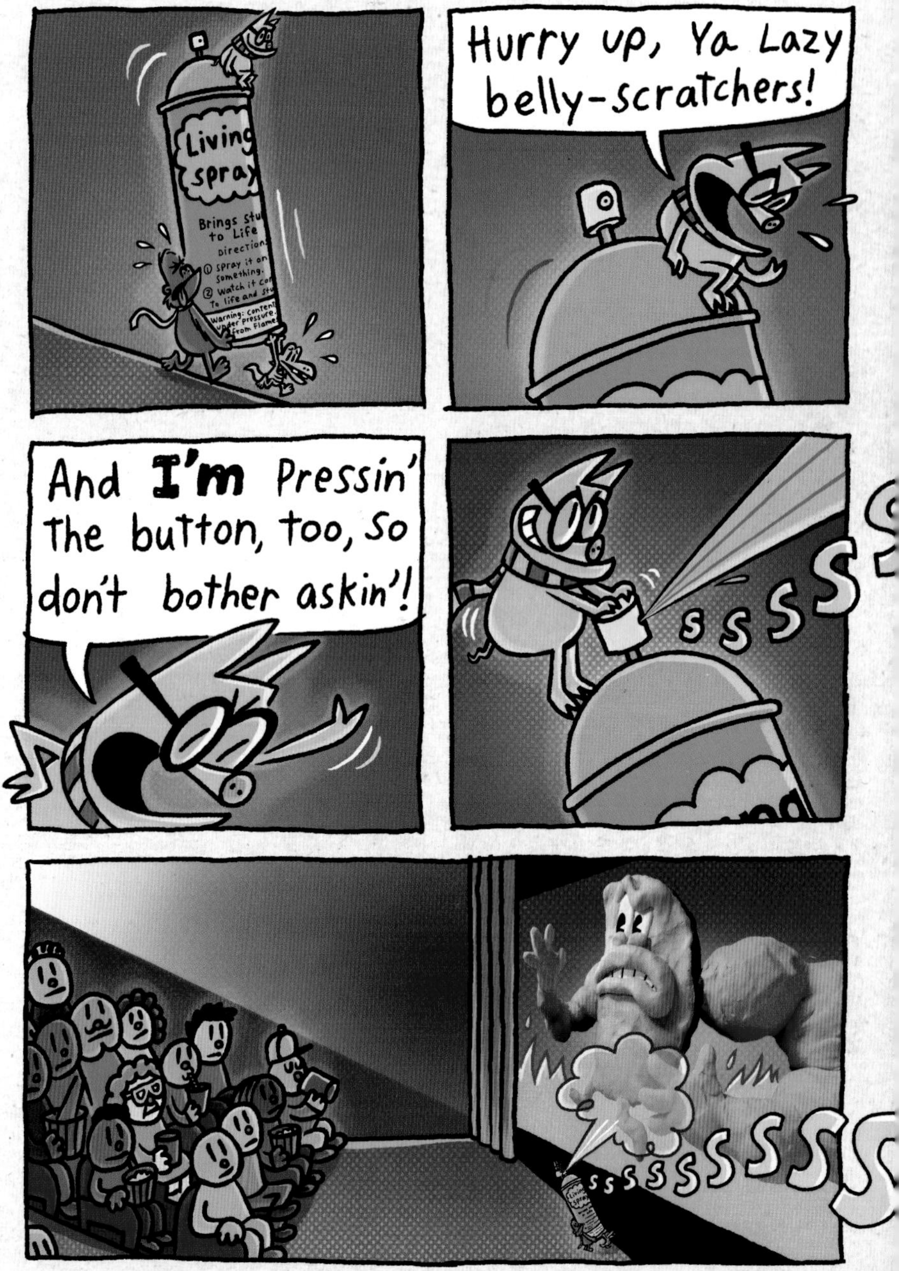
Living spray
Hurry up, Ya Lazy belly-scratchers!
And **I'm** Pressin' The button, too, So don't bother askin'!
SSSSS
SSSSSSSSSS

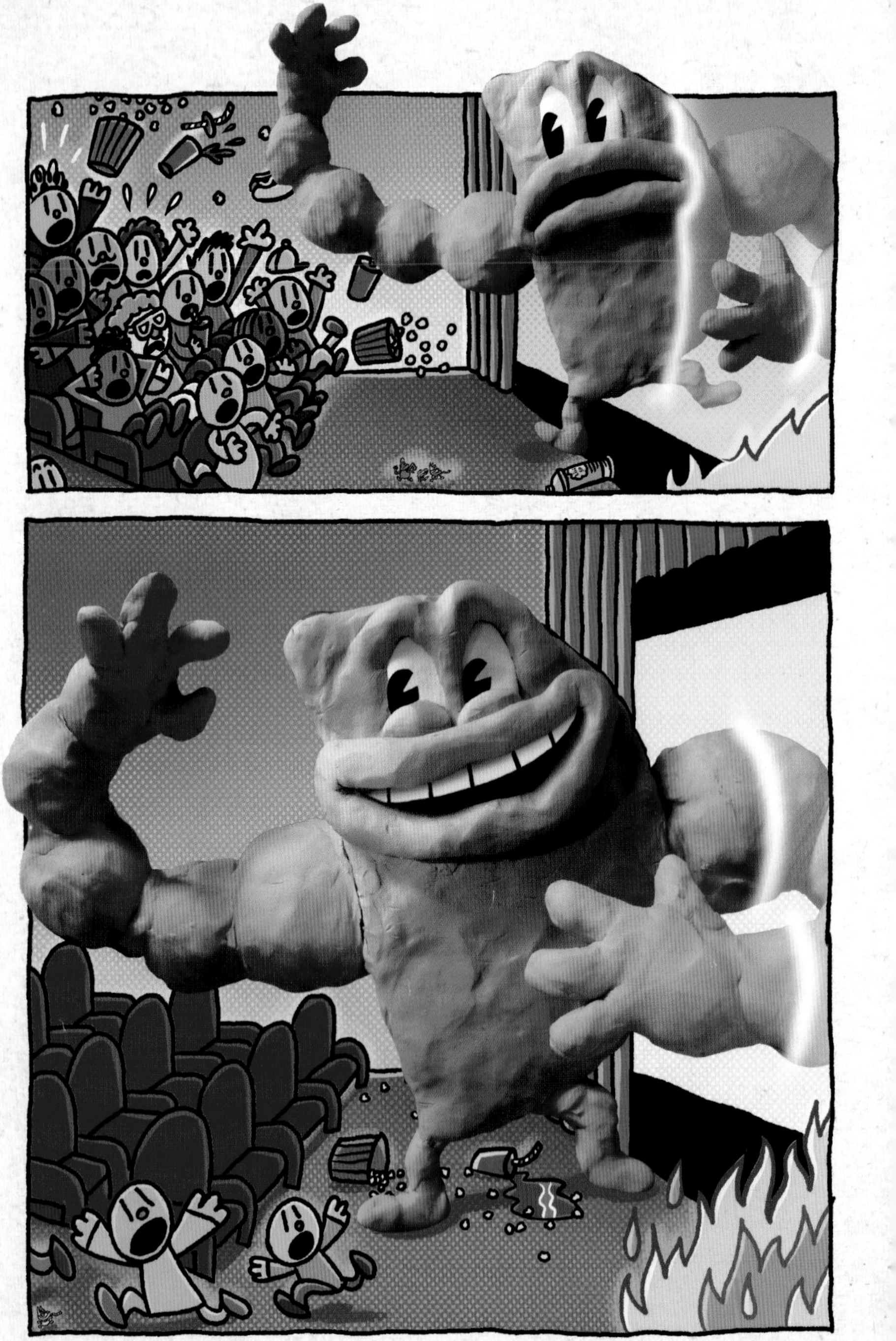

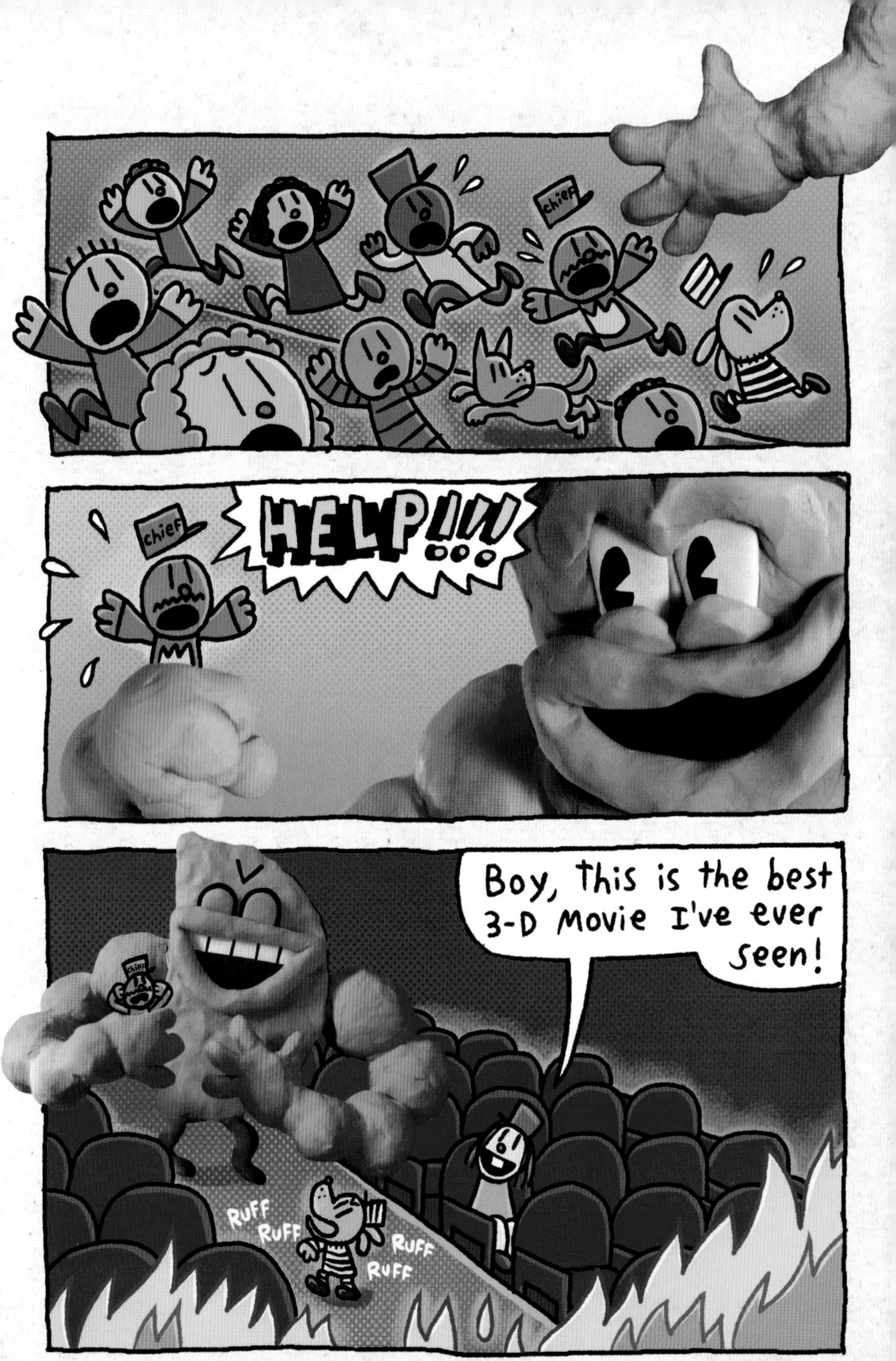
chief
chief
HELP!!!
Boy, This is the best 3-D Movie I've ever seen!
chief
RUFF
RUFF
RUFF
RUFF

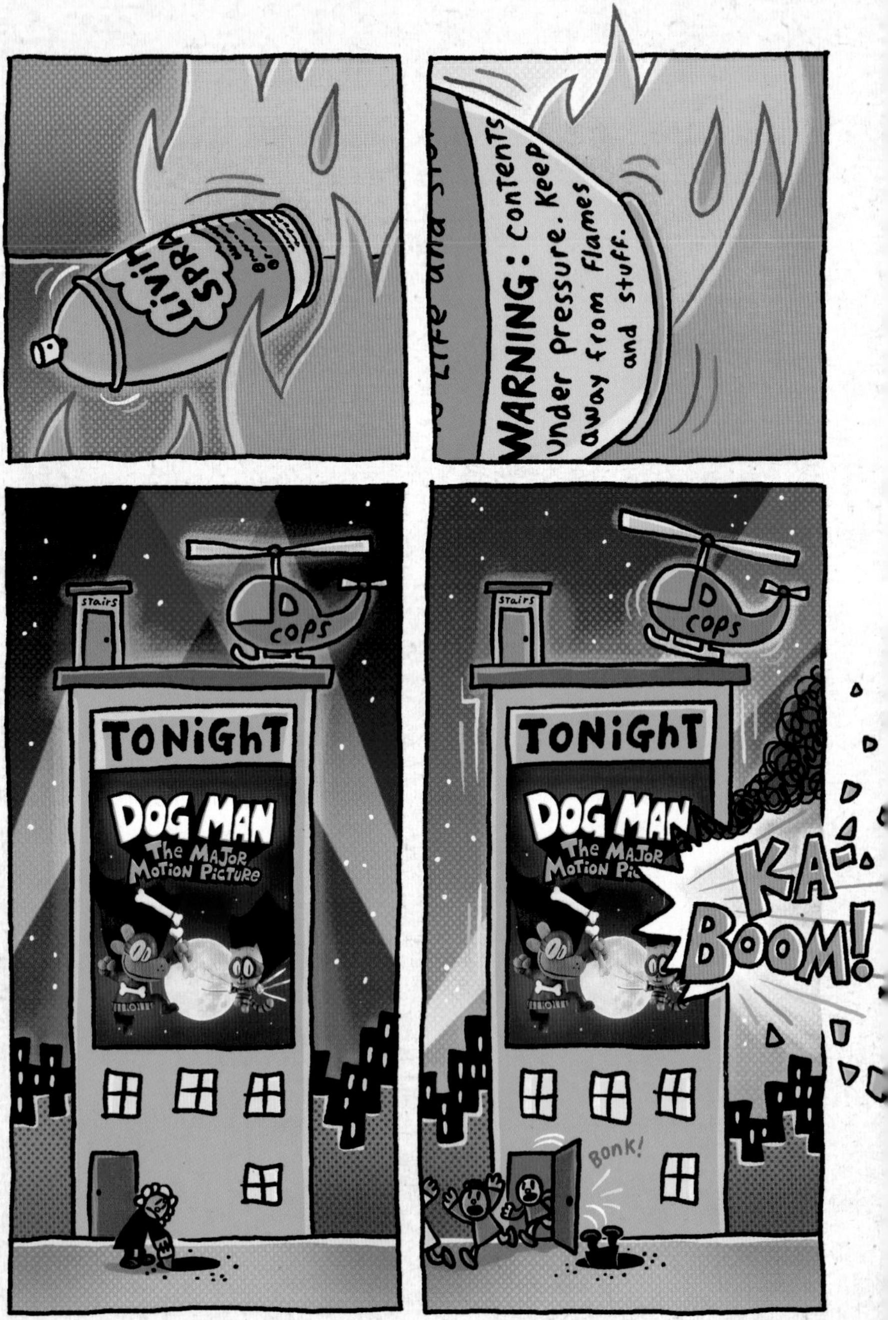
WARNING: Contents under pressure. Keep away from flames and stuff.
stairs
D COPS
TONIGHT
DOG MAN
The MAJOR MOTION PICTURE
stairs
D COPS
TONIGHT
KA-BOOM!
BONK!

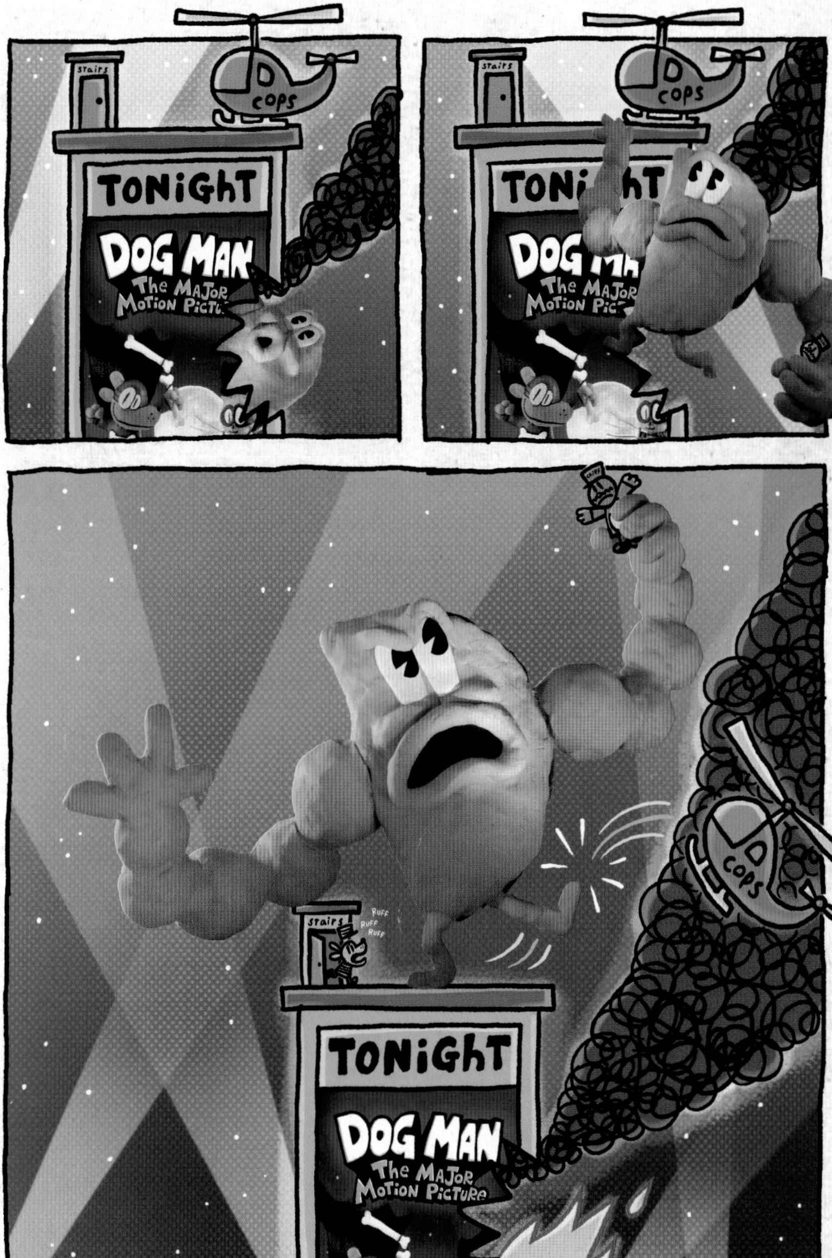
STAIRS
D COPS
TONIGHT
DOG MAN
The MAJOR MOTION PICTURE
RUFF
RUFF
RUFF

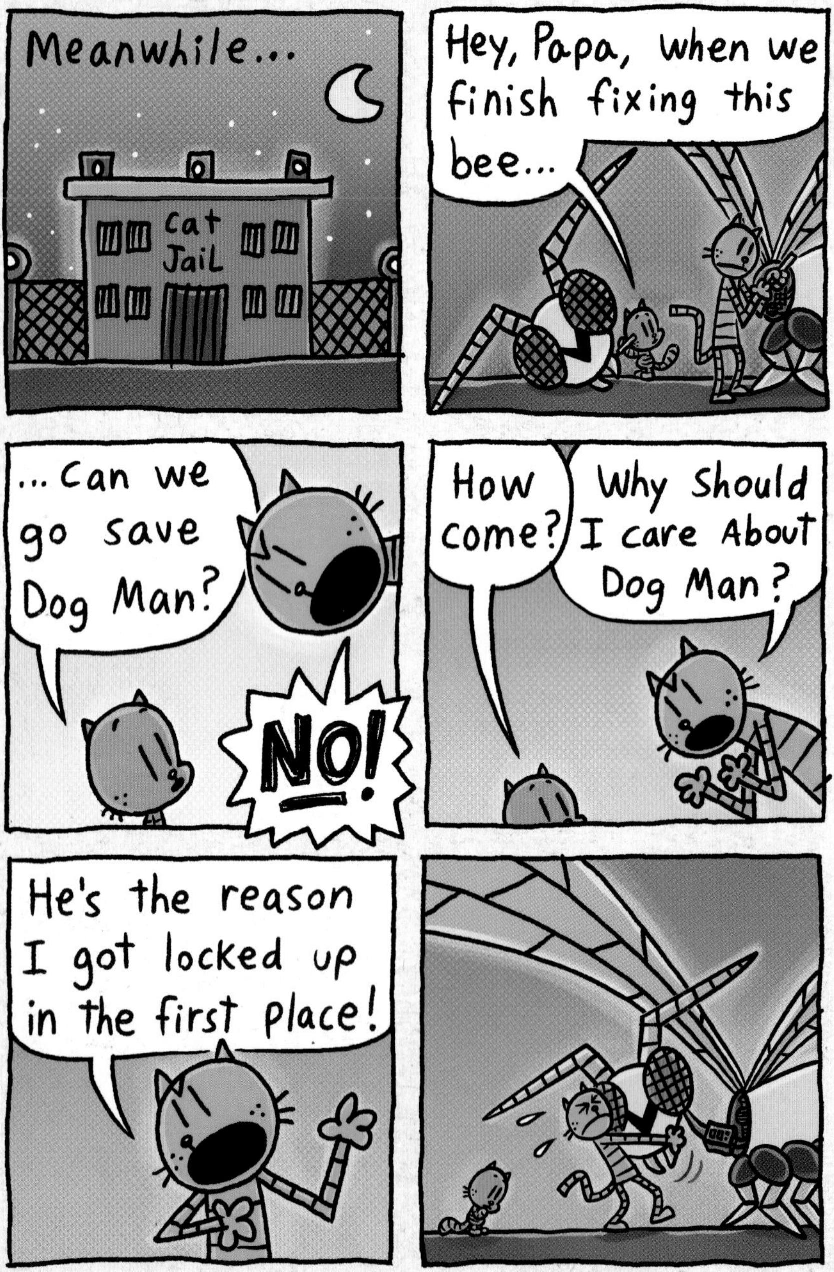
Meanwhile...
Cat Jail
Hey, Papa, when we finish fixing this bee...
...Can we go save Dog Man?
NO!
How come?
Why Should I care About Dog Man?
He's the reason I got locked up in the first place!

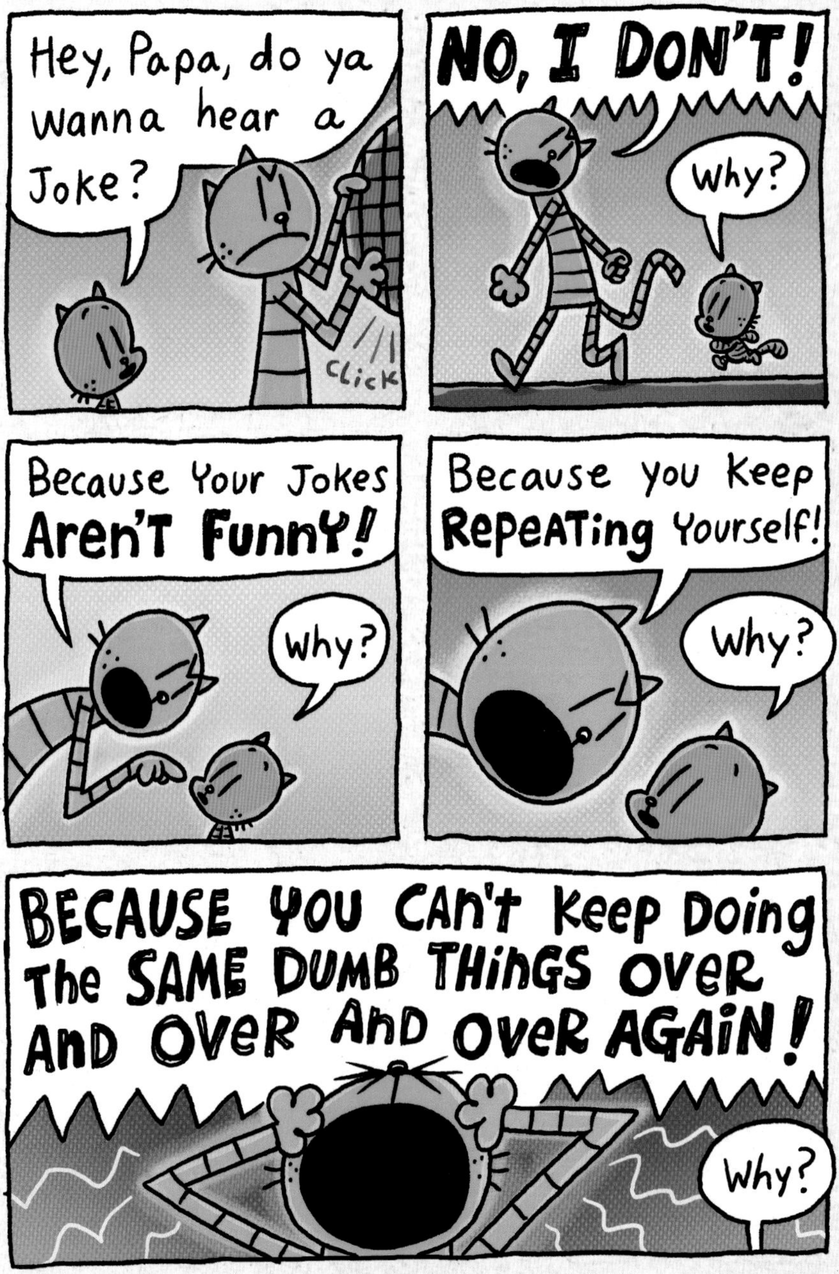
Hey, Papa, do ya wanna hear a Joke?
CLICK
NO, I DON'T!
Why?
Because Your Jokes Aren't Funny!
Why?
Because you Keep Repeating Yourself!
Why?
BECAUSE YOU CAN'T Keep Doing The SAME DUMB THINGS OVER AND OVER AND OVER AGAIN!
Why?

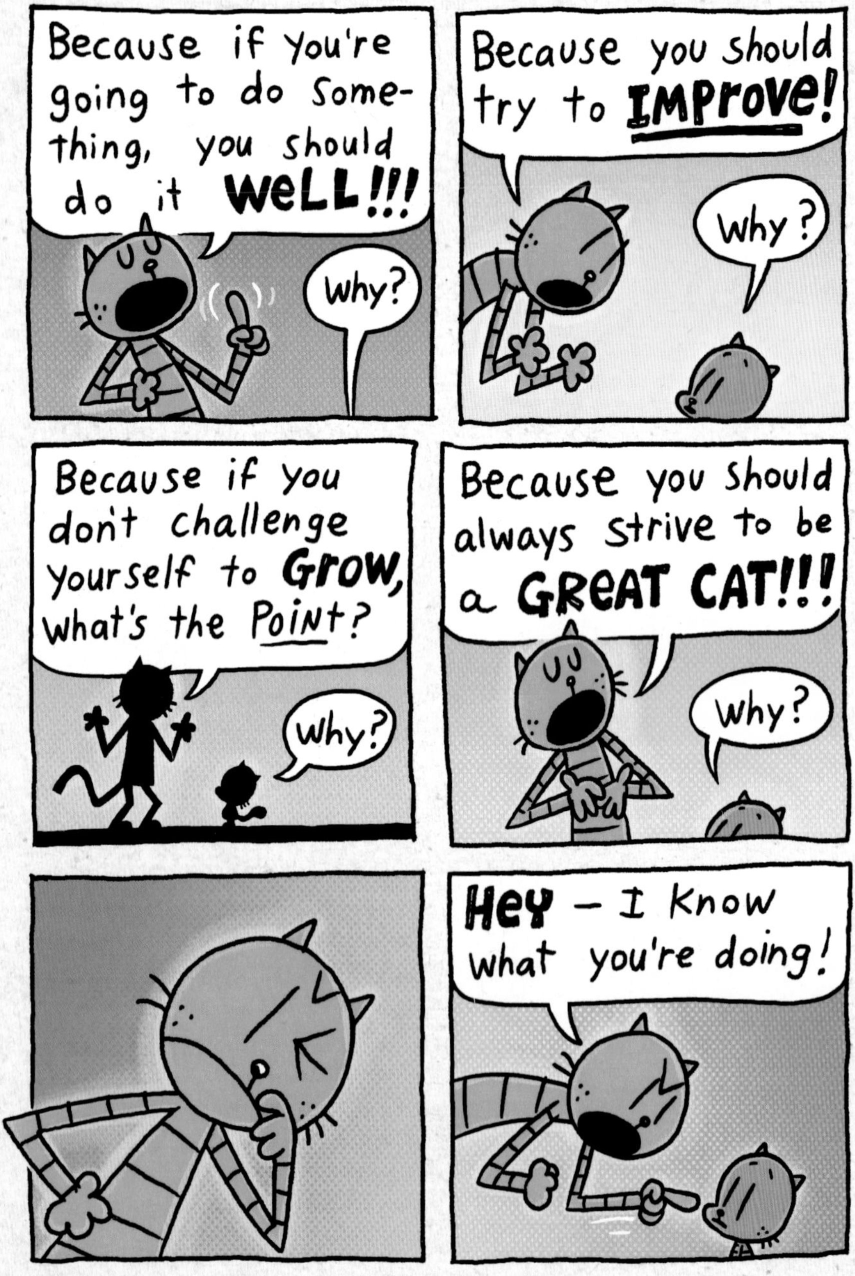
Because if you're going to do some-thing, you should do it WELL!!!
Why?
Because you should try to IMPROVE!
Why?
Because if you don't challenge yourself to GROW, what's the POINT?
Why?
Because you should always strive to be a GREAT CAT!!!
Why?
HEY – I know what you're doing!

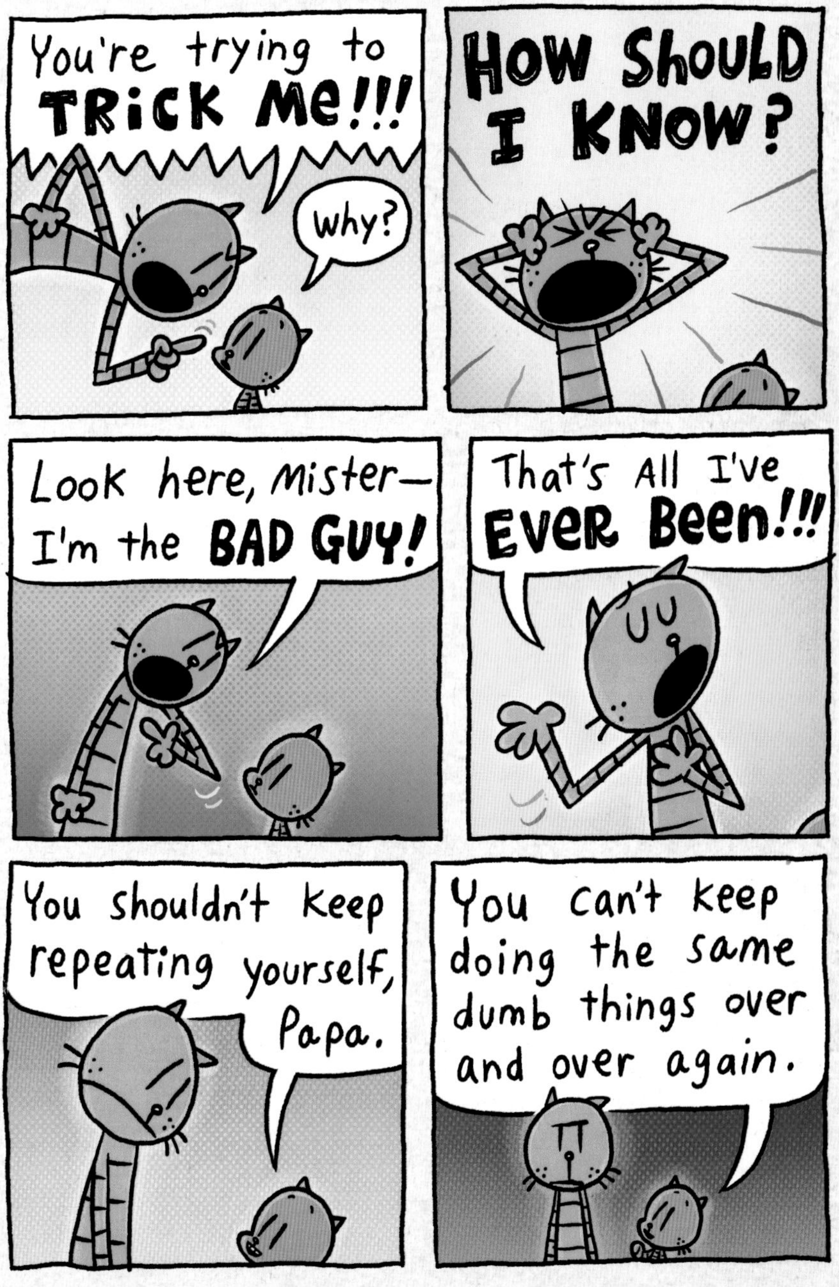
You're trying to TRICK ME!!!
Why?
HOW SHOULD I KNOW?
Look here, Mister— I'm the BAD GUY!
That's All I've EVER Been!!!
You shouldn't keep repeating yourself, Papa.
You can't keep doing the same dumb things over and over again.

If you're going to do something, you should do it **well**!

You should always try to improve!

Because if you don't challenge yourself to grow, what's the point?

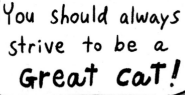
You should always strive to be a **Great Cat!**

Right, Papa?

Chapter 10
The Great Cat's Bee

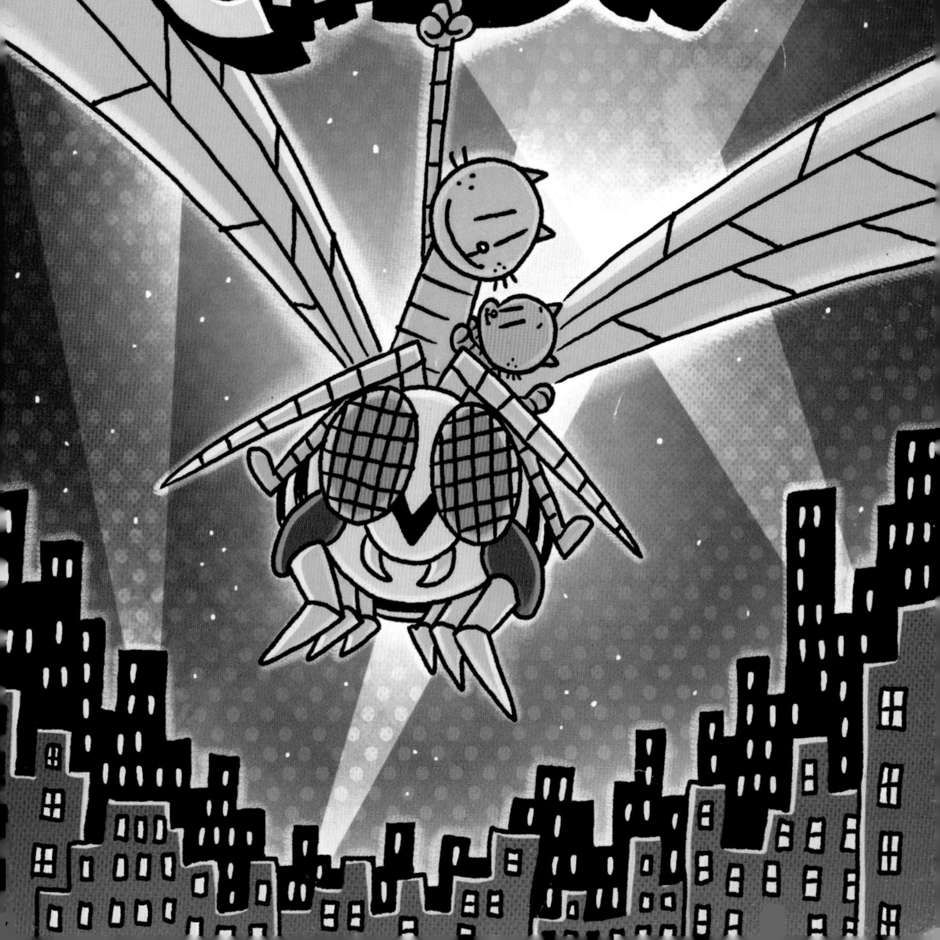

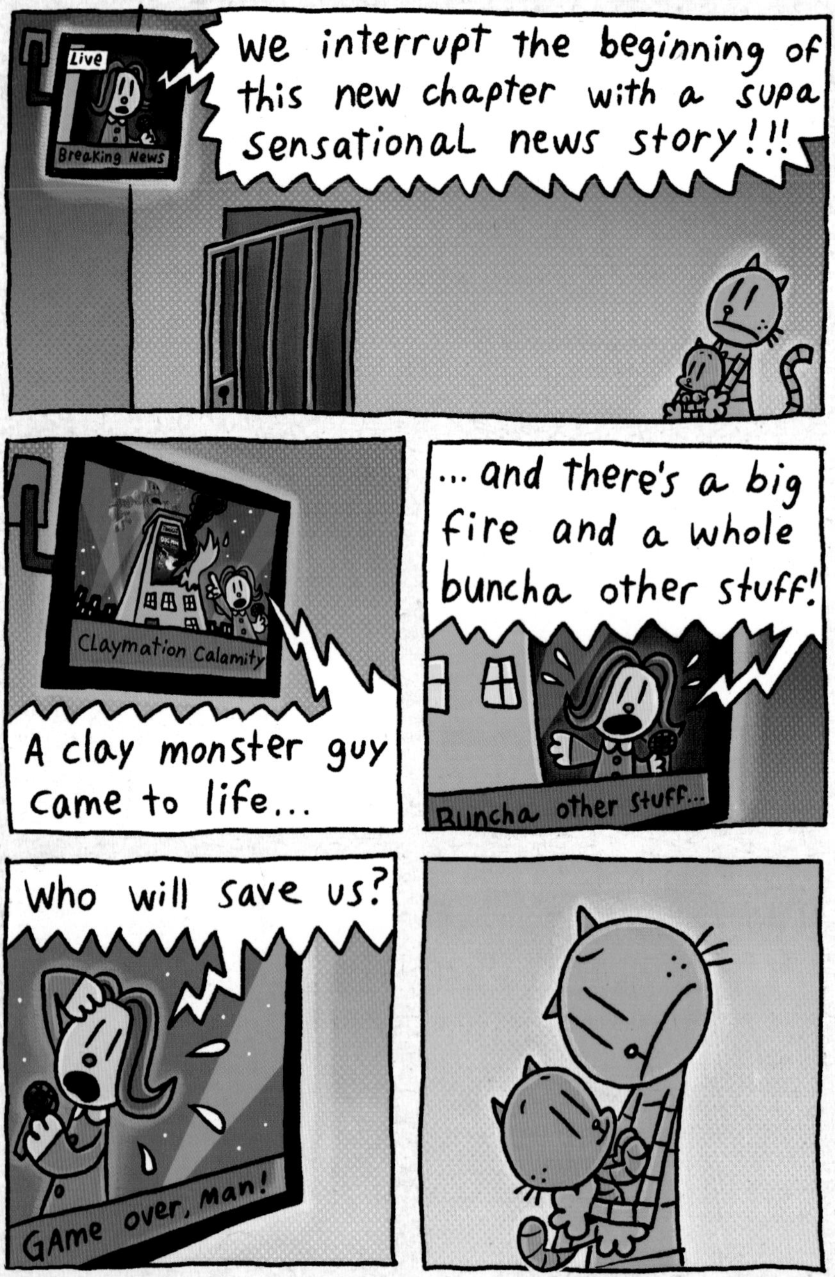
Live
Breaking News
We interrupt the beginning of this new chapter with a supa sensational news story!!!
Claymation Calamity
A clay monster guy came to life...
...and there's a big fire and a whole buncha other stuff!
Buncha other stuff...
Who will save us?
Game over, man!

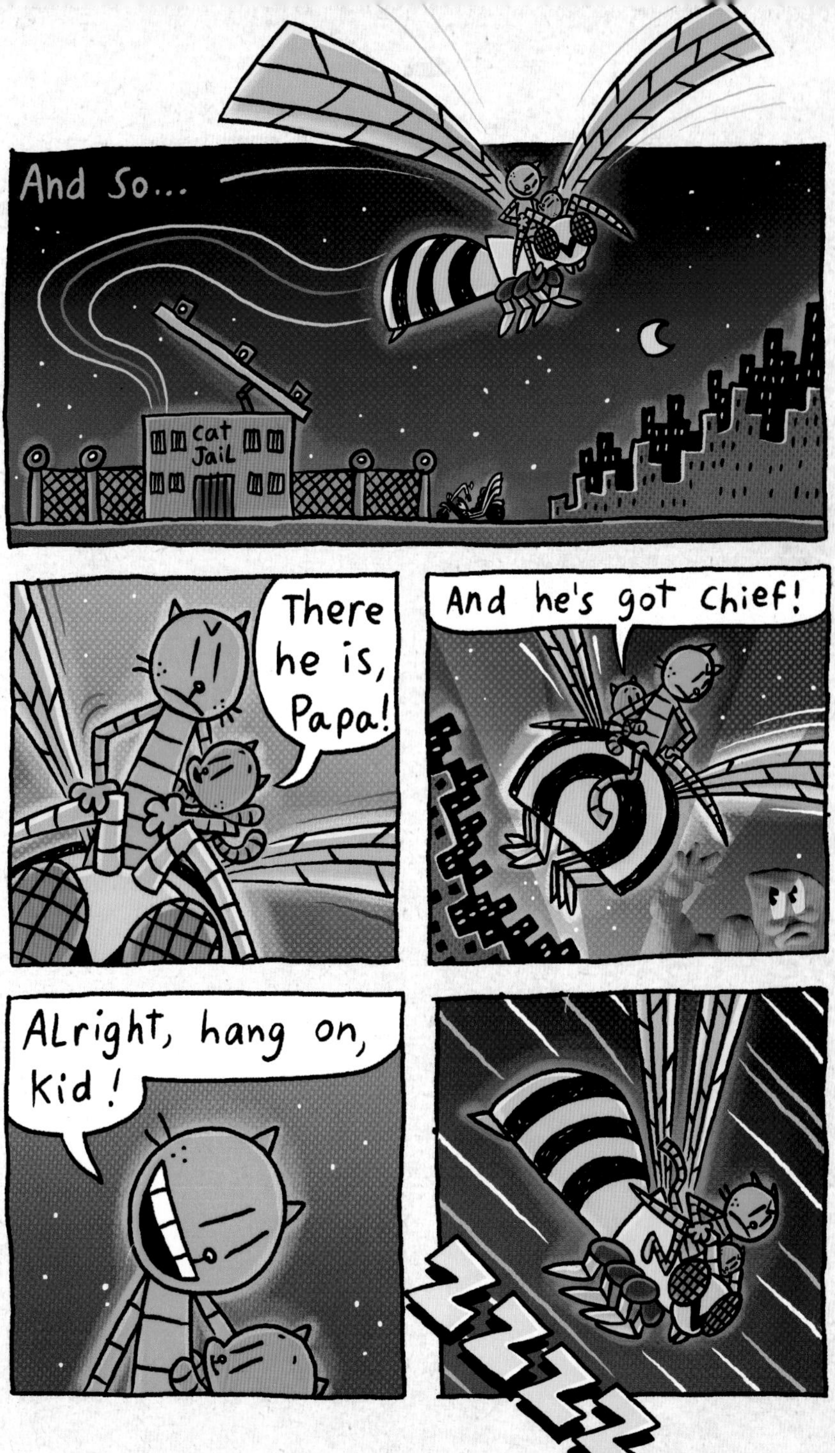
And So...
Cat Jail
There he is, Papa!
And he's got Chief!
ALright, hang on, kid!
ZZZZZ

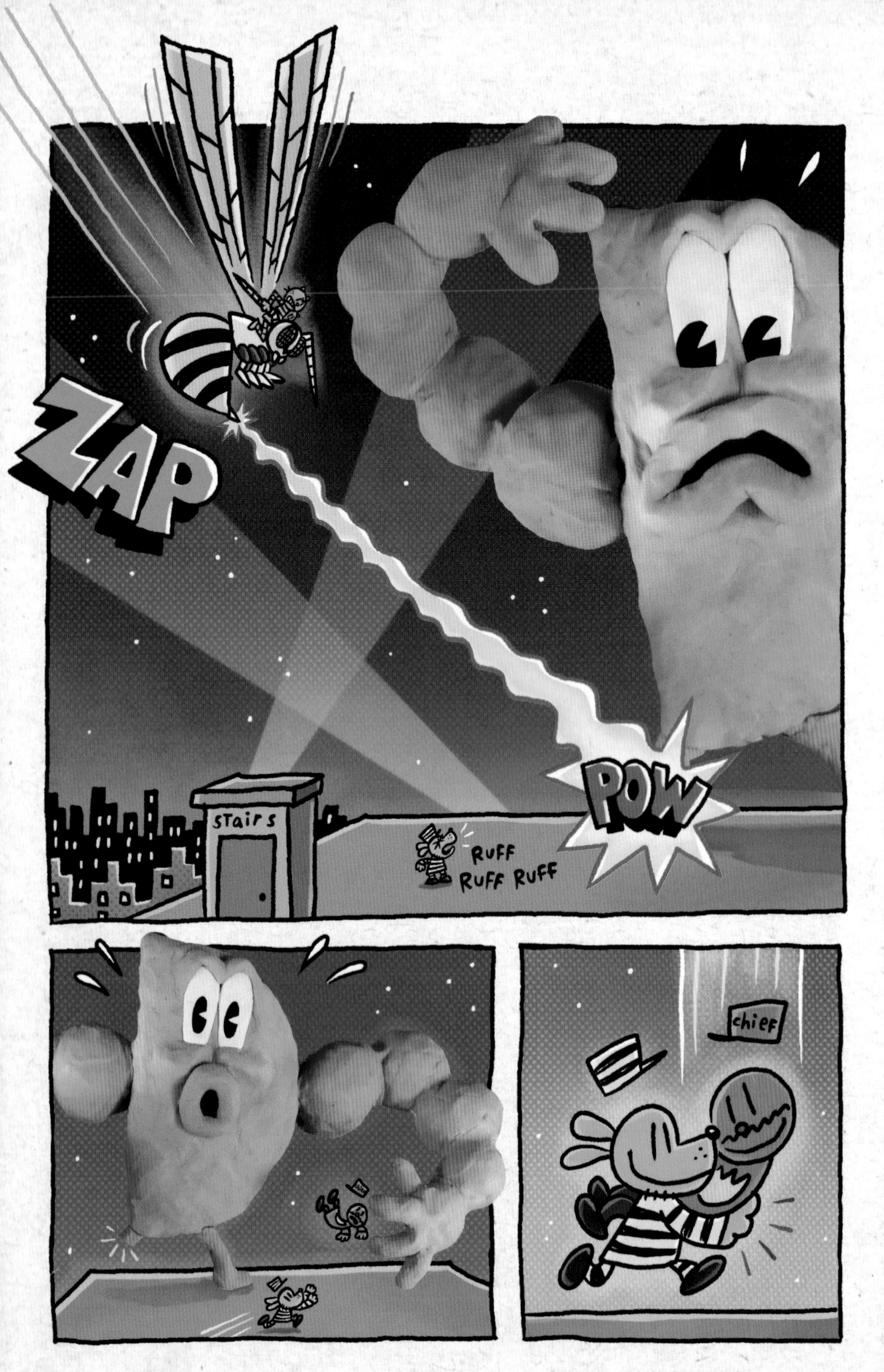
ZAP
POW
stairs
RUFF
RUFF RUFF
chief

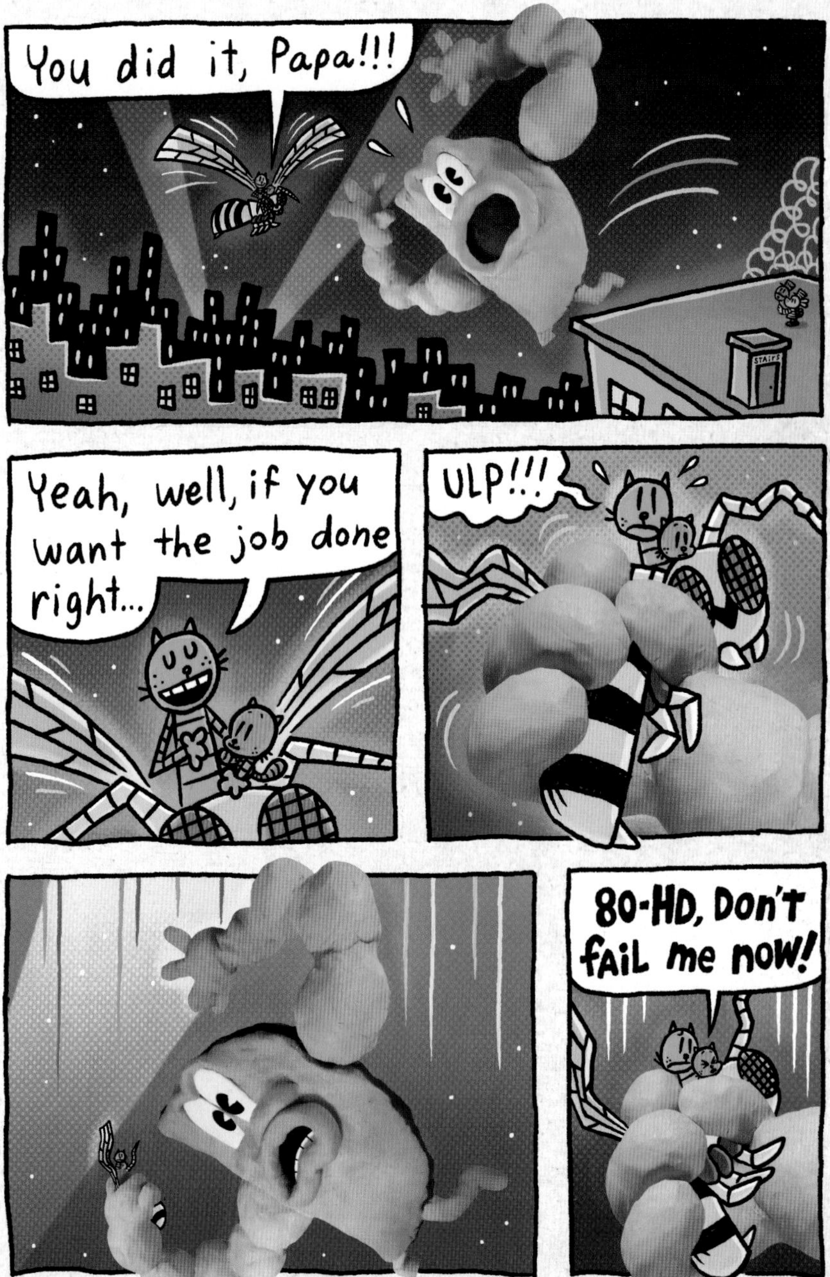
You did it, Papa!!!
STAIRS
Yeah, well, if you want the job done right...
ULP!!!
80-HD, Don't fail me now!

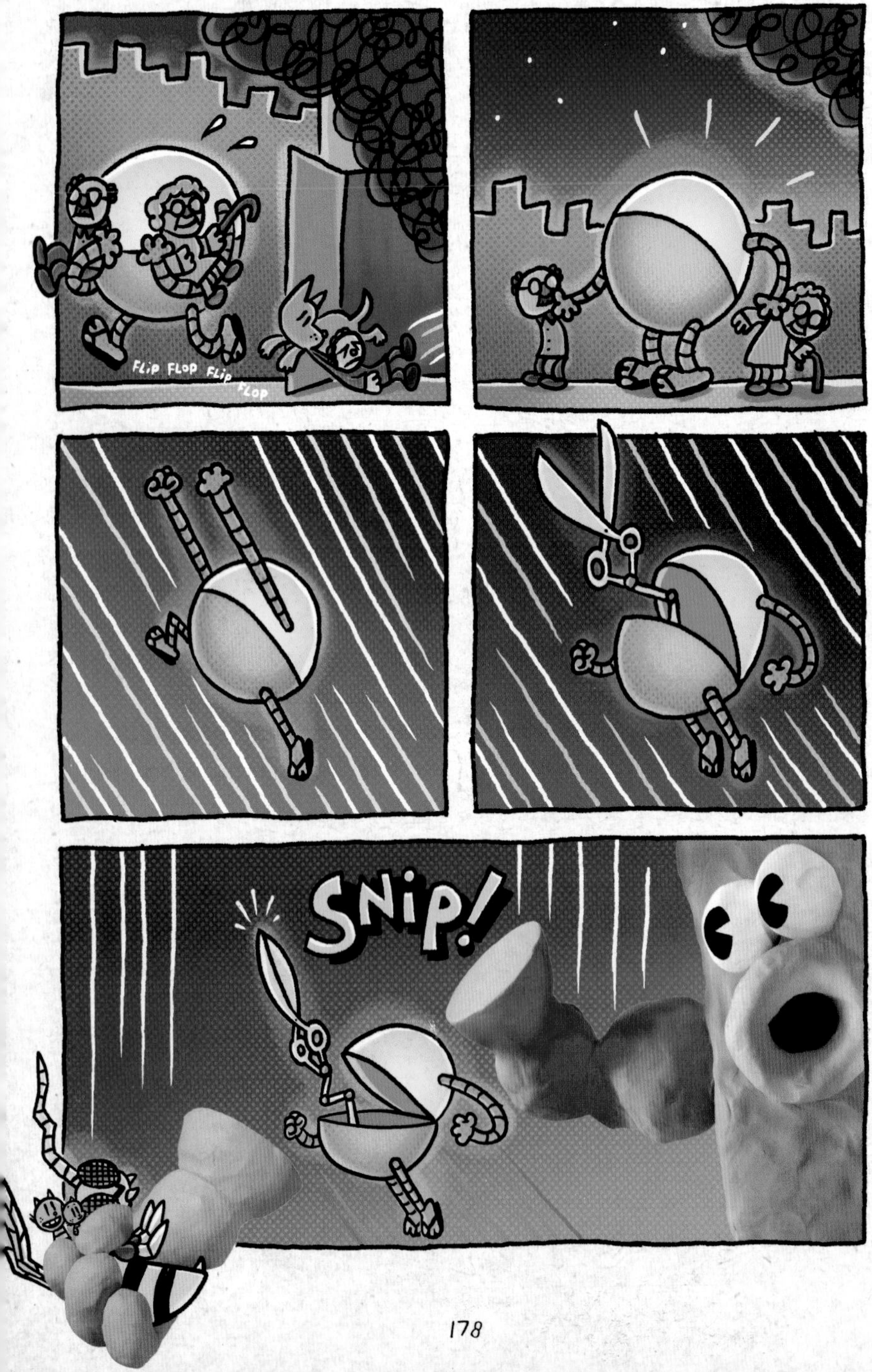
FLIP FLOP FLIP FLOP
SNIP!

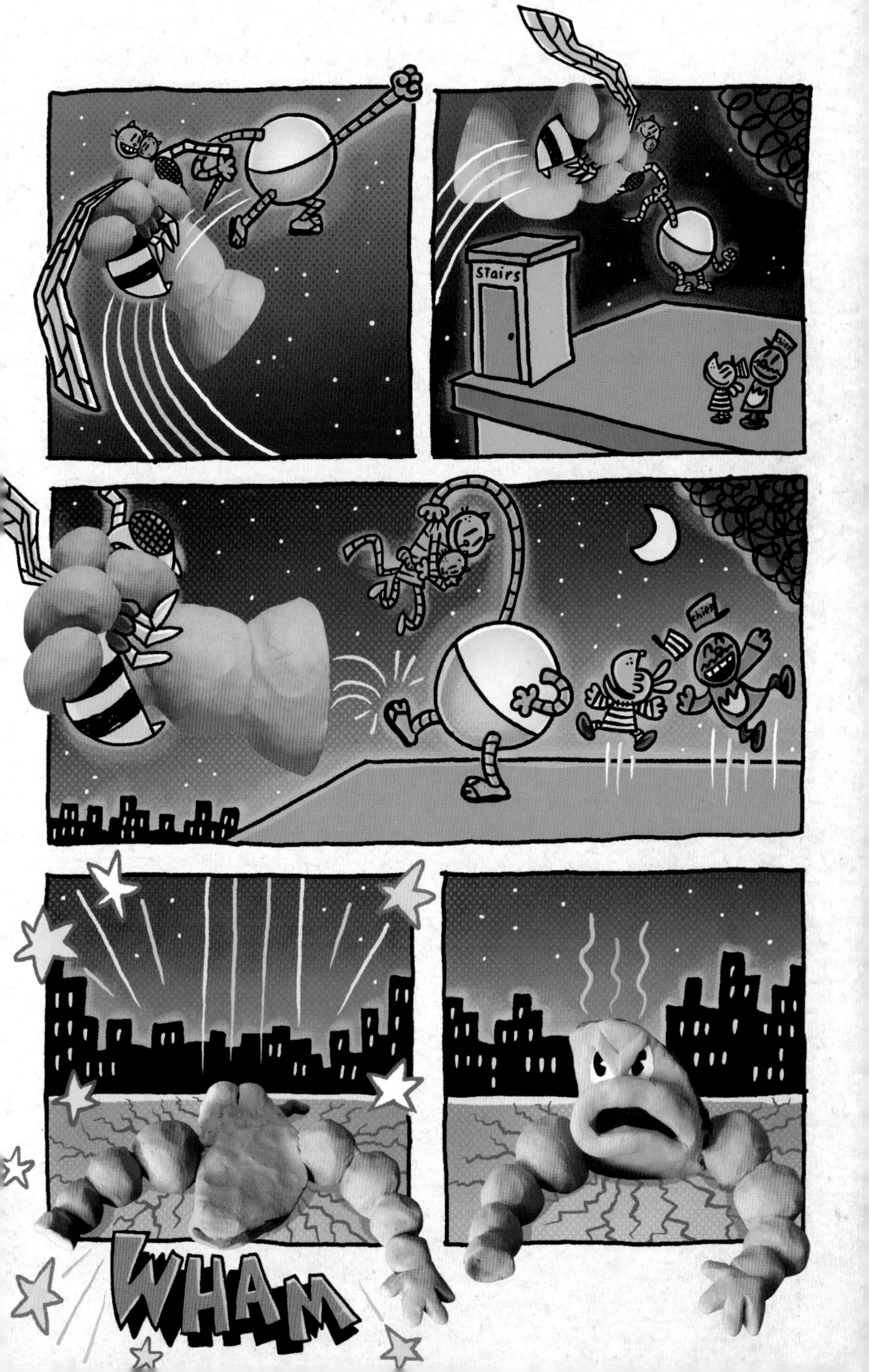

Stairs
Chief
Chief
WHAM

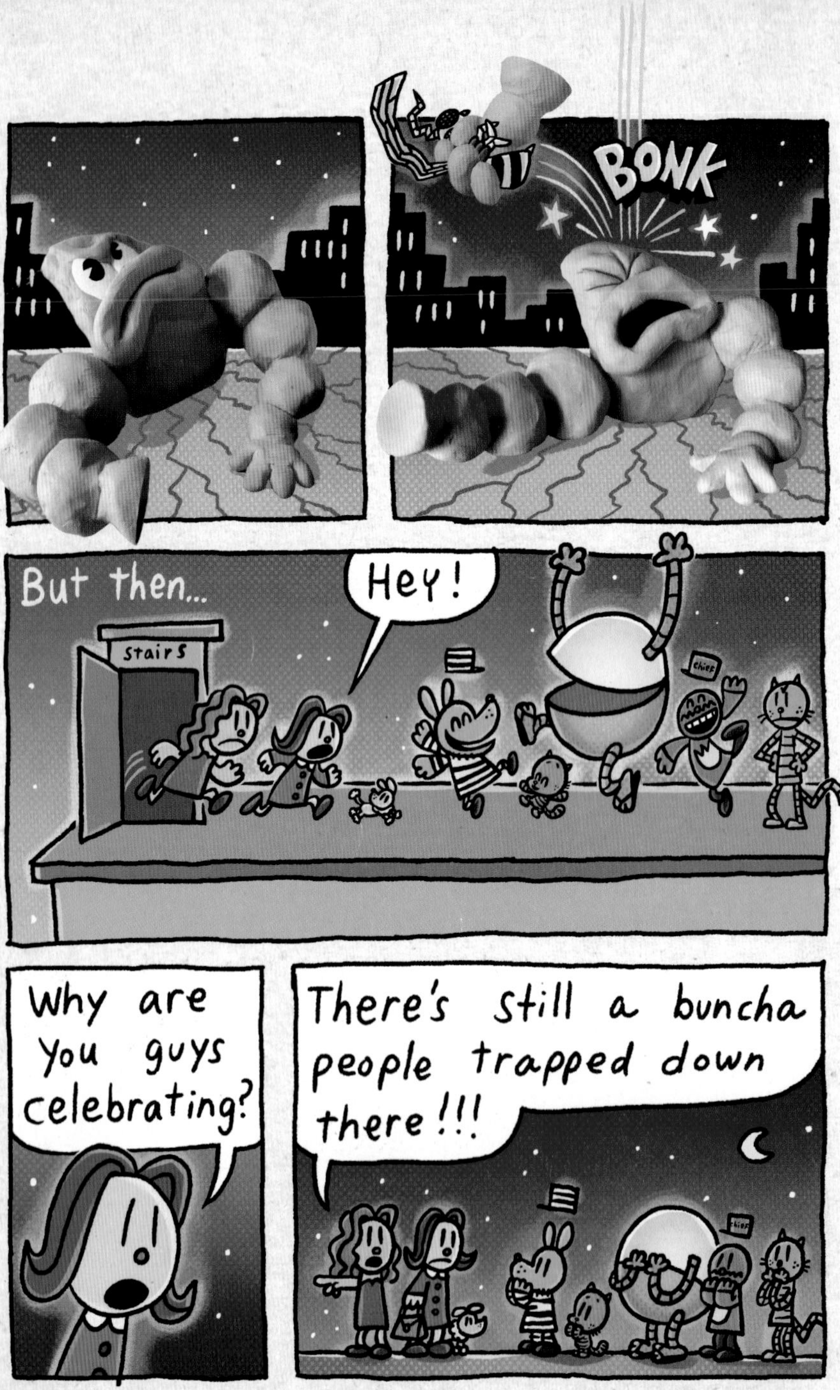
BONK
But then...
Hey!
Stairs
Chief
Why are you guys celebrating?
There's still a buncha people trapped down there!!!
Chief

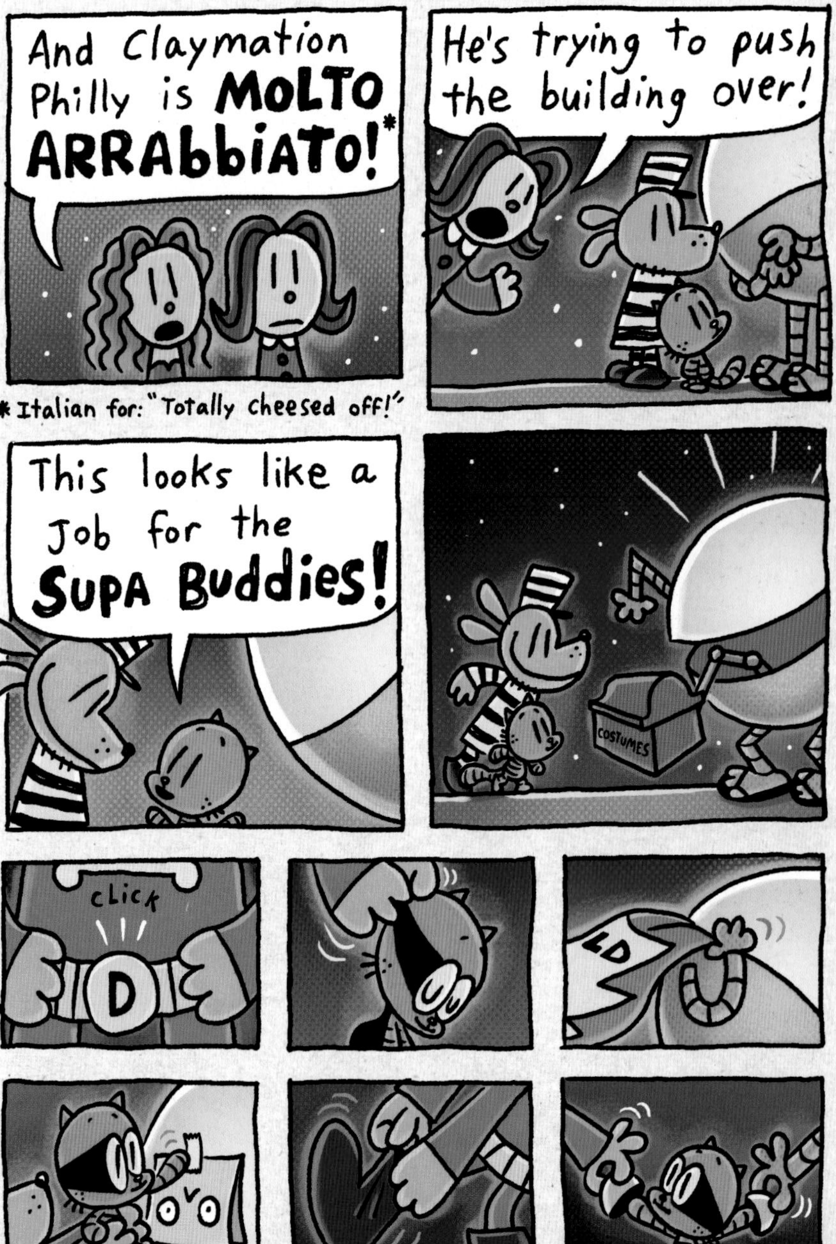
And Claymation Philly is MOLTO ARRABBIATO!*
He's trying to push the building over!
* Italian for: "Totally cheesed off!"
This looks like a Job for the SUPA BUDDIES!
COSTUMES
CLICK
D

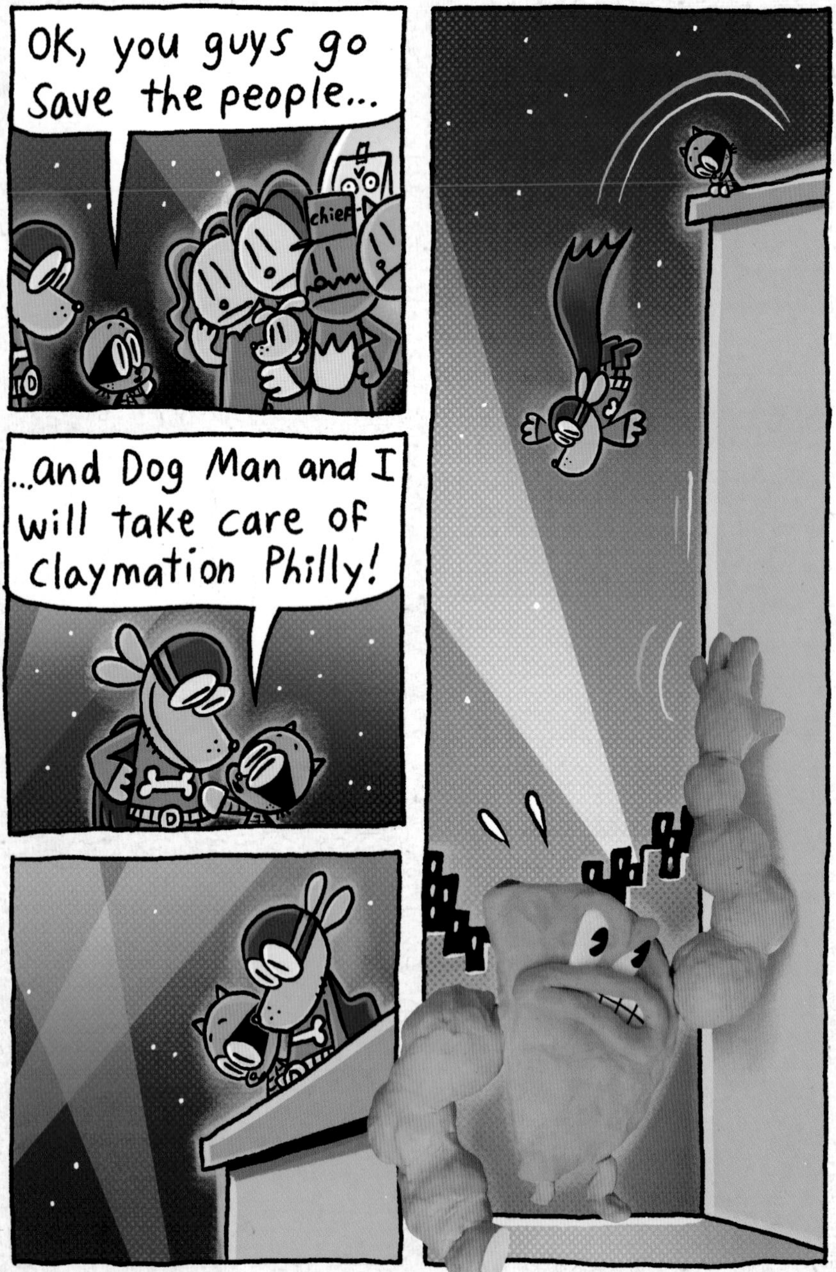
OK, you guys go Save the people...
chief
...and Dog Man and I will take care of Claymation Philly!

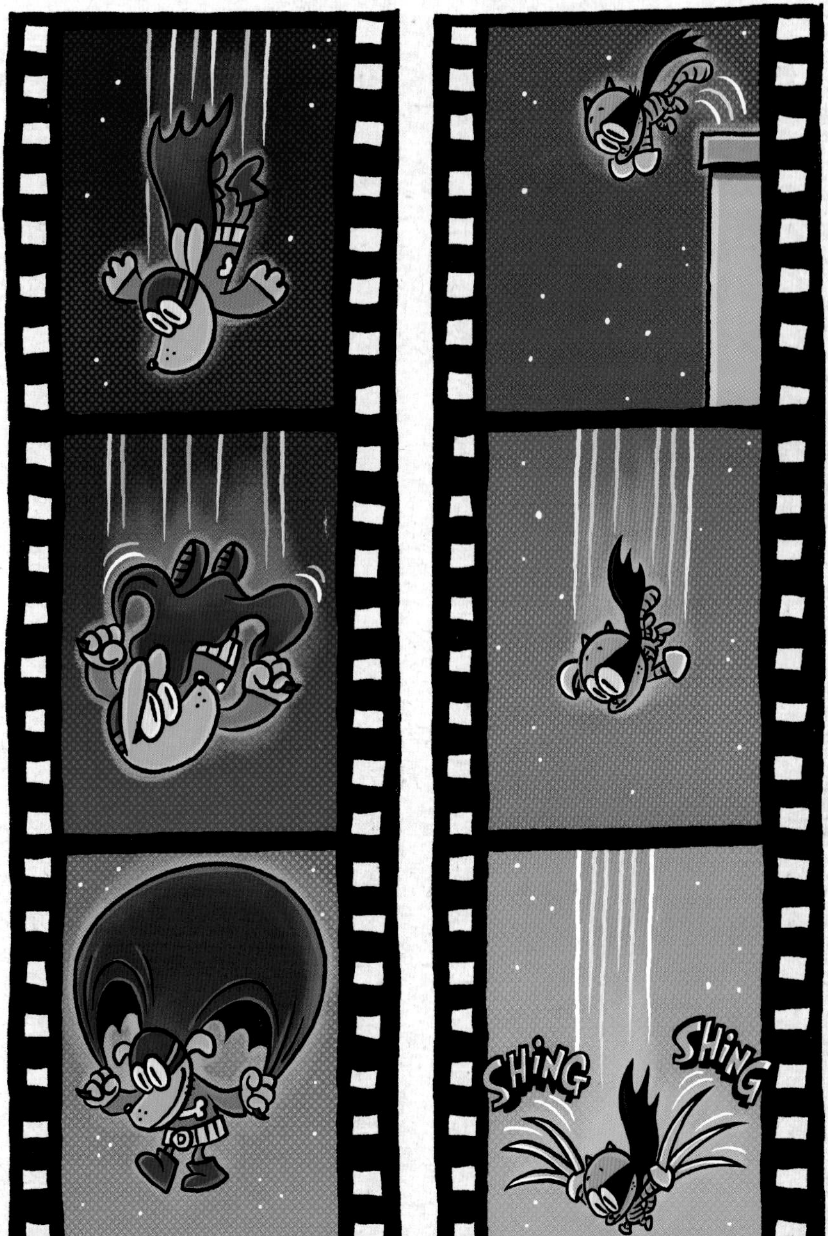
SHING
SHING

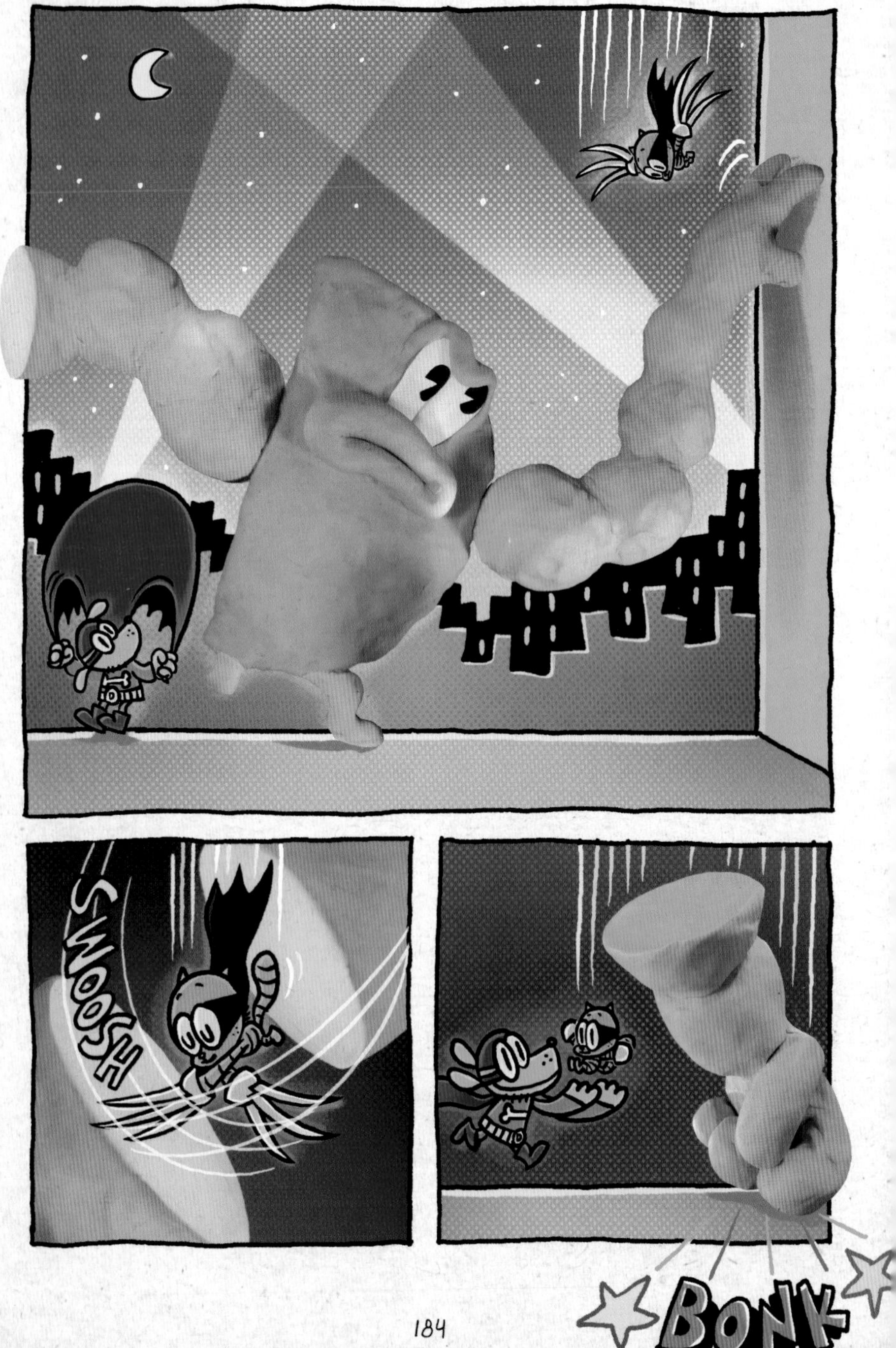
SWOOSH
BONK

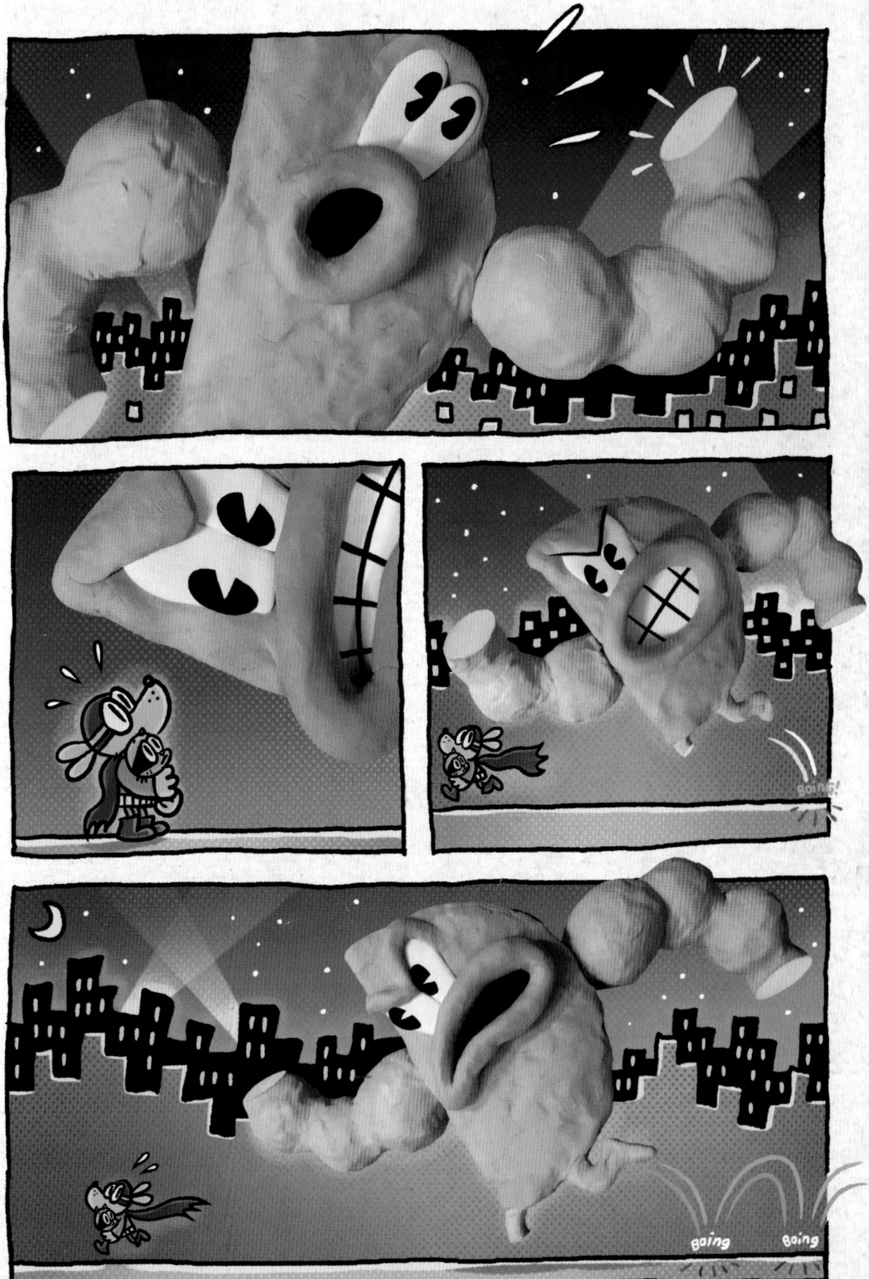
Boing!
Boing
Boing

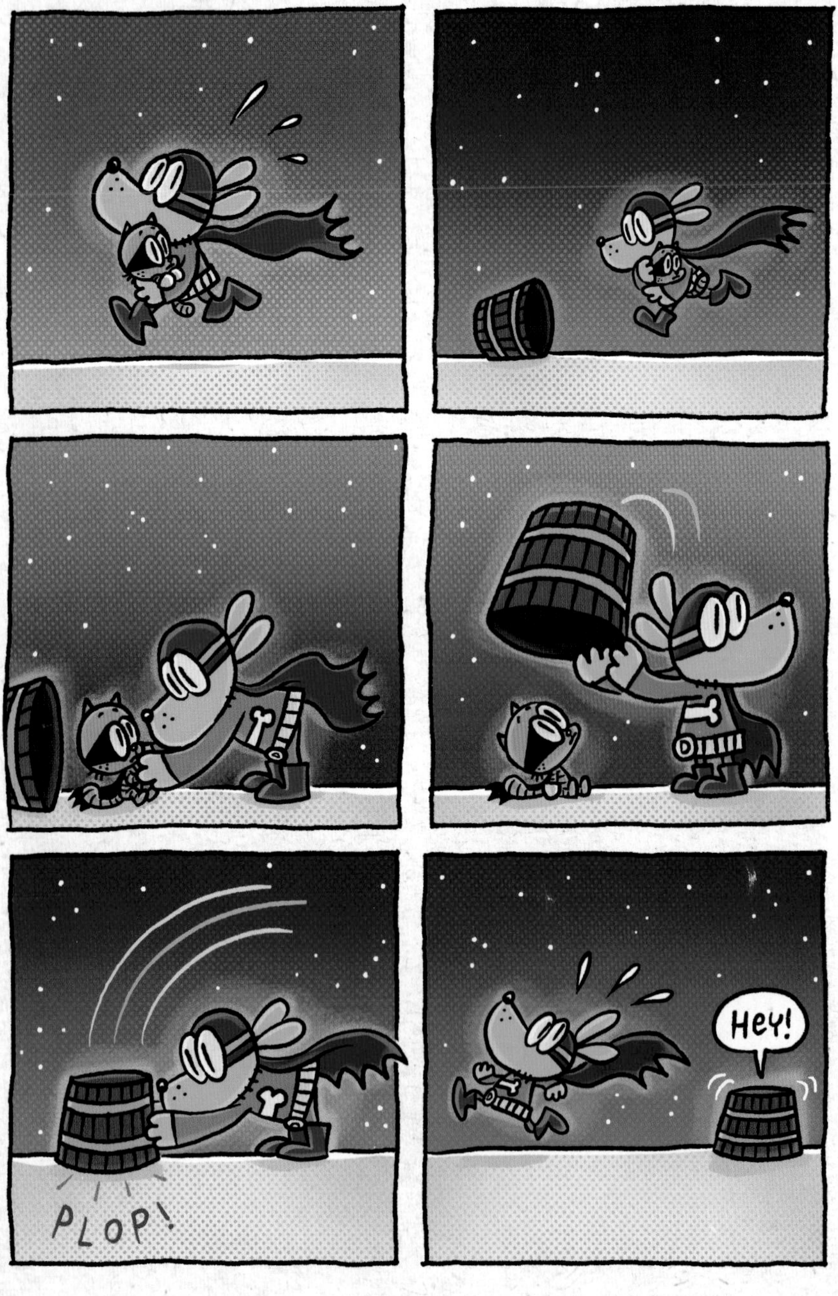
PLOP!
HEY!

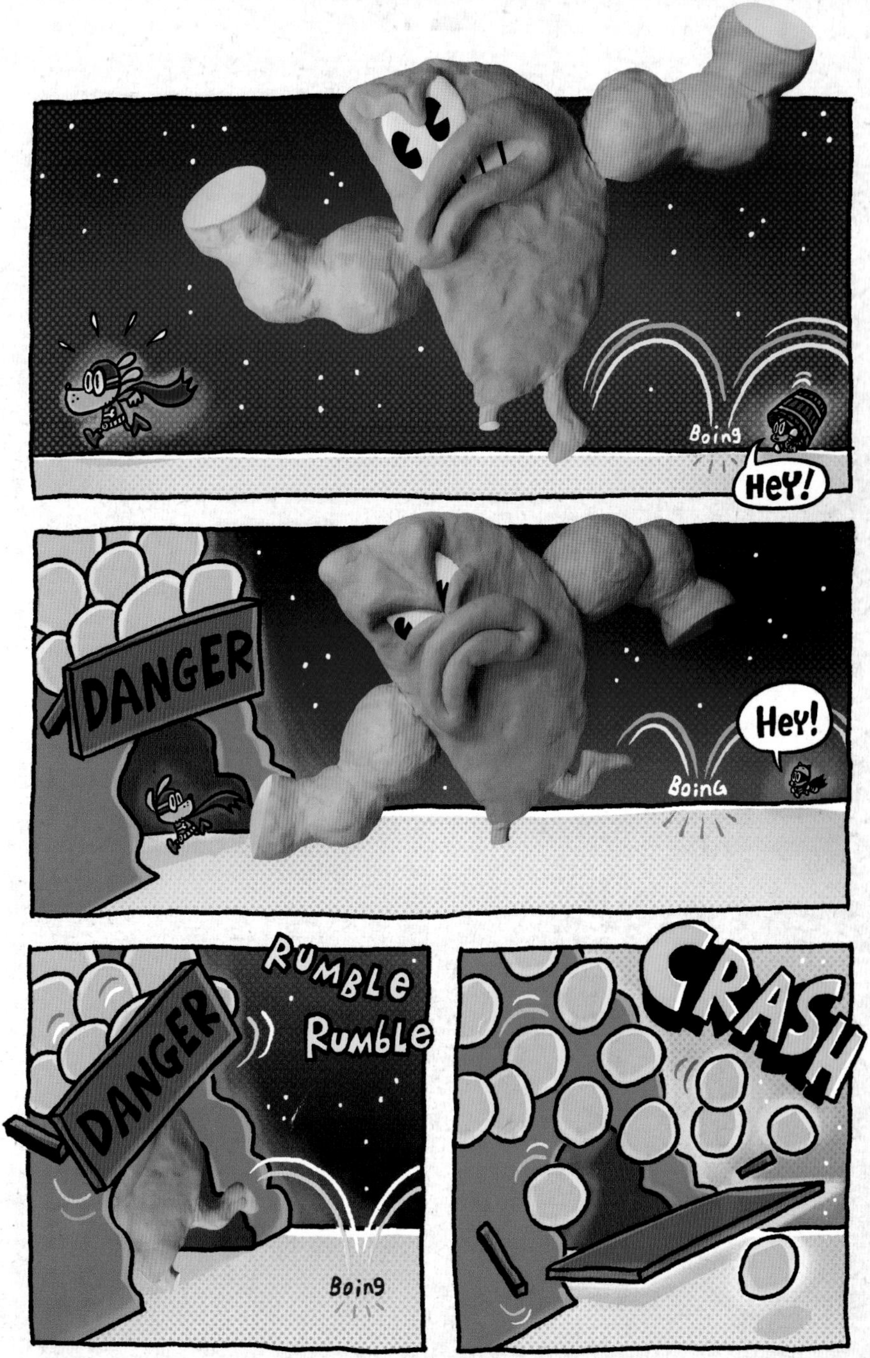
Boing
HEY!
DANGER
Boing
Hey!
DANGER
RUMBLE
Rumble
Boing
CRASH

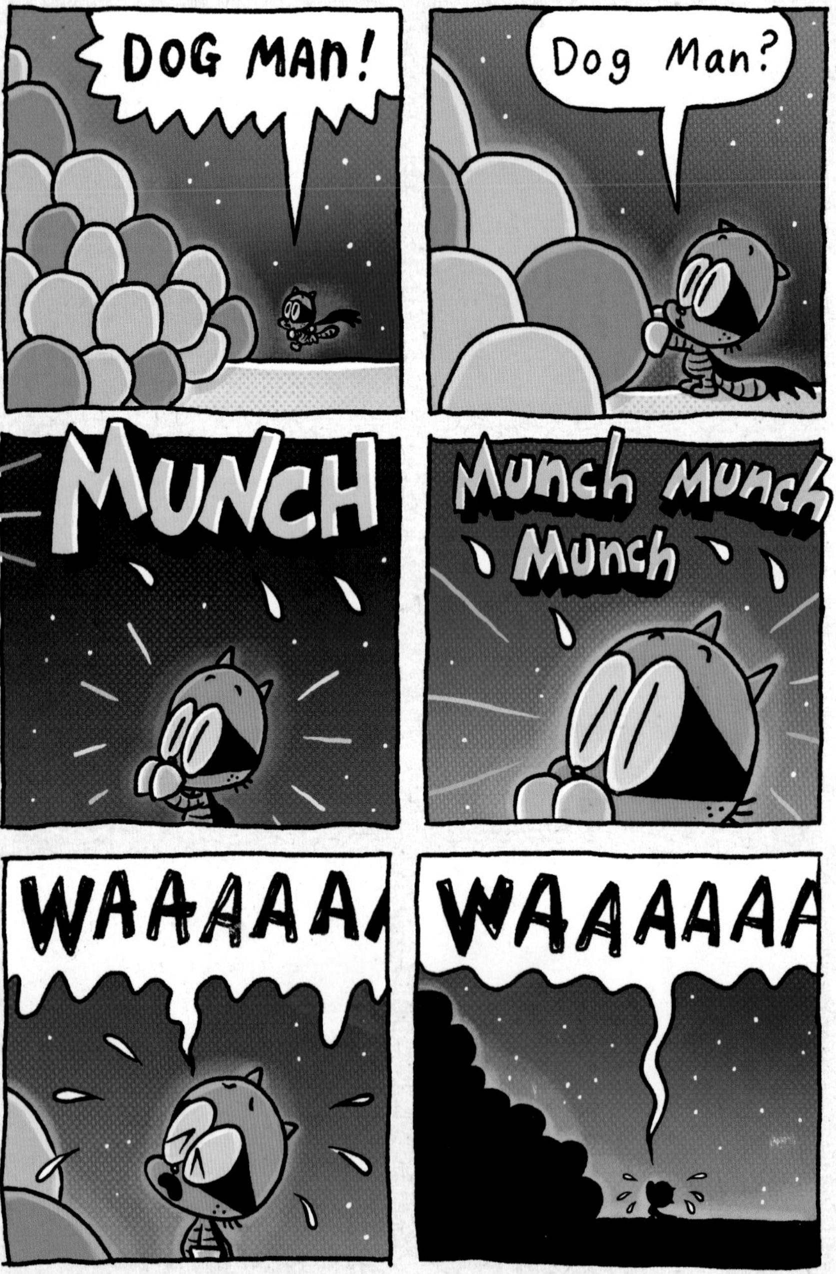
DOG MAN!
Dog Man?
MUNCH
Munch Munch
Munch
WAAAAAA
WAAAAAA

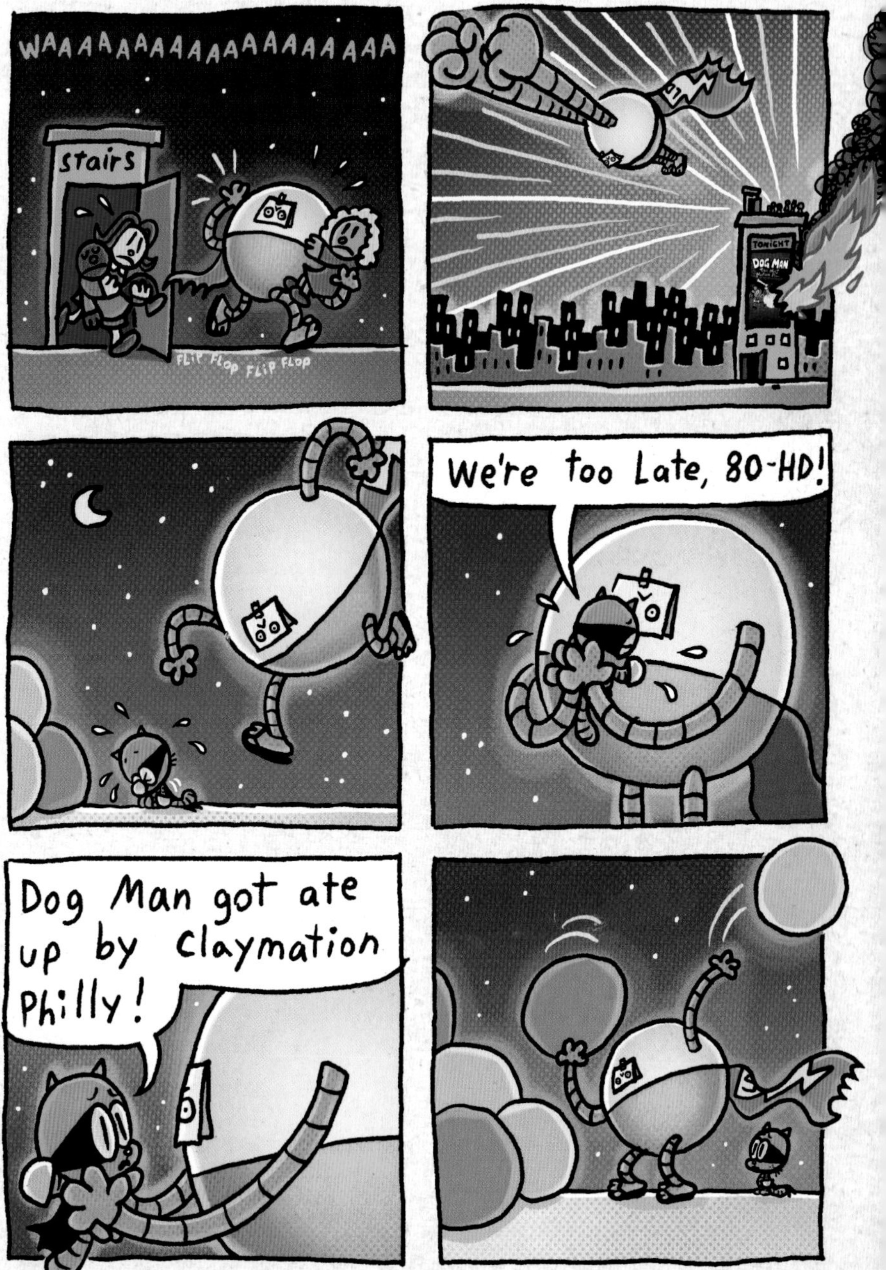
WAAAAAAAAAAAAAAAAAA
STAIRS
FLIP FLOP FLIP FLOP
TONIGHT
DOG MAN
We're too Late, 80-HD!
Dog Man got ate up by Claymation Philly!

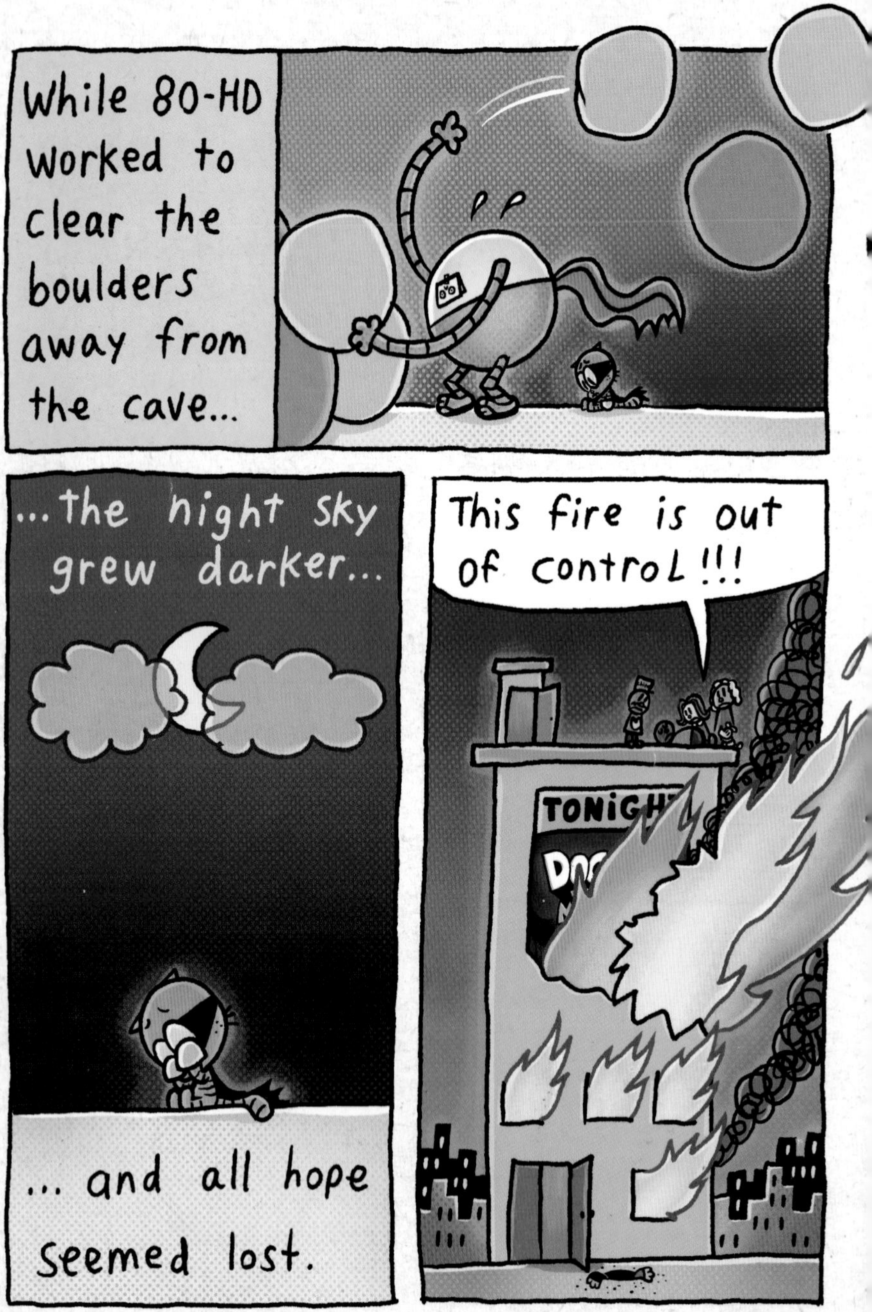
While 80-HD worked to clear the boulders away from the cave...
...the night sky grew darker...
... and all hope seemed lost.
This fire is out of control!!!

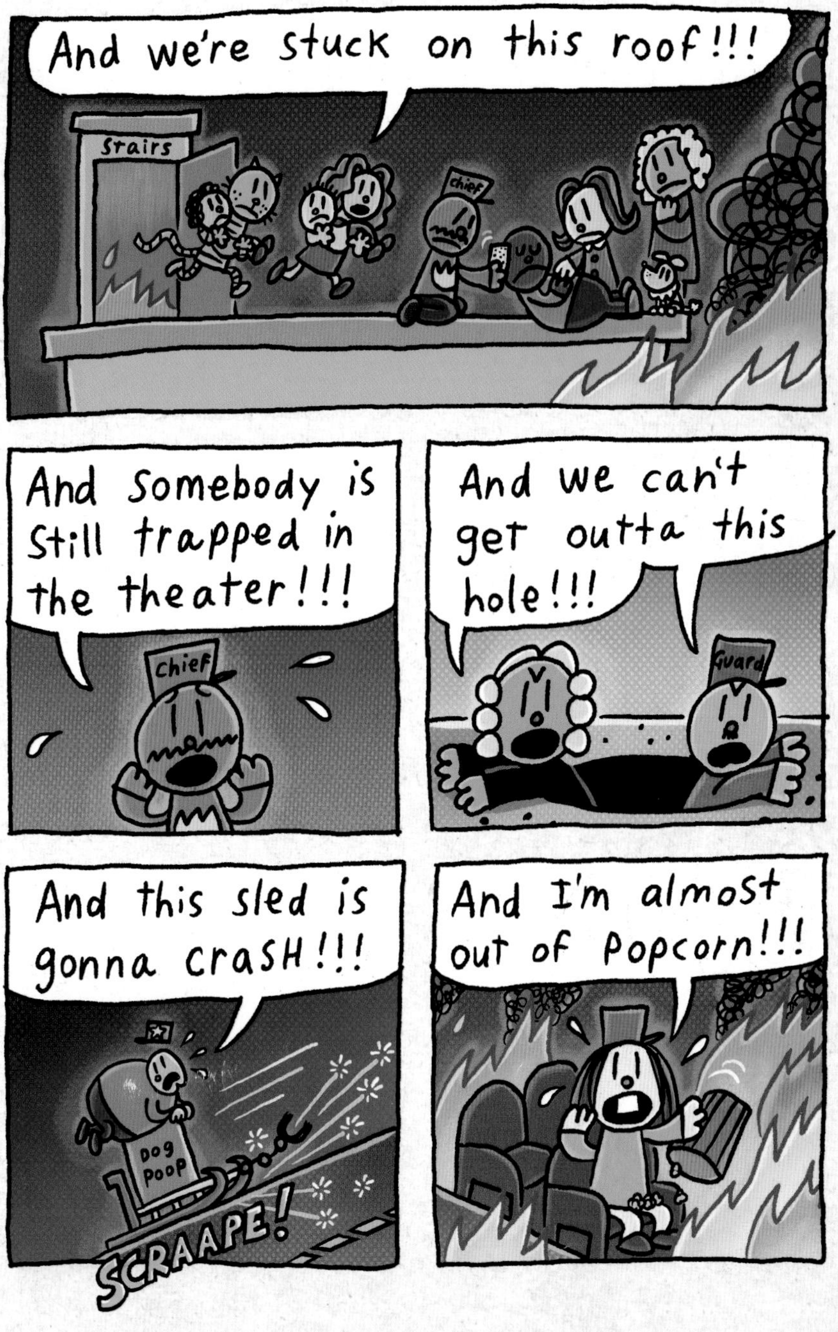
And we're stuck on this roof!!!
Stairs
chief
And somebody is still trapped in the theater!!!
Chief
And we can't get outta this hole!!!
Guard
And this sled is gonna CRASH!!!
DOG POOP
SCRAAPE!
And I'm almost out of popcorn!!!

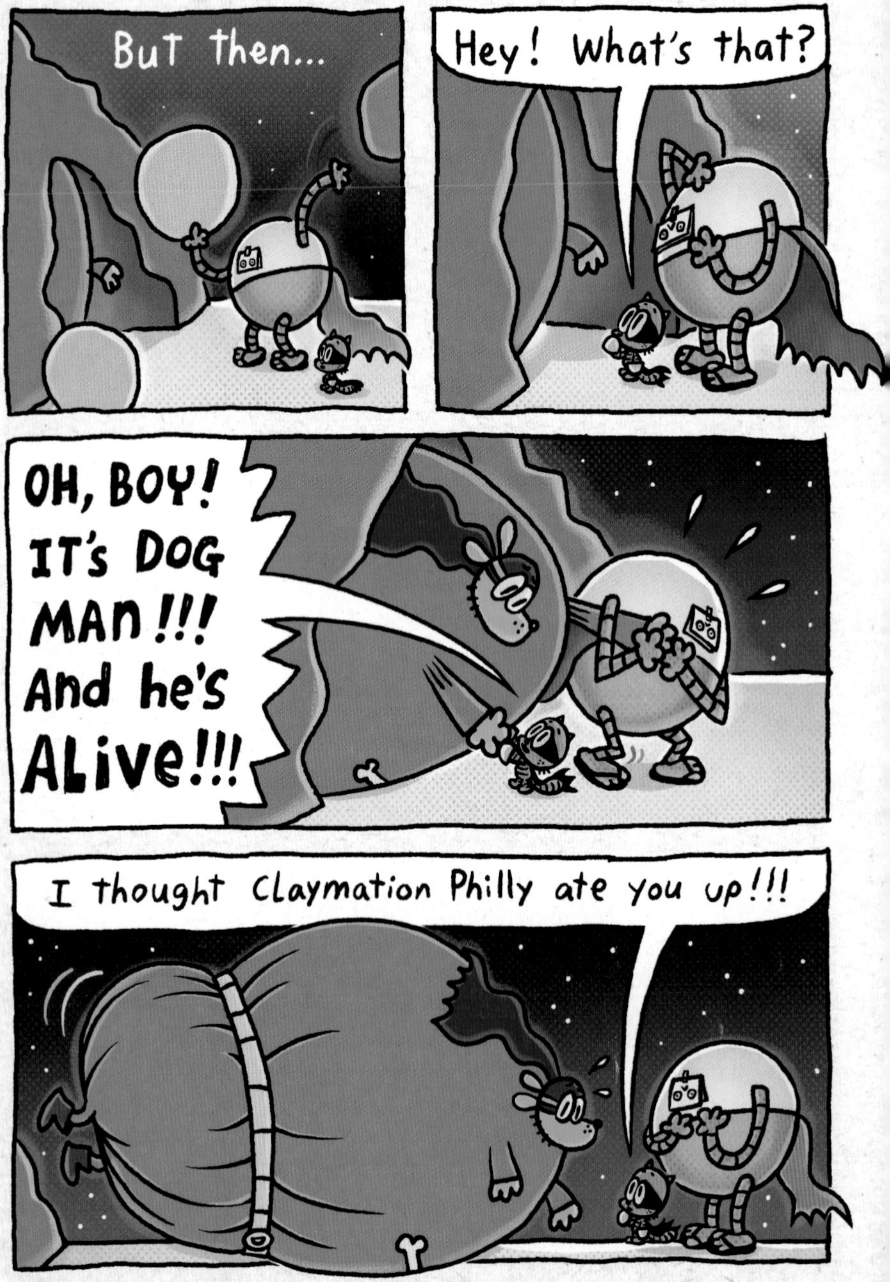
But then...
Hey! What's that?
OH, BOY! IT's DOG MAN!!! And he's ALive!!!
I thought Claymation Philly ate you up!!!

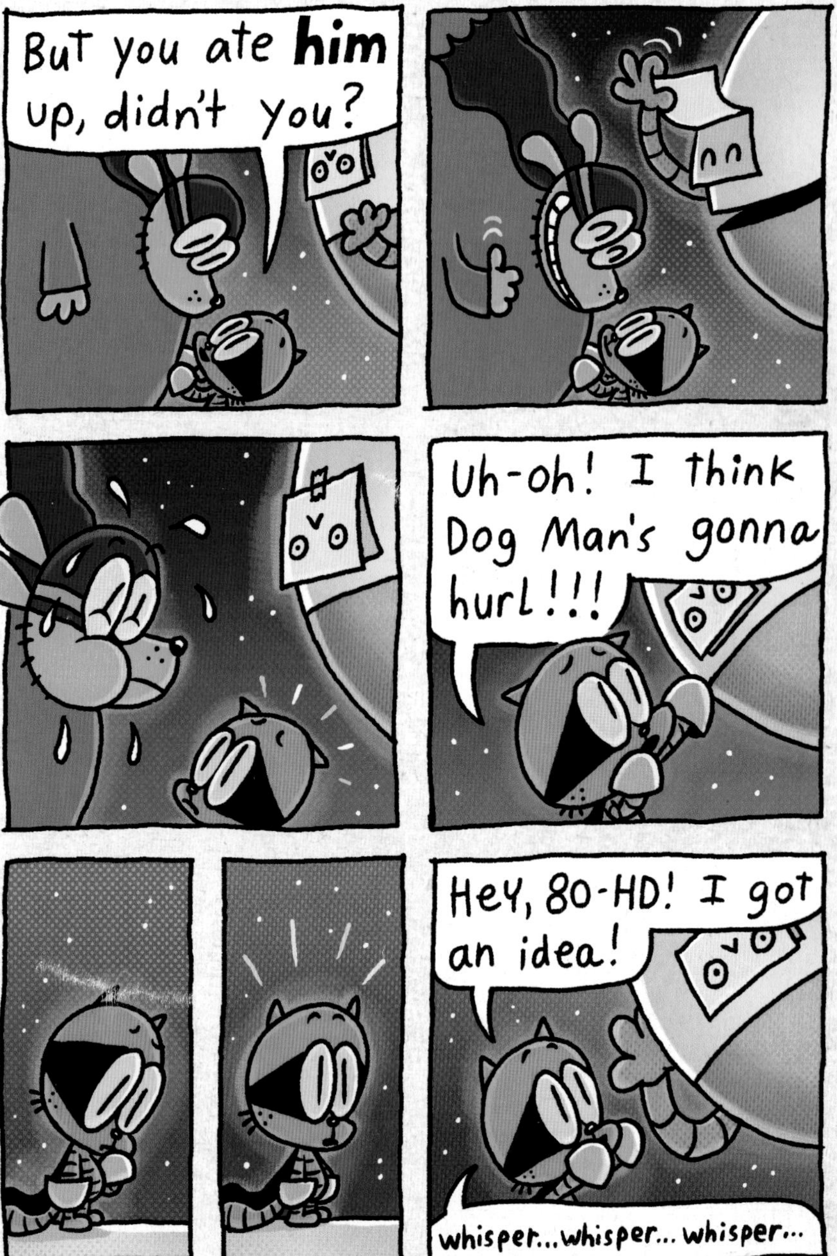
But you ate **him** up, didn't you?
Uh-oh! I think Dog Man's gonna hurl!!!
Hey, 80-HD! I got an idea!
whisper...whisper... whisper...

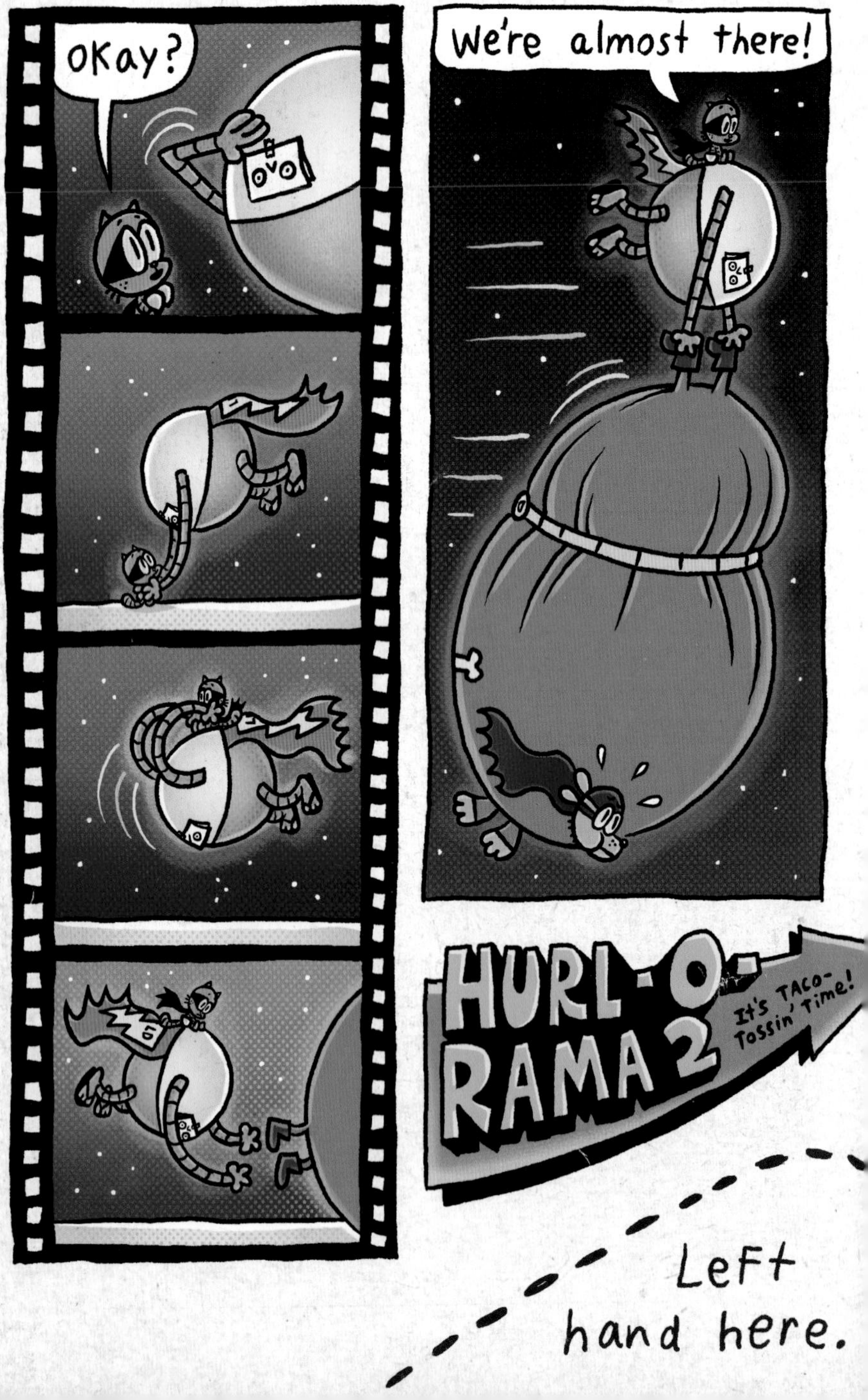
OKay?
We're almost there!
HURL-O-RAMA 2
It's TACO-Tossin' Time!
Left hand here.

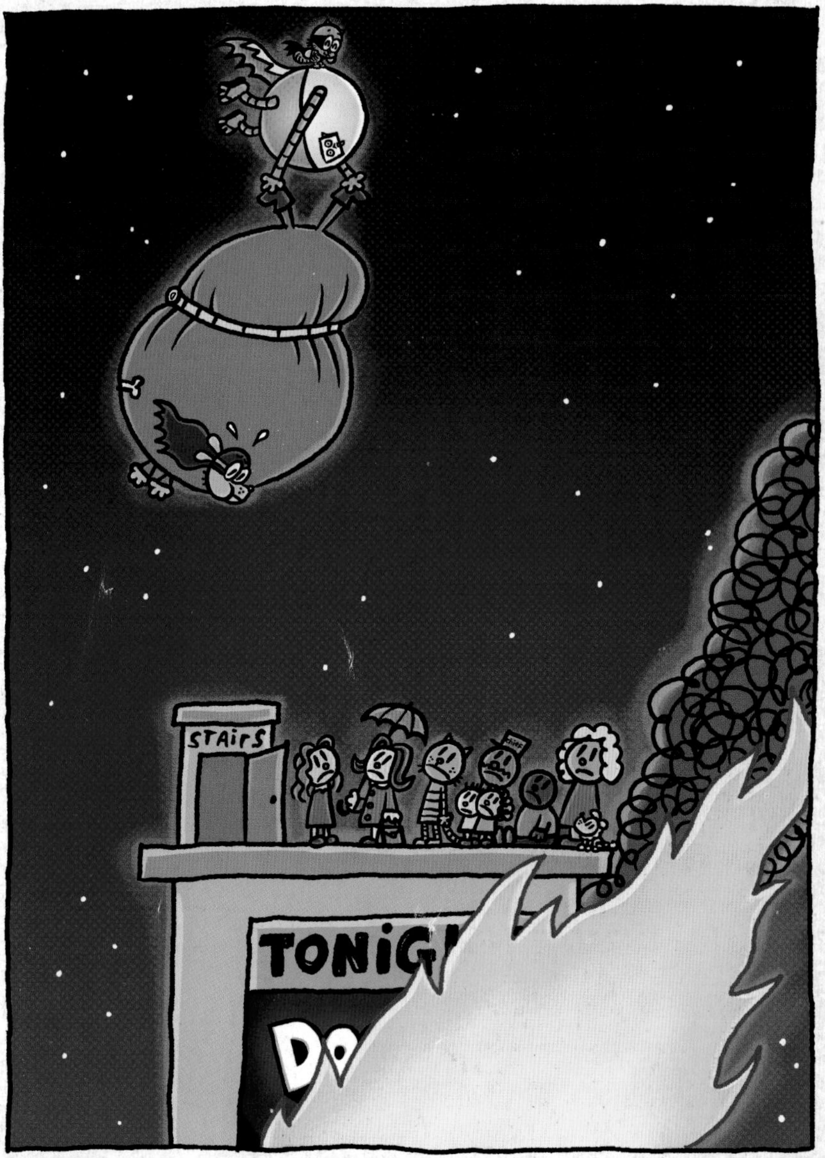
STAIRS
chief
TONIG
Do

Right Thumb here

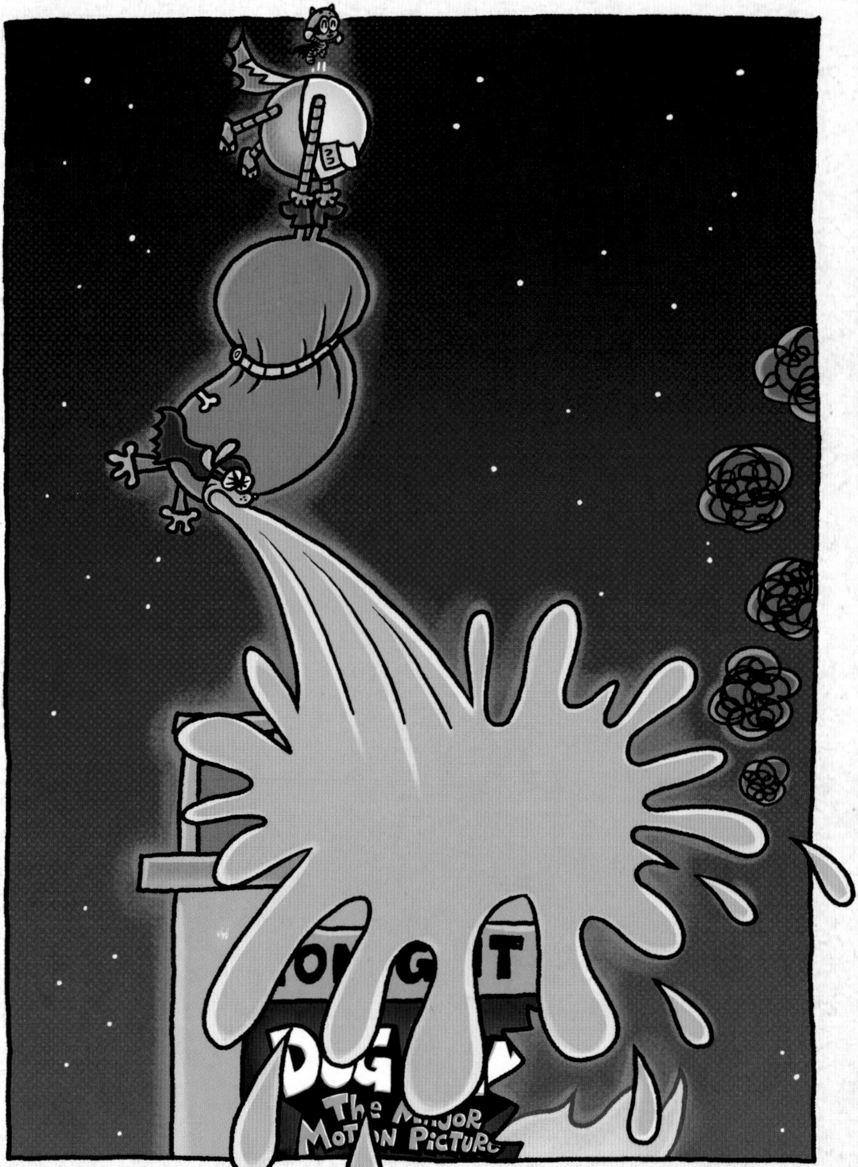

Dog Man barfed and barfed...

...until all the flames were put out.

Wow! Dog Man's Voluminous Vomit saved us all!!!

Isn't that **Great?**

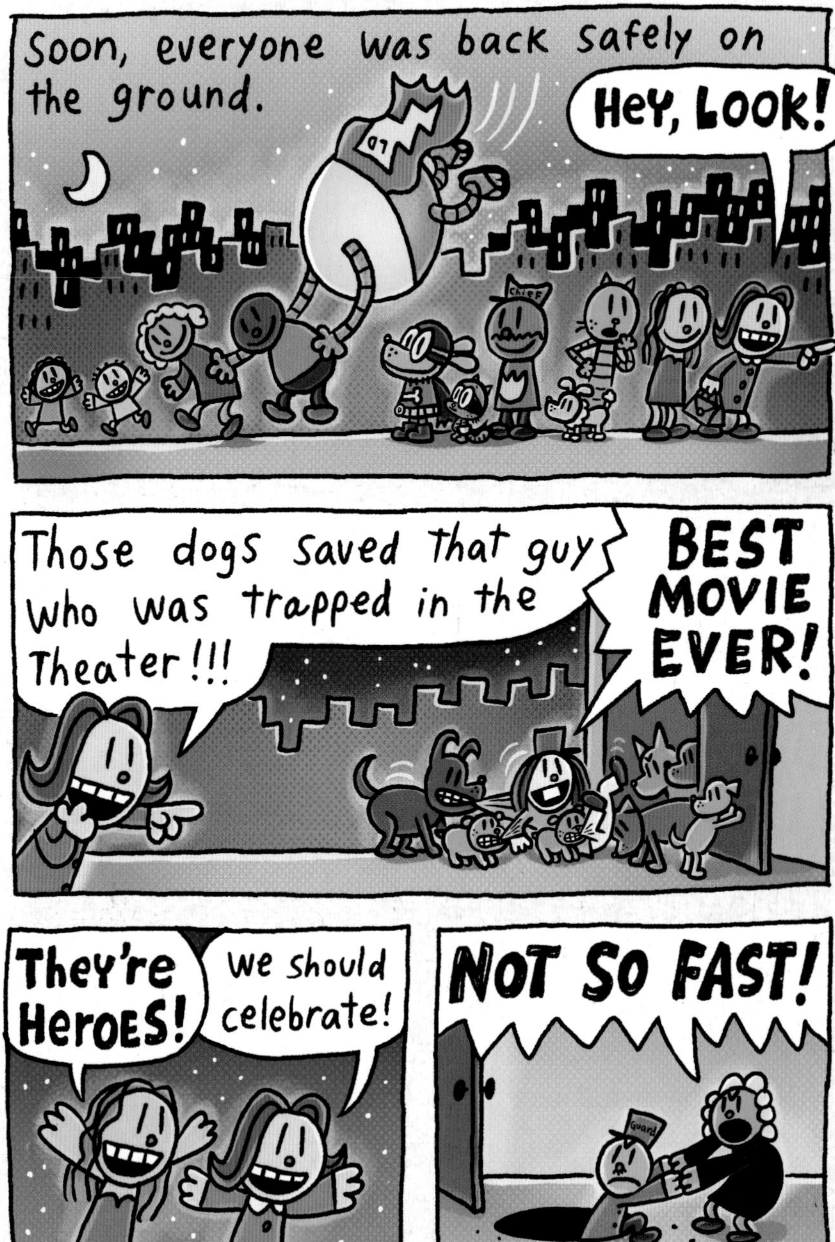
Soon, everyone was back safely on the ground.
HEY, LOOK!
CHIEF
Those dogs saved that guy who was trapped in the Theater!!!
BEST MOVIE EVER!
They're HEROES!
We should celebrate!
NOT SO FAST!
Guard

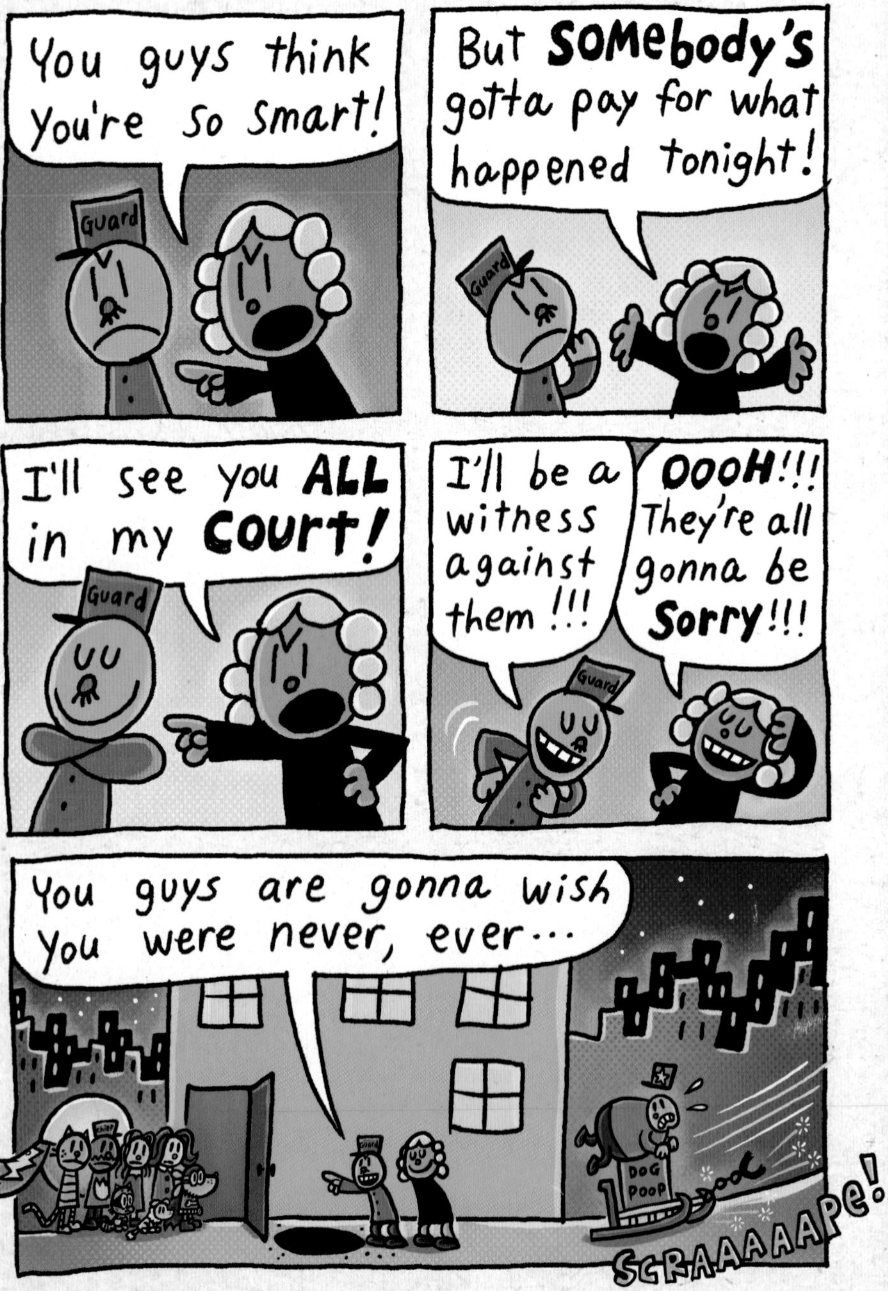
You guys think you're so smart!
But SOMEbody's gotta pay for what happened tonight!
Guard
I'll see you ALL in my COURT!
I'll be a witness against them!!!
OOOH!!! They're all gonna be Sorry!!!
You guys are gonna wish you were never, ever...
DOG POOP
SCRAAAAAPE!

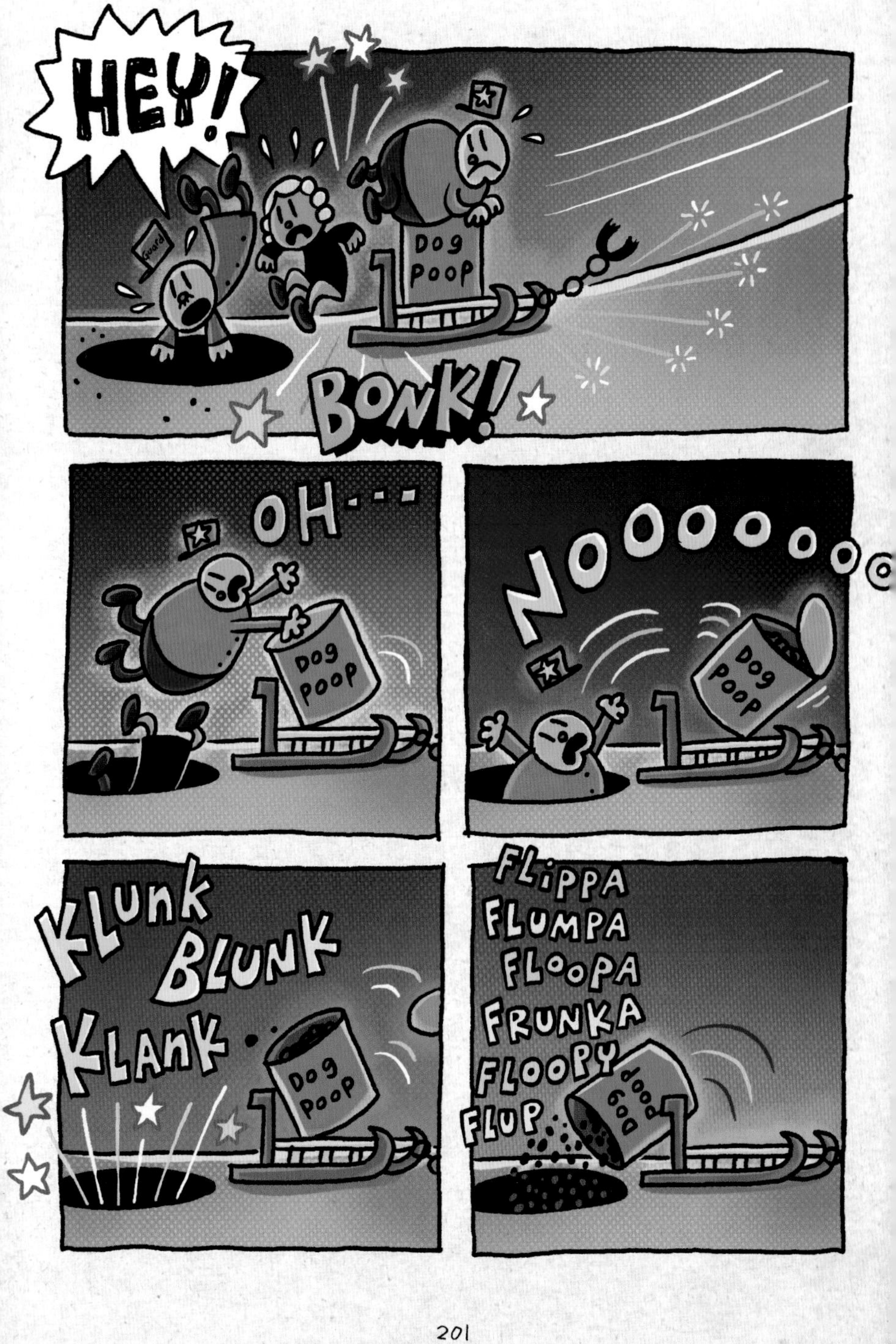
HEY!
Guard
Dog Poop
BONK!
OH...
Dog Poop
NOOOOOO
Dog Poop
KLUNK
BLUNK
KLANK
Dog Poop
FLIPPA
FLUMPA
FLOOPA
FRUNKA
FLOOPY
FLUP
Dog Poop

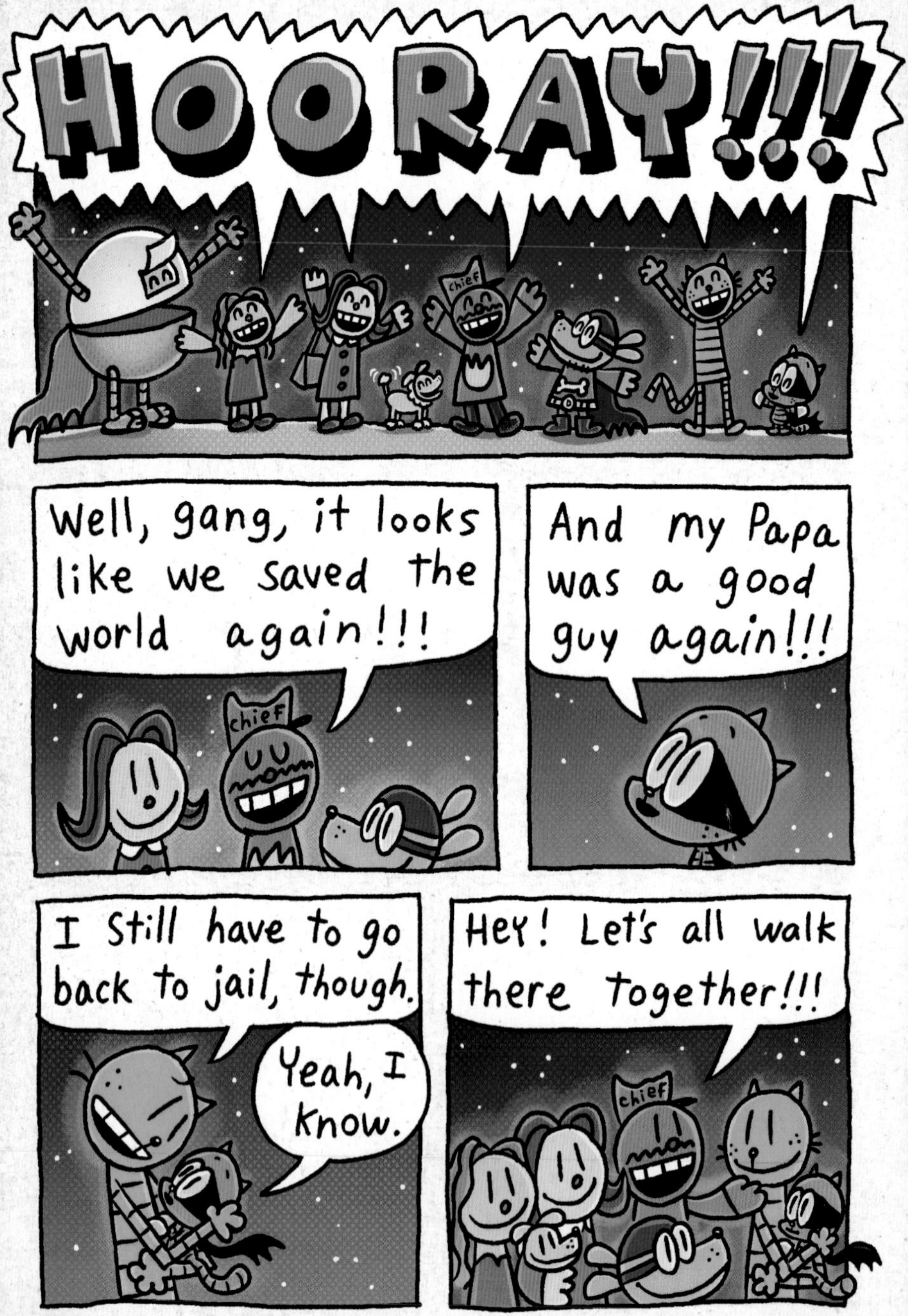
HOORAY!!!
chief
Well, gang, it looks like we saved the world again!!!
chief
And my Papa was a good guy again!!!
I still have to go back to jail, though.
Yeah, I know.
Hey! Let's all walk there together!!!
chief

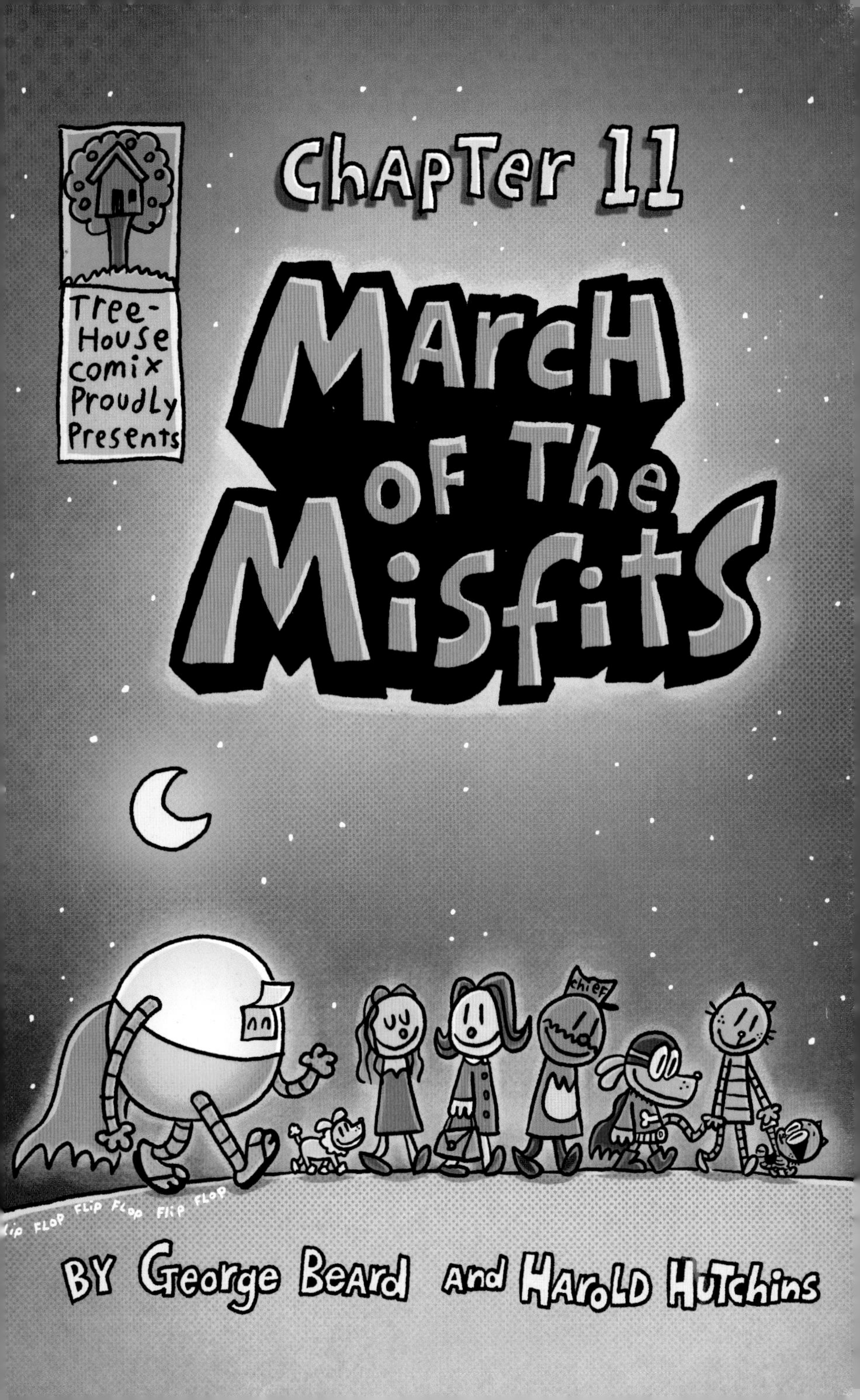
Tree-House comix Proudly Presents
ChapTer 11
MArcH of The Misfits
chief
FLOP FLiP FLop FLiP FLOP
BY George Beard And HAroLD HuTchins

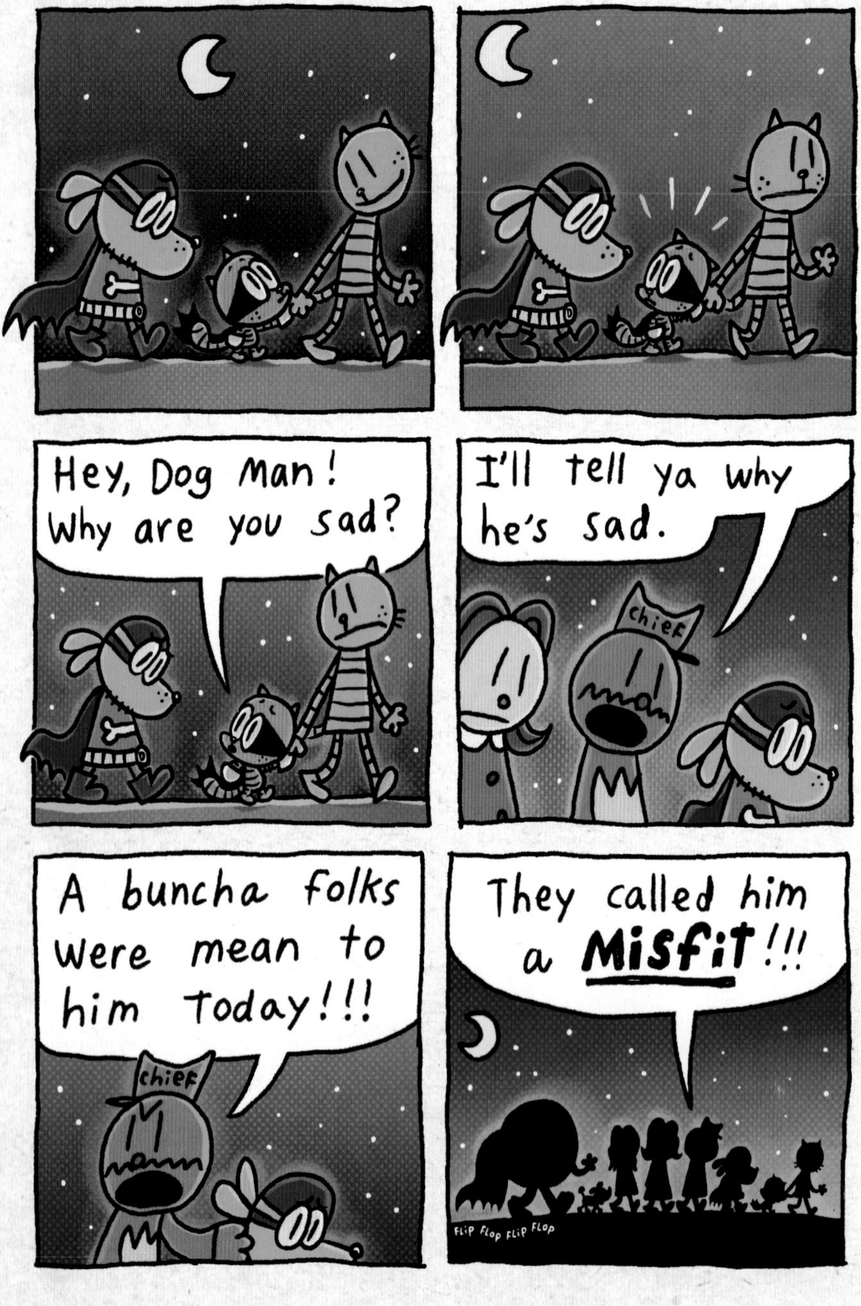
Hey, Dog Man! Why are you sad?
I'll tell ya why he's sad.
chief
A buncha folks were mean to him today!!!
chief
They called him a MISFIT!!!
FLIP FLOP FLIP FLOP

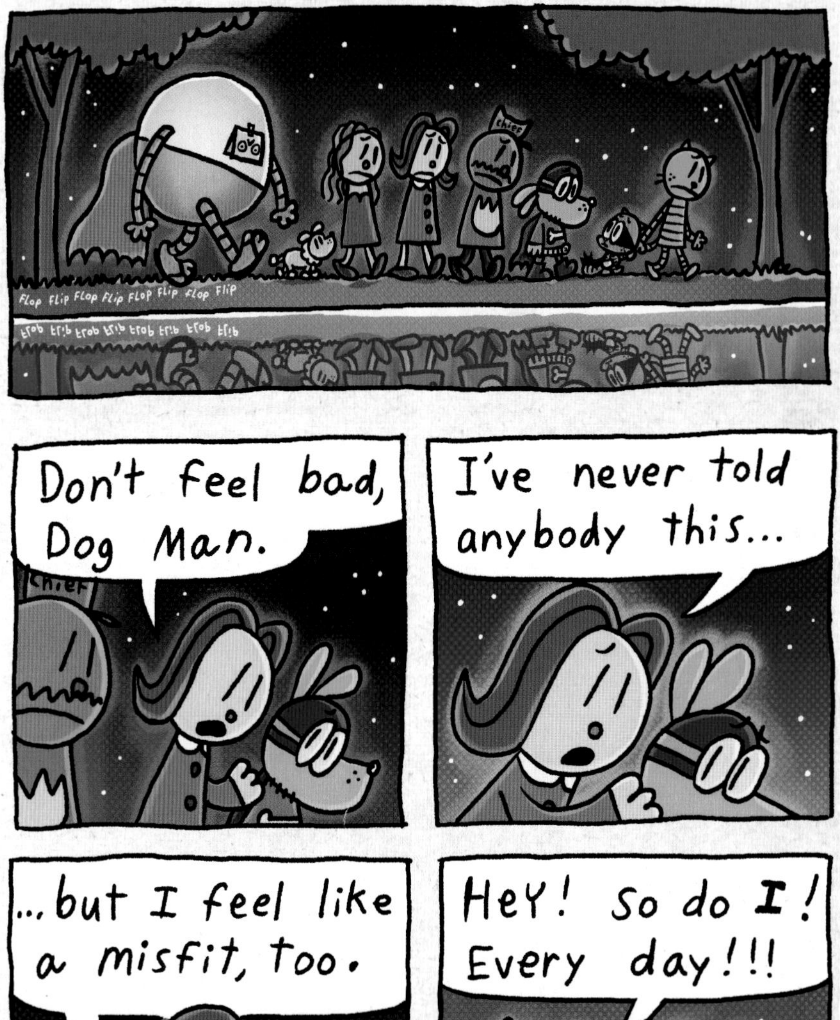
Flop Flip Flop Flip Flop Flip Flop Flip
Don't feel bad, Dog Man.
Chief
I've never told anybody this...
...but I feel like a misfit, too.
HeY! So do **I**! Every day!!!
Chief

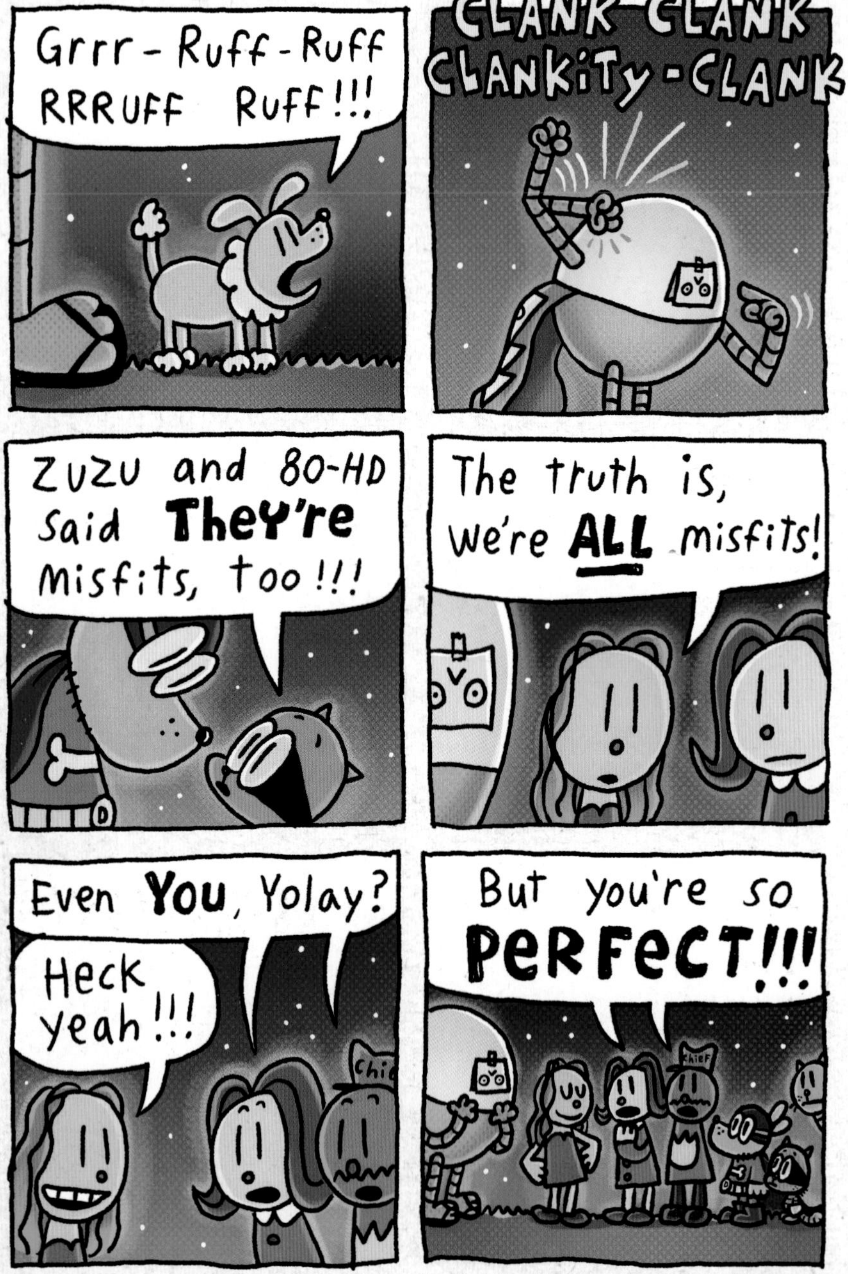
Grrr - Ruff - Ruff RRRUFF RUFF!!!
CLANK CLANK CLANKiTy - CLANK
ZUZU and 80-HD said They're misfits, too!!!
The truth is, we're ALL misfits!
Even YOU, Yolay?
Heck yeah!!!
But you're so PERFECT!!!

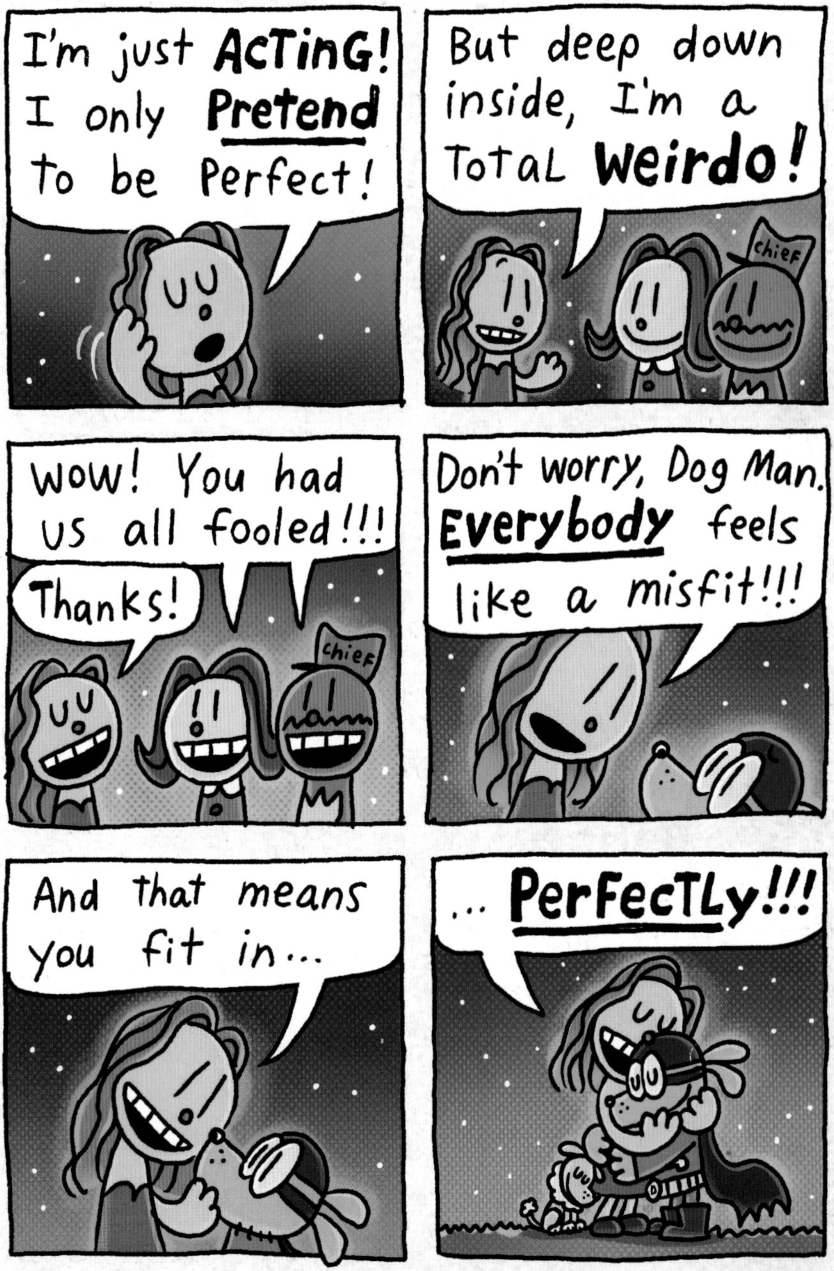
I'm just ACTING! I only Pretend to be Perfect!
But deep down inside, I'm a Total Weirdo!
chief
WOW! You had us all fooled!!!
Thanks!
chief
Don't worry, Dog Man. Everybody feels like a misfit!!!
And that means you fit in...
... PerfecTLy!!!

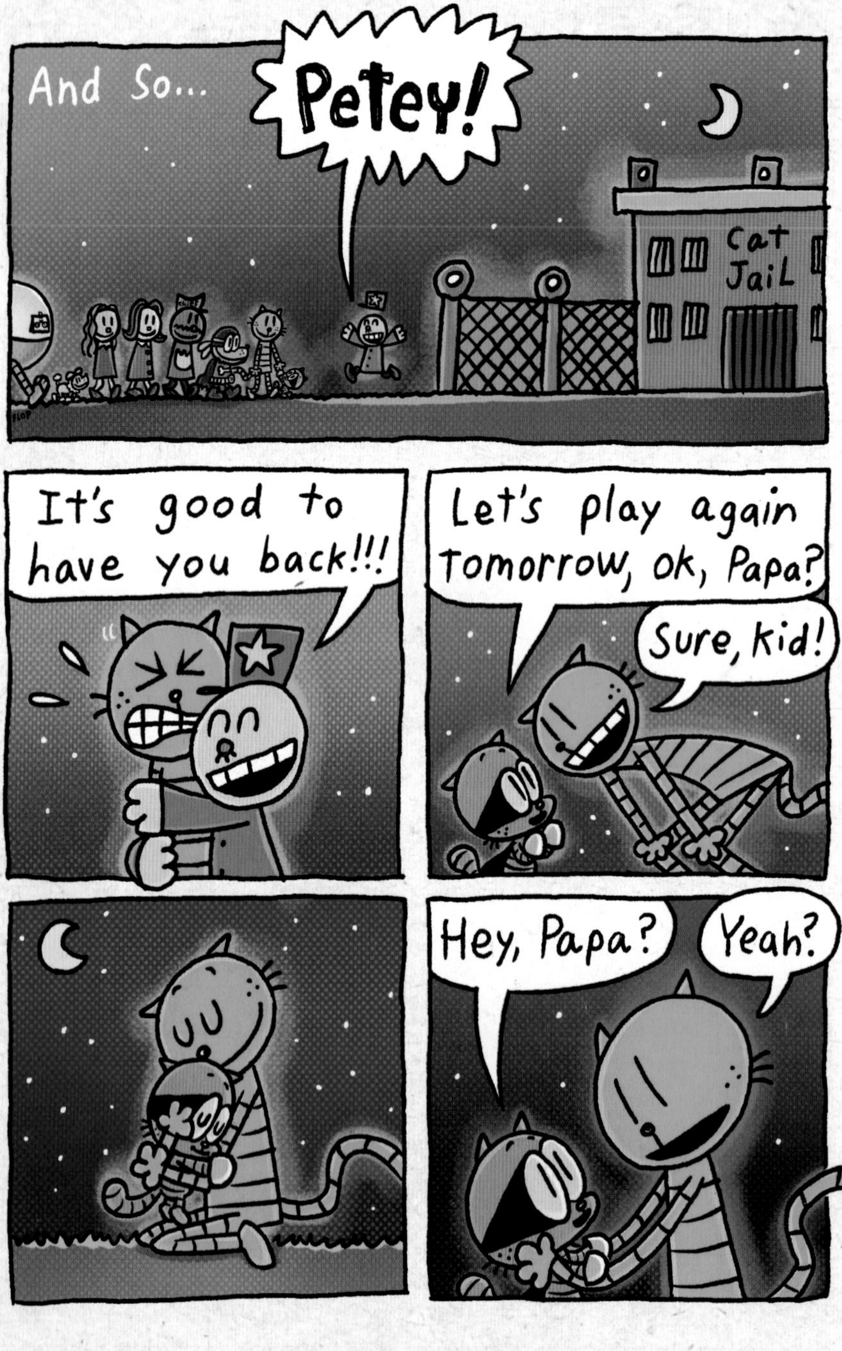
And So...
Petey!
Cat Jail
It's good to have you back!!!
Let's play again Tomorrow, ok, Papa?
Sure, kid!
Hey, Papa?
Yeah?

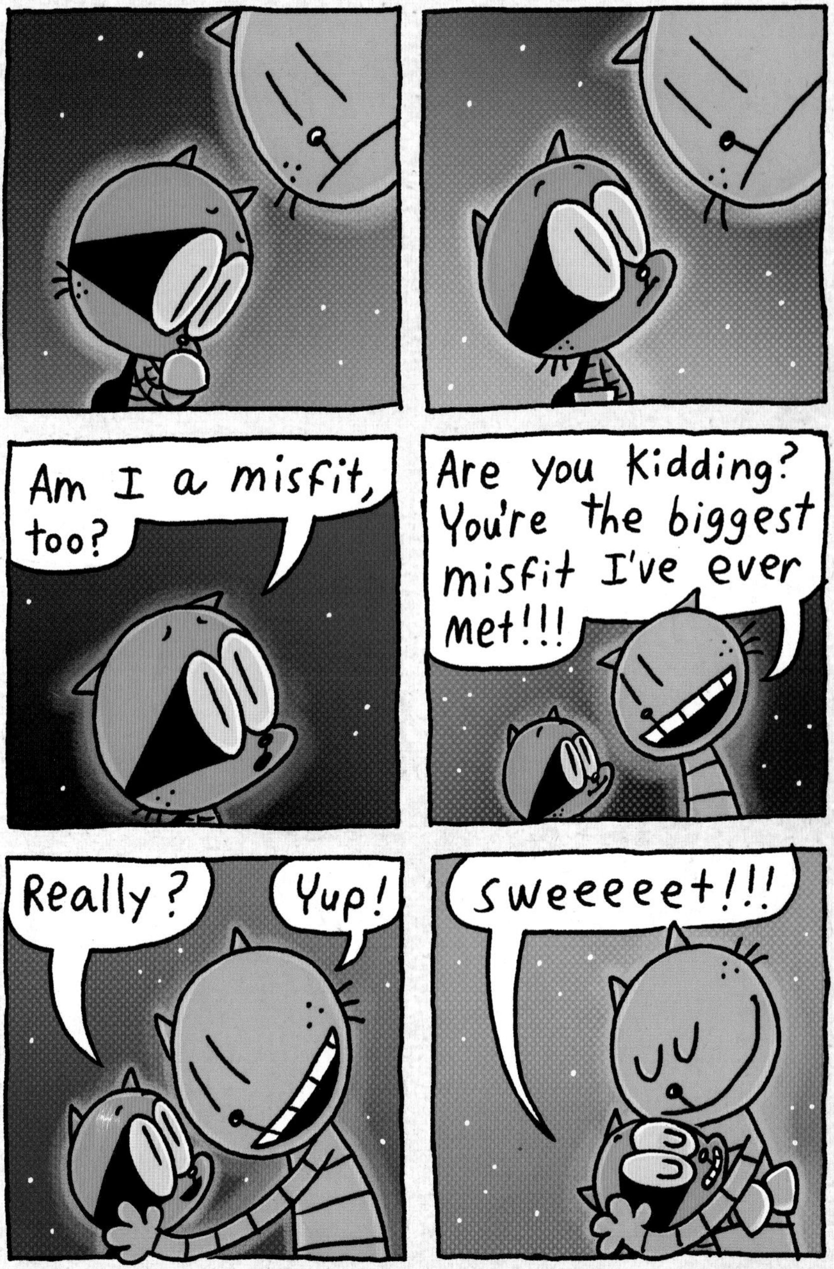
Am I a misfit, too?
Are you kidding? You're the biggest misfit I've ever met!!!
Really?
Yup!
Sweeeeet!!!

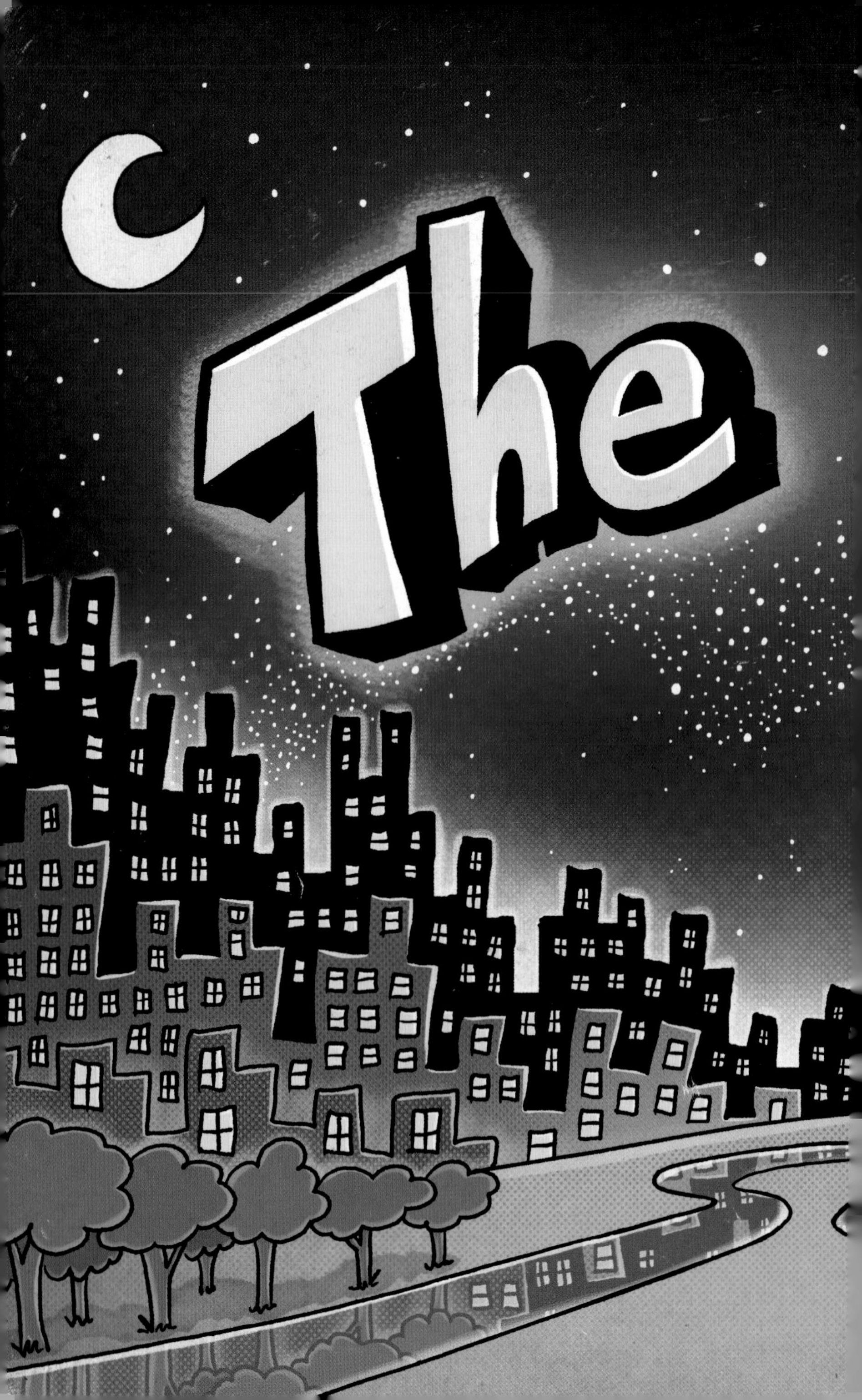
The

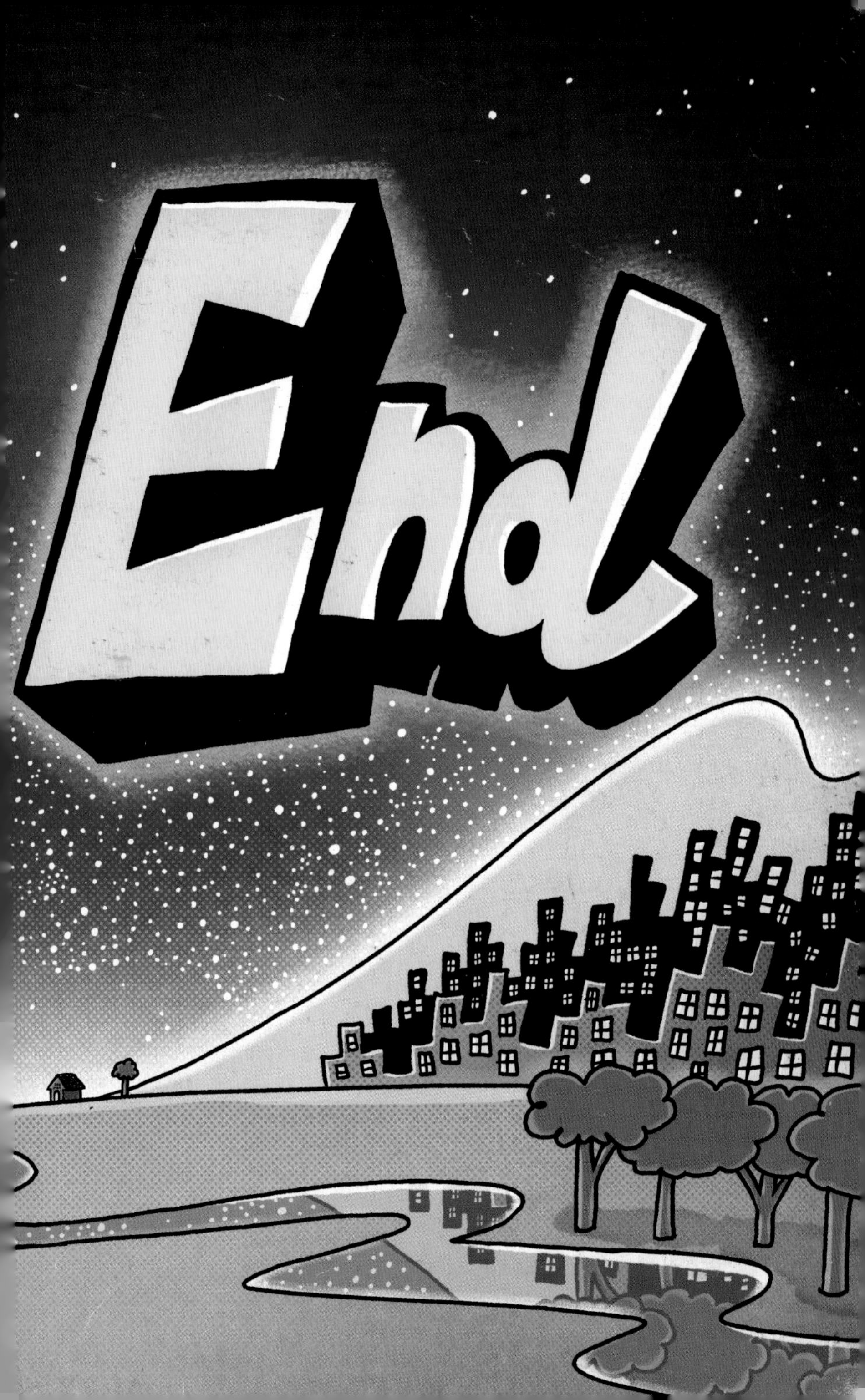
End

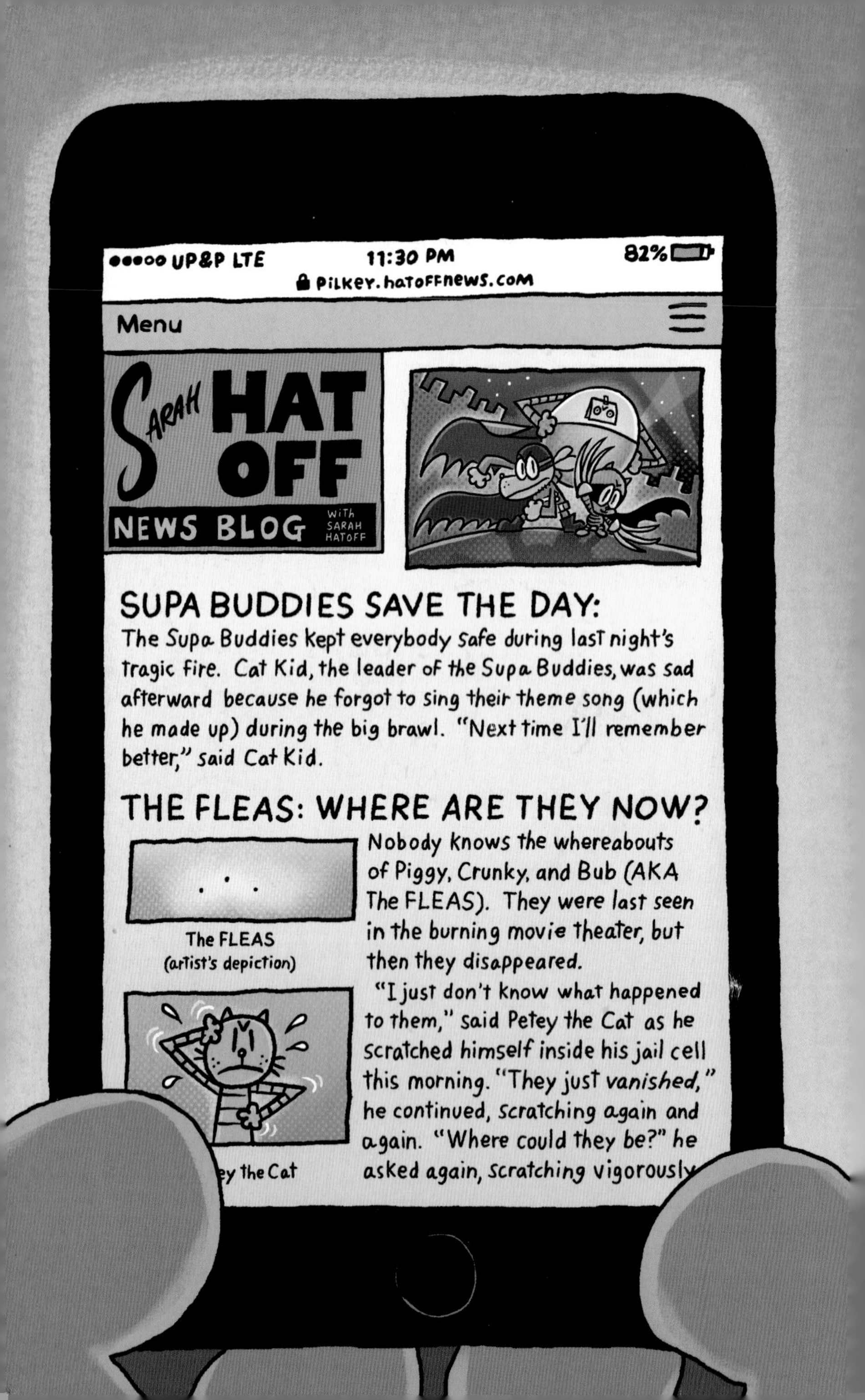

●●●○○ UP&P LTE
11:30 PM
82%
pilkey.hatoffnews.com
Menu
SARAH HAT OFF
NEWS BLOG
WITH SARAH HATOFF
SUPA BUDDIES SAVE THE DAY:
The Supa Buddies kept everybody safe during last night's tragic fire. Cat Kid, the leader of the Supa Buddies, was sad afterward because he forgot to sing their theme song (which he made up) during the big brawl. "Next time I'll remember better," said Cat Kid.
THE FLEAS: WHERE ARE THEY NOW?
The FLEAS
(artist's depiction)
Nobody knows the whereabouts of Piggy, Crunky, and Bub (AKA The FLEAS). They were last seen in the burning movie theater, but then they disappeared.
"I just don't know what happened to them," said Petey the Cat as he scratched himself inside his jail cell this morning. "They just vanished," he continued, scratching again and again. "Where could they be?" he asked again, scratching vigorousl
ey the Cat

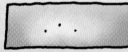

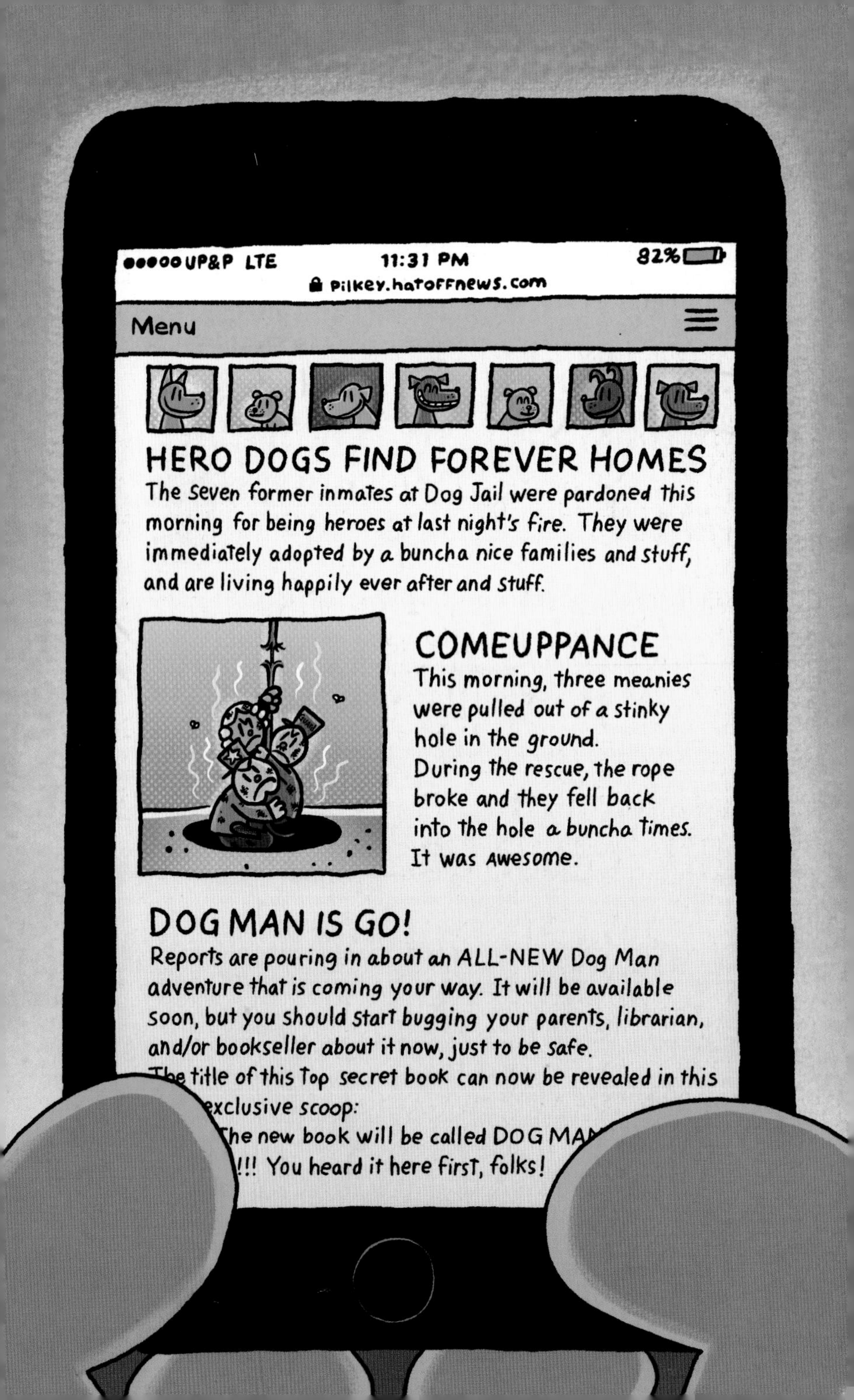
●●●●○ UP&P LTE
11:31 PM
82%
pilkey.hatoffnews.com
Menu
HERO DOGS FIND FOREVER HOMES
The seven former inmates at Dog Jail were pardoned this morning for being heroes at last night's fire. They were immediately adopted by a buncha nice families and stuff, and are living happily ever after and stuff.
COMEUPPANCE
This morning, three meanies were pulled out of a stinky hole in the ground.
During the rescue, the rope broke and they fell back into the hole a buncha times.
It was awesome.
DOG MAN IS GO!
Reports are pouring in about an ALL-NEW Dog Man adventure that is coming your way. It will be available soon, but you should start bugging your parents, librarian, and/or bookseller about it now, just to be safe.
title of this top secret book can now be revealed in this
xclusive scoop:
The new book will be called DOG MA
!!! You heard it here first, folks!

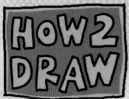

HOW 2 DRAW CAT KiD

in 49 Ridiculously easy steps!

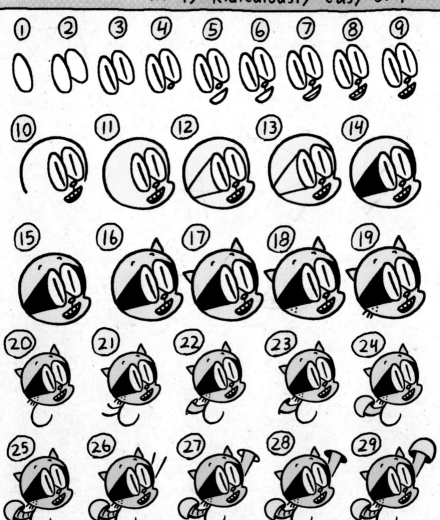

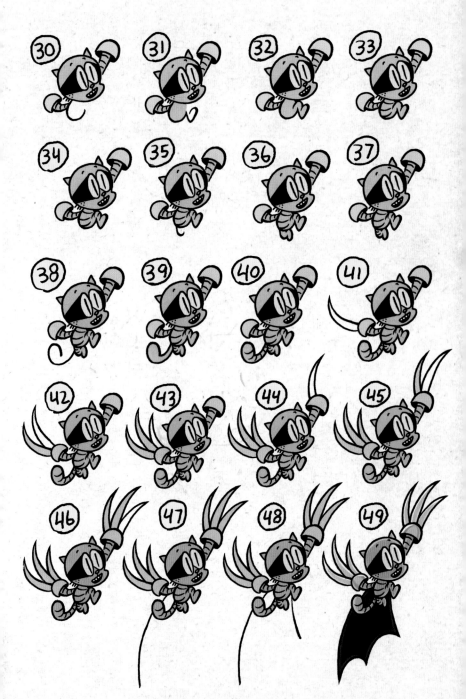

HOW 2 DRAW LIGHTNING DUDE

in 33 Ridiculously easy steps!

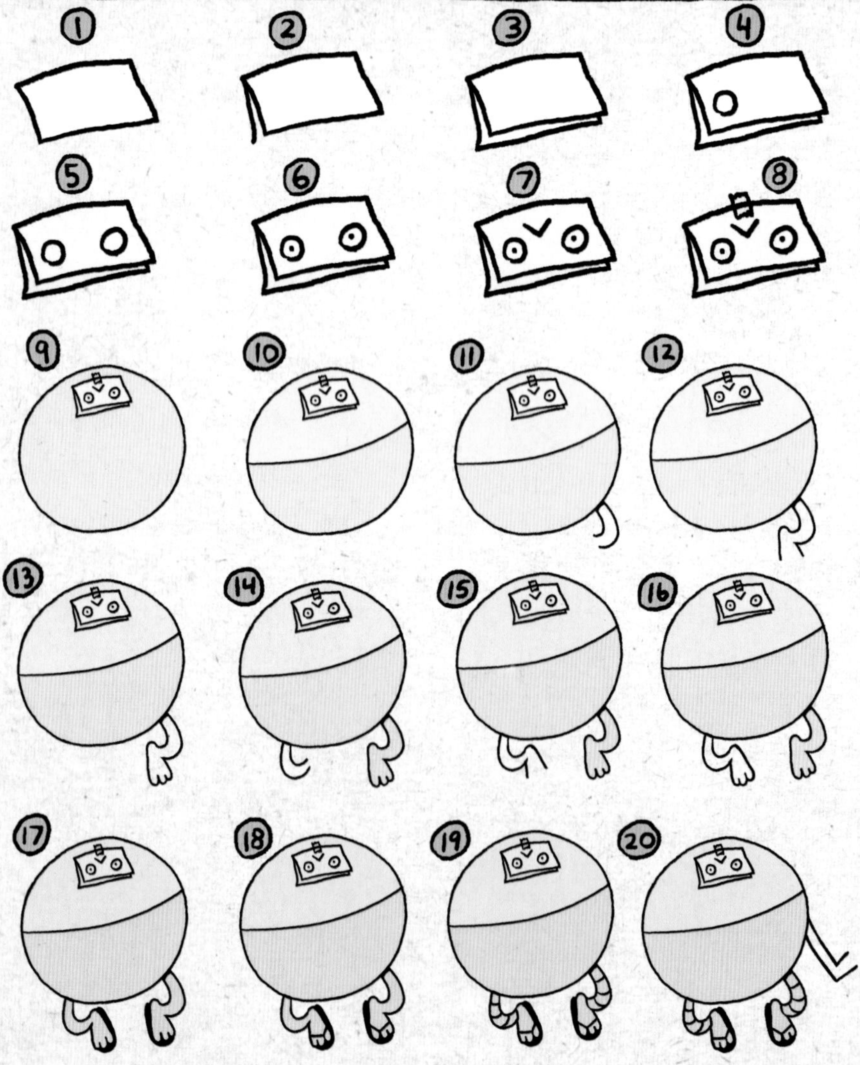
1
2
3
4
5
6
7
8
9
10
11
12
13
14
15
16
17
18
19
20

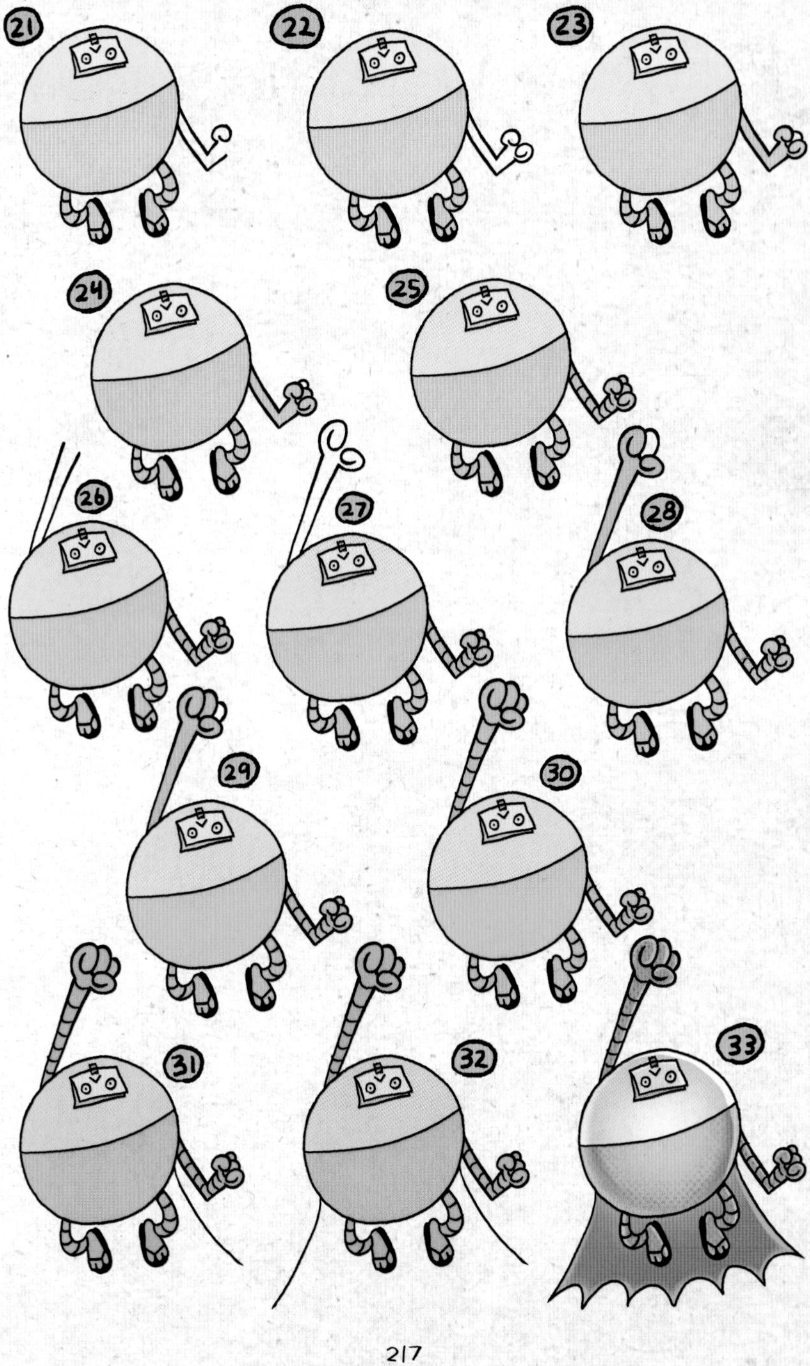
21
22
23
24
25
26
27
28
29
30
31
32
33

HOW 2 DRAW THE BARK KNIGHT

in 46 Ridiculously easy Steps!

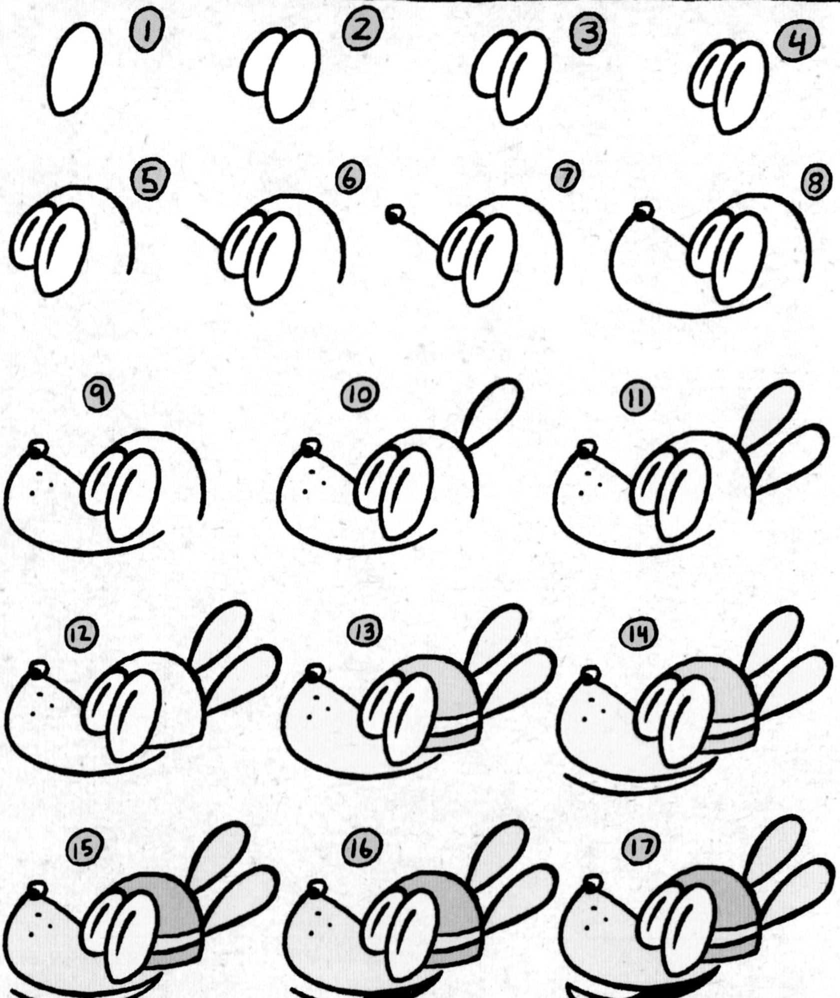
1
2
3
4
5
6
7
8
9
10
11
12
13
14
15
16
17

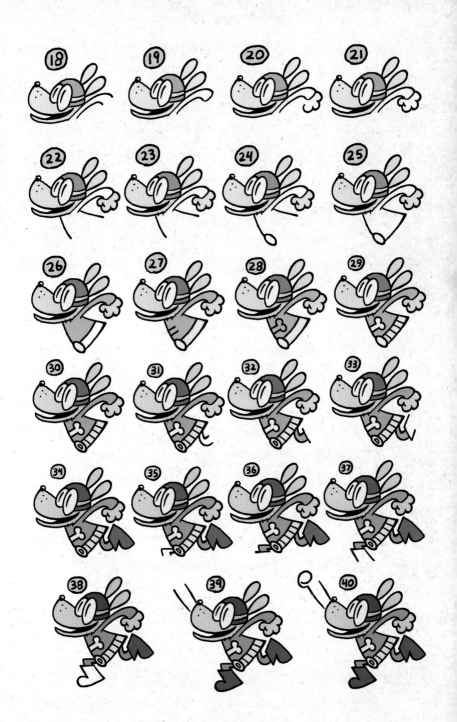

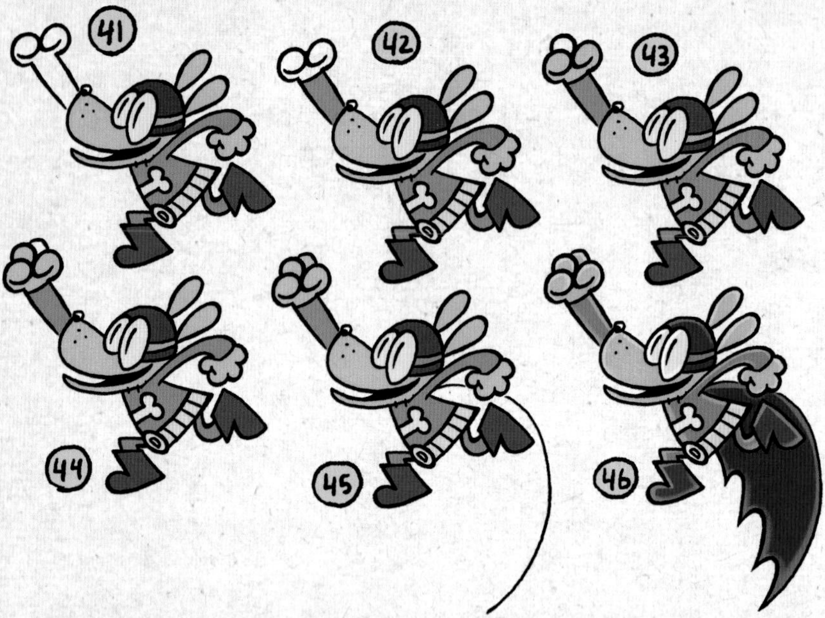
41
42
43
44
45
46

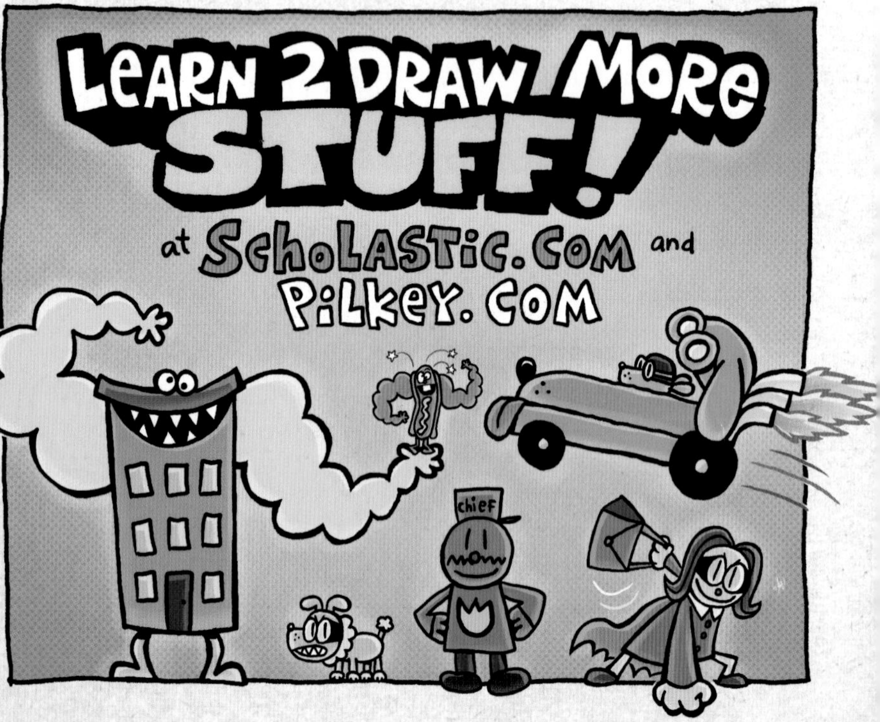
LEARN 2 DRAW MORE
STUFF!
at SCHOLASTIC.COM and
PILKEY.COM
chief

HOW 2 DRAW the FLEAS

in **3** Ridiculously easy steps!

① · ② ·· ③ ··

BONUS SECTION

Learn to draw the FLEAS
in these Exciting Natural Habitats:

in a snowstorm

at night

in the fog

at the beach

in outer space

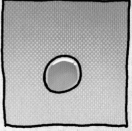

behind a grape

GET READING WITH DAV PILKEY!

The Adventures of
CAPTAIN UNDERPANTS
FULL COLOR
Action
Thrills
Laffs
THE FIRST EPIC NOVEL BY
DAV PILKEY
CALDECOTT HONOR ARTIST

FULL COLOR
CAPTAIN UNDERPANTS
AND THE ATTACK OF THE TALKING TOILETS
More Action
More Laffs
More Flip-o-Rama
THE SECOND EPIC NOVEL BY
DAV PILKEY
CALDECOTT HONOR ARTIST

FULL COLOR
CAPTAIN UNDERPANTS
AND THE INVASION OF THE INCREDIBLY NAUGHTY CAFETERIA LADIES FROM OUTER SPACE (and the Subsequent Assault of the Equally Evil Lunchroom Zombie Nerds)
Tons-o-Fun
Lots-o-Laffs
Flip-o-Rama
THE THIRD EPIC NOVEL BY
DAV PILKEY
CALDECOTT HONOR ARTIST

FULL COLOR
CAPTAIN UNDERPANTS
AND THE PERILOUS PLOT OF PROFESSOR POOPYPANTS
THE FOURTH EPIC NOVEL BY
DAV PILKEY
CALDECOTT HONOR ARTIST

FULL COLOR
CAPTAIN UNDERPANTS
AND THE WRATH OF THE WICKED WEDGIE WOMAN
THE FIFTH EPIC NOVEL BY
DAV PILKEY
CALDECOTT HONOR ARTIST

FULL COLOR
CAPTAIN UNDERPANTS
AND THE BIG, BAD BATTLE OF THE BIONIC BOOGER BOY
PART 1: THE NIGHT OF THE NASTY NOSTRIL NUGGETS
THE SIXTH EPIC NOVEL BY
DAV PILKEY
CALDECOTT HONOR ARTIST

PLANET PILKEY

Download the free Planet Pilkey app to start your digital adventure! Create an avatar, make your own comics, and more at planetpilkey.com!

Download on the App Store

GET IT ON Google Play

PLANET PILKEY

SCHOLASTIC

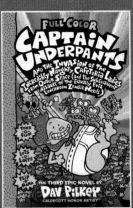

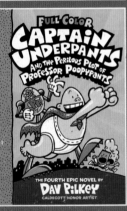

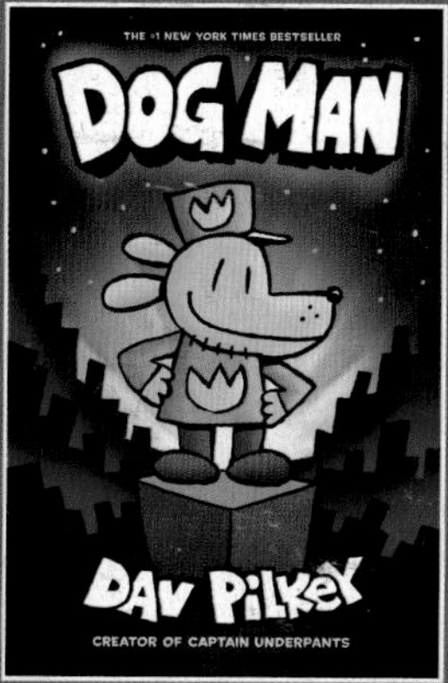
THE #1 NEW YORK TIMES BESTSELLER
DOG MAN
DAV PILKEY
CREATOR OF CAPTAIN UNDERPANTS

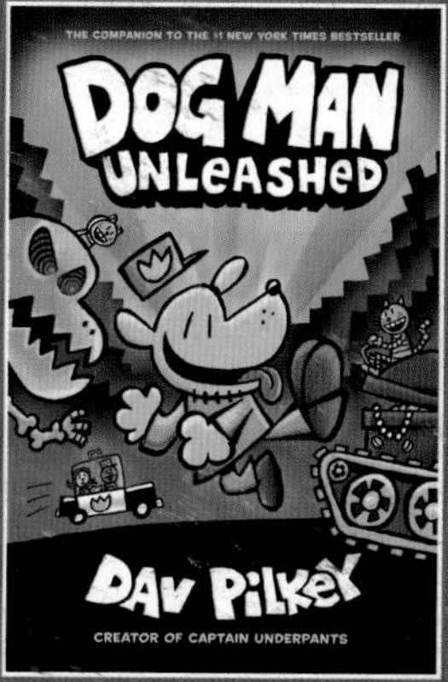
THE COMPANION TO THE #1 NEW YORK TIMES BESTSELLER
DOG MAN
UNLEASHED
DAV PILKEY
CREATOR OF CAPTAIN UNDERPANTS

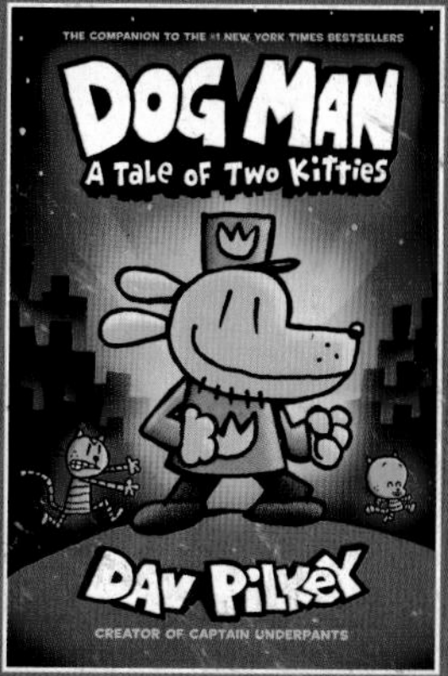
THE COMPANION TO THE #1 NEW YORK TIMES BESTSELLERS
DOG MAN
A Tale of Two Kitties
DAV PILKEY
CREATOR OF CAPTAIN UNDERPANTS

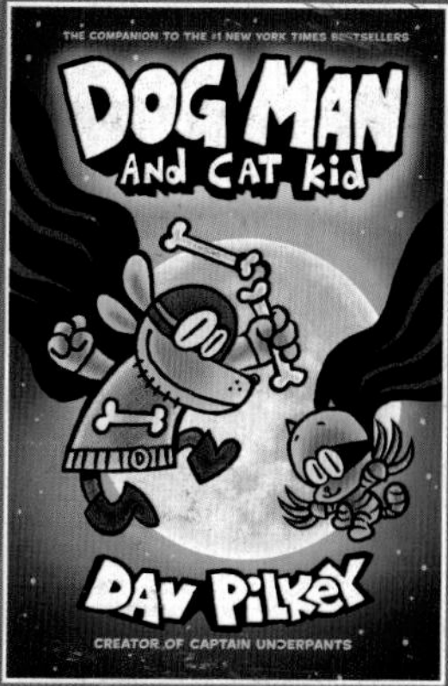
THE COMPANION TO THE #1 NEW YORK TIMES BESTSELLERS
DOG MAN
AND CAT KID
DAV PILKEY
CREATOR OF CAPTAIN UNDERPANTS

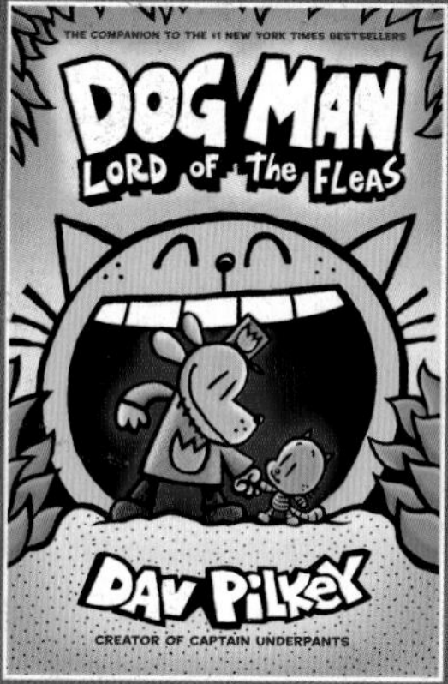
THE COMPANION TO THE #1 NEW YORK TIMES BESTSELLERS
DOG MAN
LORD OF THE FLEAS
DAV PILKEY
CREATOR OF CAPTAIN UNDERPANTS

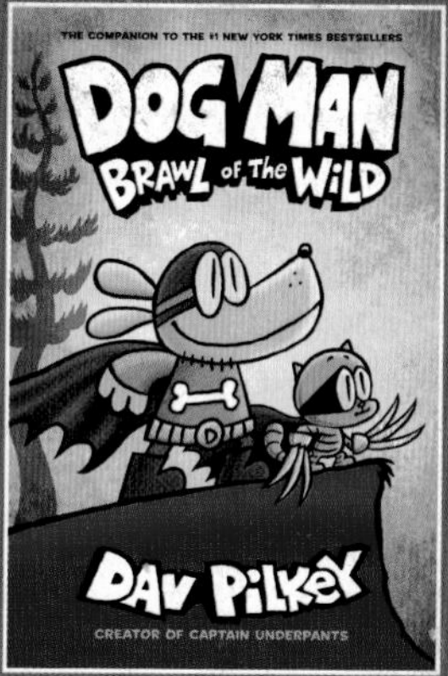
THE COMPANION TO THE #1 NEW YORK TIMES BESTSELLERS
DOG MAN
BRAWL of the WILD
DAV PILKEY
CREATOR OF CAPTAIN UNDERPANTS

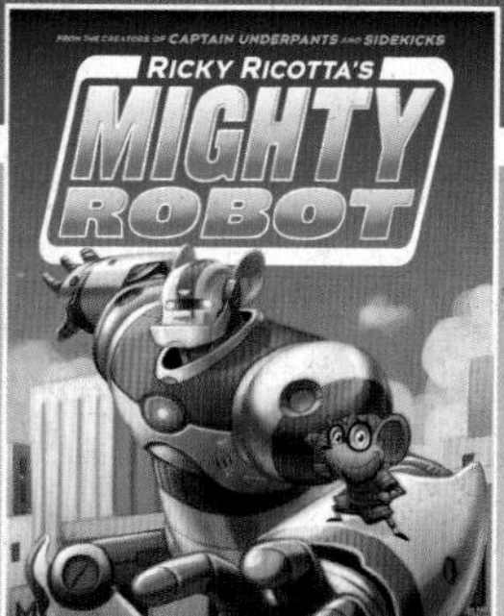
FROM THE CREATORS OF CAPTAIN UNDERPANTS AND SIDEKICKS
RICKY RICOTTA'S
MIGHTY
ROBOT
DAV PILKEY
DAN SANTAT

"A fun introduction to chapter books."
— *SCHOOL LIBRARY JOURNAL*

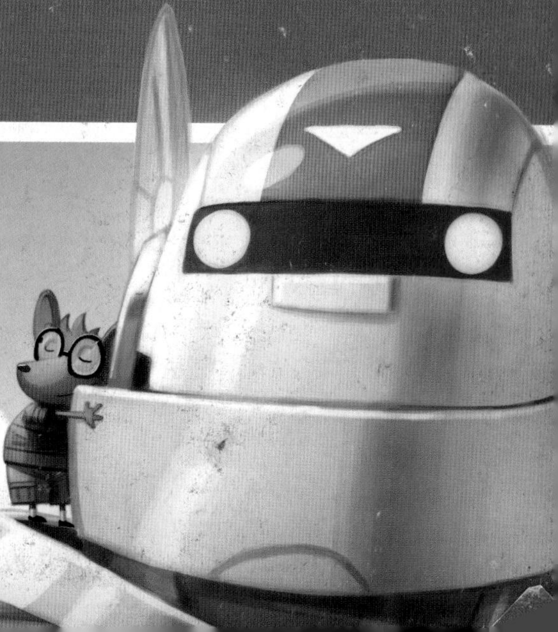

ABOUT THE AUTHOR—ILLUSTRATOR

When Dav Pilkey was a kid, he suffered from ADHD, dyslexia, and behavioral problems. Dav was so disruptive in class that his teachers made him sit out in the hall every day. Luckily, Dav loved to draw and make up stories. He spent his time in the hallway creating his own original comic books.

In the second grade, Dav Pilkey created a comic book about a superhero named Captain Underpants. His teacher ripped it up and told him he couldn't spend the rest of his life making silly books.

Fortunately, Dav was not a very good listener.

ABOUT THE COLORIST

Jose Garibaldi grew up on the South Side of Chicago. As a kid, he was a daydreamer and a doodler, and now it's his full-time job to do both. Jose is a professional illustrator, painter, and cartoonist who has created work for many organizations, including Nickelodeon, MAD Magazine, Cartoon Network, and Disney. He is currently working as a visual development artist on THE EPIC ADVENTURES OF CAPTAIN UNDERPANTS for DreamWorks Animation. He lives in Los Angeles, California, with his wonder dogs, Herman and Spanky.